THE WAR IN

HEAVEN

TEARS OF HEAVEN SERIES

THE WAR IN
HEAVEN

THE CHRONICLE OF ABADDON THE DESTROYER

KENNETH ZEIGLER

DESTINY IMAGE® PUBLISHERS, INC.
P.O. Box 310, Shippensburg, PA 17257-0310

"Speaking to the Purposes of God for This Generation and for the Generations to Come."

This book and all other Destiny Image, Revival Press, MercyPlace, Fresh Bread, Destiny Image Fiction, and Treasure House books are available at Christian bookstores and distributors worldwide.

For a U.S. bookstore nearest you, call **1-800-722-6774.**

For more information on foreign distributors, call **717-532-3040.**

Reach us on the Internet: **www.destinyimage.com.**

ISBN 10: 0-7684-2826-2

ISBN 13: 978-0-7684-2826-1

For Worldwide Distribution, Printed in the U.S.A.

1 2 3 4 5 6 7 8 9 10 11 / 13 12 11 10 09

Dedication

This book is dedicated to my wife, Mary, and all of the prayer warriors who confront the enemy on a daily basis.

Introduction
And There Was War in Heaven

And there was war in Heaven: Michael and his angels fought against the dragon; and the dragon fought and his angels, and prevailed not; neither was their place found any more in Heaven. And the great dragon was cast out, that old serpent, called the Devil, and Satan, which deceiveth the whole world: he was cast out into the earth, and his angels were cast out with him (Revelation 12: 7-9).

Chapter 1

The heat was oppressive, 114 degrees in the shade, but finding shade was the problem. It was mid-afternoon, at least it felt that way—it always felt that way. The huge reddish orb that passed for a sun hung high in the western sky; it might just as well have been nailed to the dusty amber firmament. And except for those times when dust storms obscured it from view, it was just another eternal fixture of this grim arid landscape.

This was an unforgiving land. Never as much as a drop of rain fell upon these forsaken plains. Nor did a single lichen cling to the rocks. It was the template of utter desolation.

Yet this was not a place whose silence was broken only by the occasional howling winds of a fierce dust storm. No, there was no peace to be found here. The air was full of sounds—weeping, shrieks of pain, screeching birds, and clanking chains. These sounds were a natural part of this place, as natural as the blazing sun or blowing sands.

Across the plains, a myriad of altars composed of polished black marble were laid out in orderly rows as far as the eye could see. It was reminiscent of a great city, its streets and avenues laid out in perfect geometric precision. Draped over most of these altars were rag-clad humans, their wrists, ankles, and necks securely restrained by chains and manacles. So short were these black monoliths that their occupants' heads and their legs, from the ankles down, dangled over the ends. Here, shackled and scantly clad, they were exposed to the harsh elements.

Yet the harshness of those elements went beyond oppressive heat and the discomfort of tight barbed restraints. For above this field of agony, large birds, scavengers, glided and pirouetted on the thermals. They were a savage and aggressive lot, with a 3-feet wingspan, oversized heads, and large beaks with jaws as powerful as steel traps. They were the result of evolution gone horribly wrong, scavengers with an instinct and physiology adapted specifically for preying upon a single species—humans. Indeed, the flesh of these helpless humans was the birds' sole source of nourishment and human blood their only source of moisture.

Occasionally, the birds would swoop down to claim a piece of the living flesh offered to them upon the altars. They would land upon their prone human prey, digging into soft flesh with their razor-like talons, pecking into it with their sharp beaks, and eventually coming up with slices of stringy meat that they swiftly and greedily gulped down.

So numerous were these scavengers that two or three of them might gather to feed upon one human at any given time—a gruesome feeding frenzy. Through it all, the prey would squirm and curse, scream and cry, yet to no avail, for they were shackled too tightly to their altars to offer any meaningful resistance.

It took several hours of continual feeding for the birds to reduce a human being to a mass of indigestible organs, bones, and sinew. Then they would fly off, seeking out heartier pickings elsewhere. Yet the story didn't end there. In the absence of the feasting birds, the bodies of the desecrated humans would undergo a swift yet grotesque process of regeneration, becoming whole again within the span of an hour. Then the cycle of feeding began anew.

Here, there was mortal pain and horror without the ultimate release mortality offered, for there was no death. All of these victims had already died once, and that experience of death would not be repeated. This was Hell, and Hell was forever.

Rathspith stood amid the carnage like some vulgar stone gargoyle, gazing across the flat barren plains. He looked across the myriad of altars toward a low range of mountains in the distance, mountains that seemed to undulate and ripple with the passing waves of heat. It had been a full hour since he had so much as moved a muscle.

His large bat-like wings were folded tightly together, arching a good two feet over his head and nearly touching the ground behind him. His wrinkled tan face exhibited a menacing scowl, yet his wide green eyes held a blank stare. He seemed totally unaffected by the goings on about him.

No, the cries of anguish from the altars were of little consequence to him. He had learned to tune them out long ago. If anything, he found some measure of comfort in their screams. After all, they were just humans, abominable creatures, made in the image of God, pale imitations of their Creator. They exhibited the physical perfection of their Creator, yet deep within they were creatures most foul, full of rage, hatred, envy, and avarice. No, this was the perfect place for them—a fitting destiny, an eternal supply of food for the scavengers of the air. Here, at least they served some useful purpose.

Rathspith was the lone sentinel watching over 10,000 of these loathsome creatures, the guardian who would ensure that none would escape their eternal destiny. But what was the point of it? How would one of them escape? They were all securely shackled to their altars, dehydrated, weakened by the pain and the heat. They weren't going anywhere.

No, this assignment was an act of personal retribution against him. It was the sort of assignment given to a minor demon of the seventh rank, not a lieutenant such as himself. A lieutenant? No, former lieutenant now. And these humans were to blame. Actually, it was just one human who bore the blame for his fall from grace, and ironically he had never even met her.

Six years ago, that new female arrival had been sentenced by the master himself to the most vile torment to be found in all of Hell, the Sea of Fire, a flaming ocean of black oil that fully encompassed a third of Satan's realm. There in the midst of a broiling heaving nightmare, she would come to know another definition of pain, terror, and eventual madness. At least that was the intent. Yet after only four months into her eternal sentence, she had simply vanished. It seemed absolutely impossible. After all, no human had ever escaped from that turbulent fiery realm. The shorelines around the sea were steep and rugged, the sea itself was turbulent and well-patrolled, and the humans within too weak and crazy with pain to formulate an escape. But somehow she had. An exhaustive search for her had yielded nothing.

Rathspith had been assigned the task of recovering her; indeed, his desire for power and accolades had compelled him to volunteer for the assignment. Yet things had gone horribly wrong. She had slipped through his grasp; and during the search, a demon of the sixth rank under his own command had vanished without a trace. Worse still, the human female had escaped Hell altogether by means he didn't even pretend to understand. Now she was back on Earth, proclaiming the message of salvation, stealing Hell-bound souls from the master, and the burden of the blame had been passed from minion to minion, inevitably falling squarely on his shoulders. Over the years, her name had been burned indelibly into his mind—Serena Farnsworth.

The incident had enraged the master and led to Rathspith's demotion into the company of the lowest ranks of demons, relegating him to the dirtiest and most mundane tasks in the dark kingdom. Had it ended there, things would have been bad enough. But Serena Farnsworth was just the first in a series of missing humans.

Some months later, another human disappeared without a trace. Additional months of searching had yielded not so much as a trace of her. She had vanished from Hell. Then went another and another.

Satan was positively livid. The disappearances led to the implementation of more rigorous security measures, more monitoring of the humans. That edict had brought him here, and here he had remained. All of his appeals for a transfer had been declined by his superiors, so he was stuck. And that fate, the one so cruelly dealt him, ate at him as surely as the birds ate the nearly desiccated bodies of these miserable humans around him. He had gone over it again and again in his mind. It had become his personal tormentor during these past years. This time amid his simmering rage, he hadn't noticed the small gray cloud sweeping across the plains toward him.

High above the dusty plains, a large buzzard began to descend toward a now fully restored victim who was struggling frantically upon her black altar near the edge of the field of agony. The buzzard circled the newly discovered prey, but when a small brown creature flew past him, he instinctively abandoned the descent toward the human and pursued it. Perhaps it would offer more moisture than the dried up human. His sharp beak opened wide, even as the small insect-like creature was overtaken and swept in. His huge beak snapped shut, yet he was unable to swallow his prey—it resisted, lodging itself firmly in his throat. The vulture gagged, swung his head from side to side, yet to no avail. Then came the burning stings, and a spreading of blood across the feathers of the vulture's neck. Seconds later his neck exploded. Body and head parted company and the buzzard plummeted end over end toward the desert below. The small creature continued on its way.

It was only when several other of the winged tormentors had met a similar fate, that Rathspith's attention was drawn to the aerial carnage. He stood in wonder as the birds scattered in confusion, meeting their deaths as a result of a common mistake.

A moment later, Rathspith noticed one of the small creatures fly swiftly past, only a few feet to his right. Then one passed him on the left, then overhead.

"By the lights of Sheol!" he cursed, swinging about and drawing his sword. There were no insects in this region of Hell, so what were these things? He had a bad feeling. These creatures, whatever they were, possessed a troubling aura.

Then he felt the sharp pain on his back. It was like the sting of a scorpion, only worse. Then another and another.

Rathspith screamed and swung wildly about, thrashing his shimmering sword in the air, but that was all it encountered—air. These tiny beasts were too swift, too agile to kill with a sword. Within seconds he was engulfed in a stinging, biting cloud of tiny creatures. As the battle raged, the creatures were causing buzzard feathers, body parts, and blood to rain down from the sky, even as Rathspith flapped his mighty wings wildly generating a powerful whirlwind that he hoped would sweep his tormentors away. Yet this too was a futile effort, for now over a hundred of them were gnawing ferociously at him.

He raced forward, tumbling over an empty altar and crashed to the ground, all the while flailing about frantically. He had to take to the air and get help, yet his leathery wings were already in tatters and he was being weighed down by ever increasing numbers of the six-legged creatures. For more than a minute he screamed in a shrill, unearthly voice before falling silent.

Across the plains other voices cried out as the creatures lit into victims upon the altars, yet their assaults were selective. Some of the victims were swarmed by hundreds of the creatures, while others were left in peace.

Within minutes, Rathspith had been reduced to little more than a collection of bones, shredded muscles, and indigestible organs. Yet, like the desecrated humans around him, he could not die. He gazed out at the creatures that had now ended their vicious assault and had gathered in a circle around him, observing him intently. They were furry, tan to brown in color, with six legs and a long, sharp scorpion-like stinger on their tails. Their wings, translucent as gossamer, vibrated in unison. Their heads were large and their faces had an almost human-like quality. They had long flowing hair on their heads, yet their mouths held a set of razor-sharp teeth. Never had Rathspith seen such creatures in Hell, or anywhere else. His mouth moved, but no sound came out—his vocal cords had been ripped from his throat.

About a dozen feet away, a strange apparition appeared in midair. It was like a glistening field of stars and at its very core a growing glow. From its heart stepped three angels clothed wholly in black. They had the faces of men and great black wings, like those of a gigantic crow. They approached the demonic sentry. The dark angel in the center dropped to one knee before the prone minion of Satan. The small creatures moved out of the way to make room for him.

"How far you have fallen, my dear Rathspith," he said, not a trace of emotion in his voice. He looked at his compatriot on the right. "Find him. I want us in and out of here as quickly as possible."

"I shall," he confirmed, making his way out among the city of black altars in the company of the second angel.

Rathspith was regenerating, like all beings of his kind, though it was a slow and excruciatingly painful process. For the first time in his existence, he was gaining an appreciation for the suffering of his human victims. "Who are you?"

The dark angel looked into Rathspith's one remaining eye. "Someone you probably wish you had never met. I am the voice of change, of reason. That is all that you need to know." The dark angel gazed about at the myriad of tiny creatures that still surrounded Rathspith. "I would not make any sudden moves if I were you. You wouldn't want to make my friends nervous."

The dark angel turned away from his prone adversary, gazing at the sky. The vultures, what few were left, had scattered in all directions, and the skies overhead were, for the first time in centuries, free of their terrible presence. Then he looked across the fields of agony. Most of his legion of small creatures were on the ground, apparently resting. Only a few circled overhead. The dark angel seemed anxious, nervous, as he again scanned the skies.

"We have found the one you sought," said one of the dark angels, returning from his brief quest. "He was exactly where you said he would be."

"Then fortune is with us," said the first. "Take me to him."

Dr. Tom Carson was still in a daze. He gazed at the blazing red sun behind him—the tight chain looped around his throat pulled his head back so he could look at little else. The movement of his arms and legs was accompanied by a metallic dragging sound, followed by a sudden arrest of their motion. No, he was still here. Yet the cycle of the regeneration and desecration of his body had been somehow broken. It now felt unnatural to be without pain.

His body was whole once more, of that much he was certain. The terrible itching and random sharp pains associated with the rapid regeneration of his flesh had ended some time ago. Yet the scavengers had not resumed their feast. These precious minutes without pain were a blessing. Even the screaming and wailing of those around him had nearly gone silent, reduced to a soft whimpering. In the absence of pain, he lingered in a state near sleep.

Had the end of eternity finally arrived? That was when Satan had told him that his torments would end. His time on this terrible altar had seemed like it was dragging on into eternity. It had been many months, perhaps years, but not eternity, unless Satan's definition of the term was different from his, unless time here was somehow different from on Earth.

Nevertheless, these past months had been nightmarish. This was the punishment for his greed, his lack of charity. At least that was what Satan had claimed. This precious moment gave him the time and clearness of mind to review his earthly existence. Yes he had been something less than generous when it came to his money; he openly admitted it. But more importantly, he had rejected the love of Christ and the salvation He had freely offered him.

No, he hadn't lived a perfect life, but did these flaws in his character warrant such extreme measures as these? If only he had it all to do over again. If only he had known. "Jesus, help me," he whispered, realizing that prayers were probably pointless in Hell.

There was a sudden darkness. Dr. Carson sensed the presence of someone or something standing over him.

"I am not Jesus, Dr. Carson, but perhaps I am in a position to help you."

Carson opened his eyes to see three dark angels standing over him. "Who are you?"

"Someone in need of your services," was the reply.

"My services? You need my services?" His voice quivering, almost weeping—what could he do for anyone?

"That is correct," replied the dark angel, his voice deep and impassionate. "You are an expert in the field of particle and plasma physics. Is this not true?"

Particle and plasma physics? That was an eternity ago. Right now the principles of physics were the furthest thing from his mind. Were they even still there, or had so much pain driven them away? This had to be a dream, a delusion. "Yes," was all that he could manage to say. He hoped that it was the right answer. He felt a gentle hand upon his bare shoulder.

"I know that this is difficult for you," said the dark angel. "I don't expect you to be at your best right now, not under these conditions. But answer me this, would you be willing to serve me and provide me with the information I seek?"

Carson did his best to sort out the words of the angel, to make sense of what he had just heard. He was certain that he had discerned a trace of concern, perhaps even compassion, in this strange being's voice. "I'll serve you. I promise."

"That is what I wanted to hear," said the dark angel.

Carson felt pressure on his arms like something was walking across them. He struggled to lift his head, pushing against the thick chain around his throat to see about a dozen tiny brown creatures attacking the shackles around his wrists. He watched as they dug into the heavy metal with their powerful teeth, sheering off small shards with each bite.

He could feel powerful vibrations being transmitted even through the chain around his throat. In seconds, the tight chain slipped off, severed at its base.

The shackles around his wrists and ankles grew uncomfortably hot as sparks and metal fragments were scattering. His right wrist shackle was severed first. He withdrew his brutally desecrated wrist from its barbed interior with the assistance of one of the dark angels. The left wrist shackle was next followed by his ankle shackles. As he was assisted to a sitting position upon the altar, he had never imagined rising from his slab of agony.

For a moment, he looked down at one of the tiny creatures that had freed him; it returned his gaze. "Thank you," said Carson.

He was surprised when it smiled at him. Did this strange being actually comprehend his words?

"We must move quickly," warned one of the dark angels, assisting Carson in swinging his legs over the side of the altar, and bringing him to a standing position.

The world around him grew dark. For a moment Carson was certain that he would pass out. Yet his senses quickly returned to him as he walked with assistance across the rough, rocky terrain.

"Take him back to Refuge," said the dark angelic leader. "See that he is made comfortable. He will no doubt need some rest."

"Wait," said Carson. "Who are you? What's going on?"

For the first time the angelic leader smiled, though slightly. "I am your benefactor; my name is Abaddon. You shall assist me in bringing about a new order in this place, an order of justice. Welcome to the revolution."

Carson nodded weakly as a sparkling sphere of stars and mist appeared before him. He was gently assisted by one of the dark angels into the mist. A fraction of a second later, they both dematerialized from the plains.

Their mission completed, the tiny minions of Abaddon scattered, taking flight eastward. Only those few guarding the demon Rathspith remained.

Abaddon scanned the plains one more time. Other humans had taken note of what had transpired and now begged for mercy, begged to be released from their torments. Abaddon shook his head sadly, turning to his lieutenant. "Would that we could have taken more of them with us. I regret having to leave so many deserving of our aid behind."

"We have not the time," warned his compatriot looking nervously about, "Our risk increases even now. Surely we should tarry no longer."

Abaddon hesitated. "Of this I am aware, Lenar. Nonetheless, we have one more task to accomplish before we depart. To me it is a matter of some importance, a personal matter."

Lenar looked at his leader incredulously, yet said nothing.

Abaddon returned to deal with the last loose end in this whole operation—Rathspith. By this time Rathspith had regenerated almost completely. Still, the process was apparently causing him much discomfort. Abaddon gazed at his nemesis with impassionate eyes. "My time is short, but I am obligated by conscience to deal with you as true justice would demand."

"Justice?" sneered Rathspith. "What know thee of justice? Look about ya, dark angel. This is justice, the master's justice. They are all well-deserving of the calamity which has befallen them. Not one of these is innocent."

"Yes, I know," confirmed Abaddon.

"And yet you've released one of 'em," replied Rathspith. "Don't imagine that this fact has escaped me. What gives ya the right to do this thing?"

"Compassion mostly," said Abaddon, unwilling to speak of any ulterior motives he might have had.

"But he's guilty," objected Rathspith. "Of this, you know."

"And are we innocent?" asked Abaddon. "What gives us the right to do this? Who are we to judge them? Is there no compassion or forgiveness remaining in your black heart, Rathspith?"

"None," replied Rathspith, "and I assure you that you'll come to regret this act of defiance against the master."

"Perhaps," said Abaddon, "but not today. No, today I have the duty of sentencing you for your crimes, crimes against the Father and humanity."

"And what gives ya that right?" hissed Rathspith. "You and yer kind were condemned to this place as surely as we were. You're not so different from us."

"I am nothing like you," objected Abaddon, his anger growing. "I have never been a party to the likes of this."

"Have a care, sir," urged Abaddon's compatriot. "We can linger here no longer."

There were a few seconds of hesitation. Abaddon wanted to give Rathspith a moment to consider his predicament, even as he savored this moment. But Lenar was right; they didn't have time. "Rathspith, I sentence you to the great Sea of Fire. You shall suffer like Serena suffered. I shall show you the type of justice that you have so long shown others."

"Serena!" gasped Rathspith.

"Yes," confirmed Abaddon. "Let that name sink into that pathetic mind of yours while it still can, before the agony of the Sea of Fire obliterates all other thoughts but escape."

In that moment, Abaddon swung Rathspith around, face down. He said not a word, yet his tiny minions understood only too well. They renewed their attack, yet their target was most selective. They focused their assault on the point where Rathspith's wings met his back. Rathspith struggled, cursed, and screamed, but to no avail. It took scarcely half a minute to complete the task. Amid a momentary eruption of dark red blood, the wings were sheered from his body at their roots.

Rathspith let out a high-pitched squeal as his wings were cast aside, as the last tendons were stretched and severed. For a moment the wings flapped around as though they had acquired a life of their own, then they fell motionless.

"It will take many hours for your wings to grow back," said Abaddon, pulling Rathspith to his feet. "That is, out here in the open. But in the Sea of Fire, they will never grow back. You will be like the humans, indistinguishable from them. Your own kind will not even recognize you. Prepare yourself for the execution of your sentence."

"No, you can't," screamed Rathspith as his feet left the ground behind. "I've served the master faithfully for all of my existence. Ya can't do this to me!"

"I assure you we can," said Abaddon, with no trace of emotion. "But let not your heart be troubled, you shall continue to serve your master, only in a different capacity."

The dark angels soared skyward, carrying the desecrated demon between them, screaming all of the way. They passed into a sphere of shimmering stars and vanished. The remaining small creatures followed them into the sphere, and a quiet the likes of which this place had not seen in a thousand years settled in. Yes, the remaining birds would eventually return to feed upon the only source of sustenance they had ever known. What other choice did they have? But for a brief moment in eternity, the plains would know some measure of peace.

Chapter 2

"This is unacceptable!" shouted Satan, slamming his fist upon the arm of his ornate golden throne. He rose abruptly to his feet. He carefully scanned the demons who had gathered before him. They seemed nervous. That was good, he thrived on their fear of him; indeed, he depended upon it.

He took several steps forward on the red carpet that overlaid the black marble of the great circular platform upon which his throne sat. His entourage was gathered before him at the bottom of the three steps that ran entirely around the platform.

The vast cavernous room that was Satan's audience chamber had a unique and infernal grandeur. Its lofty ceiling towered thirty feet over their heads. Its dark walls were relatively smooth and slick like melted glass, but they were hardly symmetrical. The walls and ceiling were an architect's nightmare, twisting and undulating randomly. The walls were adorned with murals etched into the rock depicting the history of this realm's demonic inhabitants—from their fall from Heaven, to their efforts in shaping this realm of pain and pandemonium, to the nature of the torments of Hell itself.

The frightening surreal atmosphere of this place was not for the benefit of Satan or his entourage, but for his human guests. This was their last stop on their road to eternal torment, the last time they would ever be without pain. Satan wanted it to be a memorable experience.

Under normal conditions, there might have been several hundred of Satan's minions in this chamber, assuming a variety of forms intended to frighten the humans summoned to this place. But today there were only six, and they appeared as Satan commanded—dark-cloaked angels with leathery bat-like wings.

Yet the Prince of Darkness assumed a very different form from those before him. His countenance was very unlike the common human concept of the devil. The only traditional aspect to his appearance was his small dark goatee. He was as tall as his subjects, yet his physical appearance was far more akin to that of a human male. He was darkly handsome and in all aspects well-proportioned. He was moderately muscular, and his flowing dark hair bore just the trace of gray around his temples. His eyes were brown, and his tan skin was flawlessly smooth and without wrinkles. He was draped in a blue velvet robe fringed with gold, and in his hand he held a golden scepter, upon the end of which was a finely cut, fist-sized gem, the very center glowing with a crimson light.

The chamber remained totally silent for nearly a minute as Satan stood before them, none so bold as to speak. "Unless I am greatly mistaken, and I never am, fifty-seven humans have vanished without a trace during the past year, and thirty-two the year before. Those are your figures, are they not?"

Only silence returned the master's query. There were times when that sort of response would have been satisfactory to the Prince of Darkness. This was not one of those times.

"Now you report to me that one of our own is also missing," he continued.

"Yes, my lord," replied Endor, his voice slow and hesitating. "One Rathspith of the Erdellan Order has been missing for two days. He vanished from his post, guarding the altars of pain on the Plains of Hegath, along with one human, Thomas Carson. Strangest of all, nearly all of the scavenger birds that preyed upon the humans were destroyed at the same time. We found…"

"Enough," roared Satan, "I read the report. Whoever did this went to a lot of trouble to take one human. Why this one? Why not take others as well? This was a carefully planned and executed operation. As with the other disappearances, no one saw anyone or anything enter or leave the area. But this time we also lost one of our own. Even if it is one the likes of Rathspith, it is one too many." Satan paused as his anger ebbed somewhat. "Over the centuries, I've lost a few of these loathsome humans, but only a few. It hasn't been like this since…" Satan stopped. He couldn't bring himself to so much as mention the name of the Nazarene and the tens of millions of souls He had stolen from him in a single day.

"This could surely not have happened at a less opportune time," noted General Krell, apparently sensing that this was a good moment to break the silence. "My people tell me that the preparations are nearly complete. Our time is at last at hand, my lord. Soon we shall be ready to break the chains that bind us to this place. Soon we shall take our rightful place." There was a few seconds of hesitation. "What I mean to say is that you shall take your rightful place, my lord."

Surely, flattery was the way to Satan's heart, or at least it usually was, but not today. "That might very well be, general, but how can we proceed with these things happening here within my realm?"

"But, my lord, what are a few missing souls compared to the billions we still hold?" asked Governor Molock, taking a step toward the monarch. "I don't see how this changes our timetable in the least. We should move ahead."

The general looked toward Molock incredulously, then back toward his master. "I still advise caution, my lord. Something is very wrong here. A new player has entered the fray. We would be ill-advised to spread our forces so thin at this time."

"A new player," scoffed Molock, "It is the dark angels who are at work here, Azazel and his followers, nothing more. They have been in hiding for centuries, and are only now striking out when the opportunity presents itself. They are but a few hundred; they can be dealt with when this operation is finished."

"The dark angels," replied Krell, "are no longer being led by Azazel. My sources tell me that they have a new leader, though I know not who. But when I speak of a new player, I speak not of them. Did you not see how the birds of Hegath were killed? The dark angels would not have butchered the scavengers in this manner. Then there was the talk of a dark cloud."

"A dark cloud?" asked Satan, turning his full attention to the general. "I've heard no talk of a dark cloud."

"Rumors, nothing more," said Molock.

"Not rumors," objected Krell. "One of my own warriors saw it from a distance, not far from the Plains of Hegath on the day Rathspith vanished, a cloud traveling against the wind. Since then, I have heard of three collaborating accounts describing this very same thing."

"A cloud that rips the heads off birds and releases humans from their torments?" scoffed Molock. "This is pure fantasy."

The other four demon lords within the chamber seemed unwilling to comment on these matters. Perhaps they perceived the foul mood that the master was in.

Satan stood in silence, considering his course of action. He had waited so long for this moment. He had dreamed of vengeance, of an invasion of Heaven, for millennia. Now that reality was almost within his grasp. His many minions' increasingly vigorous spiritual attacks on humanity had drawn ever more angels to Earth, away from Heaven. They were spread thin, very thin, and they would be totally unprepared for this eventuality. He had slowly but surely amassed the power needed to bridge the gulf that existed between Hell and Heaven. Now, at last, he could open the gate wide enough and long enough to allow his armies to stream into paradise.

Based upon his most recent conversations with the Father, Satan had become convinced that He would not interfere. After all, this would not be a personal attack upon Him; no, it was a test of the loyalty of his angels. As in the case of Job of old, Satan was certain that he had nearly convinced the Father to allow him to put His servant to the test. But this time, it would not be just one, it would be all of the angelic hosts.

It was a bold move, and it would place his very kingdom in the balance. He would be taking nearly all of his legions through the breach. But how sure was he of victory? Here in Hell, his dominion was nearly assured, or at least he thought it was. He had turned his eternal prison into a kingdom all his own. He had thwarted the design of the Father. But he could have so very much more. Still, if things went badly, his kingdom might never rise again. He could not be certain that he could open the gate long enough and wide enough to allow his forces to retreat to Hell. They would be trapped with their backs to the vast sea of space and time. Was it really worth the risk? He had asked himself that question a thousand times, and his answer was always the same.

"The Ancient of Days shall soon call me into his presence again," announced Satan, looking at his six minions. "When it will be, I can not say, but it will be soon. At that time, I shall issue my challenge. When He agrees to my proposal, and He surely will, we must be prepared to mobilize our legions at once. There will be no margin for error. General Krell, are you prepared?"

Krell hesitated. "We are prepared, my lord. Though I advise caution, yours is the word of law. I shall do as you command."

A smile came to Satan's face for the first time during the meeting. "Then it is settled. You all have your tasks, now, go. I have more pleasant tasks to attend to—the sentencing of souls."

The six wasted no time. They all bowed low before their master and prepared to depart from the audience chamber.

"Wormwood," proclaimed Satan, "I would see you in private for a moment. We have business to discuss."

Wormwood turned around as the others departed from the chamber. In an uncharacteristic move, Satan stepped down from his place of honor and walked across the chamber toward the demon. Wormwood seemed nervous.

Satan smiled as he approached his minion. "What is the status of our special project?"

Wormwood smiled, though only slightly. "All is in readiness, my lord. Nearly two centuries of our best efforts have paid off. The final alterations in course have been made. The figures have been checked and rechecked, there are and will be no mistakes. Even as you ascend the throne to sit in the presence of the Ancient of Days, humanity will come face to face with its own annihilation. They will be powerless to prevent it."

"Very well done," noted Satan, placing a hand on the shoulder of his lieutenant. "I realize that this was a long and difficult task, but now we will reap its benefits. I assure you, you and those who labored with you shall be rewarded."

The demon bowed low. "I exist but to serve you, my master."

"And you have," confirmed Satan. I have longed for this moment since the day of the creation of that loathsome creature, man. Now my revenge shall be complete."

It was in an antechamber that Lord Molock encountered one of his subordinates, a lieutenant only recently promoted to the third rank. They delayed until all of the others had departed.

"My Lord Molock," began the lieutenant, his voice soft and hesitating. "I've been going over the figures that you presented to the master, the ones regarding the number of missing humans."

"Yes," replied Molock, "what of them?"

"Well, sir, I've traveled about, conducted a study of all of the regional records, sort of on my own, checked them several times, and the numbers appear to be in error."

"Come to the point Cordon," said Molock, impatient to be away from this place.

"Sir, your numbers are very low. The actual number of human disappearances for this year alone is 539, not the fifty-seven you reported. It could even be more."

After a few seconds of silence, Molock pushed Cordon into the corner of the empty anteroom. "You think too much. You have overstepped the bounds of your authority in doing this thing. How many others know of your findings?"

"No one, sir," replied Cordon. "I brought it straight to you as is policy."

Molock's hand loosened. "And so it shall remain."

"I don't understand," replied Cordon.

"Apparently, you do not know the master as I do. Would you really like to inform him that so many humans are missing? I reported the names of those that could not be hidden, the high profile cases. In reality, there are 543 missing humans."

"Then you've purposely deceived the master," deduced Cordon. "With all due respect, Lord Molock, this is a dangerous game you are playing. What if your secret is discovered?"

Molock looked toward his lieutenant with a suspicious eye. "What are your intentions, Cordon? Do you intend to inform the master of this discrepancy? Do you have aspirations of using these statistics to further your own cause? That would be a very bad career move on your part, a very bad move indeed."

There was a long silence. It became very obvious to Molock that his lieutenant just didn't get it. How could he have lived for so long, been so clever so as to uncover the carefully guarded secret of the missing humans, yet be so stupid when it came to matters political?

"Let me spell it out for you, Cordon, in terms that even you will understand. After millennia of planning, we are finally on the threshold of ascending to our rightful place in the universe. This issue of 543 missing humans is a minor matter, but the master will allow it to distract him. He may postpone or even call off the invasion of Heaven. We have waited too long already. I want my freedom; I want out of this place. The master speaks frequently of turning this place from a realm of confinement to a kingdom all his own. But I tell you, to me it is still a prison. I will have my freedom. Of what consequence are 543 humans, or even 5,430 for that matter? The master will find out eventually, but only after we have ascended to our rightful places. When he is once more the bright morning star, coequal with God, he will accept and understand why we have done this thing. In that day, we shall all be greatly rewarded. I shall sit at his right hand, and you will be there with me, if you will but learn to hold your peace. Do you now understand?"

Cordon nodded. "My allegiance is to you, my lord; it always has been. I shall do as you command."

Molock smiled, placing his hand upon his lieutenant's shoulder. "Very well then, here is what I would have you do. Find out what you can about the vanished humans. Interrogate whoever you need to, even the humans at the scene of the incidences. Surely they saw something. Torture them if you wish...offer them enticements if you feel it necessary to do so, but bring me answers. Be discrete about it, but let nothing stand in your way.

Share your findings with me alone. If we solve this mystery, well, all the better. If we do not, it is of little consequence; we are on our way to a better place, Cordon. What happens within this prison, this burned out cinder of a world, will be unimportant once we depart. The humans and those angels who will not join us can have it for all eternity for all I care. Let them see how they like it."

The huge red sun was like a brightly burning mass of coal before him as Cordon walked across the Plains of Hegath. The slowly decomposing carcasses of a myriad of birds of prey littered the grounds around him. Only a few still pirouetted overhead and feasted upon the bodies of the humans around him. Indeed, there were many humans whose only torment now was the blazing sun and merciless heat. Merciless heat? Hardly. They didn't realize how good they had it. The environment here was mild compared to the land to the west. There, 6,000 miles beyond the horizon, in the realm of Hades, the ground blazed at oven temperatures—nearly 300 degrees. The humans sentenced to that place didn't need voracious tormenting birds to complete their suffering, the torrid environment was sufficient, reducing their bodies to desiccated husks.

Cordon had traveled there on occasion, and was always only too happy to return to the more temperate clime of Zurel or Termantus. Even the frigid realm of the Continent of Darkness was far preferable to that blazing inferno directly beneath the red sun.

His mind wandered back to this place. It would require some work before it was once more up to the master's standards. What a mess. He picked up one of the fallen birds, or at least what was left of it. He held in his hand a decapitated body. He gazed around, trying to determine which head was once attached to this particular body. Well, it didn't really matter.

What was certain was that the head had not been severed from the body from the outside by some sharp instrument. The neck had somehow been severed from within, as if something had exploded in its throat.

Cordon turned his attention to the pair of dark shredded wings that had been discovered by the demonic guard who had come to relieve Rathspith, wings that allegedly belonged to the missing minion. He examined them more carefully. The removal of these wings had not been facilitated with a sword or other straight blade. These wings had been chewed off at their roots. It made Cordon cringe. Demons and angels alike tended to be pretty sensitive when it came to their wings. He looked around nervously; nothing else out of the ordinary caught his eye.

What could have done this, and why? Cordon thought. *To keep you from flying off as you were carried away? Carried away by a cloud?* He scanned the ground around the wings; there had been a fierce struggle. Then he saw tiny prints in the sand, myriads of them, overlapping, crisscrossing, but prints of what? They were not the prints of an insect. They were almost like miniature footprints of an angel or human; they had a clubbed appearance, but a hundred times smaller. They were around the severed wings and the altars as well.

Then he noticed larger prints—the footprints of large bipeds. He knelt down to examine them. They were those of a group of angels, demons, or humans. He pondered what he had seen in the twenty minutes he had been here. This was a crime scene. There were a lot of clues, but right now they didn't quite fit together. Cordon really wasn't cut out to be a detective. It wasn't what he was made for. Under normal conditions, there was no need for a detective in Hell.

Cordon rose to his feet and proceeded toward the altar from which a human soul had been taken. It wasn't a long walk, only fifty yards or so, but all along the way the eyes of many humans were upon him. What might they know? He would begin the questioning immediately around the altar from which their compatriot in pain had been taken, and extend the search out from there if need be. He decided he would offer them a carrot rather than a stick. It was not that he had any real sympathy for humans, he did not; however, an enticement would require less effort on his part and would be more discrete, something that Lord Molock insisted upon.

As he stood before the now vacant altar, he immediately noticed the state of the manacles and chains. They had been sheered off in a haphazard way. What sort of tool cut metal in this fashion? There were tiny shards of metal scattered around the altar and even on other altars, a dozen feet away. And this wasn't just any metal; no, it was of a sort forged only by the angels and those who had fallen. It possessed an almost supernatural strength, many times more resilient than natural steel. Yet here it was, sliced to ribbons like common scrap. Cordon picked up a wrist shackle nearly half an inch thick that had been roughly sliced in two.

Incredible, thought Cordon. Even an angelic sword would have had a hard task cutting this metal.

He sat down upon the altar to ponder what he had seen here. He looked around, and a particular human, a female, apparently Hispanic by birth, caught his attention. For a human, she was rather attractive, even here in this place. She was in a perfect position to have witnessed what happened as her head was drawn back by the chain around her neck to the optimum angle. But had her mind been clear enough to have grasped what she saw? Would her testimony of the things that had transpired be reliable, or more akin to fantasy? Like many of the humans here, she was not being ravaged by the birds. Her dark eyes followed Cordon as he approached. They held such a glassy look about them. This was not a good sign.

"Please, can you take me away too? I want to go home," she said in a quiet dry voice.

Cordon knelt down before her altar. His deep blue eyes met her dark, seemingly unfocused gaze. The poor woman's neck chain forced her head back to such a degree that she gazed perpetually at an upside-down land-scape, and the altar of the missing human. Tom Carson occupied the very center of her world.

"Why do you think that I can help you?" asked Cordon, his voice soft and melodic.

The woman gazed into Cordon's face. It was the face of an angel, smooth and without blemish, framed in flowing golden hair. He was not like so many of the demons of this place, not a hideous being with a gaunt wrinkled countenance.

"Aren't you one of them? I mean…a deliverer? Yes, you must be. I knew you would come. I knew you wouldn't abandon me. I've repented, really I have. Please, give me another chance, I beg you."

The woman was rambling and confused—a product of who knew how many years of abuse on the grandest scale. Her mind might well be as chaotic and disoriented as her speech.

"What is your name, child?" asked Cordon.

"My name? I used to know my name. But I haven't needed to know it in so long. All we have to know is how to feel pain. I can do that."

Cordon waited patiently, he had time. Still, he questioned whether interrogating this wench was worth its investment.

Then her eyes seemed to come to focus upon Cordon. "My name is Julie." A single tear welled up in her left eye. "You're not going to help me, are you? You're not one of them. Your face is kind of like theirs, but your wings are not like theirs at all. You're not going to help me."

"Who is it you speak of?" asked Cordon, caressing her cheek gently with his hand. His voice was soft and gentle, the voice of an angel. "After all, I can't tell you if I am or am not one of them if I do not know who they are. Tell me about them, Julie. Tell me all that you have seen. I may yet be able to help you."

"I don't know where to begin, how to describe what I saw," said Julie, in a trembling voice. "There weren't any birds feeding on me right then. I was healing, the way we do, after they've finished with us."

"Yes, go on," urged Cordon. "Tell me all that you saw, and I will tell you if your words might hold within them your own deliverance."

"Deliverance?" asked Julie.

"Deliverance," confirmed Cordon. "No, Julie, I'm not one of them, but maybe I can help you nonetheless. I can take you from this place, Julie. Understand, your deliverance would not be permanent, you would need to return to your eternal torment, such is your destiny, but it doesn't have to be here, and it doesn't have to be now. The wheels of business can turn slowly here in Hell. I might review your files, decide that this is not an appropriate punishment for the likes of you. It is my right. In the process of transferring you elsewhere, you would be taken to a waiting cell while a new place was prepared for you, while your paperwork went through. It would be a small but quiet waiting cell, a dark place away from the heat and blazing sun, a dark corner, free of torment where you might hide for a time. And your paperwork, as it were, might become lost for a while in the shuffle. Such things happen from time to time. You might languish there for a week, perhaps more. One can never say. Then you would be taken to another place, perhaps one not so terrible as this. All you need do to get the ball rolling is give me answers. Talk to me, Julie. Tell me what you have seen."

There was a momentary silence as Julie digested all the information.

"The bugs came first," began Julie. "Lots of bugs, and they were so big. They came from the sky like locusts. Maybe they weren't bugs, I don't know. They attacked lots of people around me, but they left me alone. I don't know why. One of them landed there on the corner of my altar and just stared at me. He had a small face—almost like a man's face. I was so afraid, but he left me alone. He didn't hurt me."

Julie went on to tell Cordon about the carnage—the birds falling from the sky all around her, of the new cries of terror. Then she told of three dark angels who talked to the man in front of her. She wept as she spoke of his release. Oh, if it could only have been her. She had heard and understood some of what the angels had told him. "What's plasma physics?" she asked.

"I'm not sure," admitted Cordon. "Why do you ask?"

"Those dark angels wanted to know if that man in front of me knew anything about it," replied Julie. "I think they called him Carson. You know, I never even knew his name. Isn't that strange? We'd been here for such a long time together, but I didn't even know what he looked like, all I saw was his feet. We've never even spoken. But this one dark angel, he did all the talking. I guess he liked what he heard because he had those little insect things cut away his chains. Then they took him away. I didn't see him after that. That's all I know."

"Very good, Julie," said Cordon. "I am indeed pleased with you. You have told me what I wanted to know."

"Are you pleased enough to help me, like you said you would?"

Cordon smiled as he rose to his feet. "Yes, Julie, I am. I shall keep my promise to you. In a few hours I shall dispatch two of my guards to come for you. I will instruct them to be gentle with you. They will release you and take you to the place I have spoken of. So I have said it, so it will be."

Cordon would waste no more time here. He had learned all he needed to know for the moment. He bolted into the sky on his batwings, amid a cloud of dust, headed for home. Things had gone better than he had thought. Other demons had been here before him, seen what he saw, why had they learned so little from the experience? Because their hatred for these humans was so great that they had failed to gather information from them as he had done. Yes, he would honor the promise he had made to this human. She had greatly assisted him in his investigation, and she would assist him still more. He would question her again in a few days, once she'd had time to digest the whole experience. When the others around her witnessed her removal, her deliverance from this place, they too might speak of what they had seen. He would return to question them as well.

Chapter 3

Tom Carson's out-of-control world was reeling around him, a jumble of sights and sensations—a nightmare from which he couldn't awaken. Where was he? His mind was like a gigantic jigsaw puzzle with thousands of pieces caught in a turbulent whirlwind. Eventually the scattered pieces of that jigsaw puzzle, the events of his life, and a horrendous afterlife, began to fit together in a somewhat logical order.

He found himself in a crowded hospital emergency room, his loving wife sitting by his side. He hadn't really wanted to come here. It had seemed more like a bad case of indigestion than anything else. He'd wanted to continue playing hoops with his sixteen-year-old son Pete. He was down 7-9, but he was catching up. That was until the pain and shortness of breath hit him. He'd had to sit down. It had been his wife, Lois, who insisted that they go to the emergency room, just in case. If only he had realized the seriousness of his condition.

It came upon him abruptly. He felt the awful crushing pain in his chest. This time it couldn't be confused with a case of indigestion; it was the pain of a second heart attack. His collapse to the floor set off a flurry of activity in the emergency room. Yet for him, the pain lasted only a fraction of a minute. The next thing he knew he was rising to his feet. The pain was gone. Confused, he looked around. A doctor, nurse, and orderly were kneeling over a man lying on the floor—he couldn't see who the man was. He nearly freaked out as a second orderly rushed straight toward him and passed right through him. Then he realized that the man on the floor was him.

"Wake up, I've got to wake up!" he cried. Yet it did no good. This wasn't a nightmare, it was reality. He turned to his wife, tried to get her to see him, but it was futile. She was looking on in horror at the man on the floor. No one could see the spirits of the dead.

Perhaps they would revive him, and he would slip back into his body. Perhaps he would become just one of the thousands of people who had a near-death, out-of-body experience. But as the minutes passed and they shocked his heart again and again to no avail, it became clear that he would become a different type of statistic.

"I'm afraid I'm going to have to call it," said the exhausted doctor. "He's gone. I'm sorry."

"No, you've got to keep trying!" screamed Carson. But no one could hear him.

Then he saw the swirling violet vortex forming near the corner of the emergency room. It was more real than everything else around him that now looked dull and faded, as if viewed through a smudged lens. The swirling phantasm was not some sort of projection; it had tremendous depth. It was a corridor that led right into the wall behind it. Not to the outside of the hospital, but into some other place, some place dark and vast. And there was something else, something that went beyond the fear-inspiring visual impression of it all. There was a sensation that found its origins in the depths of his primal soul. If there was a physical manifestation of evil, he was looking at it.

He backed away, yet it was pulling him toward it. It was like some other form of gravity, and it was growing more powerful by the minute. He tried to run, but he felt so weak—this new force was swiftly overcoming the fading gravity of the world.

"Help me! For God's sake, someone help me!" he screamed.

No one responded. How could anyone in the emergency room help him? This horrible apparition was not part of their world. It was now part of his.

He reached for something to grab onto, to anchor himself. He reached for a support column that ran from the floor to the ceiling, but his hands passed through nothing but empty air. He slipped backward, toward the dark violet portal that now took up all of the space from the floor to the ceiling and more. His body was growing lighter and lighter, making it even more difficult to fight the powerful attraction pulling him into the dark undulating tunnel. Then his feet left the ground. Within a matter of seconds, he had been swept up like a piece of lint into the hose of a great vacuum.

He tumbled end over end through the billowing cloud-lined corridor, that was now very wide indeed; hundreds of yards at least. The dark clouds that rushed by him were filled with bolts of lightning that sometimes extended into the corridor itself. He screamed, but he could not hear his own voice over the roar of the wind and rumble of the thunder. He could feel the electricity, like a thousand ants, crawling over his skin.

As he watched in horror, his body looked translucent. He could actually see his own pulsing organs and bones through its milky substance. At the same time, it was becoming darker and darker around him, even as the roar of the winds began to fade. He felt a growing icy cold that penetrated his very being.

In the fading light, something moved before him, something enormous. He saw it for only a few seconds, but that was more than enough time for its image to become forever imprinted in his memory. Then it erupted from the shadows like some great leviathan from the black depths of the sea. It was like a gigantic snake, only this one had short arms and legs. It had wings too, yet they were surely too short for flight. Yet, fly it did. In an instant it towered before him. He could see its dark brown scales, its glistening red eyes, and enormous three-feet-long teeth. Carson was drenched in the creature's foul breath. It took one look at him, and as its mouth curled back into a hideous parody of a smile, it was gone.

The journey continued. For a moment, he was certain that he was tumbling through some great rocky tunnel, yet it quickly faded to black as the last trace of light was extinguished. The total darkness and intense cold that now overshadowed his fear were profound. Never in his life had he felt so cold. There was no wind here, he didn't even have the sense that he was breathing. In fact, he couldn't even draw a breath, and he very much needed to. He wasn't sure if he were flesh or spirit, so complete was the darkness. Spirits didn't feel cold or need air. At least he didn't think so. Some part of him must still be flesh and bone. He felt as if he might be going into shock.

Then the scene abruptly changed. The bright orange glare, the heat, the loud cacophony of the birds was almost too much for him to bear. What was happening? As incredible as it seemed, he must have fallen asleep for a time, reliving the events that had brought him here. Sleep on the altar of pain? It was a concept almost too incredible to believe. But now he was awake, and his waking nightmare could begin anew. His mind was awash in confusion. Something had happened, but what? The birds of prey were here. He could hear them. He could also hear the shrieks and screams of the multitude around him, yet the birds weren't attacking him. Why?

A dark shadow momentarily swept across him; he could feel the gust of wind in its wake. He was so afraid. He didn't want to be eaten again, no, not again. Tears formed. If only he could move, but he couldn't.

"Oh, Lord Jesus, help me," he cried, tears running down his cheeks. "Oh please forgive me. Please get me out of here. Have mercy on me, Lord."

He had prayed so many times on this altar, prayed for deliverance, but it had never come. No, he was past all salvation or deliverance. This was Hell.

Again the shadow swept across him, but this time it didn't depart. It seemed to hover above him. It was drawing nearer. It was a dark silhouette, surrounded by an aura of shifting light.

"No please, leave me alone," he cried, yet his voice was barely above a whisper. "Please don't hurt me, not again! Oh God, help me."

Then something touched the side of his face. It was not the talons of a bird of prey, nor the brush of swift feathers; it was soft and smooth.

"Be still, Dr. Carson," said a voice that seemed to come from everywhere. It was a woman's voice, soft and reassuring. "No one is going to hurt you here, I promise."

Here? But where was here? He wasn't sure. The world about him seemed in flux once more. Slowly a new reality began to materialize around him. It was not the harsh world of the altars of pain. He was in a small room, the lights were dim, the air cool. A damp cloth in someone's hand ran across his forehead. Beyond that hand he saw her face. It was the face of a young, dark-haired woman, a pretty one at that. Her green eyes were full of concern.

"Are you with us this time, Dr. Carson? Can you see me? Can you understand me?"

"With you? This time? Who are you?" Carson whispered.

A smile appeared on the woman's face. "You are here this time. You're coming out of it. You've had me really worried."

Carson stared at the ceiling, beyond his comely companion, into a yellowish light. The fixture looked almost like some sort of giant quartz crystal. He was lying in a bed, a brown blanket over him, of that much he was certain. "Where am I?"

"We call this place Refuge," was the reply.

Refuge? That didn't tell him very much. "But how did I get here?"

"You don't remember?" asked the woman. "Think back, the answer is there if you seek it."

There was a long silence as the last of the pieces of the puzzle, which was the life of Tom Carson, fell into place. "Those dark angels and those things that they had with them, they freed me from the altar. They took me into a pool of stars. One of them, the one called Abaddon, said something about taking me to a place called Refuge. Then there was darkness, cold, I don't remember anything else beyond that."

The woman smiled broadly. "That all happened six days ago. Since then, you've been here with me. You've had a pretty rough time of it. You've been asleep through most of it. When you were awake, you didn't make much sense. You went on about your home, about Lois, your wife, I assume."

Carson nodded.

"And Peter, your son?"

Again Carson nodded.

"It was like you were in another world. And you were a handful from time to time too, when you were in the worst of your delirium, when you were on the altar. But you aren't there anymore, and you're not going back."

"It seems that you've learned a lot about me already," said Carson, doing his best to remain awake and focused.

The woman chuckled. "Oh my, where are my manners. I'm sorry. My name is Bedillia, Bedillia Farnsworth."

"Happy to meet you, Ms. Farnsworth. Thanks for being there for me."

"Oh, please, just call me Bedillia. We're not much for titles here."

"OK, and you can call me Tom. Not Dr. Carson. I don't think I know him anymore. I think he died. And I'm sorry if I was any problem. I really don't remember. I'm just thankful that I had someone to look after me."

"No apology necessary, I assure you, and I was happy to be looking after you. I didn't mind in the least. What happened to you is normal, totally normal," Bedillia said. "So many cruel months of torment has a tendency to do things to your mind. When released, most people go into a type of shock. It is almost like the effects of withdrawing from drugs. The sudden absence of powerful stimuli, emotion, and pain creates a sort of vacuum in the human psyche. Your body gets so used to having your senses continually pressed to the limits that a sudden removal has unexpected consequences. It's like a thick rubber band, stretched to its limit for a long time, and then suddenly released—it flies apart, becomes undone. In the absence of intense pain, you feel empty. You don't see this condition on Earth because that amount of pain would kill you a thousand times over, but here the effect is only too real."

"Sounds like you've made a study of it," said Carson, who tried to sit up, unsuccessfully.

"I have," said Bedillia. "In another life I was a counselor. I have, or had, a master's degree in counseling."

"Seems to me that you've got your work cut out for you here," said Tom, trying to move into a more comfortable position. He felt weak and drained.

Tom took a moment to look around the room as best he could. It was not a large room, perhaps twelve feet on a side. Its walls appeared to be composed of hewn rock. There were two small paintings on the walls—one a stormy seascape, the other an alpine meadow. They seemed so very incongruous in what appeared to be a cave. His cave hypothesis was strengthened by the lack of any windows. There was one entryway with drapes across it, but no actual door. In the corner, another set of drapes hung from the ceiling, but it didn't look like an entryway. The chair upon which Bedillia sat appeared to be made of cut stone, while the only other piece of furniture, a small table on a pedestal, was also made of light gray stone. What caught his eye was the earthen pot in the middle of the table, a pot from which a leafy plant with several orange flowers grew. He'd never imagined that he would see a flower again. This place was absolutely bizarre. "Meet the Flintstones," he murmured.

That comment elicited a smile from Bedillia. "Betty Rubble at your service," she giggled.

Tom smiled. No, Bedillia didn't look like Betty Rubble. She was dressed in a simple brown dress, certainly nothing fancy, but it wasn't anything primitive about it either. He wondered if it were some sort of uniform.

Tom hesitated. He really didn't know how to ask the next question. "I guess I've been wishing that this whole thing was a nightmare, maybe a delusion brought about by a prolonged illness. Eternity shackled to an altar, being eaten again and again by birds of prey. It was so horrible. I'd hoped that maybe I'd wake up in a hospital, my wife waiting there by my side, praying for my recovery. She always did have more faith in miracles than I did. But it's not going to happen, is it? I'm dead, and I'm in Hell."

Bedillia placed her hand on her patient's arm. "Yes, Tom, I'm sorry. It wouldn't make any sense to lie to you about that. God's judgment is final. We are on the only island of relative safety for humanity in this horrible realm. It is the remoteness and the unpleasantness of the climate above that helps ensure our safety."

"So there is no Purgatory, no earning our way out of Hell through repentance?"

Bedillia only shook her head.

"Too bad," said Tom, who could think of nothing else to say. Apparently, the nightmare wasn't over. "It still doesn't make sense to me...Hell, that is. My trip here is such a blur now. I remember tumbling through a tunnel of clouds, then floating in the darkness. I was so cold and I couldn't breathe. The next thing I knew, two winged demons had snatched me up. Then we were in some sort of subterranean labyrinth. There were these tiny cells built into the walls. There must have been thousands of them. I remember being thrown into one of them. The demons had roughed me up pretty badly. I had lacerations that must have been half an inch deep. But they healed up in minutes. But the healing hurt."

Bedillia nodded occasionally but didn't say a word as Tom continued.

"I was dragged before Satan a day later dressed only in that awful gray loincloth and surrounded by an audience of hideous demons. I felt almost naked—it was so humiliating. Satan didn't spend half a minute on me. He rushed through the whole proceedings. He said I'd been greedy and uncharitable, and that for the rest of eternity I'd offer myself to the birds of the air. Then he demanded that I be removed from his presence. I guess I wasn't worth any more of his time. I was taken out of there through some sort of portal by two demons and shackled to that black altar. And there I was abandoned for I don't know how long. Look I don't even know where Hell is. I used to think that if it even existed, it was in some sort of cavern deep underground. But it's not, I know that much."

Again, Tom tried to sit up. This time he succeeded, with Bedillia's help.

"I'm sorry," said Tom. "I know I'm rambling on."

"It's OK," assured Bedillia, "you need to get it all out. I know how you feel, believe me."

"I'm so confused," said Tom. "I still don't even know where I am, or why things are the way they are. When you're lying there, chained to an altar, being disemboweled by an army of huge voracious birds, you really don't have the time or the inclination to consider the nature of existence."

"But that's the whole point," replied Bedillia, "Satan doesn't want you to know where you actually are or why things are the way they are. He wants to keep you as ignorant of your situation as possible. He wants you to be confused. He wants to inflict pain."

"So where are we, Bedillia? I know we are in Hell, but where is Hell?"

"I've had it all explained to me several times," replied Bedillia. "I still don't totally understand it. Abaddon would be the best one to explain such things."

"Abaddon, the angel who released me?" asked Tom.

"Yes, he is our leader," replied Bedillia. "He told me that Hell is in the middle of outer darkness, not in the middle of the Earth. He said that it was part of space isolated from the rest of space. You could go on forever from here, travel as far as you wanted, and not end up anywhere but here. Jesus talked about it, a bit indirectly, in one of His parables. He said that there was a great impassable void that separated Hell from any place else. Hell circles the star Kordor, the only star in outer darkness, the only source of light and heat. I guess that makes Hell a planet. It is the most horrible planet you could imagine, but it's all we've got. There are no stars in the night sky, only blackness, and here in the land above us, it is always night. Abaddon will explain it all to you, if you wish. You'll probably understand it better than I."

"When can I see him?" asked Tom.

"Once you've had a few days to recover. You're in no condition to see him now. His orders were to allow you to rest for a few days before a meeting is set. But before you can meet him, you'll have to be able to walk to that meeting. Are you ready to try and stand?"

"I need to sooner or later," said Tom, "might as well be now."

With Bedillia's help, he managed to place his feet on the stone floor. It was only then when he realized that even the bed was made of stone, save for a thin cushion of some other type of material. Actually, it was little more than a rectangular stone slab. He also noticed that the meager loincloth he had been wearing these past months had been replaced by a loose fitting shirt and a pair of knee length brown shorts. Being dressed was a relief.

"OK, here we go," said Bedillia, assisting Tom to his feet.

Tom swayed uncertainly. He had the strength to stand, but there were other problems. The room, rather quickly, began to fade, and Tom returned to a sitting position. "Not this time."

"We'll try again in a few minutes," assured Bedillia. "It has been over 18 months since you last stood on your feet for any length of time. You'll do it again."

Tom rubbed his eyes. Already his vision had returned. "If I may ask, how many people have been rescued by this Abaddon guy?"

"Over 1,100 at last count," said Bedillia. "Each was rescued from a terrible torment. You see, we are building an army. Eventually we will end the suffering of humanity here and become the masters of our own fate, at least as much as it is possible."

"I see," replied Tom. "And how many demons does Satan have in his service, in round numbers?"

Bedillia had to think about that one. "In round numbers? We estimate just over 180 million, give or take."

"And they're stronger than we are," noted Tom.

Bedillia nodded, "Yes, quite a bit."

"So we're hiding," deduced Tom.

"For the moment," replied Bedillia.

If Tom wasn't confused before, he was now. "OK, so they are stronger than us. I can attest to that. They have us outnumbered by 1,700 to 1, give or take, and they have one very organized infrastructure."

"Their infrastructure is Hell, Tom. And, yes, one day we are going to bring it down around their heads," said Bedillia. "We have a mission here. We may be abandoned by God, but we don't have to be under the cruel yoke of Satan. That pompous devil doesn't have a mandate from God to rule this place. He and his legions of demons are prisoners here, just like us. Maybe it's time that we take matters into our own hands. Maybe it's time for a change in leadership."

"Like this Abaddon of yours?" Tom asked.

"Why not?" responded Bedillia. "He is a whole lot better than the current management. He is more of what an angel should be—merciful, noble, worthy of our trust. I've known him for a long time; trust me, he has the qualities of a great leader. I owe him more than I can say."

"Abaddon rescued you too, didn't he?" asked Tom.

"And my daughter," noted Bedillia.

"Excuse me if it seems to be a personal question," asked Tom, "but what was it like for you. What sort of horror did Abaddon rescue you from?"

Bedillia seemed taken back by Tom's question. Her face took on a distant and fearful aspect. He was certain that he had just violated some unwritten law of etiquette. He was quick to respond. "I'm sorry if I've said something that upset you. I guess I'm still sort of out of it. I apologize, really I do."

The silence that continued between them for another few seconds was tense. Bedillia looked away from him, "It's OK," she replied, though her words were slow and faltering. "You didn't know. It is something that we don't talk about here. It is an understood thing among us. We've all experienced the torments of the damned. There are those here who experienced it for centuries before they were freed. It is a part of our lives that we want to put behind us, yet most of us can't. Perhaps it is because we all realize that we live an uncertain existence at best. We all have our horror stories here, Dr. Carson. We all know that those stories could be resumed in a heartbeat; that we could be returned to that horrible place where Satan put us if we fail. If our hiding place were to be discovered by Satan and his minions before we are ready…well, our fates would be sealed. As you have already noted, we are only a few against many. Yes we have our resources; we could put up a fight for a time. We could make Satan and his minions hurt in a big way. But in the end, we would be overwhelmed by sheer numbers. We need more power in our corner to even out the odds. That is why we need you."

"Me?" asked Tom. "What could I possibly do for you?" Then he thought back to his deliverance from the altar, something the dark angel had asked him. "Does it have something to do about my knowledge of plasma or particle physics?"

Bedillia nodded. "Yes it does. I'm sorry, I've already said far more than I should have. Abaddon wanted to speak to you about this himself. I'll let him explain to you what we need from you."

"Then that is the only reason you saved me from the altar, isn't it?"

"No, of course not," replied Bedillia. "You judge us too harshly. You are a good man, Tom. You were a bit misguided on Earth, but I believe that you see that now. The very fact that on that altar and in your delirium, you prayed almost unceasingly for forgiveness tells me that you have seen the light. You even prayed for the others. The experience of the past eighteen months has purified your character, burned away the hay, wood, and stubble. You don't realize it, but you've told me volumes about yourself in the past six days. You are a good man. I know that you yearn desperately for a second chance. We knew that when Abaddon and the others decided to rescue you. It would not have happened otherwise. You want a second chance? Well, here it is. Do you want to help change an entire world?"

Tom nodded. He wouldn't be looking a gift horse in the mouth again. He was here; he had escaped the torments of the altar. Surely whatever awaited him here beat the alternative by a wide margin.

"But I guess I haven't answered your question," continued Bedillia.

"It's OK, you don't have to," said Tom.

"No, I want to tell you. Maybe you'll learn from my experience. Unlike you, Satan gave me more than a passing glance at my sentencing, though I wish he hadn't. He spoke of my being a poison to my family, of how I abused my own children. I couldn't deny it. It was true. I had my daughter committed to a mental hospital when she was 13, not to help her, but out of revenge. She was a difficult child. I wanted her to know just who the boss in our family was and what could happen to her if she stepped out of line. Yes, Tom, that was the kind of person I was on Earth. I made my home a living hell for my husband and my children. I knew about Christ's gift of salvation, but I ignored it. I knew how I should live, but chose another path. I served myself and made no apologies for doing so. For this, Satan sentenced me to my own personal hell, a place where I would exist in isolation forever. It was a place where I couldn't hurt anyone else, but I could be hurt plenty."

Bedillia's tone of voice had changed. She was far more intense now, even agitated. Already Tom found himself wishing he hadn't asked this question.

"It was Satan himself, along with two demon escorts who led me from his audience chambers and into some sort of mystical portal…you've seen it; we call it a gate. It led right into a hot, misty tunnel. It must have been well over a hundred degrees in that corridor. I could smell the sulfur and hear the muffled roar of the flames. Then there were the screams; I can still hear the screams at night when I sleep. Along both walls of that tunnel were heavy iron doors, each with a small circular window just about eye level. Through most of those small thick windows I could see the glow of the fires that roared through the chamber on the other side. It provided the only light in that corridor. Each chamber was a furnace, a crematorium, for some damned soul, a victim of Satan's wrath. They forced me to gaze into one of the windows, to see the horror that awaited me. At first I didn't see anything, it was just too bright.

"Then I saw it…a figure writhing in the flames. It was a woman, though it was difficult to tell. She was hanging from the ceiling by shackles around her wrists that were so hot that they were actually glowing. Her skin was a charring mass of flesh, bubbling and seething. Her body was like a broiling, overcooked steak. No, it was even worse than that because it was a living, breathing human being. It was an awful sight. I think Satan showed me another woman in torment to put into clear perspective what was about to happen to me."

The mental picture that Bedillia was painting was horrendous. Tom wasn't sure what to say, if anything. This had to be far worse than the fate he had been sentenced to. "What did you do?" he asked.

"What did I do?" repeated Bedillia. "I freaked out, that's what I did. I cried and struggled, even as the demons led me to my chamber that even had my name inscribed on a crude plaque on the door. The turn of a large wheel caused the door to slide to one side. It must have weighed a ton. It was so thick. The room beyond the door was about eight foot on a side, with a bit higher ceiling. It was like a huge brick furnace. Near the back wall, a pair of heavy shackles hung from the ceiling, and on the floor beneath it was a big metal grate, upon which another pair of shackles was attached. There was a harsh yellow light coming from under the grate, and the smell was horrible. They dragged me in and placed my wrists into the shackles hanging from the ceiling. These weren't shackles with a regular lock, oh no, these things clamped shut on my wrists like they were magnetized, then they welded themselves shut. I could hear my flesh sizzling like a piece of broiling meat, at least for a second. After that, all I could hear was me, howling in pain."

Tom cringed. Why had he ever asked such a question? What could he possibly have been thinking of?

"And those shackles had a bonus effect," continued Bedillia. "They were smooth on the outside but barbed on the inside. They dug into my wrists brutally. It took only a few seconds before blood was running down my arms. Then they shackled my ankles to the grate below, stretching me out, keeping me from moving back and forth. Only then did I look down to see the flames below me through a brick-lined shaft. Never had I seen such flames. They were bright yellow mixed with blue, and they swirled like they were in a whirlwind. Being dressed only in a short gray skirt and top, my skin was exposed to the heat. But something was holding the flames back for the moment."

Bedillia paused.

"Really, it's OK," said Tom. "You don't need to go on. I see why people don't talk about it here."

"No, I need to," said Bedillia. "Sometimes I have to let it all out. Other people have to know about it. This experience is part of my life, so much a part of what I am now. There are still others there. Telling my story is telling theirs as well. Others have to know."

Tom decided not to respond.

"Here is something that might interest you," interjected Bedillia. "You could appreciate this more than most. Satan told me that the flames that I would be tormented by were flames of plasma."

"Good Lord," gasped Tom. "That would be an incredibly hot flame, much hotter than most normal flames."

"Yes, like I said, I thought you might appreciate that. Satan said that the flame had to be carefully controlled otherwise it would burn my body to cinders...and his entertainment might be cut short."

Tom gazed into Bedillia's eyes. He was certain that he could see a trace of madness there. It sent a chill up his spine.

"Satan went on about my being positioned at the very most intense core of the flame. He said that if the rest of the furnace was that hot, the walls would be slowly eroded away by the heat, or something like that. Then he and the others departed. I heard the sound of gears, cogs, and wheels as the door was rolled back into place and sealed. I kept pleading for mercy again and again, but it did no good. Then there was a pumping sound. My ears popped, then the flames came roaring up toward me. I was engulfed in them in seconds. You can't even begin to imagine how it feels to be flame-broiled for eternity. I never knew the human body could feel so much pain...continually. There was no part of me that didn't feel it. You prayed on that altar they put you on. I was so crazed with pain, that I couldn't even think what prayer was. All I felt was a sort of unfocused regret. My very most primal instincts told me that I had to get out, but that was impossible.

"For years I hung from the ceiling with the flames roaring around me. I was stripped of my humanity, leaving little more than a mad pain-crazed beast. Then all at once the flames died away. At first the pain was little relieved. The glowing walls radiated back the years of stored heat. Slowly they cooled. I hung there for hours. After a time, I felt so very cold. Then there was a noise, the metal door moved, ushering in even cooler air from the corridor beyond. I waited. I heard voices; someone had entered my crematorium."

"Mommy?" said a voice barely above a whisper.

At first I didn't understand what was going on. I opened my eyes to see a young woman dressed in gray tattered rags like mine. At first it didn't register in my mind who she was. Then my mind and heart opened and I saw her for who she was—my daughter Serena. I whispered her name.

"Yes, it's me, Mommy," she replied. There were tears flowing from her eyes. She was shedding tears for me. Then I saw who stood beside her...the very essence of evil, Satan.

"He reveled over his victory. He accused me of hardening my daughter's heart. He told me that I was the reason she was here. He now had us both.

"I was in pain, a greater pain than I had even known in that furnace. I'd sentenced my own daughter to Hell. I cried, begged Serena to please forgive me. I belonged here, but not her, not my baby.

"Satan turned to my daughter, offering to give her time to vent her rage upon me, to punish me for what I'd done. Then came the greatest miracle she refused. She reached out and touched me on the cheek. She forgave me for all that I had done. She kissed me...asked me not to cry...told me she loved me. Where such mercy had come from, I cannot say."

Bedillia sat on the bed beside Tom and started to cry. "After all that I had done, there was still love in her heart."

Tom placed a trembling arm around Bedillia. Yet he said nothing.

It was almost a minute before Bedillia continued. "Satan seemed amazed, then enraged. He nearly demanded that my daughter strike me, but she refused. She stood with her arms around me, trying to comfort me. Then he pulled her away from me and threw her to the ground. My anger soared against him…the anger of a mother toward someone who had harmed her child. I didn't care what he did to me. I screamed at him, demanded that he leave her alone. I wasn't afraid of him anymore, I saw him for what he was… detestable, an abomination. I remember his hand going around my neck to strangle me. But he didn't get far.

"My daughter rose to her feet and plowed right into him. She nearly knocked him off his feet. I wonder if any human had ever done such a thing to him, but my daughter did. She did it to protect me. Yet she was no match for his strength. He grabbed her and swung her around like an old rag doll. Then he declared his intention. He was going to sentence her to the Sea of Fire, to suffer forever adrift in its vastness…and I was going to have to watch through some sort of mystical portal. I would become a witness to the carrying out of my own daughter's sentence.

"He dragged her from the furnace. I saw him take her to the precipice of a great cliff overlooking a sea like no other. It was a turbulent sea of blackness, flames riding on its surface. He tried to get her to beg and plead before him, but she wouldn't play his game. She removed her sandals and walked right to the edge. I cried out to her. I told her how much I loved her, but I don't think she could hear me. A moment later, I watched in horror as she cast herself from that cliff into a sea of burning, boiling oil. A moment later, I saw her in the distance. The currents were sweeping her out to sea. Her hair was on fire."

Again Bedillia hesitated. "To her credit, know that she went bravely. I can say no more than that. As the door to my crematorium was closed and locked once more, as the flames returned to ravage me, my last thoughts were of her. The last of my humanity had perished. Or so I thought. In the following year I was numb, not to the pain, I still felt that, but to my spirit. I was little more than a tormented animal, occasionally howling in the fire. I was all instinct and no humanity. Then one day the flames once more died around me. The chamber had not even had time to cool before the metal door opened. They entered…three angels of a kind I had never seen before, a group of dark angels. That was the first time I ever laid eyes upon Abaddon. He shattered my chains with his sword and took me from that horrible place. He brought me here where I have been ever since."

Tom was hesitant to ask the next question. "But what about your daughter; Serena? What became of her?" He was unprepared for her beaming smile.

"She's not here, Tom. She's gone, saved from the torments of Hell by a true miracle. You see, Serena had encountered Abaddon many months before and in the process touched his heart. It was her love for this terrible sinner that brought Abaddon to rescue me. In rescuing me, he was fulfilling a promise to my daughter. Now she is practically a legend among us. She is the true author of this revolution. One life can change the course of the world and more. It has happened before."

Tom was astounded. "But where is she, Bedillia?"

"Where she can do the most good. Where the greatest battle against the prince of darkness will be fought and won—Earth." There was a pause. Bedillia smiled. "Now, are you ready to start to win your battle? Are you ready to walk?"

Tom nodded. There was more to Bedillia's story, he was sure of it, but it would have to wait for another time. Right now there were more important matters to see to. With Bedillia's help he rose to his feet once more. There was momentary dizziness. The room began to fade, but he refused to give in. No, he had things to do; he had no time to waste. He took several faltering steps, each more steady than the last. He was whole once again.

"This will be your room," explained Bedillia, walking over to the far corner, and pushing aside the set of brown drapes to reveal some clothes hanging from a short rack, also brown. "I've prepared some clothes for you. The color brown is in this year. It was the rave last year too. Still, it is vastly preferable to that gray loincloth you've worn these past eighteen months. Nonetheless, it is still in there among your other clothes."

"Why?" asked Tom. "Why would I ever want to wear that horrible thing again? It's positively indecent."

"We don't waste anything here," replied Bedillia. "I still have mine, and the top that went with it. Abaddon has asked that we keep them. Perhaps it is to act as a reminder of where we came from. Perhaps it is something that might come in useful some day, I don't know. Go ahead and select something to wear. I'll take some time and show you around. I'll be just outside."

Bedillia departed, leaving Tom to his selection and his thoughts. He sorted through the clothes. They appeared simple, but well made. A chill ran up his back when he discovered his old loincloth hanging among the other clothes. He quickly passed it by. Donning a brown vest-like shirt, a pair of long loose trousers, and a pair of sandals that looked almost Roman in design, he was ready to go. He was still a bit shaky as he turned around and prepared to head into this new world, but he wouldn't let that slow him down. In his wildest imaginings he hadn't envisioned being free again. Now he had been given a second chance. He wouldn't make the same mistakes he'd made in the past. It was time for Dr. Tom Carson to join the fight.

Chapter 4

Another set of rippling uneven stairs carved from the gray rocky floor loomed before Tom Carson. Bedillia forged on ahead. "Up, down, and all around," he mumbled, as he followed Bedillia up the 23 steps. Yes, he counted them all. They had been walking for nearly an hour. At this point, Tom was totally disoriented. This place, this refuge, as it was called, was an enormous maze of branching tunnels and oddly shaped cavern rooms. Clearly, this fortress had been carved out of an already existing cave system. Still, such a project was a considerable undertaking, of that Tom was certain.

Tom was no geologist. He could not discern whether the preexisting cavern had been formed by running water or flowing lava. It was hard to imagine water flowing in Hell, but that in itself was not evidence one way or the other.

He had seen many side passages during his tour, entrances that were covered with drapes not unlike the ones that guarded the entrance to the small room where he had awakened. Bedillia explained that these were all living quarters of those who dwelled in the Refuge. Closed drapes should be treated as a locked door. The people of this small community had little privacy, but what they did have should be respected.

Along the way, he noticed an occasional small creature fly past him that looked like an overgrown insect. He had also seen them on the day of his deliverance. He still didn't know exactly what they were, and Bedillia declined to talk about them beyond saying that they were sentries of a sort, guarding the tunnels and inhabitants of the Refuge from those who would violate it.

He also encountered people mostly dressed in clothes made of the same brown fabric. Some carried bundles of what appeared to be sticks, others had earthen jars, while still others carried nothing. Many offered a friendly smile and a hello as they went about their tasks, whatever those tasks might be.

The demographics of this place were unusual. It seemed to lack senior citizens and children. In reality, Tom couldn't bear the thought of children in a place like this. He was thankful that he saw none. Unlike the old rock song, Hell apparently wasn't for children.

He passed through a large cavern room filled with crude stone tables and chairs. Bedillia called it a community meeting room. He passed by another cavern room that contained looms and spinning wheels, the place where the simple clothing of these people was woven. There were even vast caverns where the stone floors had been ground up into a sort of rocky soil. Here, there were gardens filled with many varieties of fruits and vegetables. Some were familiar, others were not. The gardens were illuminated by brilliantly glowing crystals in the ceiling and irrigated from pools of water that found their source in the rocks around them.

Food was not a commodity vital for the survival of the bodies of those people who existed in this realm beyond death. But it served to placate their purely psychological need for sustenance in much the same way the consuming of water relieved their thirst. They were phantasmal sensations, realities that Tom's mind had problems wrapping itself around. It just didn't make sense. If you couldn't die of hunger or thirst in this place, why would one's body crave them? It wouldn't, but it did. And now, in the absence of the pain that had been a constant reality on the altar, his mind was forced to confront this enigma.

But these gardens scattered throughout the caverns produced more than food. They also produced a tough stringy plant that yielded fibers that could be woven into the brown fabric that formed the base material for all of the clothing worn here.

Tom's mind returned to the tunnel before him. The entire complex was illuminated by huge crystal lights that seemed to grow out of the ceiling. Along the way, he was forming opinions about this place based on what he had seen. So far, he was not impressed. Bedillia spoke with confidence of their eventual overthrow of Satan. How? Who were they kidding? These people were, essentially, hiding under a rock hoping that Satan or his minions didn't turn it over.

He'd tried to engage Bedillia in conversation along the way, but she was evasive about this place. Was she delusional? Perhaps all of these people were. Maybe it was the only thing that could prop up their crumbling sanity. Without some sort of hope, some vision, real or imagined, people perish. That was in the Bible, wasn't it? He directed more specific questions at her. "You've rescued about 1,100 people over the last six years or so, right?"

"I've been involved in the rescue of some of them," replied Bedillia. "Abaddon, is the real hero. He has personally rescued more people than anyone else."

"But there has to be a plan," said Tom. "I mean, what kinds of people do you rescue? Do you go for political leaders, scientists, philosophers, artists... who?"

"Whoever we need," replied Bedillia. "In the early going we've focused on builders, engineers, scientists, and military people, lots of military people. After all, we have a war to fight."

"So you have your own army?"

Bedillia laughed. "I wouldn't exactly call it an army, not just yet...but of the 1,100 souls, about 400 are military types. I'll tell you, we've got some of the best."

"Like General George Patton?" asked Tom.

"No," replied Bedillia, "he's not here. He had placed his faith solidly in Jesus Christ throughout his career. He was a bit rough around the edges, but his heart was in the right place."

"Well what about Napoleon or Julius Caesar?" asked Tom. "Surely, they would be excellent generals to lead this army of yours."

Bedillia shook her head sadly. "It's not as simple as that. You know how difficult it was for you to adjust after you were released from the altar? Now multiply that by a thousand. That much suffering does terrible things to the human mind and soul…terrible things. Four years ago, we managed to rescue the famous general, Sun Tsu, hoping that he would help us plan our strategy against Satan and his minions."

"Who is Sun Tsu?"

"A very famous Chinese military leader from the sixth century B.C.," replied Bedillia. "He wrote a book called *The Art of War*. You know, 'keep your friends close, and your enemies even closer'?"

"Oh yeah, now I know who you mean. I think it would be interesting to meet that guy."

"I'm afraid not," said Bedillia. "You see, he had been condemned to struggle forever in a horrible pit of what might best be described as boiling blood…in one of the hottest regions on the surface of Hell. There he was for nearly 2,600 years in horrible agony, until Abaddon swept down and rescued him. We had high hopes that after a few weeks of recuperation he might be back on his feet and ready to lead our human armies. But we were wrong. So much time in torment is enough to drive human reason and logic out of any man. What's left is the basic instincts, mainly the desire to escape pain. He lies in his bed, resting comfortably, yet he is a human vegetable. The great military mind of Sun Tsu is long gone. That is the ultimate fate of all humanity here…to become beings who understand only horror and the need to escape their pain."

"Ghastly," Tom said.

"There are some who do survive their long ordeal with their minds intact," replied Bedillia. "There is this Scotsman who lives among us, Kyle McCandish, a wonderful man, really. He burned within a blazing pit of fire, reduced to nothing more than bones, for over 300 years. Despite that awful ordeal, he is one of the pillars of this community, a man of considerable insight. There are a few from still earlier times among us, but the torments of Hell have reduced most of them to little more than shadows of their former selves. They are good citizens for the most part, thankful to be among us, but they are capable of only the most menial of tasks. They need continual guidance. The souls subjected to the torments of Hell for many hundreds of years become bundles of pain with no true consciousness…not like ours, anyway. Maybe it's better, more merciful for them that way. I can't imagine being tormented for eternity with my mind intact, can you?"

There were footsteps behind them, then a voice. "Dr. Carson?"

Tom turned to see a thin oriental man in what looked like a brown lab coat, running to catch up with them. At first, he didn't recognize him.

"It's me, Bill Wong," said the man, extending his hand. "The last time we talked was at the High Energy Physics Conference in Baltimore three years ago, remember?"

Tom accepted his hand. Of course he remembered him, now. Dr. William Wong was an expert in the area of manipulation of atoms with force fields. His theories had been, to say the least, controversial. He took liberties with the equations of Schrodinger and de Broglie that put him at odds with the majority of the scientific community. What was worse, he could support his claims with solid experimental evidence. Nothing disturbed the scientific community more than the suggestion that their long-held views of atoms might be fundamentally flawed.

He and Bill had corresponded on numerous occasions over the years. But the Dr. Wong he remembered had been a man in his early seventies, and not in the best of health. Wong had died of cancer a good year before his own demise. Now here he was looking so much younger.

"I heard that you'd arrived," he continued. "I'm looking forward to our collaboration on the project. I really need your help. Imagine the possibilities if we succeed; manipulating matter into any form we wish, assembling complex electronics components through the use of force fields powered by disciplined thought. It is technology largely without instrumentality, hundreds of years beyond anything we might have imagined on Earth."

Bedillia seemed almost panicked. "Bill, he hasn't been briefed yet. Tom has only been conscious for a couple of hours."

"I didn't know," replied Bill, with a more restrained tone. "Well, Tom, we've got our challenges in the days ahead. Of that you may be sure. I hope you're feeling up to it."

With those words, Dr. Wong retreated in the direction from which he had come. It was the straw that broke the camel's back. Tom could neither hold his peace nor his cool any longer.

"Bedillia, what is going on here!? You say you want my help. OK, you've got it, but I can't get a straight answer from you about what you people are doing. I know only a little bit about these monsters in Satan's service, and that's what they are. You're outnumbered a thousand to one, outgunned, and in enemy territory. The enemy is physically stronger than you. They have who knows how many millennia of experience under their belts. Did I miss something?"

Bedillia only shook her head.

"And you talk about victory? I'm sorry, but that dog just doesn't hunt. I need answers, and I need them now. Come on, work with me here, Bedillia."

Tom had expected an angry reply from Bedillia, but he didn't get it. She just wasn't that person anymore.

"Only Abaddon can give you those answers."

"Then take me to him," said Tom calmly but insistently.

"Right now?" asked Bedillia.

"Right now."

"OK," said Bedillia, "but I wanted you to have more time before discussing this with Abaddon. He tends to be fairly intense. I wanted you at your best when you met with him. Come on then, I'll take you to him."

Bedillia picked up her pace, and Tom followed. Their path took them through a series of twisting tunnels that led steadily upward. After twenty minutes, they entered a wide brightly lit tunnel with more pedestrian traffic than he had seen up to this point—humans, the strange insect-like creatures, and dark angels like those he had seen on his deliverance day. He was surprised to see a man hurrying down the corridor with what appeared to be a stack of large industrial-size blueprints under one arm and some sort of complex electronic device in the other hand. He was also surprised to see a set of metal pipes running along the ceiling overhead. They looked like electrical conduits.

The cavern walls here, hewn to much greater precision, gave him the impression of an underground high security complex. Many of the side passageways were guarded by heavy metal doors, and Tom could hear the sound of machinery in the background—including what sounded like a huge dynamo. Maybe that sound had been there all along, even in the lower caverns, but he had dismissed it as being natural. Here it was much louder.

"We call this the hub," said Bedillia. "Life is fast paced here. People might work for days without a break. After that, they welcome the quiet solitude of the lower caverns. You'll be working down there." Bedillia pointed to a long wide corridor to the left. "That is where our labs are."

"Labs where you folks are involved in manipulating matter with your minds?" deduced Tom.

Bedillia nodded. "But it's not as simple as it sounds. We need your help."

"You said that before," said Tom. "I didn't think it would be simple. But what value would there be to building things with your mind?"

"Because without it, we have no chance of defeating Satan. We can't produce all the materials we need for the coming conflict if we can't do that. We can't build factories to produce what we need, we can't conduct mining operations for the minerals we require; we lack the manpower."

"So you think you're going to make this pie in the sky technology work and save the day? Bedillia, I don't want to dash your hopes, but even if you had the best minds on Earth working on the problem 24-7 with a world of resources at their disposal, it might take a century or more to perfect such a technology."

"Tom, you are so negative," scolded Bedillia. "We've already developed the technology. It works; we just need help refining it. We need you."

By now they'd reached another wide corridor that branched off to the left. A pair of formidable metal doors guarded the entry to this rocky hallway, but they were open wide. Like all of the subterranean corridors, this one had large glowing crystals in the ceiling as light fixtures. However, these had a distinctly blue hue, compared to the yellow ones Tom had previously seen.

"This is where the dark angels live," explained Bedillia. "The doors are usually open, but the dark angels tend to be a bit solitary. They prefer that we humans respect their privacy. That is where you will find Abaddon."

"Can we go in?" asked Tom.

"Sure…we just don't want to overstay our welcome, that's all." Bedillia entered the blue corridor, and Tom followed. "The color of the crystals is to remind us that this is their home—their special place, not ours."

"They don't have something personal against humans, do they?" asked Tom.

"No, of course not," replied Bedillia. "In time, you will come to understand the angels. They are, well, different. They don't think quite the same way we do. Oh, they like us, really they do. In fact, they are somewhat paternalistic when it comes to humans. It's just that they prefer to interact with each other. It is really tough to get close to one of them."

"But you have," observed Tom, who hoped that his observation wasn't too personal.

Bedillia looked over at him, but briefly. "Yes, I have, thanks largely to my daughter. She had a very special relationship with the angels, a very rare relationship. I've sort of inherited that standing. You see, Abaddon is not one for making speeches, so I become his spokeswoman when communicating with the human population here. I also become the spokeswoman for their concerns."

"Sounds like an important position," observed Tom, as they passed a dark angel in the corridor, who offered a friendly smile, but little more.

"I suppose," was the reply. "My title is counselor. I take it seriously. I'd never betray Abaddon's trust, his faith in me."

A left turn, brought them to a partially open metal door, and behind it Tom could hear voices. They spoke a strange language that Tom had never heard before.

"This is Abaddon's audience chamber," whispered Bedillia. "It sounds like they are discussing important business. I really don't want to barge in on them right this minute."

"You understand what they are saying?" asked Tom, in a hushed tone.

Bedillia nodded. "They are speaking in the universal language of the angels. It is the language of all angels in Heaven, as well as the dark angels here."

Tom drew closer to the door to better discern the words. "What are they talking about, if you don't mind my asking?"

"It sounds like a matter of security," replied Bedillia.

It didn't seem like Bedillia wanted to elaborate on that topic further, so Tom changed the subject somewhat. "Do Satan and his brood speak it too?"

"They speak a dialect of it," was the reply. "It is a bit more harsh and guttural, but it is essentially the same language, or so I've been told. I've rarely heard it."

Bedillia paused for several minutes before stepping in. Tom followed. The room beyond was large and brightly lit, not by a single crystal in the ceiling but a multitude of them, set like candles in a chandelier of gold and fine crystal. There was another metal door, the color of bronze on the far wall, with large Chinese-looking symbols etched into its surface. The walls of the room were adorned by large almost breathtaking paintings of forests, meadows, and a dazzling city that Tom assumed had to be in Heaven. Surely no earthly city could boast of such grandeur. Upon a black marble table at the back corner of the room, a clear glass sphere, about a foot in diameter, sat upon a round metal base. To Tom, it looked like a fortuneteller's crystal ball.

Eight dark angels sat around a large rectangular table of white polished marble in the middle of the room. All possessed great black wings like that of a mighty crow, and all but two were cloaked head to toe in a black robe with long flowing sleeves. The remaining two were decked out in glistening chain mail armor. From the belts of the armored angels hung large swords sheathed in jeweled scabbards. At Bedillia's entrance, they all turned and then stood in unison.

"Selane et entraeus, carba se ling," she said to the gathered assembly, bowing slightly.

"It is quite all right," assured the angel in armor at the far end of the table. "We were just concluding our business. You are welcome here among us, as are you Dr. Tom Carson."

The other armored angel turned to see Tom and smiled. "I am pleased to see you awake and on your feet. I am Lenar."

"Yes," said Tom, "I remember you. Thank you."

"It was our privilege," assured Lenar.

Then Tom's eyes shifted to the angelic being at the head of the table. He remembered him too—the short beard, dark penetrating eyes, and burley face. That face would be engraved in his mind forever. He had introduced himself at the time of his deliverance. "Thank you for freeing me, Abaddon. I owe you more than I could ever say."

"And you'll have the opportunity to repay me," assured Abaddon, a slight smile coming to his face. "I desire to speak to you at length; however, there is a more pressing matter that requires my attention. In truth, it is a matter associated with your rescue from that altar. You humans might call it a 'loose end.' I made a foolish mistake during your rescue. Hopefully, it is not too late to correct it."

Abaddon turned to Lenar. "My brother, meet me at the ring in ten minutes. Hopefully, this will be a quick, simple mission. Hopefully. Our meeting is adjourned until the fifteenth hour, at which time I shall report on the state of the damage, if any. I pray this mission does not make matters all the worse."

The angels filed out of the room, leaving only Abaddon, Tom, and Bedillia. Abaddon turned to Tom. "Walk with me for a few minutes. I'm sure you have many questions."

The three walked from the room into the hallway. Tom anticipated getting a few answers from this enigmatic dark angel, yet it was Abaddon who asked the first question.

"Dr. Carson, why does Hell exist?"

Tom was taken aback. His experience with Hell had been on the most personal of levels. To him, the answer was obvious. Or was it? "Once, I would have said it was where the evil people of the world could be punished for their crimes against humanity. That is, if I'd believed that it existed at all."

"Now you know it exists. Tell me doctor, do you consider yourself evil?"

Tom was beginning to feel a bit nervous. He was starting to understand what Bedillia meant when she said that Abaddon was intense. "No, I don't."

Abaddon's expression remained essentially devoid of emotion. "So, why are you here?"

"I was sent here because of the way I lived my life on Earth. I should have known that Jesus was the way to salvation; I heard it often enough, but I didn't accept it. I didn't have time for God. I suppose, really, science was my god. So God commissioned Satan, master of Hell, to see to my eternal torment."

Abaddon shook his head. "An elegant explanation, however it happens to be wrong. You have much to learn about this place. Hell was intended to be a place of separation from God, not a place of physical punishment or torture. Trust me when I tell you that God is not like that, He is not a torturer. Satan, however, is. And Satan was not appointed master of this realm. Oh, he envisions his role to be that, but he deludes himself. He does it for his own sanity."

"So, why is he here?" asked Tom.

"Simple," replied Abaddon, "he is a prisoner like the rest of us. He rules by virtue of the fact that he was here first, and commands a vast number of fanatical followers. He took a relatively benign world—this world—and shaped it into a form after his own dark soul, a realm perfectly suited to torture your kind because his hate is so great and his envy of humanity so deep. Although he inflicts pain and horror endlessly, it cannot satisfy him. There is never enough. As your kind arrived, he restrained them in irons and subjected them to pain so great that they cannot think to ponder escape, to rise up against their tormentors. As your numbers have grown ever greater, the necessity to keep you occupied with your agony has steadily increased. Today in Hell, you outnumber his kind nearly forty to one. His kingdom is fragile; it has been for a long time. It simply needs someone to destabilize it. That is our task. He will make a mistake; his madness dictates it, and when he does we shall exploit it."

Tom hesitated; he wasn't as inclined to draw the fallacy of the plan to Abaddon's attention as he was with Bedillia. Still, he had to. "Humans may outnumber demons in Hell, but I don't see how that matters. They're in no position to help us. We are outnumbered, what, fifteen hundred to one?"

"That is an oversimplification of the dynamics of this struggle," replied Abaddon, who didn't even turn to look at Tom. "It also happens to be incorrect. However, I do not wish Satan to come to that realization. I want him to be overconfident. I do not wish him to realize the full extent of our resources. Know this, Tom Carson, we are able to anticipate his every move, while he neither knows our numbers nor from where we strike. We have weapons and allies of which he knows nothing."

"Like those insect things?" deduced Tom.

"Yes, but that is only part of it. There is much more. We are not ready to face him on the field of battle yet, but with your help we might soon be. Then humanity shall have its revenge upon him, as shall I." Abaddon paused. "This conversation will be continued soon. I assure you, I shall answer all of your questions. There will be no secrets between us."

A metal door opened before them of its own accord, and they stepped in. Here, they found a large room with a silvery metal ring 9 feet in diameter at its center. At the back corner of the room, upon a white marble pedestal, sat another sphere of pure glass, not unlike the one Tom had seen in the audience hall. A faint glow emanated from its center.

Lenar and about a hundred of the tiny creatures Tom had come to know only too well were already here. Lenar handed Abaddon a small sphere, about the size of a large marble. It glowed with a pure white light. It was strange, but there was something about the light—it was beautiful, peaceful. Abaddon placed it in a pouch in his belt. He looked to Lenar. "We shall use the ring to get us there, the orb to get us back."

Abaddon walked to the glassy sphere on the pedestal. He placed his left hand upon the sphere before withdrawing it. The sphere seemed to dissolve into a ball of soft light several times larger. For a moment, the soft glow was transformed into a ball of salt and pepper static, not unlike that of a television tuned between stations. Out of the static, an image was forming. It was another angel, yet this one had white wings like those of a dove and was draped in a flowing white robe. His form was like a hologram with depth and substance.

"Be well, my brother," said Abaddon, gazing at the incredible three dimensional image before him.

"And to you, my brother," responded the white angel. "Are you ready?"

"I am," confirmed Abaddon.

"The corridor is clear," said the angel. "She had a visitor several hours ago, but he has departed. She is alone, though I know not for how much longer. It would be best if you made haste. May the Father guide your steps."

"I depart even now," confirmed Abaddon, making his way to the glistening metal ring where Lenar and the small creatures awaited him.

Abaddon stretched out his hand, and a sphere of mist and glistening star-like light formed within the ring. He wasted no time. He stepped into the light. He seemed to be walking into its depths, only to vanish from sight. Lenar and the small creatures quickly followed, vanishing into the phantasmal depths.

Tom stared at the phenomenon he had just witnessed in disbelief. Never had he seen such a thing. They had stepped into one end of the ring, but never appeared on the other. What had happened to them?

The mists evaporated behind them, and Tom and Bedillia found themselves alone in the room. Well, almost alone.

Bedillia and Tom walked over to the sphere of light where the white-robed angel watched them. A broad smile appeared on his face. "Hello, Bedillia. It is pleasant to see you again."

"Always a pleasure to see you, Aaron," she replied.

"And I send greetings to you as well, Tom Carson," said Aaron.

"Happy to meet you, Aaron," said Tom.

"We need to conserve precious power," said Aaron, "so I must take my leave. I feel certain that Abaddon's quest shall meet with success. I will be with you in two days if the loving Father wills it to be so."

"We'll see you then," replied Bedillia.

The glow faded, leaving the glass sphere once more.

Tom slowly approached it, gazing into it intently. At first, all he saw was smooth glass; then he saw fine lines running through the glass. They seemed to merge near the bottom of the sphere, into a mesh of incredible complexity, into several almost microscopic black cubes. Fiber optic circuitry? If so, it spoke of a technology far beyond that of early 21st century Earth.

"We call it a telesphere," noted Bedillia. "It is not of angelic design, but was made by human hands, hands belonging to the humans who will teach you to do things beyond your wildest dreams. Get ready to open your mind to a new world."

Tom shook his head in amazement. "You're getting help from the angels of Heaven?"

Bedillia nodded, "Yes, some of them, and some of the saints too."

Tom smiled slightly. Clearly he had a lot to learn about this place and this conflict. He would not quickly dismiss the claims of this peculiar woman again. He looked forward to the future with anticipation.

Julie gazed between the gray bars of her small, dismal cell into the rocky corridor beyond. This ten-by-ten cubical offered few amenities. The small precious cup of water, now empty, had been one of them. She'd been here four days—four days without pain. The first day had been a bit rough. In the absence of the pain, she had felt so empty. It had been like going through withdrawal from heroin all over again, complete with the confusion, the depression, and even the hallucinations. She still remembered that awful week so long ago. How many years ago had that been? She didn't know. Thankfully, this time, it had passed more quickly.

Right now, she was happy to be here. Imagine being happy to be locked away in a bare, dusty dungeon cell, but she was. Never had a prison felt so good.

Actually, she had not been at all certain that this demon, Cordon, would keep his word to her. She envisioned remaining on that horrible altar until the end of time, an eternal meal for the scavengers of the air. But he had kept his word. Within a matter of hours of his departure, two demons had released her and brought her here, to this subterranean dungeon. Amazingly, they had been gentle with her, as that dark angel had promised. She would gladly have remained here within the safety of these walls for all eternity. But that wouldn't happen, would it? Very soon she would be out there again, if not on an altar, on some other device of pain. It was inevitable. She was like a prisoner on death row, only worse. The absence of pain had made the anticipation of its return all the more terrible. Had he actually done her a favor?

"Oh, God, please deliver me, a sinner," she whispered.

No, now she was being foolish, there was no deliverance in Hell. Cordon had made that only too clear. He had spent nearly an hour with her today, trying to extract more information. Right now he wanted a name, the name of the dark being who had released this Carson fellow. Yes, she had heard it that day on the fields of agony, and now, she remembered it—Abaddon. Yet she had kept it from the demon. It was the last card she held. She was stalling for time. Perhaps she could buy herself a few more days. Once she told him, there would be nothing keeping him from dumping her back into the devil's playground to continue the game. He would be back in a few hours. If she didn't give him the name, well that might be it anyway. She turned from the bars and curled up in the shadowy back corner of the cell. If only she could curl up in its darkness and disappear.

In the midst of her depression, a glowing blue cloud appeared in the middle of her cell. Within seconds the cloud was filled with a myriad of sparkling stars. It had been so long since she had seen stars. Julie gazed in wonder at this marvelous sight. It was so beautiful.

Then she saw him; a dark form emerging from the mists, then another, then a swarm of the creatures she had seen only once before, on the plains, under the blazing sun. He gazed at her, the poor girl on the floor who was illuminated by the lights of the mystical portal. She returned his gaze with a growing smile. Tears came to her eyes. It was him! It was really him.

"Please, Abaddon, take me with you, oh God, please. I didn't tell him who you were—he couldn't make me tell," cried Julie.

Abaddon smiled and extended his hand. "Then come Julie, I'll take you away from all of this. I'll take you to Refuge, a place where no one will hurt you ever again. Come, take my hand."

Julie was crying tears of joy as Abaddon lifted her to her feet and took her into his arms. "Be still, child, we are leaving right now."

"Easier than we had dared to hope," noted Lenar, who had already reopened the portal.

"You will have your own place," continued Abaddon, leading Julie toward the glowing stars. "No chains will hold you again, and no bars confine you; you are going home."

A moment later, they vanished into the soft starry mists. The small creatures quickly followed. Lenar took one last look behind them, so as to confirm that they had not been observed. Then he too vanished into the mists. Their glow quickly faded, leaving an empty cell behind.

Barely ten minutes had passed, when Cordon returned to visit Julie. His final trip to the altars had not been productive. None of the other victims surrounding Thomas Carson had been very helpful. One had no eyes with which to see, nor ears with which to hear at the time of his disappearance. Another had been beset by some sort of small creatures, which had acted to distract him. The others were simply at the wrong angle or too far away to get a good look. Julie was the only reliable witness.

Cordon was out of patience, as he walked up the corridor. Julie was the key, his only lead. He had pampered this wench long enough. She knew the name of this dark angel, of that he was certain. She admitted to having heard it. Her insistence that she couldn't remember it was a rouse. Now he would know it as well. He would do whatever was necessary to extract it. He would offer the carrot first, before resorting to the stick. He was not opposed to giving her a few more days of peace if he got what he wanted.

Still, her new place of torment was already selected; an icy resting place in the frozen wastelands of the Dark Continent. It was not the easiest ordeal to prepare, but it would be well worth the effort. A fireball or two would be needed to melt the rock-hard ground into a deep viscous slurry of mud and ice. Then, with her arms shackled behind her back, and a heavy ball and chain around both ankles to act as ballast, she would be tossed in, to sink into the yielding depths, even as they froze quickly around and over her. In the thirty-degrees-below-zero environment, she would vanish into obscurity, frozen in the ice fifteen feet down.

Was it better than the altars, less painful? Probably not. She would exchange the agony of eternal dismemberment at the scratching claws and pecking beaks of the birds for the stabbing cold pain of being forever frozen, suffocating in the dark cruel ice. Still, to Cordon, one ordeal was pretty much like another. These humans had to be put away, restrained, neutralized. Their suffering was of no real consequence to him. It was what the master demanded. Anyway, what he needed was for her to disappear, and this ordeal would certainly accomplish that. And it would be a change of scenery for Julie, a place where she could hide. The irony was amusing.

He did not immediately comprehend what he saw as he gazed into her cell. Was she there in the shadows as she often was? "Julie, come forth, we have business to discuss."

No answer; she was gone. He examined the cell lock; it was undisturbed. She had vanished without a trace from within a locked cell.

He resisted the urge to vent his rage by striking the wall or the bars of the cell. That would accomplish nothing. He was faced with another mystery, or was it another clue? He wasn't sure. Still, it might be a good idea if this incident remained his dirty little secret for now. It wouldn't be all that difficult to orchestrate. After all, his own superior had done it many times.

All it would take is a minor adjustment of the books. In the meantime, he would continue his investigation. He would get to the bottom of this disappearance—of that he was certain.

Chapter 5

Tom was restless and nervous as he paced back and forth in Abaddon's audience chamber. He'd been waiting nine hours for this opportunity, and now here he was waiting again. It had been Bedillia who had excitedly come to his room with the news that Abaddon was at last ready to see him. It had taken nearly twenty minutes for him to get here, so vast was this place. He was concerned about keeping Abaddon waiting. He was obviously a busy angel. But it had been Tom who had been kept waiting, over an hour at this point. He walked to the back of the room and gazed into the crystal tele-sphere. It appeared identical to the one in the ring room.

"I apologize for my tardiness," said a voice from behind him.

Tom turned to find the enigmatic angel standing at the other side of the table. He was surprised that so large a winged being could move so stealth-ily. "How did your mission go?"

"Perfectly," was Abaddon's reply. "I think she will make a good lab assis-tant for you."

"I'm afraid I don't even know what your mission was beyond the fact that it somehow was related to my rescue. She? Do I know her?"

"Well, you have been only eight feet apart for the past eighteen months, but I doubt you know her. I thought Bedillia might have told you," contin-ued Abaddon. "At the time of your rescue six days ago, one of the human victims on an altar close to yours overheard our conversation. I'm afraid that I introduced myself by name. Anonymity is one of our strongest advantages. A certain master demon by the name of Cordon has been investigating the incident, questioning the humans occupying the altars around you. Only one saw or heard anything of any substance. He had spirited her away to a waiting cell where he has been questioning her, yet she had resisted telling him my name. She is a most remarkable woman. She has a kind spirit, even after 14 years on the altar. Therefore, I brought her here. I think that she shall be a useful addition to our community. There are many people here who are deserving of a second chance, like you." Abaddon motioned to a chair at the table. "Please, sit, we have much to discuss."

"Thank you," replied Tom, sitting in a chair that, amazingly enough, seemed to be composed of cushioned metal. Abaddon sat across from him.

"This Cordon is not so blind a follower of Satan as most," continued Abaddon. "He employs unique methods. He thinks for himself, and he is dedicated. Now he has taken up the crusade of seeking us out. He is not as yet sure of who we are, what our mission is, or what our capabilities are. Still, he is a nemesis that bears watching carefully."

Tom nodded but said nothing.

"Never has the likes of which we are endeavoring to accomplish been done here in Hell," said Abaddon. "It is a revolution, plain and simple. It is not just a revolution of ideas or ideals, but of actions. Ideas and ideals will one day change the nature of existence here, but this place will be won through pure force, through violence and pain. This is the task set before us, and we are not alone. We have allies. The small creatures, my children, represent one of them."

"How many of those things, your children, do you have, if you don't mind my asking?"

"You may ask anything," replied Abaddon, "I am an angel; I don't have secrets. Currently the number is somewhat over seven million. They multiply quickly when they are active, and have a long life expectancy. They are not immortal; they can be killed, but it is difficult. Currently, due to a scarcity of food, most of them are in a state of deep hibernation within the lowest caverns of Refuge, but one day soon I will awaken them to begin their mission."

"And you created them?" asked Tom.

"Actually, genetically engineered would be a more accurate term," replied the dark angel. "It was a process that required centuries. They were developed from one of the native creatures that existed here at the time of my arrival, at a time when this world was not so foul. I saved it from extinction. Hell never was a world so grand as your Earth, but ten thousand years ago it was far kinder. One of our goals is to restore it if possible, and I believe it is."

"I remember that one of them smiled at me when I thanked him for releasing me from the altar," said Tom. "I was a bit out of it at the time, but it seemed like it understood what I said."

"He did," confirmed Abaddon. "They are highly intelligent."

"And you command them?"

"Yes," confirmed Abaddon, "and so can you. They are a marvelous species. They can discern the nature of the human soul by the very aura that surrounds all of us. They can sense if you are disposed to furthering the ends of good or evil. You are a good man, Tom. I knew that even before I rescued you. For much of your life you were confused; many men are, but you are now beginning to see the light as well as a purpose for your life."

"I saw the light a bit late, I fear," noted Tom, shaking his head.

"Perhaps," said Abaddon, "only time will answer that question."

"And you spoke of other allies," continued Tom, who wished to get back to the original line of discussion. "Was the angel I saw in the crystal one of them, this Aaron?"

Abaddon smiled. "He most certainly is, and he is not alone. There are currently about 5,000 angels in Heaven who share his sympathies. In addition, there are now several hundred humans in Heaven, saints who know of our struggle, and like Aaron, are willing to assist us. You see, the vast majority of your people in Heaven know nothing of those of us here. It is for their own peace of mind that it is so. After all, who would want to live for eternity knowing that a mother or father, a brother, sister, or cousin, was in torment in Hell, and that they are powerless to intervene? The Father, in His wisdom, made it so.

However, for the first time in all of eternity, there are those who seek to know. They realize that in knowing they will find both truth and despair. Yet, they do so nonetheless. They come to realize that they can no longer live in paradise with their eyes closed. Many of these have become powerful allies. The communicating device which you saw earlier, the one which allows direct and instantaneous communication between Heaven and Hell was developed by just such a group of persons. And those in Heaven send more than information. There are angels who brave the journey between Heaven and Hell to bring us other things such as tools, seeds, weapons, and power. But it is impossible for them to bring us all that we need for our struggle. We will need to learn to manufacture some of these things for ourselves, in much the same manner as they do."

"I assume that is where I come in," observed Tom.

"Very astute," confirmed Abaddon. "I am asking you to perfect an art no one here has yet mastered."

"Yes, assembling complex components from base materials, using nothing but the powers of thought," replied Tom.

This time, Abaddon seemed truly impressed. "You are more deductive than I had imagined."

Tom chuckled. "Not really, I just overhear people talking and pull it all together. Quite honestly, I can't see how it can be done. The energy required to transmute one element into another is truly enormous. The heat required to accomplish it would be on the order of tens of millions of degrees...at least."

Abaddon smiled. "Somehow, I knew you were going to say that. But as the people in your century like to say, you need to think outside the box. This is not Earth, nor is it the universe with which you are familiar. The rules of physics work somewhat differently here, as you will soon discover. However, they are not tremendously different. Your skills as a physicist, especially one in your field, make you the perfect candidate to try."

Tom pondered Abaddon's proposal for a moment. "As I promised you from the altar, I will do what I can. What sort of time frame are we looking at?"

"Of that I am uncertain," said Abaddon. "Something is happening. In the last year, Satan has nearly doubled his forces on Earth, waging spiritual warfare against your people. Despite our considerable ability to gather intelligence about him, it does have limits. His book is virtually impossible to probe. It is hazardous to any who would dare open it."

"Book?" asked Tom.

"Yes," confirmed Abaddon. "There is in Heaven a great hall of records that holds the sum total of the experiences of all beings, both humans and angels. Those records take the form of books, but they are not books of leather and paper as you understand them. They are far more. They are able to carry you on a journey with that individual, to see the contents of his or her entire life, from birth up to the present. That is how we can anticipate what Satan's minions are doing. Looking into their books is hazardous enough; looking into Satan's is too dangerous to contemplate. We see him only through the eyes of others. We can only guess what his real motives and plans are. We know that he has long contemplated an invasion of Heaven to settle scores with Michael and Gabriel, but we do not know when such might happen."

Tom looked at Abaddon incredulously. "Surely he doesn't think he has a chance of defeating God."

"He doesn't have to," said Abaddon. "He will seek God's permission to challenge Michael and Gabriel in armed conflict."

"Surely God won't allow it," replied Tom.

"Don't be so sure," cautioned Abaddon. "He allowed Satan to persecute Job. God moves in mysterious ways, as you might have heard."

"OK," continued Tom, "could Satan really pull it off? Could he defeat the angels?"

"Not if I have anything to say about it," replied Abaddon. "As Satan has a score to settle with Michael and Gabriel, so I have a score to settle with him. Revenge is not among the more noble angelic virtues, my friend; then again no one is perfect, least of all me. I will defeat him and end his reign of terror. I shall personally see that he is brought to justice, that he pays for his crimes against humanity." Abaddon paused, his eyes took on a greater intensity. "And you will assist me. Together we will change the face of Hell."

"As I said before, I'm with you all the way," assured Tom. "I owe you a great debt, and I intend to pay it. Anyway, I think I have a score to settle with old slewfoot as well."

That brought a broad smile to the dark angel's countenance. "I expected no less. From the day I saw you on that altar, I knew you were a man of honor. You had the aura of such. Your selection goes well beyond your expertise in physics, it also hinged on your character. Welcome to the fight."

Tom returned Abaddon's smile. "When do we get started?"

"I want you to take a few days to get solidly on your feet and clear your mind," replied Abaddon. "Get familiar with this place. It has over twenty miles of developed tunnels, and hundreds more that are scarcely explored. The surface above our heads is a realm of intense cold, like your Antarctica, only eternally in night. It is highly unpleasant, even for immortals such as ourselves. So for the time being, these caverns are our world, but only for the time being."

Now Tom saw where Bedillia got her confidence, her hope. Abaddon's positivity and confidence was contagious. Maybe he could really do it, as incredible as it all seemed.

"Come, my friend," said Abaddon, motioning toward the door. "Allow me to show you our facilities. Let me show you why we have hope."

During the next hour, Abaddon gave Tom a tour of sorts, a tour very unlike the one he had received from Bedillia. Tom saw the power-generating facility, a device totally alien to any technology he had ever seen before. He also saw labs, complete with many things one associated with laboratories on Earth. They had common tools like beakers, flasks, and burners, all assembled from base materials found in the very rocks around them.

"Assembling simple compounds like the silicon dioxide for glassware or the copper wire to transmit electric current are tasks that your friend Dr. William Wong has already mastered. Our problem is in fabricating more complex items like small electronic components, integrated circuits, chips, if you will. That is where you come in. I will leave it up to Bill Wong to teach you the finer points."

"But that sphere, I mean, telesphere," asked Tom, "the one that allowed us to communicate with the angel, where was that manufactured?"

"Heaven," was the matter-of-fact answer. "The artisans of Heaven have refined the creation of such things to a fine art. This particular one was manufactured by an inventor and scientist with whom you may have some familiarity. His name is Nikola Tesla."

"Tesla!" exclaimed Tom. "Yes, I sure have heard of him."

"He is one of our most dedicated human allies in Heaven," noted Abaddon. "So great are his skills that he and several others from Heaven once ventured on a mission into outer darkness aboard a vehicle of his own design. He had created a weapon so powerful as to be capable of, I believe he used the word 'disrupting,' the very bones and sinew of a demon warrior… and at considerable range. It was an impressive accomplishment indeed for a human. It took him years to master his skills. I do not know how much time you will have, but you too must master that art. Satan and his brood don't have any weapons as sophisticated as that. A large number of these sophisticated weapons, the sort developed by Tesla, would make it possible for us to face Satan's minions on the field of battle and defeat them, numerical superiority not withstanding. Still, we cannot afford to transport these weapons in vast quantities from Heaven to Hell. The abilities of our angelic messengers are being stretched to the limits as it is. Anyway, we cannot risk their being followed here, to this place. Refuge must not be discovered by Satan and his minions before we are ready."

"Please tell me you have weapons like that in your arsenal here?" said Tom.

"We have weapons like that here," confirmed Abaddon, "but not enough. That is where you come in. Currently we have only eleven…we need thousands. The lab you will be working in is unique. It has many, one-of-a-kind instruments, transported piece by piece from Heaven. You will have access to virtually all of the resources that a novice matter manipulator in Heaven would have. Bill will help you with most of the fundamentals, but you will also be able to communicate with Nikola Tesla himself using one of our telespheres. It is he who will be your actual teacher."

Abaddon's face took on a more serious countenance. "You will have all of the resources we possess at your disposal. The rest, hopefully success, is up to you. Don't fail, Doctor; we are counting on you. This revolution will likely fail without those weapons."

No pressure, thought Tom as he walked back to his quarters. *No, I just have the eternal destiny of a thousand or more people counting on my ability to accomplish something that has never been done before. No, no worries.*

Abaddon had emphasized the importance of a positive attitude, the belief that the seemingly impossible could be accomplished. Still, Tom couldn't shake the doubts that plagued him.

Satan rose from his golden throne and walked across the crimson carpet toward the large ring of metal that looked to be made of shimmering brass, fully nine feet in diameter, resting upright upon a finely fashioned golden support. Yet gazing through the ring, he did not see the cavern wall beyond it; no, its inner edge glowed a deep blue, that slowly transitioned to violet, then blackness. Within the heart of the ring, distant blue lightning flashed amid a dark sea of nothingness.

His vast audience chamber held a hundred spectators on this day. The spectators took on a multitude of grotesque forms. Those forms were, however, transient. These minions of Satan had the power to appear in whatever form pleased them, and right now they took on a form that might best strike fear in the humans called into this chamber to face sentencing. The stage was set for the next victim of Satan's wrath. The proceedings this day had gone quite rapidly. The master of Hell was in a hurry. He had more pressing business to see to today; yet, these sentencing proceedings would be conducted nonetheless. They would not be turned over to one of the lesser minions. Anyway, this activity amused Satan and reduced his stress level. He had saved the best one of the day for last.

Something appeared within the dark heart of the ring. It was still a long way off, but was approaching the threshold rapidly. It was a winged demon cloaked in black with a human in tow at the end of a long chain that coursed with bright blue electricity. He emerged from the ring and landed on his feet quite gracefully. With his bat-like wings folded up behind him, he took several steps forward.

The human's landing was far less gentle. He exploded from the ring and reaching the end of the chain around his neck, came crashing down, slamming face first onto the cavern floor. With his hands shackled behind his back his hard landing was virtually preordained. Dressed only in a gray soiled loincloth, blood dripping from his broken nose, he looked up into the face of the master of the dark realm. This man who appeared to be in his mid-twenties had a dark beard and seemed to be of Middle Eastern descent.

"Now look what you've done," scolded Satan. "You've dripped your filthy blood all over my nice clean floor. What am I to do with you humans?"

"I don't belong here," he said, his tone breathless. "I am a humble servant of Allah. I don't serve you."

"Oh, I see," said Satan, turning about for a moment, before turning to face the man once more. "You don't? I disagree. That bomb you strapped about you before you walked into that Baghdad marketplace killed twenty-two people. You sent eighteen of them straight to me. You have served me well, Ali."

"They were most assuredly all Shiites," retorted Ali. "They deserved to be sent here. They have distorted the words of the prophet, peace be unto him. I was acting in the name of God."

"Were you now?" responded Satan in a taunting voice. "God told you to slaughter a group of market goers? You humans never cease to amuse me."

"I was acting as the hand of God...I don't belong here," insisted the man, who once more tried to rise, though a boot to the center of his back sent him again to the floor. "There has been a mistake; I belong in Heaven. I have earned, with my own blood, the pleasures it offers. I will lie with the boys of eternal freshness and with the virgins. They promised it to me. I died in jihad. I was guaranteed to go to Heaven. You can't stop me."

This time Satan laughed. "I can't stop you? I think I already have. You will be pleased to learn that I have already sentenced several of your victims to dreadful ordeals within my realm. Very soon you shall join them. Oh, but your eternal punishment should be far worse. The question is, what shall it be?" Satan played with his goatee for a moment, apparently in thought. "Oh yes, of course, I have just the thing. Menlek, hog-tie this infidel, I'm sending him to the Caverns of Torment."

"Yes, my Lord, it is my pleasure," said the demon at the human's side.

A pair of barbed shackles was placed around Ali's ankles. The chain between them was looped around the one joining his wrist shackles, drawing him back into a most unnatural position. The task accomplished, the shackles around his ankles snapped shut as if magnetized, and once closed, burst into a red heat, welding themselves around his ankles permanently. Ali howled in pain as smoke laden with the smell of burning hair and broiling flesh emanated from beneath his shackles.

"Like your unsuspecting victims, you shall be rendered helpless, unable to defend yourself against those who shall become your eternal tormentors," announced Satan, waving a hand at the great metal ring behind Ali. The scene changed from that of a stormy ethereal realm to a vast dimly lit cavern in the depths of Hell.

Two demons roughly grabbed Ali by the arms and dragged him to the very threshold of the great ring. They forced him to gaze into the image before him.

At first, Ali could make out nothing, yet his eyes were adapting to the darkness. There was something strange about this place. The walls and floor seemed to be moving, undulating, ever so slowly. And there was something else, the horrified cries and screams of a great multitude. It was a dreadful yet somehow muffled cacophony. Then his eyes grew wide with terror as he realized what he was seeing. It was not the walls and floor that were moving, but the legion of creatures that crawled upon it.

They were unnatural, the largest, ugliest cockroaches he had ever seen. So numerous were they that they crawled over each other as one thick layer.

Some even flew through the twilight world of the cavern. Amid the heaving mass were dark forms engulfed by this filthy brood, flailing wildly about, yet in total futility, for they were restrained in a manner similar to Ali's constraints. A nearby yet muffled scream drew Ali's attention. He looked just beyond the portal to see a figure on the floor covered by no less than two layers of these nightmarish creatures. It was the shriveled form of a man, little more than meager flesh on bones, writhing in his shackles, trying in vain to shake off the obscene creatures. They were biting him, feeding upon him. They even swept in and out of him through his mouth, ears, and nostrils. It was ghastly.

"The Cavern of Torment," announced Satan, stepping to Ali's side. "This shall be your eternal home. You shall be a source of meager moisture for the cockroaches that will suck all of the moisture from your body. They will become your tormentors, your constant companions."

At this point Ali was blubbering and crying pathetically. In his wildest nightmares, he could not have imagined such things. "No, please don't," he cried.

"Don't be ridiculous," laughed Satan. "It is the least that I can do for one who added so many subjects to my kingdom in a single act of hate. Now get in there."

Amid his terrified screams, Ali was cast by the demons into the cavern. The cockroaches were upon him in a matter of seconds. He disappeared into a sheath of crawling horror. His flesh vanished beneath their relentless assault. The last of him to vanish was one wide-open terrified eye, a white island in a sea of pale brown. Then it too was gone, and he became like the others—buried beneath the surging blanket of insects.

The portal went black and then inert, just a ring of metal through which one could see the back wall. The entertainment was over, at least for the moment.

The great diverse hoard filed out of the room save six, those summoned by their master. Satan returned to his throne, even as they gathered at the bottom of the steps that led up to it.

"What do you have to report?" asked the Prince of Darkness.

"Fully a third of my legions are on Earth," announced General Krell. "As such, they have drawn a huge number of Michael's angels to that accursed globe. I am confident that he does not suspect that it is a rouse. I stand ready to withdraw all but a handful of them on your orders. They will be standing with you within two hours of your call, swelling the ranks of the legions I have available here in Hell. You will have a total of 122 million troops at your disposal, with an additional 12 million in reserve. We shall storm into and occupy all eleven of the angelic portals in Heaven, effectively isolating the angels on Earth from their brethren in Heaven. Even the angels in Heaven will have difficulty moving between its different levels. They will be cut off from one another, unable to communicate or mount an effective defense. It will be an operation of divide and conquer."

Satan only nodded before turning to the next demon for his report.

"Lord Satan," said Cerenak, "the power that you have required is available even as we speak." A smile appeared on Cerenak's face. "In very fact, you have fully twenty-two percent more energy than you had requested. We shall open wide the gate between Hell and Heaven. And in the case of unforeseen events, you will have vast resources, enough power to offer you many options. Never have we had such power at our disposal, and you will have more still, all that Kordor can supply. It will increase the strength and endurance of all of your warriors."

Satan pondered Cerenak's lofty claims for a moment. "Cerenak, explain to me one more time how this thing that you have created works."

"Of course, my lord," replied Cerenak. "Two of the key elements in winning a battle against the angels are strength and endurance, especially endurance. Because Michael's brood were created to be warriors and we were not, this has been a problem. But now our warriors will be able to draw upon a vast reservoir of power that was previously not available to them. The power of which I speak will be transmitted directly from the City of Sheol to seven large crystals that will be carried into Heaven with our warriors. They will act both as receivers and reservoirs for that power. As your minions grow weary, they will be reinvigorated by the power that emanates from these crystals. They will be able to throw many fireballs in rapid succession without being drained and fight tirelessly against their opponents without growing weak. They will be the super army you have always desired."

This surprise brought a smile to Satan's face. He had hardly thought it possible. He had asked much of Cerenak, perhaps more than was reasonable, and this relatively minor minion had produced even more. Satan rose to his feet. "Well done indeed, my faithful servant. When this war is won, I will personally see to it that you are well rewarded."

"It is a pleasure to serve," said Cerenak, bowing low.

"Which brings us to the matter of Earth and its demise," said Satan, turning to another of his minions. "What do you have for me, Wormwood? Is this icy shard of a world, this world I named after you in honor of your accomplishment, still on course? Will it strike Earth?"

Wormwood was taken by surprise. Never had they spoken of this before the other minions; it was a private matter. "All is as it was before. There are no mistakes. However, we might be in danger of being found out."

"Explain," replied Satan, in a surprisingly calm tone.

"There are groups of men, scientists, they call themselves, with instruments that scan the skies," began Wormwood. "One of these groups has already discovered the object, though I don't believe that they as yet comprehend the gravity of their situation. My agents have hindered their efforts, caused problems within their instruments. But they continue to scan. I fear they are about to realize the danger."

"Is there anything that they could do at this point?"

"Perhaps," replied Wormwood, "They are not as helpless as they once were."

That comment elicited a raised eyebrow from the master. "I assume that you are doing something to correct this problem?"

"Yes," confirmed Wormwood. "I am endeavoring to deal with the problem on a human level. I am anticipating success. I have not labored so long to be thwarted at this point. There will be no mistakes, rest assured. The Comet Wormwood, this Sword of Satan, if I may be so bold as to call it that, will deal a death blow to the human race. Even if some of them survive the terrible blow it deals them, they will inherit a dying world."

"Yes," said Satan, "I like the sound of that—the Sword of Satan. Thank you Wormwood."

Wormwood bowed before his master.

There was murmuring among the others at this surprise announcement, this revelation. Only Cordon seemed unimpressed.

Satan turned to Governor Molock and his new assistant, Lieutenant Cordon. "Have any more humans disappeared from their places of torment since our last meeting?"

Molock looked to Cordon, yet his lieutenant seemed hesitant. "No, no more disappearances from the places of torment," confirmed Cordon.

Satan nodded approvingly. He directed his gaze at Cordon. "Are you making any progress regarding the person or persons responsible?"

"Actually, quite a bit," he replied. "We now know that it was not the act of a single individual but a group of the dark angels, perhaps all of them. We also know that they are in possession of some new transportation technology, not unlike your ring. They also are using some new creature, perhaps some sort of small insect hybrid, to assist them. It is large numbers of these creatures that have been identified as a dark cloud by some observers. We believe them to be highly intelligent, but not invincible.

"We also know that the dark angels are selecting individual humans whom they feel might be of some use to them. But they will make a mistake—I am certain of it. Eventually a pattern will emerge, and we will set a trap for them. It is only a matter of time. We will bring this incident to an end and return the souls to you so they can continue their service of pain."

Satan turned to Governor Molock, nodding approvingly. "I like this one. You are surrounding yourself with talent."

Molock smiled, bowed, but said no more.

"Then I have an announcement for all of you," said Satan scanning his audience. "The Father will be calling a meeting of the angels very soon. It will be at this meeting that I issue my challenge to Michael. I believe that the Father will allow it." Satan turned to Cerenak. "Will you be prepared to disrupt the gateway between the worlds when I return?"

Cerenak smiled. "I am ready now my lord, or anytime you give the word."

Satan's smile grew. He was hearing everything he had hoped to hear. His day was near. He was sure of it. "Then come to a high state of alert, my friends. I cannot say when the Father will call me. It could be within a matter of days. When I depart, I want everything in readiness. You must be ready on short notice. Good work, everyone."

Satan was rarely in such a mood as this, and even more rarely so complimentary to his minions. As they departed his presence, there was on the surface an upbeat spirit, but below the surface was another matter. There were undercurrents, secrets, and hidden agendas.

Governor Molock looked toward his lieutenant as they walked into the anteroom. "In all of these high level meetings, have you noticed the conspicuous absence of someone?"

"Yes," replied Cordon, "Beelzebub has not been present at any of them. I thought he was Satan's closest confidant."

Molock chuckled. "Hardly. Satan and Beelzebub are not on the best of terms these days, though Satan would not have that fact widely known. Satan views Beelzebub as a rival more than an ally. I suspect that he is not too far from the truth. In fact, he will not even be accompanying the master to Heaven when the invasion is finally called. He will be relegated to commanding what few forces remain behind. Beelzebub is a deceiver and Satan knows it; he will not have him by his side."

"He is not the only one," replied Cordon. "Wormwood too plays a dangerous game of deception."

"Explain," bid Molock.

"Wormwood deceives the master when he claims to be the author of this impending disaster, this collision of worlds."

"Then it will not strike the Earth as he claims?" asked Molock.

"It will strike Earth," confirmed Cordon, "of that I am certain, but Wormwood is not the author of this disaster. When he began the project to alter the course of history by bending the path of an icy rock in deep space, I was with him. We had convinced ourselves that psychic force alone could bend the path of balls of ice and rock weighing billions of tons. We were wrong; when we got there, we discovered that we could hardly move a speck of dust. Yet after convincing the master to give his blessings and resources to our project, what could we do? It was then when we discovered this very special object, one already on a collision course with Earth. It was an incredible stroke of luck—so we took credit for its trajectory ourselves. Afterward, I quietly dropped out of Wormwood's team for fear that our deception would be uncovered, but it wasn't. Now Wormwood and his minions are heroes of the cause. Such irony."

"So you do not like deception, do you?" asked Molock. "Know this Cordon, you are now in the quagmire of deception every bit as deep in as I or Beelzebub, or Wormwood, for that matter."

Cordon looked toward his boss. He seemed totally calm. "I did not lie to the master, if that is what you are implying."

"Oh, is that so?" retorted Molock. "What of this Julie Rodriguez that was lost from right under your nose?"

"She was not in torment," retorted Cordon, "therefore, I did not lie. And there is something else. I know how they got her out—it was a tunnel, a portal, if you will, that leads through a fissure in space and time. I suspect that it is even more sophisticated than that possessed by the master, though I would not say that in his presence."

"I fail to see how this helps us," replied Molock.

"Oh," said Cordon. "Did I not mention that it leaves a detectable trail after it is closed?"

That brought Molock to a dead stop. "A trail?"

"Yes, and as it would happen, I am a seer. Not the best, but I am one, nonetheless. The tunnel left an ethereal fingerprint and a trail. It is a trail that can lead through solid rock for it is not part of our space or our reality. The last traces of it had nearly dissolved by the time I arrived at Julie's cell, but I could sense it. It led off into the west. I believe it led directly to the hiding place of these soul thieves. If we can identify enough of these tunnels, determine from whence they came, we will eventually pinpoint the base of operation of these rebels. Consider the loss of this Julie a gambit. We would not have learned this without her. I did not get the name of this dark angel, but I did gain a means by which we may track him down."

"Excellent," said Molock, knowing not what else to say.

"There is one other thing," said Cordon. "A device the likes of this was not built in Hell, not by the dark angels. They got it from somewhere else. Someone is helping them."

"Angels in Heaven," deduced Molock.

"Most likely," confirmed Cordon. "However, do not dismiss the possibility that other humans might be involved. We underestimate humankind, and that is a serious error on our part. They have come quite a way over the years. It is just such thinking that lost Serena Farnsworth to us. She was the first. Do you know who was second?"

Molock thought back. "Bedillia Farnsworth, her mother."

Cordon nodded. "Does that not suggest something to you?"

"Only that the two disappearances are linked," replied Molock, who was on the move again. "Clearly, the same party was responsible for both. I think that we all realize that."

"Yet, those who sought the answer to this mystery in the past were not asking the right question," continued Cordon. "I, on the other hand, am. I'm looking at all the disappearances in the order in which they occurred. There is something here, something important. It is not random. And when I figure it all out, I may also know where to begin the search for the rebels. Indeed, I will also know what it is that they are about. That too is vital information. We will get them, sir. In the end, we will get them. It is only a matter of time."

Chapter 6

Leslie Lopez leaned back against the wall of her small, dirty, south Phoenix apartment. Her green eyes focused on the small syringe still setting on the hardwood floor by her side. She had injected its load of meth 20 minutes earlier. In an act of desperation she had injected a lot, more than ever before. The total mind numbing euphoria she had once gotten from this stuff just didn't happen now. But she couldn't move onto something else; no, meth wasn't about to let her go. It was like a jealous and possessive lover. It would never allow her to pursue another, she was stuck.

She remembered the first time she'd mainlined this stuff. Wow, what a ride. Never in her wildest dreams did she expect that. How long ago was that, anyway? It seemed like an eternity ago, but it was just a year.

Back then she had a life, a career. She was a nurse, an RN, an intensive care unit registered nurse. She should have known better. But back then she believed in working hard and playing hard. To do that and maintain a demanding schedule, she had to prime the pump. Her amphetamines pumped her up in the afternoon for the long 12-hour night shift, and barbiturates put on the brakes in the morning to allow her to get some sleep. This worked for three years. It become a way of life. She knew what she was doing. She was, after all, a professional—an addict, a junky? No. Impossible. She had it all under control.

She had come face to face with the harder stuff at an upscale party. She knew well the chemistry of drugs like meth, knew their exact physiological effect upon the human body. Somehow she'd figured that meth would be little more than a super boost. It would be stimulating, an interesting experiment to be observed and monitored. Only some weak-willed high school dropout would fall prey to it. She was wrong.

For a time, she balanced her meth use and her job; now meth was consuming a large chunk of her life. When the high wore off she crashed—hard. She started missing more and more of her work shifts. She had a bout with the flu, then an intestinal bug. That is what she had told her supervisor; and he'd bought it, at least for a time.

Then came that terrible day when the hospital administration conducted an unannounced drug screening for all employees. Her secret was out; her career was over. Her salary up to this point had been sufficient to cover the considerable expense of her addiction, now it was no more. She had gone through her savings in a matter of six months. Those savings had been earmarked for buying a home of her own near Pinnacle Peak; now they supported her love affair with methamphetamine.

She eventually moved from her upscale apartment in Scottsdale, sold her car, and settled into this low rent flop in south Phoenix where she was closer to her dealer. As her savings were depleting, she had to find another source of income. Working the night shift at the local convenience market probably wouldn't cut it. In desperation, she had turned to the oldest profession in the world. Her dealer even helped her make the connections. After all, she had the looks and the moves to be a high-priced lady of the night, until meth finally took them away from her too.

She looked down at the empty syringe again. That was the last of it; and the way she was feeling now, it might have been too much. She had crossed the threshold of toxicity. Now death spread through her veins, burning her out on the cellular level.

She felt a coldness closing in around her. It wasn't the drug—no, this was something else. A spirit of darkness had entered the room. It was death;

she was sure of it. The reaper had finally come calling. She wasn't sure if she was frightened or relieved, but she knew she was slipping away.

"Come on and take me," she mumbled. "I've been expecting you, expecting you for a long time."

"Oh have you now?" came the reply.

Shocked, Leslie's bloodshot eyes opened widely. Had she just heard a voice or was it only in her mind? She couldn't tell. She looked around the room and saw no one.

"You're slipping away," said the deep voice, clearly that of a man. "There isn't much time; but I might help you if you asked me real nice. Just let me come in and I'll take you away from all of this. I'll help you experience anew the joy that drug once gave you. Let me in, let me into you."

"You're not real!" she cried, in the loudest voice she could muster. "You're not real."

"Well, if I'm not real, then there is no harm in letting me in, is there? But if you don't, you're going to die. It's your choice, but don't wait too long. You can give me reign over your body and live for a little while longer, or you can let corruption have your flesh and Hell have your soul. Believe me, I'll be a lot gentler on you. Still, like I said, it's your choice, wench."

Real or not real, the voice was right. Leslie's extremities were growing numb and cold. The chill was moving from her limbs toward her vital organs. When they shut down, that would be it. Then what? Her heart would stop, her blood would stop circulating, and her brain would starve and die. Then her body would begin to decompose, but would her soul go to Hell? Did such a place really exist? She had never given it much thought.

She had seen a lot of patients die during her career. It was the nature of the business. Still, sometimes the experience of watching them die had been pretty spooky. Some patients had gone peacefully, others with a sense of fear and horror as if they suddenly knew some terrible secret that they could not impart to her. She hadn't dwelled on those experiences. She'd done her best to put them out of her mind. She had always focused on living, not dying. The way she had it figured—at least the way she wanted to figure it—death was lights out, the end. Now, she wasn't so sure.

"You know, you really should have contemplated your mortality and what lies beyond instead of burying your head in the sand, pretending death didn't exist," said the voice. "Now it's far too late to alter your terrible destiny, for your life is nearly passed. When you enter my master's kingdom, you won't be able to pretend it doesn't exist anymore, though you'll wish it didn't. I know not what fate he might have in store for you, but be assured, it will not be pleasant. Very soon you'll know what pain really is; you'll get intimate with it, and it will continue for all eternity."

Leslie didn't respond. She was too terrified to speak. There had to be a way out, a way for redemption, but right now she couldn't see it.

"What shall it be?" asked the voice. "We don't have all night. Actually, you've got about ten more minutes. What's your pleasure?"

Leslie had a sense that she was opening the door to something worse than death. But right now it seemed the only alternative. If Hell was out there beyond this life, if it was fire and brimstone like that pastor had told her so long ago, she would do everything she could to delay it. "Come into me, then," said Leslie, her voice soft and resigning. "Come in and die with me, if you want."

A shock-like sensation permeated her entire body, then a sense of confusion. She was not alone in her own body, someone else was with her; it felt incredible. It made the high of meth pale by comparison. She rose to her feet, and as she did the room started to fade. Then she was largely lost to herself.

First she was in the shower, then putting on heavy makeup in an attempt to mask the ravages that the drug from hell had inflicted upon her. She

seemed to be fading in and out of consciousness, yet her body was on
move through it all—someone or something else was in control.

Then she was walking down Twenty-seventh Avenue, toward Buckeye
Road. She was dressed very suggestively and she moved with a confidence
she had not been able to find within her for several months. Surely she
should be dead right now, but she wasn't. She felt like a prisoner within her
own body.

Again she faded from consciousness. Then she was with a man. She was
in a hotel room standing over a man covered in blood who was lying on the
bed. There were more than six knife wounds in his chest, and she was rifling
through his wallet. She had committed murder, cold-blooded murder. She
was done for.

"Didn't you know that you should never pick up strange women?" she
heard herself say. "My, you are loaded, $468. More than enough for what
we have in mind. Thank you for your generosity, kind sir. The money will
be put to good use, I assure you." There was a pause.

"Go to sleep, little girl, this is none of your concern. We have a date with
human destiny. We are going to help bring about the end of the world. Go
to sleep."

And she did. Leslie faded away once more. This was a nightmare, a waking nightmare, sleep was her only escape.

The mighty observatory dome closed with a dull thud. Another cold
night of astronomical observing from Arizona's Mogollon Rim ended.
Twenty-six-year-old Sam Florence smiled as he looked at the electronic image
displaying the new faint comet. "At last, there you are," he exclaimed.

...ced an incredible run of bad luck when it came to this ...f study was trans-Neptunian objects, icy asteroids in ...f miles from Earth's sun. He had discovered 21 of them ... last three years, a pretty good average for a graduate student. Most of them had been discovered right here at the Discovery Channel Telescope—northern Arizona's premier astronomical instrument.

He had first seen this exceptionally faint object three months ago. Its tiny motion during the course of three nights told him that it was a member of the sun's family and not a distant star. He'd managed to get a second series of images of it two months ago. From those two sets of images, he knew that this object was special. Last month it was on the observing list again. This third set of observations would have given him a rough orbit of this newly discovered member of the solar system. But on those nights, everything that could go wrong did go wrong. One of the nights was cloudy. On the other two nights, he was plagued with a series of improbable equipment problems. The three-night observing run had turned out to be a complete wash.

This month's run was little different. Again he was plagued with a series of quirky equipment failures. Last night he had gone as far as to pray over the imaging camera. Never had he done such a thing, and he was totally serious when he did it. He was astonished when the 60-year-old telescope operator had joined him in the prayer.

"Wherever two or more are gathered, the Lord is in their midst," the telescope operator had noted. Apparently, he too had taken it seriously.

It seemed rather foolish praying over a piece of optics and circuitry, but they had done it nonetheless. Amazingly, it had worked. Fortune, or perhaps the good Lord, had finally favored him, and he had obtained one good image of the object known only as 2014F22. Normally, he would have waited until he got back to the university to get the object's coordinates and crank out an orbit for this troublesome minor planet, but not this time.

He was hard at work on the problem right there in the observatory control room. He felt a sense of urgency, though he didn't know why. Perhaps after all the trouble he had gone through to get this image, he wanted to savor his victory, but maybe it was something else. Once he was finished here, he would head to Happy Jack and get a few hours of sleep before heading back to Tempe.

"How's it coming, Sam?" asked the gray-haired telescope operator, looking over Sam's shoulder.

"Just about have it, Ken," announced Sam, as he hit the enter key.

"I reckon the prayer worked," said Ken, adjusting his bifocals and focusing on the monitor as the orbital elements popped up. "Wow, look at that eccentricity. Now that's one weird object you bagged, it looks like it is going to cross Jupiter's orbit."

Sam focused on the screen as an image of the actual orbit was displayed on the monitor. "More than that, it is going to nearly hit Jupiter…see?" He pointed to the incredibly unlikely crossing of two worlds. "Right now, this object is well beyond the orbit of Uranus, almost to Neptune; odd place for an object such as this. But it won't be out there long…it is coming inward fast. It will encounter Jupiter in 42 months. If we can believe these rough projections, Jupiter will pump down its orbit still further, bringing it in even closer to the sun."

They watched intently as the computer calculated the effect Jupiter's enormous gravity would have on this new object. A new set of orbital elements appeared, and then the altered orbit.

"This is exceptionally rough," cautioned Sam. "The actual orbit could be significantly different from this."

Rough or not, the two men almost collectively jumped out of their skin when they saw the track of the new orbit traced out on the monitor. This was not encouraging.

"Oh crap," said Sam under his breath. The computer displayed an orbit for the comet that carried it straight into Earth's path.

"That comet is going to pass mighty close," noted Ken, leaning toward the monitor. "This one will be the comet of the century all right. What a sight that will be! The tail might well stretch across the entire sky." There was a brief pause. "That is assuming that it doesn't turn around and hit us. That would ruin our whole day."

"Well, let's not jump to conclusions just yet," cautioned Sam. "This orbit is based on only three observations. I'm sure we will be able to dismiss the possibility of an impact once we gather more data."

"I reckon you're right," replied Ken, "but I'd rather error on the side of safety. There are people who need to be informed."

"Absolutely," agreed Sam. "Hey, what do you say we blow this joint and get some breakfast at Peg's?"

"Now you're talking," said Ken. "Just give me about fifteen minutes to shut down and I'll be ready to go."

Ken headed out into the observatory to shut down the telescope. Sam remained in the control room, looking at the orbital projection. He had a bad feeling about this, really bad. He suspected that Ken did too. The story of Wormwood in the Book of Revelation did a bit more than just cross his mind. He saved the data and shut down the computer. He would have one more opportunity to observe this enigmatic object next month before it passed behind the sun. Then it would be two or three months before he would be able to measure its position again.

The object was traveling fast, but it would take a while for it to reach Earth—over four years if their calculations were correct. If things went badly, was that enough time to deflect an object this size? How big was it? He wasn't sure. He smiled; he was just being overly cautious. The odds of this thing hitting Earth were ten thousand to one, at best. All he had done was discover an object that would light up the night sky when it passed by in another 54 months, that's all. He turned to pack away the rest of his things.

Quite abruptly Leslie was awake. She found herself driving a car down a dark country road amid tall pine trees. Where was she? How could she possibly have driven so far in her sleep?

"Good morning, sleepy head," she said. But it wasn't her speaking. It was her voice all right, but she wasn't in control. "It is so much easier driving when you are asleep. Still, it isn't much farther."

"Where are we going?" asked Leslie, yet not making a sound.

"Just outside of Happy Jack, to the Discovery Channel Telescope. We have an appointment with a man, no, two men, who know too much. The master would have them silenced…and that is just what we, I mean, you, are going to do."

Leslie glanced over at the 9 millimeter pistol on the passenger's seat beside her. Now she was frightened.

"The master has big plans for your world," said the demon, whose possession of Leslie was so profound. "Like the dinosaurs before you, you humans are going to become extinct. It was a comet that finished them off…so it shall be with you. We have worked so hard, hundreds of years orchestrating this event. It has taken much careful planning and nearly all of our spare resources to make this possible. A ball of ice and rock over twenty miles across is now hurtling toward your pathetic world. We had hoped that you and your kind would not have had time to develop the means to thwart our plans. However, your progress as a species has exceeded our expectations."

Leslie was horrified. What had she done?

"There are those of your people whose eyes scan the skies," continued the demon. "They are vigilant watchmen seeking to defend your Earth. Even now, two men have learned our secret. And it is our job to see that the master's plans remain a secret for a while longer, until it is too late for humankind to do anything to stop it."

Leslie was petrified. This had to be a dream; she had to wake up. But as the first light of dawn started to break in the east, she realized that what she was experiencing was only too real.

"At first we tried subtle things to thwart their efforts by screwing around with their circuitry. We might have delayed detection of our death blow had they not appealed to the Father. Imagine, two scientists praying over an electronic circuit blocked by the cold hand of a demonic spirit. The spirit was forced to flee, and their enterprise succeeded. Now we'll have to be more heavy-handed. That is where you come in, wench. You'll need to eliminate them and destroy all of the evidence of their find. It might take years before others realize the danger. But then it will be too late."

Leslie was about to become part of the most terrible tragedy in the history of humankind. She tried to regain control of her body but to no avail.

"A deal is a deal," replied the demon. "This body is mine now, and you're not getting it back. Still, you could have taken better care of it…you're a wreck. Who knows, I might return your body to you when I'm done with it." There was a pause. "No, I don't think so. You know too much. When we are finished at the observatory, I'll have to deal with you. Perhaps a final overdose will do the trick. How does that sound—one last syringe of the good stuff before you burn in Hell. Maybe we could come up with something a little more creative, more original. Well, we still have time to think about it, don't we?"

It was about half an hour before sunrise when Leslie pulled off the main road and onto the narrow drive that led to the observatory. A few minutes later she parked the car along the side of the road, just beyond the observatory grounds, and stepped out with pistol in hand.

"We'll walk from here. You don't get enough exercise." She started toward the observatory.

Deep within, the real Leslie wept silently. What had she done?

The observatory sat in the midst of the tall trees of the national forest on a gently sloping ridge. Only a fence separated it from the public lands. Leslie stopped along the side of the road.

"You are indeed fair of face," said the demon. "They'll never suspect your true intentions until it's too late. When they stop to open and close that gate, we'll pop 'em." She looked to the sky, The sun was almost up. "I doubt that we'll have to wait long."

It was less than ten minutes later when Leslie heard the sound of a metal door open and close. They were leaving the observatory. They would be here in a minute or so. She checked the gun one last time—she was ready. "It's show time," she said.

"Do you have a permit for that?" said a voice from behind her.

Leslie swung around to see a tall, uniformed forest ranger standing behind her. He stood with his arms folded in front of him. She evaluated the situation. He was clearly unarmed. Perhaps she would have to do him first. She started to raise the gun, but she couldn't. An unseen force stayed her hand.

"You've exceeded your authority here," said the ranger, a scowl appearing on his face. "This isn't your world, it was granted to man. It is not your place to interfere with his destiny."

"Who are you?" demanded Leslie.

"You know," replied the ranger, glancing into the distance to see the jeep pull away from the observatory. "Now go, and don't return. I won't warn you again."

Leslie snarled like some sort of wild animal, then bolted into the pine forests. A minute later the jeep stopped in front of the gate. Ken stepped out to unlock it.

"Good morning," said the ranger in a pleasant hearty voice.

"Morning," said Ken. "There isn't any problem, is there?"

"No sir," replied the ranger, "just making my morning rounds. It is going to be a beautiful day."

Ken looked around and smiled as he opened the gate. "Yes, I think so."

Sam pulled the jeep through and Ken locked the gate under the watchful eye of the ranger. Then the two colleagues were on their way to breakfast.

"Friend of yours?" asked Sam, as they headed down the road and around the curve.

"Never seen him before…yet there was something familiar about him. I can't rightly put my finger on it. I reckon he just had one of those faces, you know, the friendly kind."

Sam nodded; he had Peg's pancakes on his mind.

The ranger watched as the jeep disappeared from sight. He turned toward the place where Leslie had bolted into the forest; she was nowhere to be seen. He smiled and shook his head. For a moment his form changed into that of a mighty winged angel in white. Then he vanished into the chilly morning air.

A hundred yards away in the depths of the forest, a pale young woman lay motionless on the ground, an unfired pistol in her hand, a single tear poised to fall from her eye. It would be a day before the stolen car was discovered and another before Leslie's body would be found, the victim of an apparent methamphetamine overdose.

The demon Wormwood scowled upon learning of the debacle in the forest outside of Happy Jack. It was such a simple mission. How could it possibly have gone so badly? A guardian angel, obviously one of Michael's brood, had interfered. Now their secret was out.

When the plan had first been devised, man traveled his Earth in horse drawn carriages and his most powerful weapon was a cannon that could hurl rocks a quarter of a mile. In those days, he might have seen this icy messenger of death coming, but would have been powerless to defend his planet from its crushing blow. Now, however, the battlefield looked very differently. As the Nazarene had predicted long ago, man had grown greatly in knowledge and wisdom. Given sufficient warning, he might deflect the thrust of Satan's sword.

Satan's sword? That was what everyone in Hell who knew of its existence had come to call it. They had been led to believe that this object's path had been ordained by the prince of darkness himself. And why should he inform them otherwise?

Still, the problem remained. Man now knew of its existence. Now what should he do? Proceed with the plan, of course, hope that humankind's own mutual suspicions and distrust would work against them. Satan's minions on Earth would see to that. No, this plan would still work. Perhaps the panic generated by the knowledge of impending disaster would work in their favor.

However, his more immediate concern would be breaking the news to the master who might not take it well. Wormwood would find a way to turn news of their setback to his advantage. He would play upon the fear and panic angle. Yes, of course. Knowing that his world was imminently coming to a violent end, man would turn upon himself. No, this was even better. Amid the panic, Satan's kingdom would flourish. And in the end, Hell would gain six billion new inhabitants. Even if a remnant of humanity survived the fiery holocaust, they would be living on a pile of ashes that had once been their lush green world. They would be sick, weak, and demoralized—ripe for the master.

Yes, Wormwood was prepared for his impending meeting with the master. He was confident that it would go well.

Chapter 7

Tom sat quietly in the laboratory, his eyes focused upon a small glowing orb floating about an inch above the smooth, white marble table before him. Across the table, Dr. Bill Wong and their assistant Julie Rodriquez observed his progress. Beside the luminous sphere, a vastly magnified image of the goings on within the glowing orb was displayed. But this was not a display on some monitor; it floated in midair, a ghostly apparition with no visible instrumentation producing it.

Still farther up, three shimmering crystal projections in the shape of cones were pointed at the table below. They in turn were suspended from a radiating network of black tubes that ran along the rocky ceiling. The device produced a low steady hum that filled the entire room.

Behind Bill and to his right was a large glowing telesphere, within which a holographic projection of another man watched their progress carefully. "Looking good so far," he said in a calm voice. "Bring the trace out just a little bit farther."

"I'm trying, Mr. Tesla," said Bill, stress in his voice.

"Calm," said the holographic apparition. "Don't try to force it, just relax; you've got plenty of time."

Slowly, wires and components were appearing on the screen, seemingly from out of nowhere. It appeared magical—Bill and Julie were spellbound.

Julie turned to Bill, a hopeful expression on her face. "I think he's got it. He is really going to do it this time."

Bill nodded as eight layers of circuitry gradually materialized on the monitor before him. He was becoming ever more hopeful. It was looking good, real good. For six weeks they had been working on this project. Trying to build something out of seemingly nothing, using only human thought, was a daunting task.

Even with the help of this incredible instrument, it had taken days for Tom to at last materialize solid stable matter through the force of his will. Still more days had been required to move it telekinetically.

Through it all, Nikola Tesla had been Tom's guide, in much the same way he had been Bill's before him. Through this incredible communications link that joined Heaven and Hell, Tesla taught, guided, and encouraged his new students. It had taken trials and failures, small successes and disappointments, 12 to 15 hours a day, but Tom was progressing. He could create metal and even plastic-like objects to given specifications; and at this point, they had the rigidity and strength of the real thing. The patterns of their atoms were predictable and repetitive. Now creating them was easy. But when it came to circuitry, he was falling short. Its intricacies were just too daunting. They required a tremendous amount of concentration.

He had tried in vain for over two weeks to assemble complex circuitry. It seemed as if he had reached the limits of his potential. But today it looked like he was on the threshold of a breakthrough.

Bill turned back to Julie. "Remarkable. I could never even come close to this level of precision when I was on the machine. I think he's got it."

Yet, he had spoken too soon. A minute later, the newly formed wires became uneven, then breaks and twists appeared. Tom looked up, and the phantasmal screen and glowing orb vanished. What lay on the table was a small partially completed integrated circuit, singed at the one end.

"I'm sorry, I couldn't go any farther," said Tom, removing what looked like a crystalline headpiece from his temples. "I'm exhausted."

"You got farther than you ever did before," said Julie, trying to be as encouraging as she could. "I for one am proud of you."

Tom looked at Julie and smiled slightly. "I appreciate your positivity… really. The thing is, I never tried as hard as I did today. I just kept pushing, but eventually my head was pounding I just couldn't go any farther. I was at my limits."

Tesla nodded. "It's not your fault, Dr. Carson. People who do what you do in Heaven are surrounded by the power of God's Holy Spirit. It permeates their very being at all times. You are only exposed to a pale imitation of it when you are here in this room. It is a bottled version of the real thing. I think it is laudable that you have brought the science of transmutation as far as you have. Perhaps it can't be done here."

"Maybe he could do it a little bit at a time," suggested Julie, "and then, after he takes a bit of a break, continue."

Bill shook his head, "No, you have to do it in one sitting. The substrates will not align perfectly if you don't. The circuit might look nice, but it won't work." Bill turned to Tom. "Do you feel like you might be able to go farther, once you've had more practice?"

"Maybe," said Tom, "but it is going to take a long time. My accuracy is improving but my endurance, my mental stamina is not, at least not that I can see. I'm sorry. Isn't there anyone else here who can do this?"

"I can," said Bill, "so can a few others, but none of us are even remotely as good with this machine as you are. I tried for three months, but I just couldn't pick it up. We can make simple things, and we do, just not the complex, not circuitry."

Tom shook his head. "Hell is a big place. Surely, there must be someone here who could make this work. What about one of the angels, maybe Abaddon or Lenar?"

"Angelic brains just aren't wired like ours," replied Tesla. "God gave this ability to humans and humans alone."

"Look, I can fabricate the body of the weapon, even the fiber optic cables. We just need to find someone to produce the electronics."

There was a long silence. Tom scanned the room then focused upon Bill, who had a strange contemplative expression on his face. "You know of someone, don't you?"

"There might be one," confirmed Bill. "I knew her a long time ago, a most remarkable woman, Victoria van Voth."

"Victoria van Voth?" objected Tom, "Oh, you've got to be kidding, Bill; she was a crackpot."

"I won't argue that she was disturbed," said Bill, "nonetheless, she was positively brilliant and gifted in ways I don't even pretend to understand."

Julie shrugged. "I'm sorry, I guess I missed something. Who is this Victoria van Voth?"

"A real anomaly," said Bill.

"A real fruitcake," interrupted Tom.

"So who was she?" repeated Julie.

"She was a psychic, a real psychic," continued Bill. "Back in the late fifties and up into the seventies, both the KGB and the CIA were on the lookout for people who could do remote viewing."

"Remote viewing?" asked Julie. "What's that?"

"Well, it's seeing places thousands of miles away in their minds, without ever being there," replied Bill. "Now I know it sounds incredible, but there are people who can do just that. From a young age Victoria could do it, and much more. Back in the early sixties, at the age of sixteen, the CIA put her on their payroll. They practically kept her under lock and key for a dozen years. She would never tell exactly what she did for them, but when she left the CIA in 1975, they were not happy. Apparently, she had been one of their best weapons against the communists during the cold war. They put her through school, all the way through her doctorate, bought her fancy things…but it wasn't enough. She wanted to live her own life."

"I can see that," said Julie. "It must have been hard being locked away like that." She paused. "I know; Satan did it to me for twenty-three years."

Bill nodded. "I think we can all imagine it. You know, I actually saw her spin a compass using nothing but thought, and she had other powers that were absolutely unearthly."

"Sounds like you know an awful lot about her," noted Julie.

"You might as well tell her, Bill," said Tom, who couldn't help but smile.

"We were friends…close friends, for a time. We both championed unpopular ideas in the scientific community. I suppose I saw her as a kindred spirit."

"Your ideas were controversial," noted Tom, "hers, on the other hand were downright crazy. She talked about alternate realities, communicating with the dead, and ethereal time travel…really wild stuff."

"Is it?" asked Bill. "Think about what you've seen these past months. Do you still think it's crazy? Anyway, she was tormented, claimed she was hearing the thoughts of people all around her. She never had a moment of peace. I, for one, believed her."

"Then why didn't you choose her for this job?" asked Tom rising to his feet. He now seemed openly annoyed. "She died, what…eleven years ago? She's probably right here in Hell."

Bill hesitated. "You go too far, my friend. Yes, she is here. But if you must know, she was my first choice. It was where she was being held that was the problem. Getting her out would have been difficult. It almost certainly would have involved taking her out by brute force. It was too much of a risk. We were not ready for a direct confrontation with Satan's forces, not ready to show our hand, so we chose you, our second choice."

For a moment, Tom was stunned. He hadn't anticipated the conversation to go in this direction. "So, if you'd been able to get her, I'd still be on the altar, food for the birds?"

"Yes. I'm sorry, Tom."

Again silence ruled the moment. This time it was Julie who spoke up. "So, what do we do now?"

"We get Victoria here…we find a way," said Tom. "Believe me, I don't like the idea, but I don't see any other choice. If there is a chance she can pull this off, I'm in favor of it."

"It is not my place to comment on issues that might place your people at risk," said Tesla. "But I concur with Dr. Carson's opinion."

Bill looked at the others. They all seemed to be in agreement. "Then we need to take this to Abaddon, emphasize the need for this particular rescue mission. I know that he won't like it, but we have no other options I can see."

"I guess I really don't understand," admitted Tom. "Where is Victoria that makes this mission so difficult?"

All eyes turned toward Bill. He turned and walked to the wall before turning around. "She is in the Valley of Noak, about nine hundred kilometers into the daylight zone. It's not a particularly hot region of Hell, but it doesn't have to be, all things considered."

Again there was a pause. Then Tom and Julie noticed the tear in Bill's eye. "I'm sorry. I always have trouble talking about this. You see, she was more than just a friend to me. I loved her. But she left me long ago. She had needs that I just couldn't satisfy."

"You don't need to do this," interjected Julie.

"No," replied Bill, "I do. There is a place there with a steep sheer cliff, a hundred meters high. It is called the Plunge of Desolation. Men and women, thousands of them, their ankles shackled, are paraded up from the valley floor in a great dismal procession, along a trail that snakes its way through a narrow side canyon. It is a difficult and rocky trek requiring just over an hour and a half. Demons of the most hideous kind, hundreds of them, see the poor victims along the way at the business end of a whip. Eventually their victims are at the top of the cliff overlooking the desolate valley. From there they are compelled to throw themselves down. If they are lucky, they make the plunge without hitting any of the jagged rocks along the way. They end up as mangled and broken lumps of flesh on the valley floor below."

"How ghastly!" exclaimed Julie.

"But that's only half of it," continued Bill. "Once they strike the rocks at the bottom, they must somehow crawl out of the path of the next victim, who is surely not far behind. It is a virtual rain of human flesh that falls upon the blood-soaked rocks. Then, at the whips of their demon taskmasters, they are compelled to crawl back up the canyon to complete the eternal circle. Within ten minutes or so, most of them have healed sufficiently to rise to their feet and hobble and stumble up the path again. Usually their bodies are not fully restored until they have nearly completed the trip to the top, and, as you know, the regeneration process is in itself painful. So it goes on forever, without rest or respite."

"But what crime did they commit?" asked Julie.

"Their crime?" repeated Bill. "The name of the place tells it all—the plunge of desolation. They are homosexuals and lesbians. Their physical act of expressing love cannot possibly lead to conception, thus it leads to desolation. It is an act of futility, so they are condemned to an eternal act of futility…climbing to the top of a cliff, only to cast themselves to the ground, again, and again, and again."

"My God," said Tom, "only Satan would be so perverse."

"Victoria's female lover is there with her," noted Bill, "at the very same place, experiencing the very same fate. They both died of AIDS complications within a few months of each other…a strange irony. Now they will be together forever."

"A grim tale indeed," noted Tesla shaking his head. "I can see how hurtful, how very difficult this is for you, Dr. Wong. Please accept my condolences."

"Thank you," said Bill, returning to the table with the others. "We've done all that we can do for one day. The rest of you should get some rest. I will see that this situation is brought to Abaddon's attention. The final decision will be his."

"I'm sorry, Bill," said Tom, as he prepared to make the trip back to his quarters. "I really didn't know that you and Victoria had been so close. I really shouldn't have said what I did."

"That was a long time ago," replied Bill. "Over thirty years. Victoria and I drifted apart as time went by. I hadn't seen her in over five years when I learned of her death, but I still cried. Funny thing the human heart…funny thing."

"So how do you get her out of that place?" asked Tom.

"I have an idea," said Bill "but I don't want to discuss it until I talk to Abaddon. I've been going over it in my head for weeks; and I just about have it figured out."

Tom placed his hand on his friend's shoulder. "If there is anything I can do…."

"You'll be the first to know," assured Bill. "Now go get some rest."

Bill stood at the door of the lab as Tom made his way home. For a moment Bill seemed deep in thought, then he was on the move. There was a lot to be done. "I'm going to get you out of there, Vikki," he said under his breath. "I promise."

A group of four humans and four dark angels gathered around the great table in Abaddon's audience chamber. Still more watched the proceedings from Heaven through the telesphere. The atmosphere was tense. Everyone knew what was at stake.

"You all know when this operation was first proposed two months ago that we looked for a place from which Victoria van Voth might best be extracted," explained Kurt Bellows, their tactical officer and former U.S. Marine. He drew the gathered assembly's attention to a hand-drawn map on the table.

"The demon taskmasters require their human victims to walk in an orderly procession on a trail leading from the bottom of the cliff, through a canyon, along a ridge, and ending up at the top of the cliff. Along the trail from the valley to the pinnacle of the Plunge of Desolation the victims pass through a narrow and twisting stretch of canyon with sheer rock walls. Their demon taskmasters only infrequently patrol this section. There is no need. There is nowhere for their victims to escape to. There are, however, several places where large fallen rocks could conceal the gating in of a small extraction party. Dressed in a manner like the victims, so as not to arouse suspicion, members of this party would await the arrival of Ms. Voth. Then we would step out and grab her. Following which, we would reform the portal and gate out once more. The whole operation would take, at max, two minutes. If we have good intel, the risks would be minimal."

Abaddon examined the map then scanned the gathered assembly carefully. They had been discussing their quandary and what might be done for over two hours now. Everyone had an opinion as to how to proceed. Some felt very strongly about it, for they had a personal stake in the outcome, but it was Abaddon who would have the final say. One of the most difficult aspects of his leadership was to tell a member of this community that a loved one, or a person whose skills they desperately needed, could not be rescued from his or her awful torments—that the individual would have to go on suffering. If only they had more resources…that they could save all of the truly repentant souls in Hell, but they couldn't.

"I wish that I could guarantee you that we could monitor the exact locations of all of the demons at the Plunge of Desolation," said a dark cloaked man visible through the shimmering sphere, "but we can't. We can tell you where Victoria is at any given moment. We might be able to get a view of the area somewhat ahead of her or behind her, but getting the whole picture is beyond our power. No matter how you proceed, there will be unknowns, risks to take. Are you certain that you need this specific person? Are you certain that she will have the skills that you so desperately need? Aren't there any others?"

"No, there are no others," replied Bill, rising from his seat. "We have been all over this before. We took the easier road last time, and now, six weeks later, we are little better off, little closer to solving the problem at hand. We need Victoria van Voth…that is the long and the short of it."

"But you would have us take a terrible risk that could expose this entire community to discovery with no real guarantee of success," said the dark angel Eleazar who also rose to his feet. "Suppose one of the team is captured, tortured. What sort of guarantee can you offer me that they wouldn't reveal all, give Satan the location of Refuge. Even if this van Voth person can do as you claim, and I find that dubious, can one person with this gift make that much difference?"

"Yes, she could," interjected Bedillia. "It would make all the difference in the world to us. Within a month we could significantly turn the tables on old slewfoot." Bedillia turned to Abaddon. "This is a mission for humans.

We're the ones who will take the risk. I for one want to go on this mission, regardless of the danger."

"As do I," said Bill. "Vikki knows me, trusts me; it will make it simpler."

"Sit down, people," said Abaddon in a calm yet firm voice. "Assuming that I understand this mission correctly, you are asking me to send my chief liaison and the head of my scientific staff without the assistance of my children or any angelic backup. You want me to send you on a mission from which you may not return?"

"That's about it," replied Bill. "But we won't be interrogated. We will all be carrying a power sphere in the shape of a stone to provide the energy for the trip back. If we get caught, we destroy it. The energy released will forever remove that accursed place from the map of Hell. Dr. Kepler has calculated that any soul within about thirty to fifty meters of the explosion will have his or her atoms scattered so greatly that they shall never reconstitute. They will be gone forever. That also includes demons. If things go badly...well, we're out of the equation, and we take out some bad guys with us."

Abaddon turned to the glowing holographic projection, their link to Heaven. "Is that correct, Dr. Kepler?"

Kepler nodded. "Assuming that my understanding of the nature of outer darkness is correct, yes it is. Our best estimates indicate that you would be dealing with an explosive force of just over a quarter of a kiloton. That is equivalent to setting off about 250 tons of dynamite in one place."

"That's one huge antipersonnel device," noted Kurt. "Talk about overkill...nothing short of a nuclear bomb has that kind of yield."

"I don't think you want to make a habit of setting those things off," noted a young man standing behind Dr. Kepler. "In Hell, it would have the explosive force of a small nuclear device including the residual radiation. If you have hopes of establishing a new post-Satan order there, it might be nice if it weren't a radioactive wasteland."

"Amen to that, David," said Bedillia.

"And there is one more thing to keep in mind," said David. "This is not your typical nuclear detonation; it is the result of the combination of absolutely pure energy with an indeed exotic form of matter. In reality, you couldn't even begin to produce spheres like those on Earth or anywhere in the known universe. In Heaven they would be inert. If broken there, their power would disperse harmlessly into the great sea of power that is God's Holy Spirit. But in Hell they would release a true cataclysm. Understand, the explosion will not occur in three dimensions, but will extend into hyperspace as well. There is no way of determining the exact consequences of such an explosion in Hell. We have no way to run a simulation…I'm not sure I'd even know how. Detonating those things should be considered only as a last resort. But if you do it, do me a favor and take notes."

That off-the-wall comment drew raised eyebrows and the like from both sides of the crystal. It was a Davidism. You had to know him to understand it.

Abaddon again scanned the faces of those in attendance, the faces of those awaiting his decision. The silence was long and tense.

"All right, I will agree to this mission, but only on certain conditions. One: at least one of the members of the team is armed. I do not want this operation to end up in what you humans call a firefight; but if necessary, I want you to have the means to cover your escape. Two: we set the maximum time on the ground at two minutes. If Victoria does not show up, or if demons enter the area, you are to do battle with them only as a last resort. Three: and I pray to the Father that it doesn't come to this: if a member of the party gets separated from the others and is discovered, play the part of a victim. Be demure, submissive. Don't give them any reason to suspect that you are anything but a condemned soul doomed to the Plunge of Desolation. The demons won't suspect you as long as you play the part.

I know that it will be difficult, but you'll make it. We'll get you out of there on the next pass, I promise."

"After we take a three hundred foot plunge from a sheer cliff to the rocks below," noted Kurt. "That is why we stay together and play this thing by the numbers. At the first sign of trouble we pull out."

"I have a bad feeling about this," said Eleazar. "If one of the humans is discovered, and we have to get them out of there by force…"

Abaddon smiled, though slightly. "I appreciate your concerns, my old friend, but my decision stands. This risk must be taken." He turned to Kurt. "You will be in command. Your team will consist of Bedillia, Bill, and yourself. Make sure they are totally familiar with the plan and adhere to it. If all goes well, you will leave within the day."

Kurt only nodded. He had wanted to do this months ago. Now, at last, he would have his chance.

Tom parted the drapes of his quarters to find Bedillia standing in the rocky corridor. He was immediately taken aback. She looked so different from the Bedillia he had become acquainted with. She was wearing a very becoming knee-length black dress made of a velvet-like fabric; hanging from a fine gold chain around her neck was a small shimmering cross.

"Wow," said Tom who could think of nothing else to say.

"Bill made the fabric for me weeks ago," explained Bedillia. "And the cross and chain too. I wear it for my daughter, in humble thanks for what Jesus, Son of the Father, did for her."

"Very nice," said Tom. It had been so long since he had seen a woman dressed so nicely as Bedillia was right now. For a moment, his mind wandered back to the wonderful green Earth.

"You up for a cool walk," asked Bedillia, a broad smile on her face.

Tom was a bit wary of the offer. It had been the better part of a week since his counselor had dropped in to see him. Apparently Abaddon had some concerns regarding the long-term effects of using the matter trans-muter on the human brain and had assigned Bedillia, their resident psy-chologist, to check up on him from time to time. "This is not another long, dark hike into the undeveloped caverns for a psych evaluation is it? I assure you, my emotional condition is fine. Using that matter transmuter is not having any adverse effect on me. If anything, it has sharpened my ability to focus my thoughts."

Bedillia's smile faded. "No, Tom, it has nothing to do with that. I just wanted to talk to you." There was a pause. "I need to talk to you."

Right now Tom felt about six inches tall. He'd jumped to conclusions. Maybe the stress and frustration of the work was getting to him. "I'm sorry, Bedillia, I didn't mean it to sound like that. I'd love to take a walk with you, even a cool one."

Bedillia's irrepressible smile slowly returned. "I have a place I want to show you; it won't take very long. I promise that there will be no evaluation along the way."

Tom stepped out into the corridor and away they went. Bedillia reached for Tom's hand; he didn't mind in the least. Yet, he sensed that something was wrong.

"Did you hear that we are going to go after Victoria van Voth?"

"I figured that was coming," confirmed Tom. "I guess we have to. I'm not making much headway with that instrument."

"Tom, don't beat yourself up over it," objected Bedillia. "You tried your best. Bill spent months trying to make that thing work. He is a brilliant man, but in all that time he didn't get half as far as you did. We don't know that van Voth will do any better, but we have to try. It might be that we don't have that thing set up right. Maybe it just won't work in Hell."

"Maybe," said Tom. "Who is going to go after Victoria van Voth, anyway? Are Abaddon and Lenar going to go in with a bunch of his flying buzz saws, cut down the bad guys, and rescue the fair maiden?"

Bedillia hesitated. "No, we can't risk so heavy-handed an operation as that. This is a surgical strike, not a firefight, as Kurt likes to call it. We are going to sneak in, grab her, and then run before anyone even realizes that she is gone."

They turned a corner, walked up a corridor lined on one side with metal pipes and what looked like electrical cables. They could hear what sounded like the hiss of steam rushing through one of them.

"We?" asked Tom. "Who is we?"

"Bill, Kurt, and myself," replied Bedillia. "We will go in dressed like humans in Hell, in the very rags that Satan himself provided us. We will be sure and look the part, dirty and pretty battered. We will even be wearing ankle shackles, just like those worn by all of the humans sentenced to the plunge. The thing is, ours will look genuine enough to fool the demons, but are not barbed on the inside, and can be sprung open in a second with the push of a small pin, thus releasing us."

Tom abruptly stopped and turned to Bedillia. "No, you can't...it's way too dangerous."

"I've done this sort of thing before," replied Bedillia, who seemed anxious to move on. "Not exactly like this, but I've been in harm's way before, and I've come back, just like the bad penny."

"You're no bad penny," objected Tom, "you're special...at least to me."

"Thank you very much, kind sir," replied Bedillia with a smile.

"But why do you have to go?" objected Tom. "I know that there are former soldiers here, a lot of them. Wouldn't they be a better choice?"

"And one of them will be leading the mission," replied Bedillia, who was now almost pulling Tom along. "The thing is…I have experience with this sort of thing, a lot more than most. Anyway, there should be a woman on this mission for Victoria's sake. I'd explain the psychology of it, but it might be better if you just took my word on it. Bill is going because Victoria knows and trusts him. Trust me; I know what I'm doing."

The two moved steadily upward, following the trunk line of pipes and cables that ran along the wall. As they did, it seemed to become ever cooler. Now the corridor was downright chilly, perhaps in the fifties. Even the crystal lights that were found throughout the caverns were unusually dim in this corridor.

"Where are we going?" asked Tom.

"Out to get a breath of fresh air," replied Bedillia. "It is unusually warm on the surface right now. I've rarely seen it warmer, eighteen degrees below zero. It's almost unheard of. A breeze is blowing in from the south. Normally the mercury doesn't rise above forty below."

"A real heat wave," replied Tom.

Before them the cavern seemed to end in a solid rock wall, while on their left in a small alcove hung a variety of long black cloaks and boots. Here the cables and pipelines vanished into the wall.

"You'll need to dress for the weather outside," noted Bedillia, making her way toward the alcove.

She picked up a pair of black boots and slid her small feet into them, then wrapped one of the cloaks around her. Tom followed her lead, searching for a pair of boots and a cloak that he figured might fit him.

"You know, there are a lot of people here who have never been outside of Refuge since they arrived," noted Bedillia. "They have no real desire to."

"I suppose I can understand that," replied Tom, who had finally found a pair of boots to fit his size 12 feet. "After what happened to them out there, I can't blame them for wanting to hide."

Within a few minutes, they were bundled up for the severest of weather. Tom was amazed at how warm the cloak really was. They walked back into the corridor. Bedillia picked up a small rock and threw it at the wall before them; it bounded off. Again Bedillia took his hand.

"Just follow my lead and don't lose faith…we are going to walk through that wall. Tom, keep your eyes on me and don't doubt, not for a moment."

Tom looked at her incredulously, then followed her instructions. He gazed into her eyes, deep into her eyes. He had never noticed just how pretty they were. Then they were moving. Suddenly a dense fog seemed to block the way. He could barely see her. Then he understood why; they were walking straight through the wall! But he'd watched the rock bounce off the wall; it was solid. This was impossible. Yet he kept his cool. He had faith in Bedillia—he kept on walking.

About 20 seconds later, he felt intensely cold air. He was out in the open, but he couldn't see a thing. From her cloak, Bedillia produced a small glowing crystal that illuminated the cold, dark cavern around them. Patches of frost and ice covered the ceiling, walls, and floor. Tom turned to look behind him to see the rock wall from which they had just emerged.

"That was freaky," said Tom. Bedillia smiled, amused.

"Try to explain that one using your science," she said, the trace of mirth in her voice.

"I can't," admitted Tom.

"Just another way this place is different from Earth," said Bedillia, turning toward the wall. Again she picked up a rock, threw it at the wall, and again it bounced off.

"A force field?" asked Tom.

"Something like that," said Bedillia.

Tom walked to the wall and placed his hand on it; it was very cold and very solid. Bedillia went to his side. She reached out, her eyes half closed. Her hand passed through the rock as if it were a phantom. Tom just shook his head.

"You have to have faith," said Bedillia. "I have the faith that I can pass through that wall…while you had faith in me. That is why it worked, how we passed through fifty feet of solid rock."

"It can't be that simple," objected Tom.

"It's not," replied Bedillia. "But that is not important. There are people in this community that, try though they might, cannot pass through that wall. On Earth, as a child, you believed in gravity, though you didn't know how it worked. People fly on airplanes every day but don't know how they fly. They just have faith that the airplane will take them to where they want to go. They have faith to step down that jet way and put their lives in the hand of the pilot. It is the same with that wall. I know I can pass through it…there is no doubt in my mind about it…so I do. I guess it's a little bit like faith in God." Bedillia lowered her head. "If only I'd had that sort of faith on Earth, I would not have ended up here."

"Then you wouldn't have been here for me," said Tom. "I don't know what I'd have done without you."

"Let's move on," said Bedillia turning from the wall. "It's not far now."

Tom followed, wondering if he might just have said the wrong thing again.

The winding, irregular rocky tunnel was a good 20 feet high, and even wider than that. Frequently they had to step around rocks and boulders as they made their way along. It was only a few minutes before Tom saw a shifting green glow reflecting off the icy wall ahead. A moment later they stepped from the cavern and out into the open to behold the most glorious display of the aurora he had ever witnessed.

The aurora took on hues of green and blue, and forms ranging from shifting glowing curtains, to dancing filaments of light. How high they were, Tom couldn't say, but it was certainly 50 to 100 miles or more. They illuminated the vast plain of ice and rock before them in shimmering ethereal light. Never had Tom seen such a sight.

There was not a cloud in the sky; yet beyond the dancing lights, there were no stars, no stars at all, only blackness. It was an empty void, an outer darkness beyond the wonders of the starry universe. And it was cold here. The icy wind seemed to blow through him.

Yet for all of its cold, there was surprisingly little snow. It clung here and there in icy patches, yet nowhere was it more than a few inches deep. The ground was mostly a frozen mass of soil and rock. What a wasteland. It made Antarctica seem welcoming by comparison.

"I occasionally come here to think," said Bedillia. "Demons rarely frequent these climes. It is dark, quiet, and peaceful, except for the wind... there is always wind."

Tom didn't need to be told about the wind, but there was something else. "Bedillia, what is it? You didn't bring me out here just for the air and the view."

Bedillia looked at Tom in surprise then quickly looked away. "In part I did," she finally said, slowly turning back toward Tom. The glow from the aurora danced across her cold face. "But there is more. I'm afraid, Tom."

"You, afraid?" asked Tom. "Afraid of what?"

"This mission," said Bedillia. "I have this feeling, this bad feeling, like I'm not coming back from it."

That sent a cold chill down Tom's back, a chill that went beyond the harshness of the climate. "Then don't go."

"But I have to go," said Bedillia, "that's the thing. I have to go."

Tom was confused. This didn't make any sense. "Why?"

"Call it destiny, fate, or the will of God, but I have to go. I still pray, you know. I pray a lot. I ask God to give me strength, to help me make right decisions. This mission is a right decision…I know it."

"I used to pray a lot," said Tom, "back on the altar."

"But you don't now," deduced Bedillia.

Not so much now," admitted Tom.

"Why not?" asked Bedillia. "He answered your prayer, didn't He? He delivered you from that terrible place."

"I'm not sure," admitted Tom. "Abaddon was the one who rescued me, not God."

"But it was in God's plan," said Bedillia, "that's why you're here. Abaddon was simply His instrument. Let me tell you something. Call it foolish, if you like. I ask God for forgiveness for the many mistakes I've made. I ask it all in the name of His Son, Jesus. I ask every day. Even in that horrible furnace I prayed, or at least I tried. He spared my daughter, that prayer straight out of the furnace, He answered. I'm very grateful for that. Now I try to do whatever I can to relieve the suffering of others. Call it trying to pay for all the hurt I caused those around me, if you will.

"You see, even if I am beyond forgiveness, I have to do this…I have to go on this mission." There was a long pause. Bedillia didn't look directly at Tom for awhile. Only the wind passed between them. Then she looked up. "Tom, will you be there at the ring with me until I leave? Will you be there, waiting for me if I do return?"

For a moment Tom was stunned, but it passed quickly. He took a step forward and held her close. "Of course I will, Bedillia. But I won't have to wait long…you will be coming home."

"I hope…I pray that you are right," said Bedillia. "I feel like I draw strength from you. I don't think I've ever felt like that about anyone else. Too bad we couldn't have met on the other side."

Tom nodded. "I feel the same way about you."

After a moment, they turned back toward the cave, hand in hand. When they finally came to the wall at the end of the cavern, Tom didn't hesitate; they both passed through it as though it was made of air.

Along with Abaddon and several others, Tom watched as the team pre-pared to depart. They were all dressed in gray rags. As Tom watched, they each attached a pair of heavy shackles around their ankles. Each tested the release mechanism to confirm that it functioned properly, then latched the shackles once more. These shackles would allow them to blend into the crowd of damned humans if necessary. But in an emergency, the shackles would offer them little mobility, barely allowing them a slow shuffling walk. The release had to work quickly and perfectly.

Each of the three appeared dusty and bruised, with just a trace of blood on their ragged gray clothes. Kurt handed his two team members a small oval-shaped rock about an inch and a half across.

"Whatever you do, don't lose that," he warned. "It's your ticket home." He hesitated, "or your ticket out. If all goes well, we'll hardly get a breath of the air in that place before we're on our way back." Kurt checked his pistol one last time before sticking the barrel under the loincloth at his hip.

"Remember, if you have to use it, make every shot count," warned Tesla who watched the preparations through the telesphere near the corner. "That particle pistol is every bit as potent as the rifle I developed…with one important difference—the smaller power module is only good for about four shots, not sixteen. Its effectiveness also drops off quickly with range, more so than the rifle, so take that into account if you have to use it."

Kurt nodded. He knew all of these things already. He was ready to go.

"It looks clear," said a voice from behind. "She will be there in approximately one and a half minutes."

"Activate portal," said Abaddon.

The ring burst into life, its interior glowing and shimmering then fading to a billowing fog with a scattering of glimmering stars. Kurt looked into its depths then back at his team. The portal was stable. "OK people, here we go."

Bedillia looked back at Tom. She smiled slightly.

"See you in a couple minutes," said Tom, trying to stay as positive as he could. "Have a nice trip."

The three moved into the portal. They seemed to be walking into a fog, then they faded away. The fog vanished, and all that Tom could see was the far wall of the room. Now the waiting began.

Chapter 8

The light of the bloated sun cast eerie shadows across the rough barren terrain of the Valley of Noak. The side canyon lay in shadows as it always did, offering little respite from the heat of the blazing orb that bathed the landscape in its deep amber light. Yet the canyon echoed with crying, moaning, and the crack of whips, as the shackled ragtag multitude continued single file on their dismal and eternal procession.

They all knew the fate that lay ahead. It was the same that lay behind. Until then, bones would realign and heal, even as scars and abrasions shallowed and vanished. Through it all was the pain, the itching pain that always accompanied the regeneration of their eternal flesh.

Out of sight of all, a field of glistening stars appeared amid the red rocks. Out of this misty phantasm stepped three humans. The apparition behind them quickly faded.

"Bill," whispered Kurt, motioning for him to come up to the front.

Bill almost tripped over his own shackles as he joined their leader at the edge of the huge boulder. Beyond, scarcely 15 feet away, he saw the dismal procession. Most limped and hobbled along, the restoration of their legs still incomplete. They traveled with their heads down, as the demons commanded. Their backs were to them as they passed by. The team had gone totally unnoticed.

Kurt turned to Bill. "I've seen an image of van Voth in the sphere, but I'll need you to pick her out. You'll need to move out and grab her. She'll be here within thirty seconds. Just follow the plan, and we'll be out of here in a minute. Good luck, buddy."

Yes, they'd practiced this a few dozen times. Bill knew how to make the move, but he was frightened. No, he had to do this.

"Go," repeated Kurt, concern in his voice.

Bill stepped out about eight feet from the rocks. Here he could see more clearly as they walked past him. Amazingly, he had still not been noticed. He scanned the faces for Vikki—no sign of her.

"Get back in line," whispered a man as he walked past. "Do you want us all to be whipped?"

Something was wrong. Where was Vikki? Bill's heart beat faster and his muscles became more tense.

Then, there she was—right in front of him. He had nearly missed her. Her head was bowed, her long dirty black hair covering most of her face. He reached out, nearly missed her, then pulled her out of line. A second later he was looking into a face he hadn't seen in many years, a young face with eyes filled with tears.

"No, let go of me," objected Vikki, in a hoarse voice. "I've got to get back in line."

"Vikki, it's me," whispered Bill. "Look at me."

Their eyes met. At first Vikki's eyes held only a blank stare. Then they cleared and focused on him.

"Bill?"

"Yes, Vikki, it's me."

By now, Kurt and Bedillia were at their side, pulling them back behind the rocks and out of sight. The procession continued without Vikki.

"But how?" asked Vikki. "Bill, how are you here?"

"Later," said Kurt placing a hand gently over Vikki's mouth. "You can have your reunion later. Right now we've got to get out of here." Kurt turned to Bill. "Use your sphere. Get ready to gate us out of here."

"We're leaving?" asked Vikki.

"Yes," confirmed Bill as he pulled the sphere from beneath his loincloth. "It's like Star Trek, beam me up Scotty."

"No," insisted Vikki, "not without Joan."

"Who's Joan," asked Kurt, trying to quiet Vikki.

"She's my wife," insisted Vikki, who was now struggling. "I won't leave without her."

"We don't have time for this," objected Kurt.

"She can't be far behind me," insisted Vikki, "you can't leave her here."

Kurt surveyed the situation for a second. "All right, we'll take her."

"I know what she looks like," said Bill, putting the sphere away. "I can get her."

A few seconds later, Bill was in position, searching the procession for Joan. This was the last thing in the world that he wanted to do. Joan had taken Vikki from him. If he had his way, she could stay here. No, he couldn't do that, no matter how he felt about her personally. He waited. A minute went by, then two.

Kurt was getting nervous. The longer they stayed, the greater the probability of being discovered. From time to time demons checked this area, it was a favorite hiding place for humans seeking just a few minutes of rest from their torment. To make matters worse, occasionally demons patrolled the sky here. They were sitting ducks. Still, they waited.

"I'm stepping out to help him," announced Bedillia, moving several steps forward.

Kurt's hand was on his sidearm as four and then five minutes passed. Then suddenly she was spotted. Bill reached out for the limping, blonde woman—but missed. "Joan," he said in the loudest voice he dare use; yet she continued walking.

Bedillia moved forward to intercept Joan, but the shackles restricted her. Nevertheless, Bedillia walked after Vikki's lover.

"No," said Kurt.

Bill prepared to take up the pursuit, but Kurt pulled him back into the cover of the boulders.

By now, Bedillia was over 30 feet away, slowly catching up with Joan. "Oh, these shackles," she cursed, under her breath, as she shuffled and clanked along. She was tempted to release them, but it was too big a risk. Anyway, she had almost caught up to Joan.

By now Bedillia was out of sight. Kurt drew his weapon. "Get ready to gate out," he said, turning to Bill. You need to get Victoria out of here, she is our first priority."

"What about Joan?" objected Vikki.

"I'll get her," said Kurt. "You two just get out of here, *now.*" Kurt cautiously moved out from their hiding place. He got sight of Bedillia just as she laid her hand on Joan's shoulder.

"Let go of me," said Joan, turning to the unfamiliar woman. "I don't want to be lashed because of you."

"Neither of us is going to be lashed," said Bedillia. "Victoria sent me. I'm getting you out of here."

"Vikki can't save me," objected Joan, "no one can."

"I assure you, we can," said Bedillia, who had noticed the small outcropping and another large set of boulders on the left side of the trail just ahead. She and the team had noticed it yesterday on the map. It offered almost as much cover as the spot they had finally selected for their gate in. After this place, however, the canyon widened, they would be out in the open with no cover at all. If she were going to gate out with Joan, it would have to be here. They would be upon it in a matter of seconds.

"Look, I don't have time to argue with you, are you coming with me or not? I can take you away from all of this, but this is your last chance."

Joan hesitated. "OK, I'll trust you. What do I do?"

"We're going to duck behind this boulder on the left," said Bedillia, who had already pulled out the sphere hidden in her short, tattered skirt. "Just go to where I point. We'll be out of here in seconds."

Joan nodded. She saw the boulders. She had once tried to hide there for a few minutes, though, unsuccessfully.

"Here we go," said Bedillia, taking Joan by the left arm, and directing her toward the boulders to her left. As she turned, she saw Kurt out of the corner of her eye. She motioned to him that everything was under control. He nodded. This little wrinkle in the plan seemed to have ironed out nicely. They would only be a few minutes late on their return.

"Almost got it," said Kurt, under his breath. Bill and Vikki had already gated out. Once he had confirmed that Bedillia and Joan had done the same, he could blow this place. Using three rather than just one sphere to get the team back was a waste of limited resources, but at least they'd accomplished their mission objectives.

The two women had barely ducked out of the line of doomed souls when they came face to face with a seven foot tall leviathan, one of the most frightening looking demons Bedillia had ever encountered. The horned obscenity that towered over her was covered in coarse brown fur. He had sharp claw-like hands and feet and large glistening black eyes that appeared insect-like. His mouth was filled with black razor-sharp teeth, and his ears were exceptionally long and pointed. He was truly like something out of a nightmare. Apparently he had been watching the procession from behind the boulders, keeping those within it on track.

"Lost, ladies?" he said, in a deep guttural laugh. "Yes, that must most assuredly be it, for you'd not be seeking escape from your fate, would you? You know the penalty." He drew out his massive whip, a whip whose business end held not just one single leather lash, but nine, each with a small jagged metallic ball at its terminus.

Bedillia was caught by surprise. She thought to open the gate here and now, pull Joan in with her, and hope that in the confusion, they weren't followed.

The demon saw the sphere in Bedillia's hand. "You'd throw a rock at me, would ya wench?" The whip struck out at her in an instant, wrapping around her arm, its nine terrible spiked balls digging into her flesh. Then he pulled it back, ripping flesh with it and dislocating her shoulder. As she cried out in pain, her sphere flew from her hand to become but one of many small stones scattered along the pathway. Bedillia stepped backward but was tripped by her shackles, and she fell to the ground.

Then the demon took the lash to Joan who had already turned in an attempt to reclaim her place in line. Its balls dug into her back and side. She howled in pain.

Nearly 100 feet away, Kurt watched in horror, as the beast encroached upon Bedillia, then pulled her roughly to her feet. He disengaged the safety, took aim with the pistol, but he didn't have a clear shot. Even if he did take this beast down, popped the shackles, how long would it take him to reach Bedillia? Too long. Even now, a second demon farther up the trail had taken an interest in the goings on. Kurt didn't think the demon had seen him. But by the time he would reach Bedillia, the second one would be practically on top of her. He would be in a firefight. Four shots wouldn't get him very far. He should have brought the rifle.

The demon placed Bedillia back in line and watched the blood pour from her wounds. "An unusual amount of blood for one of you," he snarled. "You must be new. Learn from that, wench...I might not be so merciful next time. Now get moving, your wound will heal before you make the plunge, allowing you to fully focus on the anticipation, horror, and agony of that experience."

The demon placed Joan directly in front of Bedillia, then walked at their sides, laughing at them, mocking their efforts to seek refuge, if only for a moment. "There is no hope for you," he said. "Never will you escape this place, neither one of you. Unnatural were your affections; unnatural shall be your eternal fate."

Kurt put his weapon away and drew back into the cover of the rocks. There was nothing he could do for now. He couldn't leave her behind, he had never left a brother or sister in arms behind, but he could do nothing else. She would be back this way again, in about an hour and a half, but only after experiencing a fall that would have instantly killed her, had she been mortal. He couldn't stay here and wait either. He would most surely be seen. With no other option, he drew out the sphere and opened the gate back to Refuge.

Kurt emerged from the mists to find Bill and Victoria among those awaiting his return. That, at least, was a relief. It took but a few seconds for those in attendance to realize that something had gone horribly wrong.

"Where's Bedillia?" asked Bill, fear in his voice.

"They got her, but I don't think they realize who they have." replied Kurt, who was quick to appraise the others of the details.

"If they do come to realize who she is, we are all in dire peril," noted Abaddon. He looked into the telesphere which still had an open link to their allies in Heaven. The looks on the faces there were not encouraging.

"OK," said Dr. Kepler, turning away for a moment to communicate with someone out of their view. "We should be able to appraise you of Bedillia's situation in a few minutes. Beyond that, there is little that we can do here. Whatever is to be done must be done from your side."

"She's almost certainly in the procession with the others, when she takes the plunge, those shackles might bust open," said Kurt. "They were designed to be easy to remove in an emergency…not to resist hard falls. Once they discover that her shackles are fake, they'll be onto us, unless they are just stupid."

"They're not stupid," said Abaddon, "but I don't see how we're going to free her before the plunge. We will have to hope that the shackles hold together on impact."

Tom could remain silent no longer. This was Bedillia they were talking about. "You mean she's going to have to fall a hundred meters from a cliff, be bashed and crushed on the rocks at the bottom, before we are able to rescue her? No…no, that's not acceptable."

Tom felt a hand on his shoulder—it was Lenar. "Tom is right; we cannot allow her to fall from that cliff…for many reasons. She has about half an hour, maybe more before she reaches the cliff. Johannes Kepler and his people will be able to tell us exactly where she is and what the situation is in less than ten minutes. I say we take twenty of our best warriors and five hundred of your children in, and attack in force to secure her, even if it means revealing ourselves to them."

"I can have my rapid response team ready to go in fifteen minutes, armed with Tesla particle beam rifles," said Kurt. "It's about time we tested them out under combat conditions anyway. Whenever we go on a mission, my rapid response team is on high alert. No loincloths and shackles this time. They go in wearing full battle gear. I'm tired of pussyfooting around with these demons. Sneak in, sneak out, enough already. It's time these demons learned some respect. Let's go in there and kick butt—give them payback for a change."

Lenar nodded, smiling approvingly. He liked this human.

Abaddon scanned the room. There seemed to be general agreement on this issue. Even those he could see on the telesphere nodded in agreement.

It was tempting. "You want me to approve a spur of the moment mission, just send in the troops and see where the chips fall?"

"Exactly," said Kurt. "No one under my command is going over that cliff, and we'll have the element of surprise on our side. Anyway, it's not a spur of the moment decision. My men have trained for this contingency. They're marines; they'll get the job done. Abaddon, we've never done battle with these guys. We need to size them up, and this is the perfect way to do it."

Again, there was the rumble of general agreement.

"We are wasting time, my friends," said Abaddon. "Prepare your forces; have them assembled here in fifteen minutes in case we need them."

"In case we need them?" asked Kurt. "What's that supposed to mean?"

"If those shackles come open on impact, if those demons come to realize that she is not what she seems…we need to get her out of there. We will grab Bedillia and Joan, as well as any others we can reach. We will cut down as many demons as possible, make them feel our wrath, then withdraw."

"No, we've got to get her out before she falls," objected Tom. "For God's sake, Abaddon, she's one of us."

"You speak as though you think I have no heart for her," replied Abaddon, his tone calm yet firm. "I have known her longer than any of you. She is my friend. But I have a responsibility to this community, to our mission." He turned to the others. "Set things in motion people. You all know what needs to be done. We have precious little time."

Bedillia stumbled barefoot up the rocky trail, following the grim procession. After just three minutes the bleeding had stopped, and the terrible itching that was part and parcel of the healing process had begun. The hairy demon still walked by her side, observing her closely, yet he hadn't said anything until now.

"So, yer a bleeder" he observed, turning to her, eyeing her over carefully. "Rarely do I see so much blood coming from one of your kind. This place, this ordeal, wrings it out of yer kind pretty quickly. Why is there so much in you? You must be one of the new ones. Is that not so?"

Bedillia didn't respond. She kept her head down, hoping that this beast would tire of her and leave.

"Answer me when I talk to you, wench!" he growled angrily, digging his claws into her shoulder, then shoving her dislocated arm roughly back into its socket.

The pain was tremendous, yet she held her peace. "Yes," said Bedillia, "I'm new."

"Yes, master," corrected the demon. "You'd best be watching your manners, little girl."

"Yes, master," replied Bedillia.

"I don't remember you arriving," said the demon. "Strange…not many details miss my eyes. Nonetheless, I don't think you realize just how easy you got off back there. There are hundreds of places like this throughout Hell, places for the likes of you and your unnatural sexual appetite. I'll tell you now, most of 'em are far worse than this. Most are much hotter. You don't know what real heat is until you end up at the Plunge of Desolation in Xarin. The ground there could nearly boil water, if there were water. Then there is the Valley of Krull. They shackle both your ankles and your wrists there, and the rocks at the bottom of the cliff are rough and jagged, not smooth and round like ours. You don't realize how good you got it."

"I'm very grateful for your mercy, master," replied Bedillia.

"That's better," said the demon, a hideous smile coming to his face. "I shall help you get acquainted with our procedures. I am called Drelleth, Master Drelleth to you. And what is your name, human child?"

There it was. What was she to do now, lie? "My name is Bedillia, Bedillia Smith."

Drelleth's smile grew even wider. "Very well then, Bedillia Smith, now we are acquainted. From now on, I'll be keeping an eye on you."

"Yes, Master Drelleth," said Bedillia, lowering her head once more. "I appreciate your concern. I'll do better in the future."

"I'm sure you will," said Drelleth.

Several minutes passed before Joan spoke. "Why did you do this to me? What did I ever do to you?"

"I take it that he is gone," said Bedillia, almost under her breath.

"Yes," confirmed Joan.

"I'm still going to get you out of here," said Bedillia.

"You've done enough to me already," replied Joan, in an angry voice.

Bedillia wasn't going to argue with Joan, not now. She knew help was on the way, and when it arrived, she'd grab Joan, and they would be out of there, one way or the other. But when would it come? Would she end up making the plunge? The thought caused a chill down her spine. She had spent years amid the flames of that hot furnace. Surely this wasn't going to be nearly as bad as that. But she wasn't ready, not now.

They were making their way up the side of the canyon through a series of switchbacks toward the top of the ridge. It wasn't very steep, but the shackles and bare feet on sharp rocks made the going difficult. The trail was well-worn here by who knew how many feet over the centuries.

"How much farther is it?" asked Bedillia.

"You don't know?" said Joan.

"I've never been here before," replied Bedillia.

"Would the two of you just shut up," said a man behind them. "You'll bring them down on us."

"Maybe twenty-five minutes," replied Joan, "I know every rock of this place. You'll see it coming a long way off. The ridge flattens out there. You can see the people ahead of you disappearing over the cliff. I'm terrified every time I see it. I don't deserve this place. I was a good person, really."

"And you are getting out," said Bedillia. "I promise you."

"Are you mad, woman?"

Bedillia looked around to see the dark, sad-eyed man behind her. "No, I'm not mad. If you want, I can take you too."

"I saw you and the others among the boulders," he said. "I have been here for many years. I know almost everyone here, but I've never seen you before."

Bedillia knew enough not to give out too much information, but right now she didn't care. "That's because I have never been here before. This is my first trip up this trail."

"They haven't brought anyone new in here in almost a year...I know, I remember."

"They didn't bring me in here, I came here of my own free will...on a rescue mission. My friends have already taken one from this place, and we can take more," said Bedillia.

There was a long pause before the man spoke again. "I have much to answer for in my life. That is why I'm here, I'm no saint. I knew the message of Christ; I even preached it, but it didn't take hold in my heart. If I only had another chance, I'd change...I swear I would. I'd make up for all the things I did." Again there was a pause. "Please, if you can do what you say, take me with you, I beg you."

"Then you're coming with me," promised Bedillia. "Stay close, and when I give you the word, follow."

"I will," said the man.

"This is madness," said Joan.

"Just keep your eyes open," said Bedillia. "When the time comes, you will know what to do."

"Can I come too?" asked the woman directly behind the dark man.

"Just stay close," said Bedillia.

They arrived at the top of the gently sloping ridge. The well-worn trail followed the slowly rising crest of the ridge for some distance then crossed onto a flat stretch of land beyond. In the distance, Bedillia saw a grouping of demons. Here, the procession seemed to break up and vanish.

"That's it," said Joan, "the plunge. There is no way we're going to get rescued between here and there, is there?"

Bedillia didn't know what to say. She could only imagine what was going on back at Refuge. She was confident that they were planning a rescue, but not here. She would have to take the plunge. "I very much doubt it. Hold on, just this one last time."

"I've faced it often enough," said Joan. "My body is completely healed. I have about ten minutes before my pain begins all over again."

Bedillia looked at her arm. It was covered with dry blood, but it was otherwise whole. Then she thought, *Suppose my shackles spring open when I hit the ground at the bottom of the cliff?* It was a very real possibility. The demons would surely realize something was wrong. They might suspect something already. Somehow she had to protect them on impact. What an insane concept, but she had to do it. She prayed for strength, for the courage to face what was ahead.

"Bedillia is approaching the cliff," announced Dr. Kepler. "She is a very brave woman. I think you need to make provisions to retrieve more lost souls. Bedillia wants to assist some of those around her."

"Very well," replied Abaddon, "we will make room for them."

Abaddon glanced at the now full ring room. Kurt had 12 armed marines suited in battle gear that looked very much like the battle armor worn by contemporary soldiers. Lenar also had a dozen dark angels ready for battle, and hundreds of Abaddon's tiny winged children had gathered on the walls, awaiting their orders.

Tom had never seen the likes of this. He turned to Bill. "Where did the uniforms and the battle gear come from?"

"I made some of it," replied Bill. "I'm not as good as you are with that machine, but I do have some abilities. Interestingly enough, so does Kurt and about half a dozen others. They just don't possess your level of skill. They use two less sophisticated versions of the machine to manufacture such things as daggers, clothing, and body armor…that is, by the way, several times more resilient than that used by the U.S. military."

A hasty battle plan was drawn up. Now it all depended on what happened when Bedillia hit the ground. If only they could help her before she took the plunge, but they didn't dare.

The edge of the cliff grew ever closer, and the cries and weeping of those around Bedillia increased. Some even prayed, though they must have realized that it did no good, not here. There were four demons standing near the threshold—more than enough to handle the multitude of shackled and defeated humans in their charge.

The line was vanishing as one by one, the poor damned souls threw themselves from the precipice. Most of the ragtag multitude stepped off the cliff without being coerced by the demons, beyond their endless cruel taunting. It appeared to be a conditioned response, the result of years of intimidation, retaliation, and hopelessness. To hesitate more than a few seconds at the threshold was to invite the wrath of the masters. Consequently, the line moved smoothly.

"It's better if you try to land on your feet," said the man behind Bedillia. "Try to absorb as much of the impact as you can with your legs. Your legs will be shattered like you can't imagine, but you might come out of this with your arms and neck unbroken. That way you'll be able to drag your body away from the cliff more quickly. The demons won't whip you as much if you get moving quickly after you hit the bottom. Landing on your stomach isn't as good. It breaks your ribs up real bad, messes up your innards too. It's particularly bad for you women, if you get my meaning. Never land on your back, side, or head; that's the worst. You might end up paralyzed for ten minutes or more. Then the demons will have to drag you away from the cliff themselves. They don't like to do that. Trust me, they'll take it out on you later. And don't hesitate at the edge, push outward if you can. That way you'll land a bit farther away from the cliff...be less likely to hit rocks on the way down, and have less distance to pull yourself to get out of the way of others."

"Thank you," replied Bedillia. "I'll remember that."

"Please remember me when the time comes," continued the dark-skinned man. "My name is Leland."

"I will," replied Bedillia, "I promise."

Bedillia was drawing closer to the front of the line. Though it must have been over 90 degrees up there, she was shaking. She wasn't ready for this. If only Abaddon would come and rescue her, yet she knew that he couldn't, not here.

How should she make the plunge? Going feet first was out of the question unfortunately. The pin in the shackles would most assuredly be triggered, and her deception would be discovered. Going belly first seemed the only option, though that didn't seem too appealing either. "God give me strength and wisdom," she murmured, "in the name of Jesus."

She could see the edge clearly now. It was a sharp rocky drop-off. The cliff beyond seemed nearly vertical, at least from here. She could see all the way across the valley—magnificent desolation. There were three people ahead of her, then two. Then Joan took the plunge. It was Bedillia's turn. She felt sick to her stomach. She was looking straight down at the carnage below; then she was airborne.

She felt the wind growing stronger, saw the cliff face passing her even more swiftly. She was tumbling; she had to gain control. She stretched out her arms…her spin stopped. She would try to hit belly first if she could. The ground was coming up so fast. There were so many twisted and broken bodies. She prayed that she would neither hit a large boulder of which there were many, nor another damned soul of which there were even more. She took a deep breath.

The impact was violent and traumatic but it paled in comparison to the resulting tremendous pain. She had hit the ground on her belly. She had missed the boulders and impacted on a stretch of level hard soil mixed with small rocks. She couldn't breathe, she was suffocating, yet she was incapable of passing out.

She tried to move her right arm; the attempt was accompanied by a horrible sickening pain. It was broken in several places. One bone, the radius, appeared to have shattered in two and the tip had penetrated her skin.

She tried to move her left arm; it worked, although it was badly lacerated and bleeding. But what was the condition of her legs, and more importantly, what about her shackles? She could feel her legs; her back wasn't broken. She looked around and saw at least seven or eight demons, though none had taken any particular interest in her. She rolled on her side and looked at her feet—the shackles were still attached, the illusion had survived.

Not far away, Joan fought to pull herself along with her arms. Her legs had literally been telescoped into her hips. Ghastly. Somehow Bedillia had to stay with her. Amazingly, her right leg had survived the fall unbroken, though her left leg was twisted around 90 degrees. She struggled to move, though it was pure agony. She tried to cry out to Joan, but the attempt to open her mouth was accompanied with intense pain—her jaw was broken. Other bodies were falling around her. She had to move. Like all of the others, she was a broken mass of flesh, but she was moving enough to avoid the whips of her taskmasters. The road ahead would be more difficult than she'd ever imagined.

"Bedillia's shackles survived the fall undamaged," announced Kepler, to those assembled in the ring room. "I wish that the same could be said about her. She is in very grave condition, but she is moving."

"Very well," said Abaddon, turning to Kurt, "you and your men have about forty minutes before you go through. Your main objective is to get Bedillia. If you can get others as well, you have a go. I am sending the first wave of my children through once Bedillia gets on her feet. Their mission will be to protect her, if necessary, until she reaches the extraction point. I'll send a second group through just ahead of you to establish the bridgehead—then you will follow. Lenar and his warriors will stand by in case they are needed." Abaddon paused. "Until then, it's up to Bedillia. She is in the hands of the Father."

Bedillia was on her knees now, crawling as best she could. She saw that her left leg was nearly straight, but the pain was unbearable. Tears ran down her cheeks, but she kept moving on. She was getting closer to Joan who had risen to her feet, only to fall again to her knees. Bedillia's radius bone was now covered by skin, though it was still broken. It had been nearly ten minutes since the fall. During half of those minutes she had been unable to take a breath, and yet in that time she had covered nearly 50 yards.

But the demons around her were becoming impatient. They were using their whips to encourage their prisoners to rise to their feet. Soon Bedillia would have to make the attempt. Again Joan rose to her feet. She stumbled repeatedly, but managed to stay there. Bedillia attempted to do the same; she succeeded.

The line of lost souls was forming again, though it was moving far slower than before. Bedillia managed to get in line behind Joan. Amazingly, the dark-skinned man she had met before the plunge, entered the line behind her, though the woman who had been behind him was nowhere to be seen.

From a distance, the demon Drelleth watched Bedillia suspiciously. Something was wrong here, though he knew not what. Right now, he was searching for Task Master Sargoth. He would know more about this mysterious woman. To Drelleth's knowledge, they had not acquired a new human here for nearly a year. They were at capacity. The new souls were being directed to Krull and other newer facilities. So who was this Bedillia? He would find out.

Behind a pile of boulders, in the narrowest portion of the canyon, a glowing blue fog began to form. A moment later, more than 100 tiny creatures flew out of the shimmering mists. They scattered, most taking up positions on the canyon walls. Still others flew down the canyon in search of Bedillia. They would circle high above her until needed.

The procession around Bedillia was picking up the pace, driven on by the whips of their taskmasters. She limped along as best she could, even as her arm slowly straightened itself. She was moving into the entrance to the side canyon. Amid the pain, a terrible depression was setting in. Would there be anyone waiting for her up ahead, or was she doomed to make this trip again and again throughout eternity? Right now, she wasn't sure.

In the midst of her depression, she heard a low fluttering sound; then she felt something land on her right shoulder. She turned her head to look into a tiny face smiling back at her. Her heart soared. "Hello little friend," she whispered, tears welling up in her eyes. "I'm *so* happy to see you."

It settled into the nape of her neck, hiding beneath her long hair, and stroking its soft fur against her skin. She had never felt such a wonderful sensation. She had not been abandoned. How could she ever have thought otherwise? She felt at peace now. The cavalry had arrived.

It was several minutes before the man behind her looked up to see Bedillia's tiny friend. The small creature turned about to face him. At first the man was alarmed.

"Oh my…what is that thing?" he gasped quietly.

"Don't be afraid," said Bedillia, "he's a friend, a very good friend. He is going to help get us out of here."

"Then it's all true," he said. "You're still taking me with you, aren't you?"

Bedillia didn't immediately respond, yet the small creature smiled at him as well, made a soft purring noise, and Bedillia knew. "I can tell that he likes you," she said. "He senses your repentant heart. Yes, you're coming with us."

"Thank you, sweet Lord Jesus," said the man, as tears wet his face. "Thank you for having mercy on me, a sinner."

Bedillia had been gone from the bottom of the cliff about 20 minutes when Drelleth at last located Task Master Sargoth, only to learn that Bedillia had been deceptive.

"There are 4,211 souls here in this place, Drelleth, 4,211," said Sargoth, turning to see a pair of souls make the plunge from the cliff together. "We are at capacity. No humans have been brought here in a long time."

"So who was she…this Bedillia Smith?" asked Drelleth.

"There is no woman by the name of Bedillia Smith here," confirmed Sargoth. "Perhaps for reasons of her own, she was lying to you."

"But her blood flowed so freely when I struck her," objected Drelleth. "No human here could still have so much blood flowing through their veins, not after so much time in the procession."

"Wait," said Sargoth. "I overheard others talking about a bleeder not twenty minutes ago, a woman."

A dark-haired woman?" asked Drelleth.

Sargoth just shook his head. "I hadn't given it much thought until now."

"She is on the trail back to the top," said Drelleth, "I saw her not long ago. I will find her and discover what has happened here."

Drelleth was on the trail, and Sargoth was close behind. They were going to get to the bottom of this. She couldn't have gotten very far.

Farther up within the canyon, Abaddon's children had drawn the attention of the humans. It had been a long time since any of them had seen a flying creature. Some watched in awe, others in fear, but there was a sense that something was about to happen, something unusual. As the minutes passed, the creatures grew more numerous.

The aerial display had caught the attention of the demons as well. Several had already transformed themselves into their more natural form—a bat-winged angel better able to take to the skies and investigate this strange phenomenon.

"Something is happening up ahead," said Sargoth as a winged demon, then another took to the skies. He and Drelleth quickened their pace.

A minute later they witnessed three small creatures streak over their heads flying out into the valley. A bat-winged demon was in hot pursuit.

"By the lights of Sheol, what is happening?" asked Sargoth. He stopped to observe the mad pursuit as Drelleth forged on ahead.

They were almost to the middle of the valley when the three children of Abaddon split up in different directions. The demon followed the center one. He was gaining on him, but slowly. The others swung back around and were now closing on their demon pursuer. A few seconds later, the first turned on him. The demon tried to defend himself but the tiny creature was too fast. It hit him straight in the face, clawing and biting. The other two joined him a few seconds later. The demon drew his sword, swinging it about wildly, yet its blade met empty air.

Seeing his plight, another demon bolted into the air and made for the middle of the valley, not realizing that he too had been pursued by several creatures. All the while, Sargoth watched in amazement.

Drelleth continued past the endless parade of humans, looking for one specific woman. Then in the distance, he saw her. He quickened his pace.

Another of Abaddon's children landed on Bedillia's other shoulder then another. Bedillia laughed as best she could amid her still lingering pain. "Easy guys, there is only so much of me to go around."

A minute later, a dozen were circling about her. Something was wrong. She turned to see Drelleth rapidly encroaching upon her. He was going to reach her long before she reached the boulders and the nearest extraction point. Something had happened, her secret was out. She reached down and popped open her shackles. They both opened easily. Then she picked them up. They were heavy; perhaps she could use them as a weapon.

Drelleth had drawn to within a dozen feet of her when two things happened almost simultaneously. The children of Abaddon attacked him, and so did Leland. Leland drove into Drelleth as hard as he could, with all of the strength remaining in his being. He did the unimaginable; he drove the mighty demon to the ground.

Leland scanned the ground and picked up a rock the size of a small melon. "No more!" he screamed, driving the rock into Drelleth's skull. "I'll never follow that road again, never again. I'll never allow you to hurt my friends again. It ends here!"

An air of growing confusion was falling all around. Abaddon's children were everywhere and more were joining the battle.

By the time Bedillia stayed Leland's hand, the demon's head had been pulverized. "Leland, that's enough, we've got to go."

Leland relented, rising to his feet. He was out of breath, almost out of strength, and his anger had ebbed. "God forgive me, but that sure felt good," he said, throwing the bloody rock aside and walking with Bedillia.

Bedillia turned to Joan who appeared nearly frozen. "Come on, Joan, time to go."

Bedillia looked up the canyon. As best she could figure, they still had 200 yards to go to the most likely extraction point. The procession of slaves was becoming more disorganized as the people began to realize what was happening. Behind her, Drelleth convulsed and shuttered, as Abaddon's children lit into him savagely.

Bedillia, Joan, and Leland picked up their pace, and others began to follow.

Suddenly Bedillia began to sing loudly. She didn't know why she was singing or why this particular song, but she sang, "Onward Christian soldiers, marching as to war, with the cross of Jesus, going on before…"

Amazingly, others began singing. The chorus was swelling, echoing from the rocky canyon. Never had such a sound been heard in Hell beyond the precious cavern walls of Refuge.

Demons were rushing in from all quarters, only to be intercepted and attacked by Abaddon's many children. It had started—war in Hell.

Bedillia and the others pushed on, yet her friends' shackles were hindering them, slowing their pace. This wasn't working; but Bedillia had an idea. There were still three of the children perched upon her shoulders. It was time to put them to work. She stopped, pointed to the shackles around Joan and Leland's ankles—that was all it took. In an instant the children had attached themselves to the heavy metal restraints. In seconds, four others swept in to assist.

"Don't be afraid," said Bedillia, "they won't hurt you, but they will free you."

It required half a minute before the first shackle fell from Leland's ankle. Within a minute, both Leland and Joan were free. It had been over 70 years since Leland had seen his ankles without shackles, since he had been free.

"OK, folks, we gotta go, go, go," urged Bedillia.

They took off. Not running, not yet, but moving much faster than had been possible before.

Others cried out for mercy, for deliverance, as Bedillia passed. If only she could free them all. Perhaps she could, but not right now.

Bedillia looked around. Still more demons were coming, sweeping in from all directions. They were being met by Abaddon's children, but the children were being quickly overwhelmed. There just weren't enough of them. Some were even falling to the claws and swords of the demons they had attacked so fearlessly. Yet they fought on, regardless of the odds. Despite encouraging beginnings, this rescue was starting to fall apart.

All the while the three moved up the canyon. How much farther? She wasn't sure now. There was a sound of flapping wings above as a demon descended toward them. The three children who had accompanied them moved to intercept the attacker. But it seemed like a David and Goliath battle. Suddenly a dazzling beam of light, then another, bolted skyward striking their would-be attacker. The demon exploded in midair, in a blinding flash. What was left was a boiling rain of blood and shattered body parts scattering over a wide area. Then out of nowhere someone stepped into her path.

"Nice of you to join us, Bedillia," said Kurt, a broad smile on his face and a Tesla rifle in his hand. Three other soldiers stepped out of the shadow of the rocks, weapons drawn. "We're getting you out of here right now—your friends too."

Tears welled up in Bedillia's eyes; he was really here.

Kurt took Bedillia's hand. "Remember what I told you? No one gets left behind, no one. Now go with Corporal Lawrence. He'll see to it that you get gated out of here."

"No, I can't leave until I see these other people to safety," objected Bedillia.

"Yes, you can," corrected Kurt, "getting these people out is my job, soldier. Your job is to gate out of here right now and report straight to Abaddon. Appraise him of our situation. I can't spare anyone else. Tell him I'm going to need backup. He'll understand what you mean."

"Yes, sir," said Bedillia, the slightest smile coming to her face. "I'll pass the message onto him."

Kurt smiled then kissed Bedillia on the cheek. "Welcome home, Bedillia."

Bedillia's smile broadened. She and the others followed the corporal into the cover of the rocks. He handed her a sphere.

"Can you make the trip back to Refuge alone?" asked Lawrence. "We're kind of busy here."

"We'll manage," said Bedillia. She took the sphere in her hand. In a few seconds, a foggy field of stars appeared before them. "Take my hands," she said, turning to her friends, "we're going home."

"Thank you Lord, thank you Jesus," said Leland, over and over again. He was weeping for joy.

The three stepped into the cool fog together. Their surroundings faded into the mists. This place felt awesome. It was like walking on a cloud. A moment later they stepped through the ring into Refuge.

A cheer broke out that was wonderful to hear. Bedillia walked into the midst of the assembled crowd. She was still in considerable pain and could hardly believe that she was back. It took only a few seconds to find Abaddon.

"Kurt says he needs backup," said Bedillia, her tone cold and distant. "It's a mess over there. You've got your first battle of a new war."

Abaddon nodded to Lenar who had also heard Bedillia's words. A minute later, 20 armed dark angels, eight marines, and another hundred of Abaddon's children entered the ring and vanished. This thing was rapidly escalating into the thing that so many had feared—war. Abaddon placed an arm around Bedillia hoping that it would help. "You've had a terrible experience. I want you to report to your quarters. And I don't want you to be alone; that wouldn't be good right now. Take as much time as you need." He placed a finger under her chin, looked deeply into her eyes. "Thank you, Bedillia. You did a wonderful job. We all love you very much."

Bedillia nodded and walked toward the door. She found Tom just two steps away. She practically fell into his arms. She had been so strong up to this point, but now her lips were trembling.

"I was afraid I was going to lose you," said Tom, holding her tight. She was shaking all over. "I'll take you home and stay with you, if you like."

"I'd like that," she said. They vanished into the corridor, arm in arm.

"Where is this going to end, Abaddon?" asked the dark angel Eleazar, stepping up from behind. "Are we just going to keep sending men, angels, and your children into that bottomless pit of a ring? And that's what it is, my friend, a bottomless pit that will consume as many of our people and resources as we send into it. We're not ready for this, not yet."

"Perhaps not," replied Abaddon, turning to his old friend. "But the time has come to send a message to Satan. Perhaps he needs to know that his hold on this place is not as absolute as he would like to think." Abaddon paused. "I will not allow this to go too far, I assure you. We needed this, and it will pay dividends."

Within a minute, the first of many dazed human refugees stepped from the ring. They were greeted with applause.

Abaddon watched as they were guided away to the commons, their largest meeting area. Most of them already had their shackles sheered off by his children. The others would be done presently. He wondered just how many of these poor souls he could manage to free before he was forced to withdraw his forces. This had been a major and not very well thought out change in strategy. He only hoped that it would yield favorable results.

Chapter 9

The skies above the Valley of Noak were calm now. Twenty minutes ago, they were ablaze with the flashes of angelic swords, demon fireballs, and human particle weapons. Lenar looked skyward with concern. He now had nearly 2,000 of Abaddon's children, and 47 dark angels patrolling the area. An additional 28 humans, mainly in support roles, were also here, reassuring and guiding the rescued slaves of this dreadful place through the gate, and into Refuge.

They had rescued 257 repentant souls at last count, and rejected so many more. Abaddon's children found a second calling in this task. They could discern which of the victims of this terrible place had truly repentant hearts. These people alone would make the journey to Refuge. It was a tragedy as to how many human hearts had not been driven to repentance by this terrible experience. But one way or another, this operation had to come to an end. The demons of this place had largely retreated, but reinforcements were surely on the way. They didn't have much time.

"We'll eventually need to begin an organized pullback," said Abaddon, standing by Lenar's side. He looked over at a group of humans who stood guard around their staging area, Tesla particle rifles in hand. They had played an important role in today's battle. "So like children with a new toy they are," he said, smiling slightly.

"That is some toy," said Lenar. "Some of those demons knocked down at short range an hour ago by those very weapons have not even regenerated yet—they remain as dismembered parts. I'd not thought that possible. The weapon might be more potent than we had at first imagined."

"All the more reason to build them in large quantities," replied Abaddon. "That task will fall to this Victoria van Voth. I pray that this operation was worth it." He turned his attention to more pressing issues. "We shall pull the human aid workers out first. Then the angelic and human warriors shall withdraw from the field. My children shall bring up the rear." Abaddon again considered his options. "Perhaps I should allow several thousand of my children to roam Hell freely, live off the land. We have not the means to feed their numbers properly at Refuge. They might well become a potent curse on Satan's minions, gorging themselves on demon flesh. They might enjoy that."

"An intriguing concept," replied Lenar, gazing up toward the ridgeline above them. "I have sentries up there. They will give us plenty of warning in the event of a counterattack. It will take only a few minutes to evacuate our forces through the gate. I want as much time as possible to get these victims to safety. In truth, I am surprised we haven't been attacked as yet."

Abaddon nodded. He could remember a time when Lenar was anxious to pull out once the mission objectives were accomplished. Now he was pushing the envelope. "Don't wait too long."

Abaddon turned to the other problem in their staging area, the place where those who could and could not go through the gate to Refuge was decided. He had stationed several of his dark angels here to enforce the decisions that were often unpopular. Those selected were sent into a cordoned off area where their shackles were removed, and they were sent in groups into the gate with a human volunteer from Refuge to guide them.

Those rejected were escorted down the canyon, still shackled, into the open valley to await the return of Satan's minions and the continuation of their eternal sentence. They would be confined to a small region of the valley by Abaddon's children until they were ready to withdraw. Abaddon regretted the necessity of this; he desired that none should continue to suffer, but he couldn't have such people as these in Refuge. They were unpredictable, lovers of self over others, potential liabilities to a community that worked for the common good.

Abaddon bolted skyward toward the top of the canyon to survey the situation from a broader perspective. Here he encountered one of Lenar's sentries. The sentry bowed his head in honor of his commander.

"Are they still there?" asked Abaddon, gazing across the valley, toward the mountains on the far side.

"Yes, they remain," said the sentry, pointing to a high mesa on the far side of the valley, about four miles away. "But now there are far more of them than there were just half an hour ago, perhaps a thousand, at this point."

"What are they waiting for?" asked Abaddon, almost under his breath.

"Perhaps they are sizing up the situation," suggested the sentry. "They are certain neither of our numbers nor our capabilities. They were routed rather severely by our initial attack. I would imagine that they will only counterattack once they can be certain of victory."

Abaddon nodded. He knew they needed to withdraw. This terrain would be difficult to defend against a force so large. Yet he still delayed. He had to evacuate as many slaves as he could. It was inhumane to do anything else.

On the far side of the valley, Cordon scanned the abandoned Plunge of Desolation using a glowing sphere that acted to greatly magnify the enemy camp. This attack came as a complete surprise to him. It was out of character with the tactics the rebels had used up to this point. It was bold, perhaps a bit too bold.

There had been a steady stream of humanity up and down the narrow canyon, escorted by dark angels. He turned to his aide, Rolf, then pointed to the growing group of humans on the valley floor. "They're separating the wheat from the chaff."

"What?" asked Rolf.

"Somehow they are discerning which souls are worthy of being saved and which are not," replied Cordon.

Rolf shook his head. "How could they possibly know that?"

"If we knew that, my friend, we might be one step closer to bringing an end to their rebellion," said Cordon.

Cordon turned to review the growing force Governor Molock had assembled on the mesa. They were over 1,400 strong right now, seasoned warriors all. Very soon he would have double that number. For reasons totally unknown to him, Molock had placed him in charge of this assault. Cordon had not complained, but he had found it curious.

"This couldn't have happened at a worse time," growled Molock, approaching Cordon and Rolf. "The master has summoned me to come at once. He has been called to stand in assembly before the Father and with the other highest angels. General Krell and I are to stand at his side. I believe this will be the day. He is going to make his challenge to Michael and Gabriel; I am certain of it. Now what am I to tell him?"

"Why tell him anything?" asked Cordon. "If I may be so bold as to advise you, my lord, speak of it only if he asks you directly. The position of these rebels is in flux, and the territory they occupy virtually indefensible. I have already sent a force of 300 on a long loop, to engage them from the south. We shall move on them from the north within the hour, and they will retreat through their portal or be annihilated it is that simple. And we shall learn much about them before this is all over. Perhaps I will even learn the whereabouts of their hidden base."

"That may be," replied Molock, "but if all goes well, you will have but a fraction of the resources you have now to accomplish it, for we will be at war with the angels of Heaven. Both General Krell and I will be fighting at the master's side." There was a momentary pause. "I am placing you in charge of my territories, of the forces under my command that remain. Bring this rebellion to an end Cordon…I am depending on you."

"I shall do my best," promised Cordon.

"I expect no less," replied Molock, placing a hand on Cordon's shoulder. "I did not always hold the trust in you I have now. At one time I considered you a liability; but in the time since, you have earned my trust and my respect. Don't disappoint me."

Not much surprised Cordon, but that statement did. It was almost moving. "I shall endeavor to live up to the faith you have in me, my lord."

Governor Molock departed, leaving Cordon to his plans. He was in control now.

"Fate has smiled upon you this day," said Rolf.

Cordon nodded approvingly but said nothing. Rolf was right. No longer would he have to deal with an incompetent bureaucracy. Now he could get this task done efficiently, his way. But by the same token, he could not blame the failings of this campaign on someone else should it go badly. That blame would fall on him.

"There are massive enemy forces approaching from the north and the south," warned the sentries. The warning sparked frenzied activity in the valley below. Abaddon's children swept out of their resting places amid the cliffs and soared skyward to meet the encroaching demon units. Still, their task was only a delaying action. They would buy the ground forces a few minutes, no more.

"If we only had more time," lamented Julie, as she prepared to escort the last eight refugees into the misty corridor and freedom. "It felt so wonderful to give to others the gift that had been given to me, the gift of freedom from the torments of Hell."

The marine sentry at her side nodded but said nothing. It was time to go.

Julie was the last volunteer still here. They had gotten out so many, but there were so many still left to go. Beyond the cordoned off area, a great multitude's joy turned to horror as they realized that they would not be escaping this place after all.

"You've got five or six minutes," warned the sentry, "go!"

Julie led the last eight refugees, hand in hand, into the mists, followed quickly by the last of the marines.

Abaddon turned to the gathered humans that he would have to leave behind, even as his own dark angels began their retreat through the gate. "Please, do not lose hope, never lose hope. I swear to you in the name of the Father, I will return to take you home."

In the midst of the crowd, Tim Monroe looked on in horror. He had been just a few feet from going over the cliff again when the attack came and the assembly line of agony had been suspended. Then followed the confusion and the realization that freedom might well be at hand. It had been an arduous journey from there to here, wearing the dreadful shackles much of the way. But hearing the rumor that freedom might be at the end of the journey made it worth the shackled trek.

Along the way he had met a pair of marines in full battle gear. Imagine that, real marines in Hell. They had been amazed to encounter one so young as himself, little more than a child, really. Even now after a year in this awful place, he had not yet turned 17. With the help of several small creatures of a kind he had never seen before, his shackles had been sheared away, right there on the spot. It had been a trial of sorts, or so he had been told. These creatures, Abaddon's children, had judged him to be worthy of salvation from this place. The marines had told him to come to this place, told him to hurry. Now he was so close, but not close enough. He had gotten lost in the shuffle; and now as just one among the surging crowd, he couldn't reach the leader of the dark angels.

"Please, take me with you!" he cried. "I'm all ready; they said I could go." But his voice faded to insignificance amid the growing din of lamenting and pleading voices.

Then even Abaddon retreated into the starry portal, leaving thousands of defenseless humans behind. What was Tim to do? He began to run. Many times as he made his way up the switchback trail to the ridge then onward to the precipice, he had looked down at the narrow canyon. It snaked its way through the rocky plateau to he knew not where. Might there be hiding places out there? He had to find out; it was his only hope.

It was difficult for him to make his way through the still shackled multitudes, but at last he broke free and ran into new territory. In high school he had been on the track team. The 440 was his main event, yet after a year of this place, he had become so weak and dehydrated that he was in no danger of breaking his personal record. Yet, he pushed on ahead of the crowd.

There were no demons overhead yet. Apparently, they had been waylaid by the many small creatures that still flew around the canyon. The canyon made a sharp turn to the left. He lost sight of the other victims, though he could still hear their lamentations bouncing off the nearly vertical canyon walls around him.

A brightly glowing ball of dazzling light rocketed across the sky, hitting the cliff a few hundred yards behind him with a powerful detonation. "A fireball," he gasped. Yes, he had seen these powerful demonic weapons before. The demons used them to demonstrate their superiority, to remind their slaves of the power they possessed.

Rocks from the canyon wall were blasted away to plunge to the canyon floor in a terrible torrent, forming a barricade of rubble across the canyon floor behind him. Still more lit up the sky, dropping beyond the ridgeline, followed by a series of titanic explosions. The fading voices behind him turned to screams of terror.

His bare feet hurt, as they were brutalized by the maze of rocks that made up the canyon floor. He was running so hard; he had to stop, yet the thought of what lay behind, the fate that could be his again were he not swift enough, gave him incentive to push on.

Tears ran down his cheeks as he pushed onward. At any moment he expected to hear the flapping of wings or feel the sharp talons of a demon digging into his flesh—yet neither became a reality. Through it all he prayed, over and over again, even as he wept.

Still, his endurance was not without its limits. In the end, he found himself kneeling on the ground fighting for his breath. He didn't have the strength to do this, yet he could do nothing else. It was several minutes before he rose once more and continued his trek, though more slowly.

Then there was a sound coming from the rocks ahead of him. He stopped. All he heard was the wind blowing through the canyon. But wait, he heard it again. He advanced cautiously. It sounded like an animal of some sort. It sounded almost like a faint cry of pain. But he had never seen animals of any sort in Hell, not once in the year he had been here. He peered behind the rocks to see an amazing sight. There, on the sand, was one of the tiny creatures that had come with the rescue party. But this one was not in good condition. Apparently it had been injured during the battle. There was dried blood in its fur, and its wing on the same side was sliced open. From the faint trail of blood, it was obvious that it had been trying to reach something, but what?

Tim looked in the direction it had been moving to see a cave about three feet up on the canyon wall. The creature had been trying to reach it, but it lacked the strength. It appeared to be a very small cave indeed. Tim wondered if he might be able to squeeze through its narrow entrance. Time was running out. Demons would surely search this canyon to regain any lost souls that might have slipped through their grasp. He had to try, but he hesitated. He knelt down before the small being.

"Hey there," he said softly.

He was surprised when it lifted its head to look at him with weary eyes. It looked so sad, so helpless.

"I'm not going to hurt you," he said. "I promise."

He knew it was a bad idea to reach out to a wounded animal, especially one as powerful as this tiny one, but his love for animals allowed him to do nothing else. Gently, he picked it up in his hand. It didn't resist, it just whimpered softly.

"You poor thing," he said softly, stroking its fur. "I'll try to help you, I promise."

He gently set the creature upon a ledge near the mouth of the cave, yet it seemed to lack the strength to move any farther. He then climbed up to the cave and peered in. It was round and narrow indeed. About 8 or 10 feet back, it made a turn to the left. Beyond that, he could not tell in which direction it went, or if it went any farther at all.

Then there came a new sound echoing from the canyon walls—the sound of demon wings. They were coming. This was his only hope. He would enter the cave feet first. There might not be any place in there to turn around, and he wanted to be able to scan his surroundings when he exited the cavern. He slipped his feet in and began to crawl backward. It wasn't easy. He reached out and picked up the tiny being in one hand, even as he struggled through the narrow opening.

He had barely disappeared into the shadows when three winged demons swept through the canyon. He went undetected. He continued crawling backward on his belly. At first the tunnel narrowed, then it turned and widened, much to his relief. Within another minute, he had slipped around the bend in the tunnel and out of sight from the entrance. About another 15 feet back, he found a small elongated room, roughly 4 feet high, 5 feet wide, and 8 feet long. He stopped to rest, placing the small creature at his side.

"We'll be safe here, I hope," he said.

It responded with a purr, almost reminiscent of a cat. He and his companion just laid there in the dark for about 20 minutes.

Then he heard noise beyond the cave. There were voices, demon voices. They spoke a language that he didn't even pretend to understand. The light faded; one of them was standing at the entrance. Then another light, a bright beam, like that of a powerful flashlight illuminated the tunnel, yet he and the little creature remained in shadows. A small stone, then another bounced off of the rocks around him, but neither hit him. There was a scratching sound, as if something was trying to crawl into the tunnel. Again, the beam of light shown. This time it seemed more focused, nearer. The demon was at least partway into the tunnel, though from the scratching of his claws and the grunting sound he made, it was clear that he could go no farther.

Through it all, Tim remained completely still, not even daring to breathe. Even the tiny creature remained totally quiet.

A moment later the scratching sounds ceased, and daylight once more shown into the tunnel; the demon had withdrawn. The voices continued for a few more minutes, though farther away. Then the voices stopped entirely, followed by a fading sound of flapping wings.

It was over an hour before Tim even moved. He was not about to stick his head out of the tunnel. Did they suspect he was here, or had it been a more or less routine check? He couldn't be sure.

By now, his eyes had adapted to the darkness well enough that he could see the rocky walls and his tiny companion quite clearly. He found a more comfortable position. He had no intention of leaving the cave. Here, he was relatively safe. As far as he was concerned, he could stay here forever.

He examined his small companion more carefully, he didn't look too good. He was breathing, but in small labored gasps. Tim's heart went out to his newfound friend, his only friend.

"Come on, you can make it, I know you can," he whispered softly, stroking its fur. "I don't want to be alone here, I need you. You're my only friend. Please, don't die."

The creature didn't respond. Tim knew that it probably didn't have much of a chance. If there was only something that he could do for it. He kept his eyes on it for a long time, expecting each breath to be its last, yet it hung on. Eventually, the creature's eyes grew just too heavy to keep open. In the absence of pain, he curled up and partook of a blessing forbidden him for nearly a year—sleep.

Cordon was on the ground now, surveying the damage done by a hundred fireballs. It was wasted firepower. They had not hit the enemy, for the rebels had withdrawn five minutes before the first one had hit its target. But that wasn't what concerned him now. He wanted to know from where the rebels had gated out. With the help of his lieutenants, the information was extracted quickly from the humans who remained. As he had figured, those who had been rejected were more than willing to tell all that they knew.

There had been three places from which the dark angels and their human allies had gated out. Cordon and his lieutenants fanned out to examine each one before their ethereal signatures faded. The one amid the boulders of the canyon had left the most distinct trail by far.

"Yes, this is excellent," said Cordon to a lieutenant as he walked away from the gate out point. He held a small dark sphere in his hands, one that held an ever-changing set of symbols on its surface. "The trail is very warm indeed. Counting these three, we now have four good ethereal trails. With this information, I should be able to greatly narrow the search for the hiding place of these dark angels and their human allies."

"My lord, with what you know right now, do you have any idea where they are hiding," asked the lieutenant.

"My best guess is somewhere on the Dark Continent," said Cordon, gazing again into the darkened sphere.

"An awful lot of territory to search," said the lieutenant. "Conditions there are harsh; it would be a difficult search."

"I should be able to narrow the search to a smaller region within the next few days," said Cordon, placing the sphere in his cloak. "What we really need is to get another bearing. We will have it if they gate in and out somewhere else, and we get a bearing soon enough afterward." The direction of the conversation abruptly changed. "Have you completed a sweep of the area for escaped humans?"

"We have…several times farther out than we felt it would be possible for them to travel. I feel fairly confident that we have them all," said the lieutenant. "And we have these as well." The lieutenant held up the body of one of Abaddon's slain children. "My people are finding them all over the area. They are difficult to kill, but they can be killed."

"Collect several for me," said Cordon. "They will need to be studied. I suspect they are a creature from the old age of Hell, altered by the dark angels, of course."

"Yes sir," said the lieutenant. "My forces have continued to question the humans, and we now have a name, perhaps their leader…Abaddon."

"Abaddon, yes of course, I've heard that name some years ago," confirmed Cordon. "A great deal is starting to make sense to me now. We must question these humans carefully. If offering them an incentive, perhaps four or five days in a cool dry cell away from their torments will loosen tongues, so be it. I will authorize it. See that a report of the information gathered is brought to me when the questioning is complete."

"I will, my lord," confirmed the lieutenant. There was a long pause. "One thing troubles me greatly, sir."

"What would that be, lieutenant?"

"One of the taskmasters assigned to this place was literally blown apart by a weapon held by one of the strangely attired humans. Even after many hours he has not reconstituted. His blood dries in the sun, and his flesh decomposes. Never have I heard of such a thing. I know not even if his spirit has survived."

Cordon nodded. "Yes, that is troubling, but I can not say that I have never heard of an incident such as this. I have read of such a thing in the archives. It is not a loose piece in the puzzle; it does fit. Let me give you some advice, lieutenant. Be not so quick to come to a conclusion about what you see here. The quick answer is not often the right answer. Neither should you take the events you see this day in a vacuum. Ask yourself as to whether something like this has happened before. The events of this day have been building up for some time, perhaps six or seven years, perhaps even longer ago than that. Abaddon and his followers may have won a small battle here, but in doing so they have exposed themselves. The war shall be won by us."

"What of this place?" asked the lieutenant. "What would you have me and my minions do about the purpose it serves and the humans that serve it?"

"The damage is not extensive," said Cordon, looking around. "Although I fear we used the fireballs rather liberally, it seems to me that most of the humans are still here, and others can be added to reinforce their ranks. It is time to organize them, give them a purpose. Let it be their responsibility to clear away the rubble that blocks the paths and rebuild the trail where it has been damaged. Then they will be free to resume their service to the master. I doubt that they will be much trouble. They might even view it as a welcome vacation from the boredom of their eternity. I suspect that three or four days will see things back to normal."

The lieutenant nodded approvingly. "I'll see to it at once my lord."

The lieutenant and his subordinates departed, leaving Cordon to his thoughts. No, he hadn't caught any of the rebel angels or humans today, but he had nonetheless learned a lot about them. He needed to do some more research before he proceeded. He would need to peruse both the historical records as well as make some important mathematical calculations before he continued this operation. There was much to be done.

Corporal Lawrence and Private Higgins worked their way through the crowded commons a second time without results. Surely he had to be here, but he wasn't. He hadn't made it out.

"I knew we should have kept him with us…had him gate out with us," said Higgins. "He was just a scared kid. Tim didn't belong there."

"You can't beat yourself up over it," said Lawrence. "You didn't know. You were following proper procedures."

"Heck of a rationale to leave a sixteen-year-old kid behind," continued Higgins.

"If it bothers you that much, then take it to the counselor," replied Lawrence, "but she'll tell you the same thing I did. Look, every time we step through that ring we're walking into harm's way. I don't need to tell you that; you know it as well as me. The longer we stay out there, the greater the chance of getting nailed, and if that happens, we're all in a world of hurt.

We're going to end up leaving a lot of people behind before this is all over. We'll never be able save as many people as we would like."

"I know, I know," said Higgins, scanning the room one last time. "It's just hard, that's all. I mean…I know what kind of stuff these people went through. I went through it for twelve years myself. No one should have to go through something like that. I just don't like thinking that an error I might have made doomed someone to more suffering."

Lawrence shook his head and placed a hand on his friend's shoulder. "I understand, really I do. I was out there for nearly forty years. Look, we're only human, we're going to make a lot of mistakes, but in the end we're gonna win this thing…we have to. Come on, we've got other things to do before we turn in."

As Lawrence and Higgins left the commons, most of the refugees were settling down to get the first night of sleep they'd had in years. This war was just beginning. Who could say how long it would go on or how many good people would have to be left behind in the dungeon of the damned before it was through.

Chapter 10

Satan and three of his highest ranking minions stood before the gray marble ring, a monument that seemed so incongruous here on the plains of Heckath. It was an enormous monolithic arch, 100 feet across and 8 feet thick, partially buried in the reddish soil. Engraved deeply into its smooth surface, written in the angelic language, were the solemn words: Abandon All Hope Ye Who Enter Here. The red sun stood low at their backs, glistening off the surface of the 10-foot band of arching granite, an eternal sunset on the barren landscape.

Satan remembered this place well. It was from here that he had first viewed this realm that was to become his eternal kingdom; his eternal prison. It seemed little different now, really. The only things missing were the few meager desert bushes and patches of yellowish grass that once populated this windswept plain. He stretched out his arms to the great ring. "It was through this very portal that we arrived in this savage land so many years ago, and it is through this very same portal through which we shall ascend once more to our rightful place in Heaven." Satan turned to his closest confidant, the enigmatic and mysterious minion Metastopholies. "What say you old friend, shall we succeed in our endeavor?"

Metastopholies turned to his master. He was cloaked totally in black and was a good 6 inches shorter than his prince. His head was bald and he had no facial hair whatsoever. His eyes were an unnatural yellowish green and his lips thin and pale. For that matter, his whole complexion was unusually pale. From a natural perspective, he did not appear at all healthy, yet this was an illusion. He was as potent an adversary as any of Satan's minions. In fact, his mental powers were second to none in the kingdom.

"The signs do bode well, my master," he said slowly. "I believe that the Father shall consent to your proposal."

"But shall the day be ours?" asked Satan.

"I discern that it shall," replied Metastopholies. "Michael shall not suspect what this day holds for him and those who follow him. He has become too confident in his power. The events of this day shall render the victory unto thee. The pillars of angelic power in Heaven shall shake, and the saints shall tremble."

Satan's smile grew at the words of Metastopholies. "Then our enterprise shall succeed?"

"I say only that this day shall belong to thee, my lord," replied Metastopholies. "As for the days that follow, I cannot say the future is not so clear. I bring to you one warning. Heed it, and your fortunes shall be more favorable. Do not disregard the little things. Like ants they are, small in stature, and seemingly insignificant as individuals. Yet in sufficient numbers, they make a formidable enemy. They can bring down even the greatest of the beasts of the forest and make of them nothing but bones. Even a few can foil the best laid plans if they attack at the right place and time. Do not underestimate them, for that may be your undoing."

General Krell and Governor Molock looked on in amazement at this ally, so small in stature. They had always felt uneasy in his presence. He seemed to look right through them when he spoke, as if he knew their every secret. His words made sense enough, but the context and relevance were somewhat unclear. What or who were the ants?

"When you speak of the ants, are you speaking of the humans?" asked Satan. "I say, surely, that is all they are to me."

"Then you perceive the meaning of my warning?" asked Metastopholies, not the slightest sense of emotion in his words.

"Yes," confirmed Satan, "and your words will not be lost on me."

Before them, the distant hills viewed through the aperture of the great ring began to ripple and distort. In but a few seconds the ring had become a misty doorway into the realm of Heaven. It was time.

The four proceeded into the mists and faded from sight. It didn't seem like a long walk through the glowing mists. For a time, it seemed as if they were walking on air, as light as a breath of wind. A minute later, they stepped from a side corridor and into a vast rectangular arena, measuring about a 100 feet wide by 150 feet long, whose floor was made of seamless white marble. They were surrounded on all sides by a wall of the same material, perhaps 10 feet high. Rising in stepwise fashion beyond the wall were rows of empty seats rising to a glistening white wall interspaced with towering marble columns that supported nothing, for there was no ceiling. Above and beyond the columns were billowing clouds rising to an azure sky.

"It's always someplace different," said Satan, turning to his compatriots. "Last time it was in a great pine forest, in the third Heaven. The time before that, it was on the shores of the Crystal Sea. The Father rarely has these meetings at the same place twice in a row. This is the Hall of the White Throne Judgment, where the humans are weighed in the balance to be sent to Heaven or to us. To them, this is the closest to Heaven they will ever come. Impressive, isn't it? The Father has always had a passion for the dramatic. He tries to impress these humans for reasons I do not fully understand. It is strange to see this place deserted. Normally the seats around us would be filled with saintly spectators."

Before them was the Great White Throne itself. Clearly, it was meant for a being who must have stood 15 or 20 feet tall. Yet, it was empty. At nearly the center of the great arena was an oval-shaped table composed of the finest cultured marble. Chairs that appeared to be made out of fine crystal were positioned about it. Normally this region of the arena-like hall was open, reserved for the human facing judgment.

Around them, about a dozen angels dressed from head to toe in white milled about, talking in groups of two or three. They noted the arrival of the newcomers dressed in black but made no attempt to greet them, with the exception of one. A blonde, blue-eyed angel approached the group, a slight smile on his face.

"I bid you welcome, Lucifer. Welcome to the assembly," said the angel.

"Michael," said Satan, bowing but slightly.

"I am surprised to see that you have not come alone," said Michael, scanning the others. "Saral, Otimus, and Metallis, I bid you welcome."

"We no longer go by those names," objected Molock. "Those were the names the Father gave us, but we have taken on new names since our departure; surely you must realize that."

Michael shook his head sadly. "Yes, I know. I'm sorry, I did not mean to offend."

Satan smiled broadly. "No apology necessary, my old friend. I wish no ill will between us, not on this day. I know that your heart is in the right place, and I for one am glad to see you. I bring a proposal to the table this day... one that I think will interest you."

"Indeed," said Michael, his smile returning. "I await your words with great anticipation."

Michael rejoined the other angels. No others came over to speak to the four who seemed so very different. Even here they were shunned by their peers.

God's arrival occurred with no fanfare, no blowing of trumpets. He simply materialized as the others had. He took the form of a human man, just over 6 feet in height. He did not have the long beard so often ascribed to him in the classical and renaissance paintings. Nor did one gain any sense of

His actual physical age, so smooth were His features. His hair was long and curly, and at first glance, it looked to be blonde. Yet any discerning of color with respect to God's physical form was subjective at best, for His entire being was aglow, from His flawless skin to His long white robes.

At His side was a very human looking man with long flowing hair and a short beard. Like the Father, He too was dressed in white. He appeared to be in His mid-30s, a very handsome man with kind blue eyes. He and the Creator of the universe were discussing some issue between them, though the others did not hear the essence of their conversation.

He did not glow physically, as God did, yet one could sense the invisible spiritual aura that surrounded Him. It was as if a portion of God's divine spirit had been placed into a vessel of flesh. He was well-known and respected by this assembly, the only true son of God the Father—Jesus, the Nazarene.

All of the angels, even Satan and his minions, bowed low before them. God and His Son responded with wide characteristic smiles. God walked over to the large table and stood at one end, His Son to his right. The angels approached, standing before the other chairs.

"This is different," noted Satan, turning to his followers. "It reminds me so much of a corporate business meeting, so common among the humans of this age. I believe that the Father has become the President of Heaven, and His Son the Chairman of the Board."

When the group was assembled around the table, the Father sat down and His angels followed suit. For a moment the Father scanned the assembled angels carefully, then he began. "My children, I have called this assembly not to speak unto you, but to give you the opportunity to address me. Some of you have concerns to address, others have proposals. Speak what is on your heart, my children; I am here to listen."

It was Iseus, an angel under Michael, who spoke first. "Good Father, I must object in the strongest terms to Lucifer's meddling in the affairs of humankind. Since our last assembly, his minions attempted to murder two of your earthly children, children sanctified by the blood of your Son. They attempted to do so through the possession of another dying and downtrodden human whom they found easy to control. Only the quick actions of one of our own saved their lives."

"You distort the truth," objected Satan. "It was but a random act of violence, nothing more. As it happens, it was an act of violence you prevented through your meddling in the affairs of humanity."

"Random?" asked Iseus. "There was nothing random about it. It was deliberate and calculated." He paused, scanning the faces of the others. "And why did they do it? Why did Lucifer himself order this to be done? He did it to prevent the discovery of a celestial body on a collision course with Earth. He attempted to steal from man his freedom to choose his own destiny. Humankind has a difficult enough path to tread without your interference, Lucifer."

"And through my 'interference' as you call it, man becomes stronger," argued Satan. "He needs me more than you think. I am essential to his survival and you know it. It is I who has driven him to improve his lot in life, to find a better existence through technology. I lit the spark of curiosity within his mind. You cannot deny it, for it is a truth we all must acknowledge."

"Pure fantasy," objected Gabriel. "You are the enemy of humanity."

"And do you serve the best interest of humanity?" continued Satan, who seemed oblivious to Gabriel's comment. "I had not intended to offer my challenge so early in our meeting, but you have forced my hand."

Satan turned to the Father, his eyes full of sincerity. "Father, I have not always been faithful to you as I should. For that, I beg your forgiveness. But I question if Michael and his followers are themselves worthy of serving you. If put to the test, I do not believe that they would remain loyal to you. I beg your permission to test this."

He turned to Michael. "I challenge you to armed conflict."

Michael looked at Satan incredulously. "Surely this is not the place for jest."

"I jest not," assured Satan. "I propose a battle that will continue until only one side remains, no matter how long that takes."

"Yes, and what shall we do after the first minute of the battle, once you have fallen?" said Iseus, barely loud enough for the others to hear.

"You are no warrior," said Michael. "Iseus is right. You would not last long in single armed conflict against me. Surely you must know this."

Satan smiled. "I speak not of single combat. I speak of a war the likes of which has not been seen in one hundred centuries. I speak of war in Heaven—a war between those loyal to me, and those loyal to you—a war to determine who shall serve the Father."

Satan turned to the Father. "I ask Your permission, O Lord. Should I prevail, I vow to serve You forever. It will not be as it was before. I promise to be obedient to Your will. I will not question Your wisdom again; I swear it. I will rule the angels with wisdom and justice. Once again angels shall sing unto You songs of worship in Heaven. There shall be a new golden age of angels in Heaven."

"And what of our human brethren?" objected Gabriel. "It was their creation by the Father that led to your revolt, the revolt that inevitably cast you and your minions from the Father's presence. After tormenting them in Hell for so many millennia, how can I believe that you would be willing to serve them now?"

"There shall be a place in Heaven for them too," vowed Satan. "I have tormented only those who rejected God's plan of salvation, those whom He Himself condemned to the realm of outer darkness. I have acted as His avenging hand, and I will continue to do so. Those loved by the Father, those who have found a place in the Father's presence will be loved by me as well."

All eyes turned to the Father. Surely he would not agree to such a challenge. The Father's eyes were upon His most wayward angel; He seemed to look deep into his very soul. Then He scanned the others.

To his right, Jesus said nothing. His eyes did not move from His Father.

When the Father at last spoke, even the winds whistling through the mighty columns grew still. "These are my words. The house of the angels, my loyal servants, has been divided for a very long time. You do not know how this grieves me."

Once again He turned to Satan. "I will agree to your challenge, but know this: the war is between your angels and those of Michael and Gabriel. It is not with the saints of Heaven. Should you lift your sword against them, you will suffer the consequences. Be assured, those consequences will be indeed grave."

Satan was quick to raise an objection. "But what shall I or my legions do if the saints raise up arms against me? They have no love for me or my kingdom. May we not defend ourselves?"

"You may," replied God. "But it must be they and not you who makes the decision. If they choose to enter the battle, fight on the side of Michael and Gabriel, then you may war against them as well."

"And you will not take sides?" asked Satan.

"I will not," confirmed God.

Gabriel looked to the Father in disbelief. "But we have been Your obedient sons. Surely You can not abandon us and open the door to our enemies."

God looked to Gabriel with sympathy in His eyes. "My dear Gabriel, you have served Me faithfully…all of you have…but this thing must happen. Since the Fall, it has been within your power…all of you…to seek reconciliation with each other. During these many thousands of years the house of angels has been divided. I have allowed it to be so up to this point, but it will be so no longer. This conflict must be resolved.

"That I allow this to happen does not mean I do not love you. I loved Job, but I allowed him to be tested. Never since the Fall have your brethren been put to the test; you have been spared. The time of trial has been postponed, but no longer. Now is the time. When this battle is over, an age will have ended and a new order of peace will be established. All of you will determine the shape of that new order."

"But a war in Heaven?" objected Magar, a lieutenant of Gabriel. "We have all worked so hard to build the infrastructure of this place. We have had millennia of peace. Now we face the real possibility of seeing much of it destroyed, seeing much of Heaven reduced to a wasteland. It might take decades…even centuries to rebuild it." He turned to Satan. "Have a care, sir."

"You could surrender," suggested Satan. "My terms would not be unreasonable, I assure you. In the case of your surrender, many if not most of you would remain here in Heaven with my minions. In many ways it would be as it was in the first time, the time before man. We would all live together once more.

"You would assist in the day-to-day operation of this place as you have always done. Others of you would assist us in seeing that the humans in Hell, those who did not accept the gift of salvation offered by God's most holy Son, got all that they had coming to them. I assure you, it is not a task without its rewards. You shall come to see what I mean."

"You are asking me to become a torturer," replied Magar. "That, I could never be."

"This assembly is adjourned," proclaimed the Father, rising to his feet.

The others quickly stood with the Father. Never before had an assembly been so brief.

With no fanfare, God and His only Son entered a starry mist and vanished from the others' sight. As They walked through the mists, Jesus turned to the Father. "Then this is the time?"

"Yes," replied the Father, glancing only briefly at His Son.

"I knew the day was coming," replied Jesus, "I preached it to My disciples two thousand years ago, though I find no satisfaction upon its arrival."

"Nor do I," replied the Father.

There was an uncharacteristic moment of hesitation before Jesus spoke again. "I do not see the coming events so clearly as You, Father, what shall I expect?"

"Let Your heart not be troubled, my Son," said the Father, who had come to an abrupt halt in the mists. "I have always been ready to point out the path to You, although You have most often discerned it on Your own. But for now we must wait. It is for the angels to determine their next course of action; we must not interfere. The saints also have choices to make, but we must trust them to make the right decisions as well. They do, after all, have free will, and I shall not take it from them."

Back in the great hall, Satan and his minions had also made a hasty departure, leaving the other angels to ponder their situation. It became quickly apparent that there was no consensus of opinion.

"We must take the offensive," declared Iseus. "We can ill afford to allow Satan to dictate the venue of the initial thrust of this war. We must attack Hell with what forces may be quickly assembled."

"This was no sudden impulse of Satan's part," replied Michael. "You can rest assured that his forces are even now prepared to strike. If we strike out at him without a well-thought-out plan, then we place ourselves at an even more perilous disadvantage. No, the move is his, we can only respond. However, we must recall the majority of our forces from Earth at once. We shall set up our command post at the great angelic hall in Zion—time is of the essence. We should all use the portal here in the judgment hall to gate there at once."

The angels moved quickly to the corridor behind them, only one of two corridors that opened directly into the vast arena. It came to an abrupt end 30 feet back. It seemed like a tunnel to nowhere. Usually, this was the route through which unsanctified human souls bound for judgment entered the great hall. But now the angels would use it to gate back to the city of Zion. An angel could open it to the destination of their choosing through an act of pure will. The angels had now stood before it in silence for over a minute.

"What's wrong?" asked Magar, turning to Michael.

"The gate to the angelic hall in Zion won't open," replied Michael. "Something's wrong."

"Try to open the gate to Elesia in the second Heaven," suggested Gabriel.

"I've already tried," replied Michael. "This gate works...it responds to me. But the gates on the other end appear to be open to somewhere else."

"Lucifer," gasped Iseus.

"Let's not jump to conclusions," cautioned Michael. "There could be any one of a number of possible explanations."

"You don't really believe that, do you?" asked Gabriel.

"Try to gate into another angelic hall—any other hall," suggested Magar.

For more than 20 minutes these highest leaders of the angelic hosts attempted to access the other portals but in vain. Then it became only too clear what had happened.

"Satan has done this," said Michael turning to the others.

His compatriots were surprised that Michael had referred to their former friend as Satan and not Lucifer. Michael had always held out the hope that one day Lucifer might return to them. Apparently that hope had finally died.

"We can't fly out of here," noted Iseus. "All of Heaven lies on different planes from this place. Beyond outer darkness, there cannot be a more isolated place in the universe than this."

"So we're trapped," deduced Gabriel.

Michael just nodded. Never had he felt so helpless.

"Perhaps the Father shall return," suggested another.

"Perhaps," replied Gabriel, "but I fear we might be in for a long wait."

Up until this point, the angel Moriah had held his peace. More than any of the others, he had seen these events coming. "There is another portal in the fourth level of Heaven," he said in a cautious tone. "I have used it numerous times. It is a secret portal known to a few of us. It is, in reality, a private portal designed by one of the saints."

That revelation caught the group by surprise. A mere human building a thing that even the angels could not fashion? It seemed impossible.

"A portal built by a human?" asked Michael, confirming what he thought he heard.

"Yes," said Moriah.

"What value would a portal be to one of the saints anyway?" asked Iseus. "Humans can gate from one place in Heaven to another at will; they have no need for a portal."

"He built it for me and others as a courtesy," replied Moriah. "It allows us to travel directly to his home. He has actively worked to oppose Satan for years. Some years ago, he confronted the father of lies right there on the plains of Hell. He is one of our greatest allies. Would you like me to attempt to open it? From there he could take us to Zion."

"By all means," said Michael, motioning to the corridor.

Moriah stood before the corridor for only a few seconds before it burst to life. The blank wall beyond vanished into sparkling mists then to what appeared to be a study within a home. Moriah entered and the others quickly followed. They had found a way out.

They stepped through a glistening metal ring into the large study. The walls were made of fine wood, as was the floor. The walls were adorned with beautiful paintings of the starry universe while before them was an old-fashioned blackboard with a myriad of mathematical equations of a complexity that would even challenge the mind of an angel. In front of the blackboard two men stood on either side of a wooden table gazing at their newly arrived guests.

One wore a long gray cape of a sort that was centuries out of fashion on Earth. He had hair of black with a distinctive receding hairline and a short pointed beard. In very fact, his head seemed a bit large, as if designed to hold an unusually large brain.

His companion was dressed in a pair of dark trousers and a loose white shirt. He had a mustache, curly dark hair, and dark eyes that seemed to look right through their unexpected guests.

"Please forgive the intrusion," said Moriah.

"Not at all, my good friend," said the cloaked man, a broad smile on his face. "You are always welcome in my house, you and your distinguished colleagues."

"Johannes Kepler," said Michael, smiling slightly, who then turned to Kepler's companion, "and Nikola Tesla. I should have surmised this. Few others could have accomplished so great a feat as building a dimensional portal."

"We had considerable help," replied Kepler. "What you see is the work of eight men and women, and four years of labor."

"Dr. Kepler, we need your assistance," said Michael. "We have been unable to gate from the Father's great judgment hall to our angelic compound in Zion. I fear we are in great jeopardy…all of us."

It took several minutes for Michael to tell the two men of science about the cataclysmic events that might even now be occurring in Heaven. The two saints stood in amazement. Yes, they had been expecting something like this, but not so soon or so drastic. With the telling done, Dr. Kepler turned to the silvery metallic ring near the corner of his study and attempted to establish an ethereal corridor to the angelic compound in Zion, though without success.

"We will have to travel to the gates of Zion and go on foot from there," announced Johann. "We cannot gate directly into the city itself…it is forbidden."

Michael nodded. "We are indebted to you for your assistance."

"Not at all," replied Johann. "You and your angels have certainly come to our aid often enough. We are very much indebted to Moriah for all of his help over the years. We shall help in any way we can."

Nikola nodded in agreement. "It sounds like we need to get moving." He momentarily left the room, returning with two very sophisticated looking rifles. They had the look of weapons straight out of a science fiction film. He handed one to Johann. "If we encounter one of Satan's brood, I want to be ready. I hope these are as effective in Heaven as they were in Hell."

"I wouldn't recommend that," cautioned Gabriel. "Satan is forbidden to harm any human. That is…unless they are attacked first."

"I'm not about to stand by while Satan attacks our allies," said Nikola. "We're in this with you for the duration."

"Amen to that," said Johann, quickly checking his weapon.

That response brought hope to the heart of the angels. Perhaps other humans would feel as these did. Perhaps they would not need to face this trial alone.

As 24-year-old David Bonner looked up from the bustling street toward the sky, all that greeted his eyes was a clear blue firmament. He was sure he had heard thunder, but in Zion? Yes, from time to time it did rain here, but he had never observed a thunderstorm.

There it was again. He could discern a direction to it now. It seemed to be coming from the Great Hall of the Angels, one of the tallest buildings in the city. He could see it from here, over a mile away, a great windowless marble structure, better than two miles wide on each side, rising nearly 300 feet above the busy streets. He was horrified when a third blast rocked the building. A section of the imposing structure, at least 20 feet on a side, exploded from the nearest corner, some 200 feet up. The huge fragments rained down onto the street below.

"Oh, sweet Lord, no!" cried David. His mind was catapulted back to the event that sent him and his mother from an 89th floor office in New York's World Trade Center to their mansion in Heaven on September 11, 2001.

There were cries of alarm in the city street around him as balls of fire erupted from the newly formed gash in the great building. A second and third explosion blasted out two additional gashes along the east side of the building. Again there was a shower of rubble. Most of the people in the street could do little more than watch in horror; yet there was a growing surge of people moving in the direction of the most Holy Place in all of Zion; that place where the citizens of Heaven communed directly with the Father.

Within a minute, thousands of angels were flying above and around the building amid brilliant flashes of light and roaring spheres of fire. At first David did not comprehend what he was seeing. But whatever it was, the region in which it was occurring was swiftly expanding and growing closer. David began to retreat toward his home that was half a mile away. He turned to see figures in black and in white, closer now, apparently in the midst of battle. He put it all together. "War in Heaven," he gasped, "an invasion." He ran toward home.

By the time he reached home, the battle filled the skies, a battle between angels and demons. There was a steady stream of people migrating toward the center of the city and the perceived safety of the Holy Place.

"Oh thank God you're safe!" said David's mother wrapping her arms around him. June Bonner was in a hurry to get out the door. "We've got to get to the Father. He'll protect us. We've got to get to the Holy Place. How can this happen in Heaven?"

How could it happen? That thought had been on David's mind for the past ten minutes. But now he remembered a passage in the Book of Revelation about war in Heaven. So many people interpreted it as a reference to Lucifer and his angels being thrown out of Heaven thousands of years ago, but suppose they were wrong? Suppose this moment was the fulfillment of that prophecy?

David heard a loud clashing in the street just outside the house. He looked out the window and saw a battle between an angel clad in white and a demon in black. The clashing of their gleaming swords was accompanied by a near blinding flash of light. Never in his life had he been witness to such a thing. A few seconds later, others joined the fray. It seemed that the few angels were being quickly outnumbered by the demons. "If only I had one of Tesla's particle rifles," lamented David. He might have to do something about that. He turned to his mother. "Mom, I think we better stay inside…it might be risky to be out in the streets right now."

His mother looked from the window in horror, and backed toward the living room. "I think, you're right...we'd better stay inside."

As the battle escalated around them, it was clear that they would have to wait it out at home. June sat down at the kitchen table with her son and prayed that God's protection would be upon both of them.

At the great ring on the plains of Hell, Satan could hardly contain his glee as demons by the thousands poured through the portal and into the swirling mists beyond. They had already sent nearly two million through this ancient archway to every angelic portal in Heaven. He felt confident that he now had control of all of them. Most would be deactivated. He would only keep those that he absolutely needed. Divide, isolate, and conquer—that was the plan.

He gazed toward Metastopholies, who watched the advance dispassionately. "Our day has come," he announced.

Metastopholies only nodded.

"Soon, very soon, we shall set foot in Zion once more, breathe the air of Heaven again," continued Satan. "I shall ascend to the place of honor I once held...to the throne of angelic power, second only to the Father. I shall be the bright morning star as it is my destiny to be."

Satan turned to see General Krell approaching. Krell bowed low before his master. "My lord, I have confirmation that we now hold all of the angelic portals in Heaven. We have deactivated seven of them, leaving only the four that we need for this operation. The minions of Michael and Gabriel are in full retreat. Thus far, things are going better than we had anticipated. I congratulate you, my Lord."

"Very good, General," said Satan, a smile on his face. "May I assume that the Hall of Angels in the City of Zion is sufficiently secure for me to make the crossing?"

"Almost," assured Krell. "We are sweeping the complex for what scattered pockets of resistance remain. I suspect that it will be safe for his lordship within two hours…perhaps less. However, be aware that it has been heavily damaged. It was there that resistance was the greatest."

"So much progress," said Satan, turning to Metastopholies as Krell returned to directing the forces streaming through the portal. "With the war but three hours old, we have nearly secured our principle targets. It has been almost too easy."

"Proceed with great caution, my lord," cautioned Metastopholies. "Do not count the victory before it is truly won. Do not underestimate your adversary. While it is yet dying, the venomous snake might strike one last deadly blow, pulling its attacker down in death along with it."

For a moment, Satan seemed frustrated, perhaps even a bit angry. "Why are you so negative, Metastopholies?"

"Because you need me to be," retorted Metastopholies. "Whether you realize it or not, it is true nonetheless. I will speak the truth to you when others fear to. I do not fear your scorn because I wish for you to succeed above all else."

Satan nodded as he watched his forces continue through the great portal. He gazed out upon the plains blackened by the sheer numbers of his forces. The words of Metastopholies continued to rattle around in his head. They rang true. Military logic and tactics had to rule this war—not emotion, not his rage. The humans said that revenge was a dish best served cold. He would have to remember that wisdom, despite its dubious source.

Chapter 11

The group of angels and humans emerged from the misty portal into a war zone at the east gate of the City of Zion. The skies above the city were literally ablaze with angelic and demonic weapons, and the air rumbled with their report. Before them, a flood of people were streaming away from the city gate, vanishing into starry mists.

"Refugees fleeing a battle in Heaven," noted Johann, shaking his head sadly. "The last time I saw such a thing was four centuries ago, Protestants fleeing from the Catholic persecution in northern Europe. Never had I thought to see the likes of that here."

"Our forces are being routed," noted one of the angels.

"They were caught by surprise," replied Gabriel. "The fault was ours. We had no contingency plan. Never in our wildest imaginings had we envisioned such a thing as this."

"We thank you for your assistance," said Michael, turning to Johann and Nikola, "but we must take our leave."

"And do what?" replied Johann. "Your forces are in disarray. You must fall back and regroup."

"But we must make contact with our angels if we are to bring order out of chaos," said Michael. "They must know where we are to regroup. The word must be spread to our forces. If the twelve of us must do it one angelic warrior at a time, so be it."

It took a few minutes for the angelic leaders to develop a contingency plan. They would meet near the edge of the forest, 20 miles to the south, at a rocky hill called Ceranda. They would have to spread the word to their forces.

Moriah turned to his human friends. "We must part company now. I have concerns for your safety. Right now, the safest place for you might be at your home in the forest."

"We appreciate your concern," said Johann, "but we have pressing business here in Zion."

Moriah nodded. "Take care, dear friends."

"And our prayers are with you as well," said Nikola, "all of you."

They took to the air in groups of two, into the fray overhead. Johann and Nikola watched them vanish into the pure chaos.

"We need to find David," said Johann. "If Satan's minions realize what he knows, what he has done, they might decide to detain him."

"But how will we locate him?" asked Nikola. "It is, after all, a big city."

"We shall go to his home," replied Johann. "If he is not there, then I can only assume he has gone to the Holy Place, or perhaps is trying to make his way back to our lab."

"It will be indeed difficult to navigate the city streets moving against the flow of so many people," said Nikola.

"We have little choice in the matter," said Johann. "He is my student, my friend. I can't abandon him."

"Of course," replied Nikola. "We might be able to make our way in by squeezing our way along the walls, out of the main flow of the refugees. Still…it may take many hours."

"All the more reason to get started now," said Johann heading toward the gate.

Getting through the huge arching gate and into the walled city was the toughest task. What under normal conditions might have taken ten seconds now required several minutes moving against the surging crowd. At last they moved into the wide golden streets. The going got easier as the crowds thinned out. A mile into the city the streets were practically deserted. Yet, here they faced a different peril. This was a war zone. Before them, an errant fireball discharged from a demonic sword struck the side of a street side shop. Bits of shrapnel flew in all directions causing the two to seek cover. Up ahead there was a battle in the street as fierce fighting between angels and demons raged. Their weapon blasts had reduced the buildings on either side of the street to rubble.

"We might want to consider going up that narrow side street," suggested Nikola, pointing to a street half the width of this main avenue. "It shouldn't take much longer."

The two men moved cautiously across the street and into the alley. They had traveled only 100 feet when a loud explosion overhead drew their attention. Scarcely 50 feet ahead of them an angel with one wing ripped to shreds collided with the wall of a building on their left and fell to the street. A bat-winged demon dressed wholly in black alighted on the street before him.

"Get up, minion of Michael," he snarled, his dark sword in hand. "Fight me."

The angel tried to rise but collapsed. His white robes were soaked in blood. Never had Johann or Nikola seen an angel in such a condition.

"So all of the fight is gone from you, is it?" said the demon in a taunting tone. "Then it's time to slice your wings from you. Then you'll look more like the humans you protect. But more importantly, it will make you lighter, easier to transport."

The demon tossed two pairs of shackles before the angel. The angel looked up with dazed eyes at his attacker but did not speak.

"And once I remove those wings, I'll shackle you up good and tight and leave you here to be picked up later like the garbage you are. You'll spend the rest of this war in our prison, formerly known as the Hall of Angels, to await Satan's pleasure. But first things first, let's get rid of those wings."

The demon approached the helpless angel, swinging his sword menacingly.

"That will be far enough!" warned Johann, his weapon raised.

The demon turned to see the two humans, their weapons raised. "I advise you not to interfere," he snarled. "This is none of your concern. The master has ordered me to leave your kind in peace, so long as you take no hand in this fight."

Again the demon took a step toward the angel. He stopped when he heard the hum of the particle beam's charging capacitor.

"If you want no trouble from us, then you had best walk away," warned Nikola. "That angel is our friend. If you have an argument with him…you have one with us too."

There was a moment of hesitation. The demon stared intensely at the two humans challenging him. Demons had never feared humans. What could a human do to oppose them? The demon turned to strike his angelic opponent but he never got the chance. The brilliant trail of two particle beams homed in on him, hitting their mark. A loud explosion scattered boiling demon blood and pulverized flesh and bone across the width of the alley. When the flash subsided, the remains gave not so much as a clue as to what sort of creature had stood here just seconds before.

"What a mess," said Nikola, looking about at the carnage in amazement. Yes, he had designed this weapon, but he had never fired it at a living target. "That was far more effective than I had dared to hope. I'd like to see that demon try to reconstitute itself."

"I don't think it will," replied Johann. "That was incredible."

The angel looked up in dazed confusion and noticed the two humans approaching. "What happened? Where is that demon?"

"He has returned to the dust from which he came," said Johann.

"We need to get him out of the open," said Nikola, pointing toward a small shop just ahead.

They slung their rifles and assisted the injured angel into the shelter of the small shop. The angel looked around to see what little was left of his demonic opponent—it was a frightening revelation. The shop provided special musical instruments to the musically inclined people of Zion, a place where artisans made instruments through the power of thought. Already the angel's wounds were healing, yet it was a slow process.

The angel looked toward his two human benefactors. "You have my thanks. I dread to think of what might have occurred had you not happened by."

"We are all in this together," said Johann. "I can assure you, Heaven's human inhabitants will not abandon our angelic brothers. Your fight is our fight."

"You destroyed that demon," deduced the angel. "You destroyed him with that weapon."

"That is correct," said Nikola. "Angels have swords and we humans have, well, this. Perhaps we can turn the tide of the war with this weapon. As the artisans of this shop make instruments that create beautiful music, I make instruments that disrupt the bonds between atoms, weapons that destroy rather than create."

"There is a time to create and a time to destroy," noted the angel. "Perhaps, now is the time for the latter. How many of those weapons do you have?"

"Nineteen, including these two," said Nikola. "I didn't see any need for more."

"How many can you make in a day?" asked the angel.

"I'm not sure," replied Nikola, "maybe five or six."

"Are there others that can do it?"

"Yes," replied Nikola. "Niels has made a couple, so has David. David could probably build eight or ten a day, maybe more."

"I cannot say that this weapon, despite its power, will be of much help if they are so few in number," noted the angel. "If Satan has launched an all-out assault upon Heaven, the number of his forces will surely be over a hundred million. He caught us completely by surprise. I was preparing for a journey to Earth when his minions began streaming out of our gate. There were so many…and they just kept coming. I cannot say how many angels are still in the hall being tormented and imprisoned by his legions. They ripped the wings from so many of my brethren. They are doing horrible things to those they capture. They rolled over us like a plague of locusts. They give us not a moment to rest, to regroup."

"Blitzkrieg," noted Nikola, "the lightning war. It was a tactic employed by Hitler in his war in Europe."

"We need to be moving on," said Johann. "We have to reach David. My friend, you should be safe here. We will try to come back for you, if we can."

"No need," assured the angel. "When I am fully restored, I shall fly from this place on my own."

A moment was taken to inform the angel of the regrouping place selected by his commander, the place from which they might mount an organized defense. Then Johann and Nikola headed out into the street. The way Johann had it figured, they were about 12 blocks from David's house. He prayed that fortune might favor them.

The route they followed was indirect and torturous, avoiding raging battles and streets full of rubble. It was over an hour before Johann and Nikola reached David's house. Many of the houses here had been heavily damaged, although David's house seemed to have weathered the storm well.

"Please be here," whispered Johann, knocking on the door.

Nearly a minute went by before they heard footsteps beyond the door. The door opened just a crack, then wide.

"Johann, Nikola, welcome," said June, hurrying her son's two best friends into the house.

Just inside, they found David who was smiling broadly, a particle rifle in hand. Johann knew only too well how fortunate they had been.

"I'd wanted to go on to the Holy Place," said June, "but David insisted that we stay here. Somehow he knew that you were coming."

"I wasn't sure," admitted David, "but I had faith that you would come for me."

"Now we can all go to the Holy Place," said June. "We'll be safe there."

"We'll see that you get there, Mom...but I've got to go with Johann and Nikola; we have work to do."

"But those are demons out there," objected June. "What can you do?"

Nikola couldn't help but laugh, just a bit. He told June and David of their demonic encounter. "I cannot say that the demon was utterly destroyed, some fading spiritual remnant might still exist, but his physical form is not likely to rise again."

"We need to make more of those rifles," said David. "I made this one about an hour ago."

"I didn't realize that you had a copy of the blueprints here," said Nikola.

"I didn't," said David.

Nikola looked at David incredulously, "You made that without any blueprints, no schematics?"

David smiled his oh so characteristic devious smile. "Sure, I'd made several of them before. I helped you work on the design. I did this one from memory. I've checked it out; the capacitor charges fine. I haven't tried to fire it yet, but I'm confident that it will work."

"I never watched my son create something with his mind," noted June, placing her arm around David. "I'm so proud of him."

"We might want to consider getting the group together and creating these rifles as an assembly-line program," suggested David. "If each of us only had to focus on creating one part, we might be able to create a hundred a day, maybe even more."

"We'll have to get them all together," said Johann. "Given our current situation, that might be difficult."

"We could form a militia," announced David, "Kepler's irregulars, we could call them."

Johann smiled slightly. "I question if Michael's forces will be able to hold out long enough for us to get organized. They took a beating today, to be sure. Anyway, we've got to get your mom to the Holy Place and safety. Then we can concentrate on this problem."

"I'm going with you," announced June. "Maybe I can help."

"Mom," objected David, "this is too dangerous. This is a war."

"I sat it out the last time you got involved in something like this—rescuing Serena—but not this time. I'm not going to let you have all of the fun. Wonder woman is coming along."

June's comments elicited a round of laughter from the group. David walked back into the kitchen and returned with a second particle rifle.

"You guys were running a bit late so I made a second one while we were waiting," said David. He handed it to his mother. "Here Mom, you might need this."

June took the rifle in hand, tried to get the feel of it. "My own father taught me how to fire a rifle. I'm a pretty good shot, really. This thing is really light."

"David, how long does it take you to build a rifle?" asked Johann.

"About forty-five minutes," replied David. "If I got more practice, I'm sure I could do it quite a bit faster."

"We really need to get going," said Nikola.

"I wonder if we could gate out from here," pondered David. "It would save us a lot of time."

"You're not supposed to gate out from inside the city," said June.

"This is war," said David. "Anyway…look around, this city is dying. I believe that the Father established that rule due to the shear number of people in the city. If they were constantly gating here and there, it would undermine the space time of this region. That would be a bad thing. The city, beyond the Holy Place, is nearly deserted. It should be fine."

"That seems reasonable to me," said Nikola. "If it can be done, we really should do it."

David turned to the center of the room. "To your lab, right Dr. Kepler?"

Johann nodded. "Yes, go ahead and try."

Almost instantly, the misty field of stars appeared before him. David proceeded in and the others followed. They emerged in the middle of Johann's study.

"Our friends at Refuge need to be appraised of our situation," said Johann, walking over to the telesphere setting on the middle of the table. He stood there for several minutes before turning back toward the others. I can't make contact…and I'm not sure why."

"Let me try," said David, walking over to the telesphere. He examined it carefully. To its left a cryptic display appeared floating in midair. He examined it stretching out his hand to page through several different displays. The sphere began to glow, then was transformed into a much larger sphere that displayed video static in three dimensions. Slowly an image began to materialize out of the static. It was the dark angel Lenar. The image swayed and rippled and was full of snow. "That is the maximum power I dare use.

I don't dare open the wormhole wider. I've never seen the density of the dimensional barrier between Heaven and Hell so high."

"It's good to see you, David," said Lenar. His voice was very distorted barely readable. He made another comment, but it was indistinguishable.

"I'll try to clean up the audio," said David, making additional adjustments.

By now, a second dark angel had joined Lenar; it was Abaddon. "We've been trying to contact you for hours, but without success," said Abaddon, his voice faint and distorted, but understandable.

"Satan's forces have invaded Heaven," said Johann, stepping up to the sphere. "The angels were taken by complete surprise and are in full retreat."

"So it finally happened," lamented Abaddon. "What's wrong with the telesphere?"

"It must be the work of Satan, directly or indirectly," said Johann. "He is sending millions of his demons through the portal and into Heaven. That open gate might be the cause of our problem, we're just not sure."

"I can hear you, Dr. Kepler…but just barely," said Abaddon. "I do have some good news to report here. Victoria van Voth is already making dynamic strides using that machine. She didn't even take time to rest after her ordeal; she got right to work. Tom and Bill taught her the basics, but she needs a good tutor to master the more advanced techniques."

"I can't hold this wormhole open much longer," warned David. "I'm running way more amps through this circuit than it was designed to withstand. For the moment, I don't see how we can communicate with our allies at Refuge for more than a few minutes at a time."

"I'm afraid your people will have to manage on your own for now," said Johann. "Communications problems won't allow us to do tutoring sessions by telesphere, and travel to outer darkness is impossible for the time being, so we won't be able to supply you. I'm sorry, my friend."

"We will manage, my friend," said Abaddon, his image rapidly fading. Then the image faded completely. The sphere returned to its normal size, then went dark.

"We're going to have to get as many of our people here as we can," said Johann. "We'll have to work with the angels. They won't be able to move from one level of Heaven to another, and nearly a third of them are trapped on Earth. We can't transport the angels on Earth back to Heaven, but we can act as pilots, ferrying angelic forces from one level of Heaven to another. That might be a good job for you, June."

June nodded. "I'll be glad to. I just can't sit around when all this is going on. Captain June Bonner at your service sir."

Johann nodded. Now he knew the source of David's off-beat humor.

As if an answer to prayer, a starry mist appeared near the corner of the room. From it stepped three men and a woman. One of the men held one of Tesla's particle beam rifles.

David took his mother by the hand and walked over to the man with the rifle. "Mom, I'd like to introduce you to Dr. Niels Bohr, the father of the science of quantum mechanics. Doctor Bohr, this is my mom, June."

The dark-haired man smiled broadly and extended his hand. "You have a brilliant son, Mrs. Bonner, you must be very proud."

"And I've heard a lot of wonderful things about you, Dr. Bohr," said June. "Thank you for tutoring my son. I'm glad to finally meet you in person."

"My pleasure," replied Niels.

"And these are students of Dr. Bohr," continued David. "This is Don, Karen, and Hari."

"We'll have time for introductions later," said Johann. "Right now we have to come up with a plan...and we have to develop it fast. Within the hour I need to meet with Michael, assuming I can find him. We have to figure out what we're up against. We have to know how the other levels of Heaven are faring. That means that we are going to need to open the gate to allow the angels to go there, perhaps, even go there ourselves. The days ahead will neither be easy nor safe. We may be putting our eternities on the line."

"I think we all realize that," said Niels. "Fill us in on what's happened up to this point. All my students and I know is that there are demons loose in Heaven. They were going door to door in our village. One of them actually walked right up to my door and advised me not to interfere. It was more a thinly veiled threat, really. Stay in your homes, he warned us. He said we wouldn't be harmed if we didn't interfere. I didn't openly confront him at the time, not with my wife and students in the house; but there is no way we are going to cooperate with his kind. I sent my wife off to the Holy Place; and we came here. We are ready to do whatever needs to be done."

"Very good," said Johann. "Please…let us sit together and discuss the situation. I am certain that the Father will give us guidance."

The discussion had been under way for about 45 minutes, and a course of action had been agreed upon. They would rendezvous with Michael's forces at the hill called Ceranda in two hours.

As they continued to talk, David proceeded to the transporter ring that linked to the other rings in Heaven. He tried to link to one then another without success. He wasn't surprised. Satan's forces had either destroyed them or linked them solely with the great ring in Hell. He was, however, shocked when he got a solid link to the ring in the Hall of the Angels in the City of Elesia, on the second level of Heaven. He could see through the ring clearly. The room on the other side was largely in ruins. He was surprised when he saw half a dozen angels step up to the portal, their swords drawn.

"Dr. Kepler," he said, turning to his primary mentor.

Johann stepped up to the ring, scanning the scene beyond. His eyes focused on one of the angels. "It's Marlith...I know him well. He was one of the angels who flew into Hell to support our rescue of Serena."

Marlith apparently recognized Johann. He sheathed his sword and raised his right hand in greeting.

"I'm going over," announced Johann. "I need everyone to remain here until I can ascertain what the situation is over there." Without so much as a second thought he stepped through.

"Greetings my good friend," said Marlith. "I can't say that your arrival is a surprise. In very fact, our ring is set to accept transport only from yours. We had prayed that you would come. I suspect that we will need your assistance."

"My friend, we will help in any way we can," assured Johann.

"I take it that the forces of Satan have invaded all of the levels of Heaven," deduced Marlith.

"Apparently," said Johann. "Surely, they must have hit here too."

"They did," confirmed Marlith. "What saved us was our contingency plan. We had suspected that something like this might happen for some time. Our commander, General Moriah, suspected that if such an attack occurred, it would happen during or immediately following a meeting of the angelic council. He had a standing order to place additional forces within the gate room at these times and place our forces on high alert. Several hundred of Satan's minions, an advanced force, stormed through our gate early this morning. They seemed quite surprised to encounter our forces waiting for them. Initially, they pushed us back, but we inevitably got the upper hand and secured the gate once more. We shut it down to prevent additional troops from arriving and reinforcing their position. Two of Satan's minions escaped, but we captured the rest. Eventually we will track down those who escaped as well. Currently, darkness is hindering the search, but it will resume come morning."

"Nice work," said Johann. "What have you learned from the prisoners you captured?"

"Quite a bit," replied Marlith. "We discovered that they were an advanced party. Their mission was to secure this gate until additional forces arrived. This was their plan at each of the seven angelic halls throughout Heaven. By controlling the gates, they would be able to isolate our forces, rendering them ineffective. However, as you humans say, we rained on their parade. We have made this level of Heaven a fortress that is, at least for the moment, impenetrable."

"You have made my day," said Johann. "This is wonderful news. How many angels are here under your command?"

"Just under three million," said Marlith. "Many of our angels are on Earth or in Zion."

"It's a start," said Johann. "Your victory here has provided a safe haven for the rest of the angels, a place to mend and regroup. We need to find Michael; his will be the final decision, but for now, I fear we have no option but to retreat before our losses become even greater. Then we shall choose the time and place for the next battle."

Sister Elizabeth sat quietly by the fire reading a book of poetry—the collected works of E.E. Cummings. She was alone, and the room was dark save the light from the old stone fireplace and that of an oil lamp on the table by her side. She wore a long frilly dress, of a sort that was five centuries out of style, dating from the time when she walked the green Earth. She pushed her long brown hair aside and turned the page.

Beyond the open window, the crickets chirped in the darkness, as they usually did on a summer's evening. By her soft comfy chair, seven additional books were arranged in two neat stacks, those that she had read, and those she soon would.

It was late, but she wasn't tired. After five centuries in Heaven, she had nearly evolved beyond the need for sleep or even food—both of which she partook of only once or twice a week.

Her mansion was not a large one, at least not by heavenly standards. She had a kitchen, this modest study which held all of her books, and a small bedroom, which she rarely used. The house, constructed from local stones, stood in a one-acre-wide clearing in the vast green forest, a truly isolated venue. She liked it that way. It gave her time to reflect, to appreciate the goodness of God. She would have been totally lost in a large mansion.

She received few visitors here. Her encounters with others occurred most often on her biweekly trips to the City of Zion. There, she would commune with the Father and afterward visit one of the city's many libraries.

Interestingly, her last visitor had passed by this way only two weeks ago—a very special visitor. It had been her Savior—Jesus Himself. Indeed, since her arrival here, He had dropped in to see her frequently. They had even taken walks through the forest together. They discussed matters of the spirit, philosophy, even poetry. How she loved His visits. However, during His last visit, He had spoken of spiritual strength and courage. He had reminded her that He was with her always, even in times of danger. He also spoke of the power she possessed through the Holy Spirit. How strange, what sort of danger was to be found here? He told her to show no fear in the face of that danger, though He declined to tell her what that danger might be.

On Earth she had lived the cloistered existence of a nun. It was a lifestyle ideally suited for her personality. In very fact, she even had two long black habits in her wardrobe, though she seldom wore them anymore. No, she preferred to dress comfortably.

It was nearly midnight when she laid the book down and looked out the window into the night full of fireflies. Everything looked normal, but it wasn't. Something was wrong, very wrong. For one thing, the crickets had gone silent, and there was something else, a darkness that went beyond the darkness of the night.

Elizabeth rose to her feet and gazed out the window. It was growing darker, even the sparkling of the fireflies seemed subdued. A chill went through her body. She heard a flapping of wings as if some great bird had flown over her house. Then there were voices, deep and guttural. There were footsteps on her wooden porch, then a knock at the door.

"Visitors at this hour?" she murmured. She made her way to the door.

Opening the door, she saw a frightening sight—a pair of bat-winged demons dressed head to toe in black stood on her porch. Their faces were those of two very old men, wrinkled and practically gray. Indeed, they looked like the faces of a pair of dead men.

"Do not be afraid," said the one on the left, "we will not harm you; however, we require that you perform a task for us."

Yes, Elizabeth was frightened, but she was not about to let these two know it. "You have no right to be here, leave at once."

"Now don't be so rude, human," said the other. "We will trouble you but a minute and be on our way."

"OK, what is it you want?" asked Elizabeth, wondering if being diplomatic might be a better approach."

"We require your assistance in taking us to the City of Zion," said the first. "It is but a small thing, a simple thing. Do it and we will trouble you no further."

"Now wait a minute, how could it be that you are here in the first place," asked Elizabeth. "How can you be here?"

"You will need to get used to us being here," replied the demon. "Heaven shall be the dominion of our master, Satan. So long as you cooperate, cause us no trouble, you humans of Heaven will have little to fear from us."

Elizabeth looked at the demon incredulously. "Cooperate with Satan and his followers? I think not…and I won't take you to Zion."

"Obviously, you don't understand the situation you are in," said the second demon, grabbing Elizabeth by the arm and pulling her onto the porch. "We are not asking for your help, we are requiring it. You are a pretty one for a human, I wouldn't want to have to do anything that might mar that beauty. I am very accomplished in the art of doing just that, and doing it in a most painful manner. Trust me, you wouldn't want that, and it doesn't have to happen." He pulled her out into her front yard. "You can form the portal right there."

Elizabeth was terrified. Never had she imagined such a thing happening to her. Then her mind went back to the last time she had spoken with Jesus on this very spot. She was fortified by His words. Her fear turned to righteous anger. "How dare you touch me in that way! You have overstepped your authority."

"We will do far more than that if you do not help us," said the other.

"I'll give you one more chance to leave," proclaimed Elizabeth. "I won't ask again." Quite honestly, she had no idea as to whether she was bluffing or if she could make good on her threat.

"The only asking you will be doing is asking for mercy," said the demon.

Elizabeth extended her hand toward her attacker and she felt a surge of power flow through her body. It was not a frightening sensation. Actually, it felt good. Her hand was glowing with a bright blue aura. A wide beam of blue light left her hand and struck the demon. He was quickly shrouded in a field of sparkling light. He let out a terrible scream as his flesh began to dissolve away from the outside in. He fell to the ground writhing in pain.

Gray flesh gave way to dark red muscle, then dissolving bones and internal organs. Within 30 seconds little remained beyond a pile of soot scattered across the ground. Then she turned to the second one.

He drew out his sword and swung it at Elizabeth. She grabbed its blade in midair with her glowing hand. It instantly liquefied and flowed to the ground like glowing quicksilver.

He tried to take flight, but was swiftly engulfed within the deadly blue aura. Half a minute later all that remained of the demons was two piles of dust.

Elizabeth looked on in amazement as her hand returned to normal. Then she dropped to her knees crying. "Oh, thank You, Jesus," she wept.

The sounds and sights of a summer night returned. The crickets resumed their song, the fireflies their light show, and the frogs their croaking from a nearby pond.

Elizabeth rose to her feet and returned to the house in a state of mind somewhere between the elation of worship and the numbness of shock. She extinguished the oil lamp and went straight to bed. She would try to sort this whole thing out in the morning.

Chapter 12

It was 45 minutes later when Johann, Nikola, and Marlith emerged from the cloud of misty stars at the hill called Ceranda. They didn't know what to expect. Perhaps they would emerge into the midst of a great battle—but they didn't. They found themselves surrounded by a countless number of angels, many still badly injured. They appeared exhausted and forlorn. Never had they known a defeat as they had on this day. To the north, flashes of light and the rumble of thunder told of a raging battle. It was a few minutes before the archangel Gabriel approached them. Johann appraised him of the situation.

"I have no great desire to withdraw from this battle," lamented Gabriel, "yet to do anything else is to yield to defeat. We have just a rudimentary battle plan. We are only a few hundred thousand here against millions, and their numbers grow every minute. Many of our angels have already been captured and imprisoned…perhaps millions. Our position here is in jeopardy. This place will be overrun within an hour…two at most. Many of those around us are in jeopardy of being taken prisoner. They can neither fly nor fight. It will take many hours for most of our warriors to mend. If you have a way to get our wounded to safety, we would appreciate your help."

"It will take more than just the two of us," said Johann, turning to Nikola. "Return to the lab. Bring as many of our people as you can. We will have to form multiple gates to the second level."

Nikola nodded and quickly gated out. Within two minutes, seven members of his team had arrived. They immediately formed passageways to the

Hall of Angels on the second level of Heaven, each leading a long train of wounded angels hand in hand into the ethereal corridor.

"How many can your people take at a time?" asked Gabriel.

"At least a hundred, safely," replied Johann. "After which the person forming the corridor can return for more. If we have an hour, I feel confident that we can evacuate thirty thousand or more."

"That's barely a tenth of the angels we have here," lamented Gabriel. "If they are here when Satan's forces arrive, they will surely be captured."

"I don't know what else we can do," admitted Johann, "and the longer we delay, the fewer we can evacuate."

Gabriel looked to the north. He was convinced that the battle was drawing closer. "Do what you can."

It took less than a minute to begin the evacuation. Each of Johann's people led a group of angels through the portal, hand in hand, as if in some children's game.

As the minutes ticked by, other humans gated in and joined in the effort. Some were members of Johann's science team; others were his neighbors who had heard of the plight of the angels. Still others were from the local area, people who had heard news of the angelic crisis and wanted to help. Within half an hour, there were more than 40 people guiding the angels to safety, and more were arriving by the minute. Still, they needed more time. The battle in the sky was growing nearer. It was time to take a radical step. Every particle rifle in Johann's arsenal was brought from his lab to the battlefield.

Johann gathered his team together. "My friends, I have a plan, but it carries with it considerable risk. Gabriel informs me that we have about half an hour before the demons are here. Well, I think it is about time that we put the particle rifles to the test. No point in building more of them until we can be sure that they are worth building. You've all test fired them; well, this won't be a test, this will be actual combat. We'll take up positions around the evacuation area. When the demons get close enough, we will all open fire simultaneously. I doubt that we will be able to hold them off long with 21 rifles…but maybe we will be able to throw them off balance. I warn you, they will probably respond with a barrage of fireballs. There is no telling how those will affect us or the rifles. We might have to pull out in a hurry."

"Sounds reasonable to me," said Niels.

"And me," said David.

There was total agreement among the ranks. For years they had supported the struggle of the people of Refuge against Satan. Many had loved ones within Satan's grip. Now, Satan was here among them. It was time for determination and hard work to become courage.

They returned to the task of ferrying angels to safety, waiting for the moment when they would find themselves on the front line with their angelic brethren. Many were afraid, all prayed for strength, but none would waver from what they saw as their responsibility.

Another 50 minutes passes. The angels still in the fight had held out longer than any had dared to hope, but their strength and numbers were fading, and the front line was half a mile away.

By now, 80 volunteers had become pilots carrying the wounded angels to safety. Over 100,000 had been evacuated so far, but so many still remained.

The demons were closing in on three sides, in numbers too great to calculate. It was time. Within two minutes, 21 human defenders had taken up their positions in hastily excavated foxholes and behind mounds of earth prepared by the angels.

"Show time," said David, turning to his mother who had taken up a position behind the earthen mound at his side. "Mom, I don't like the idea of your being out here. This is war. I can't bear the thought of something happening to you."

"It won't," replied June, charging up her rifle. "If God is with us, who can possibly stand against us?"

Individual demons were clearly visible now, like bats against the clear blue sky. The angels' defense line was crumbling. The demons seemed to hover for a moment, pirouetting on the thermals; then they descended upon the defenders from all directions.

"Wait," urged Johann. "Let them get closer. Now!"

Brilliant beams of highly ionized atoms swept out in all directions. Then came the explosions as they hit their targets. The massacre was legendary as the minions of Satan exploded in midair. The beams kept slicing through a dark mist of incredible carnage. In some places the sky turned red with their blood. Yet the demons continued their relentless descent. They hit the ground and drew their swords to be met by angelic swords and deadly beams of atomic particles.

Johann had not envisioned the battle occurring at such close quarters. One demon, sword drawn, approached to within a few feet of the great scientist but was cut down by a blast from Karen's particle rifle. Johann was knocked to the ground by the explosion, splashed in boiling blood and lacerated by fragments of bone.

The pain was terrible. Johann removed a shard of bone that had penetrated over an inch into his arm, and another into his chest. He struggled to rise to his feet, but collapsed. A shadow loomed over him. He rolled over to see another demon descending upon him, sword drawn. He swung his weapon into position and pulled the trigger. The resulting explosion was deafening. It left Johann dazed.

Fifty feet away, David and his mother stood back to back, trying to hold off the onslaught of no less than a dozen angry demons. Both were spattered in blood, bruised and lacerated by the debris falling everywhere, but their determination was unwavering.

Still farther down the defense perimeter, Hari and Niels continued their aerial barrage knocking dozens of attackers from the sky. Yet they too were being splashed and lacerated by the hot caustic remnants of their vanquished demonic targets.

The defense line wavered uncertainly under the ruthless assault. It was worse than any of them could have imagined. Yet, as quickly as it began, it ended. The confused demons were retreating as particle beam fire continued to cut them down by the scores.

The angels still aloft pursued the retreating demons. All the while, the evacuation continued. They had won the first round.

Nikola rushed to Johann's side. Johann was badly burned and lacerated.

"What happened?" asked Johann. "How did it go?"

"The battle was a success," replied Nikola. "We put them to flight…at least for the moment."

"They'll be back," said Johann, his voice weak and faltering, "and they won't make the same mistake twice. They will probably try to bombard us from long range with fireballs next time. We can try to hit the fireballs with the particle beams. They might disrupt them. If not, we will need to withdraw."

"We'll cross that bridge when we come to it," said Nikola. "For now, we need to get you out of here."

"No," insisted Johann, his voice suddenly stronger, "I'm staying. If Bedillia can brave a fall from a hundred meter high cliff and stay in the fight, I can handle this."

"We really waxed them," announced David, coming to Johann's side. David was badly scarred and in considerable pain, yet he managed a smile. "We must have knocked down five hundred of them!"

In the background, the blasts of particle beams finishing off those fallen demons not totally destroyed by the original battle commenced. None of these minions of Satan could be allowed to regenerate and rise again.

At the far side of the defense perimeter, Niels looked on with pained concern as an angel reattached the arm of his student, Don, an arm which had been severed during the battle by a demon's sword.

Don did his best to remain calm. He was sure that his God-given body would heal swiftly, yet that didn't reduce the pain he was feeling right now. In his 30 years in Heaven he had been free of all discomfort. Its return with such intensity was a terrible shock. It made him think about the fates of those poor souls in Hell, especially that of his father. He had willingly sought the restoration of all of his earthly memories, though sometimes, he wished that he hadn't. This experience only highlighted for him the consequences of contact with the forces of Satan.

Another hour passed and the number of wounded angels in the field around them began to visibly decrease. They had moved a staggering quarter of a million of them through the portals to safety. And now having nearly 100 humans guiding them through was accomplishing miracles. More and more angels were gathering in the skies above them, strengthening their defenses. Still, Johann knew that they were living on borrowed time. He was right. Another ten minutes found a virtual armada of fireballs hurling in their direction. They appeared as an orange glow on the northern horizon, growing brighter by the second.

"There must be tens of thousands of them," said Johann, gazing at the encroaching apocalypse. "Even if our particle beams can detonate them, we won't be able to stop a tenth of them. They'll reduce this area to cinders."

The order was given. The angels were taking flight, heading south, even as the last of the injured fled into the portal.

"We have less than two minutes. We need to pull out," said Gabriel. "Those angels who remain can fly. You evacuated all of the most seriously injured ones. We will retreat to the Mountains of Sarval, five hundred miles to the south, at the confluence of the Marten and Salba rivers. Meet us there in three days, if you can." Gabriel bolted into the sky. He was one of the last to leave.

"Everyone…we have to get out of here," warned Johann. "Right now, go!"

The volunteers didn't need to be told twice. They vanished from the field of battle like puffs of smoke. One quickly gazed at a beautiful mansion just to the north, probably for the last time. It had been his home for over a century. It would be difficult to leave it. Then he was gone.

Less than 30 seconds later the fireballs hit the now abandoned field like napalm bombs. They exploded on contact. The fire rushed out in all directions—flames rising 100 feet into the sky and smoke turning the sky orange. By the time the last fireball hit, four square miles of meadows and forests were in flames. The fire would, no doubt, spread to encompass much of the timberland around this ground zero.

Satan leaned back on his new throne on the highest floor of the Hall of Angels in the City of Zion. This throne was not nearly so grand or comfortable as the one he had in his audience chamber in Hell. He would have to have that throne transported here once things got a bit less hectic. This had been Michael's audience chamber. It was illuminated by four skylights that provided adequate illumination before the throne, but left the area behind it a bit shadowy. It was rather Spartan for his tastes. It had a few decorative columns along its walls and a tall set of deep blue curtains covering the bare walls behind the throne, but not so much as a single piece of artwork adorned its blank white marble walls.

No, that too would have to change. Fortunately, it had sustained no serious damage during the assault. If the same was true about the rest of the building, he would have been happier. Collapsed ceilings, blown out walls, and rubble-filled corridors were but a few of the problems of this place. He was not even certain that the building could be salvaged. Again, that could be dealt with at a later date.

Right now he was in his glory. Things had gone more smoothly than he could have dared to hope. Sure there were some problems, some setbacks, but they had been relatively minor. At last count, he had captured and imprisoned over 1.5 million angels here in Zion alone, and that number would surely grow. There were still countless numbers of shackled wingless angels to be picked up from the streets of Zion by his minions. This operation had gone very well indeed.

General Krell entered Satan's new audience chamber. He bowed low. "My lord, forgive the intrusion, are you busy?"

Satan smiled. "Not too busy for you, my friend. What do you have to report?"

"My forces have searched over half of the city," began the general. "Most of its human inhabitants have fled to the Holy Place for fear of us. Those who remain were reluctant to allow us to search their homes for angels who might be hiding from us. I had thought that the angels would fight us house to house and street to street, but they haven't. They appear to have retreated from the City of Zion entirely."

Satan nodded. "I'm not surprised. They no doubt hoped to minimize property damage within the city. They value these humans and their culture here far too much. I suppose I can respect that aspect of their character. What about the battle I've heard of south of the city? Scattered reports tell me that there is a new weapon in play, a weapon wielded by human hands."

General Krell scowled. "It would appear that at least some of the humans are aiding the angels. They are gating them from one place to another, helping wounded angels to evade capture. This could prolong the war if it is allowed to continue. In addition, they have a weapon that appears to be able to permanently destroy the bodies of our minions. We estimate that no fewer than eight hundred of our forces have been permanently removed from eternity in this battle alone. The weapon has considerable range. It can destroy our forces before they get close enough to use their swords. Therefore, I took the initiative of destroying the entire region with a fireball attack. It was effective in destroying or scattering this pocket of resistance."

Satan pondered the situation for a moment. "And what news is there regarding the attack on the second level of Heaven on the fortress of Elesia? Do you have any new information?"

Krell shook his head. "The first surge penetrated their defenses. However, it would seem that the angelic forces there were on high alert. I fear that our troops were neutralized. That gate is now closed...or perhaps destroyed. Unfortunately, it has provided the angels with a place of refuge, and the humans are providing them with a means of getting there."

"Well, we can't do anything about that now," noted Satan. "As the humans say, it is the fly in the ointment. Let us do our best to consolidate our position in the levels of Heaven we *do* control, and then concentrate on this problem later."

"I fully agree," said General Krell.

Satan smiled. "Good work, general; that will be all."

The general bowed and left the chamber. Beyond the chamber, he encountered one of his chief aides. He seemed deeply concerned.

"My lord, how did the master react to the news about the setback in Elesia?"

"He was amazingly calm," noted the general. "Apparently, the master is in a good mood. He even took the bad news in stride. There were no fits of rage and no tangential ramblings. It was curiously refreshing."

The aide nodded. "It would seem that the angels have abandoned the city. None of their numbers have been spotted within its bounds for over an hour. They appear to be moving southward."

"I suspected as much," replied the general. "They will try to regroup, but we cannot allow that. Send out the order to the field commanders—keep pushing them, keep engaging them. Give them not a moment's rest."

"It shall be as you command," replied the aide, continuing down the hall.

Krell turned his gaze back toward Satan's chamber. "Remarkable," he murmured, as he headed toward his meeting with the rest of his staff.

"Very good, my lord," said Metastopholies, stepping from the shadows near the back corner of the audience chamber. "You are in control. Continue, and you might well win this war."

"The humans trouble me," noted Satan. "I can't have them interfering in this conflict."

"But they might very well be playing right into your hands," suggested Metastopholies. "There is undeniable evidence that they took part in the battle to the south of the city. This might well provide you with the justification to move against them as well. At least, it gives you a reason to confine them."

"Yes," said Satan, "very good."

"You must identify the party or parties responsible for building those weapons," continued Metastopholies. "Hopefully, only a few humans know how."

Satan smiled a most devious smile. "I think I already know who is responsible. There are eyewitness reports of a weapon like this being used before, on a remote island in the Sea of Fire. I met the inventors once…six years ago. A reunion is much overdue. I think that it is time to pay a visit to Johannes Kepler and Nikola Tesla."

It was very late at Johann's mansion on the third level of Heaven. Twenty-seven of the best scientists and engineers in Heaven were crowded in and around the mansion. It looked chaotic, but in reality it was a series of very focused and organized pursuits. One group of 11 were hard at work assembling particle rifles and pistols, sending a shipment of the completed units through to Elesia for safe storage every hour or so. Others focused on solving the problem of opening reliable communications with Refuge once more. Still others worked on a strategy to assist the angels.

"What we need is a method of bringing angels from Earth back to Elesia," noted Niels. "The ring in Elesia is not powerful enough to open a wormhole between Heaven and Earth. Satan has somehow increased the dimensional density. I think if we could link our ring with that at Elesia, we could open the barrier and start bringing them back one at a time."

"But, it would take so long," objected Johann. "At best, we might be able to transport ten or twelve an hour. What we need to do is find out why the dimensional barrier is so dense now. If we could solve that problem, we could bring home all of the off-world angels in a matter of days. Then, Michael's forces could confront Satan's on the field of battle."

Niels nodded, but said nothing.

"I believe that the density of the dimensional barrier is being altered by some power source in Hell itself," said Nikola, who was sitting with David at the end of the table. "I've looked at the data we gathered so far, and I'm convinced of it. Destroy that power source, and we open the dimensional barriers that are blocking us."

"That sounds like a job for Abaddon and his people," said Niels.

"If they knew what they were looking for," interjected David. "We have a plan. We have calculated just how much energy would be needed to punch a hole through hyperspace from here to Hell and fly our Spirit shuttle through. It can be done. Once there, we could map the density of the inter-dimensional medium and figure out where the power source is. Then Abaddon and his forces could destroy it."

"Then fly back with the information?" deduced Johann. "No, David, it's unacceptably risky."

There was a pause. "No, not fly back" replied Nikola. "With capacitors fully charged, we would have enough power for a one-way trip. Once we located the power source, we would rendezvous with Abaddon, most likely at Refuge. His people would then destroy the target. Assuming that the density of the dimensional barrier returned to normal, the flight back could be made with the remaining fuel, with about a fifteen percent margin of error."

"That works," said David. "It's an acceptable margin of error. Nikola and I would probably be back within the week."

"It would also allow us to ship Abaddon's people much needed supplies, mainly power spheres," said Nikola. "And I would be there to tutor Victoria van Voth directly, get her up to speed using the instrument. We would kill a lot of birds with one stone."

"And get yourselves killed in the process, or worse," noted Johann. "Also, the Father told you never to go there again, or have you forgotten?"

"No, I haven't forgotten," replied Nikola.

"And you want to take David?" continued Johann. "It's just crazy. No, it's worse than that, it's irresponsible. And you want to put David's life on the line in addition to yours."

"No, I *want* to go," objected David. "No one is twisting my arm."

"No, David," objected June, emotion in her voice. "You're talking about flying straight into Hell, not knowing if you can ever get back."

"It's too risky a journey for either one of you," said Johann, "we need you here."

"And you have any better ideas?" objected Nikola.

"No, not yet," said Johann.

"But we have to move now," insisted David. "How long do you think it's going to be before Satan comes a calling on us? His minions are probably combing the globe right now looking for us. We can't stay here."

"The issue is closed," replied Johann. "The answer is no."

The group continued pursuing other options. To them, Tesla's plan was dead in committee, but to David and Nikola, the plan was far from dead. Already, they had loaded up the Spirit with most of the equipment they needed.

The Spirit was a strange looking craft—a perfect glassy sphere, 16 feet in diameter, with four spidery legs extending out from the bottom. There were no engines, in the conventional sense, protruding from its hull. A narrow stairway led from the ground and into the belly of the craft. It was designed to seat ten people comfortably, but right now, it was full of supplies for the defenders of Refuge.

It flew by creating small distortions in space time, gravity wells that moved the craft in any direction they wished. It was like pulling yourself up into the air by your bootstraps. It sat parked about 50 feet from Johann's home, the only one of its kind in Heaven, or for that matter, anywhere else.

"It will be light soon," noted Nikola, looking toward the cloudy sky overhead. "You won't have much time…be careful."

"I will," said David, placing the particle pistol under his cloak. "I'll try to gate into my own bedroom in Zion. From there it's only a half-hour walk to the Holy Place. Somehow, I'll convince the Father to give us permission to go."

"Don't take any chances along the way," warned Nikola. "At the first sign of trouble, gate out."

"You know me," said David, "I'm a natural chicken."

David opened a portal before him and vanished into the mists. Nikola stood for a minute in silence. "Sorry, David," he whispered, as he made final preparations in getting the Spirit ready for launch.

David emerged from the mists and into his second floor bedroom in Zion. Nothing here had changed beyond there being a bit more dust than when he had left. He walked to the window and looked down toward the street; all was quiet. There was not a soul as far as the eye could see. The neighborhood had suffered some damage, but all in all, it was minor. It was time to get moving.

He practically ran down the stairs and stepped into the quiet streets. He made his way toward the Via de Gloria, one of the main avenues leading to the holiest place in all creation. He stayed out of easy sight as much as possible. Ahead, he could hear the singing of the multitudes, songs of praise to the Creator of the universe. That, at least, was normal for this place. Otherwise, it seemed like a ghost town. Even the skies overhead were empty.

Five blocks from home, he was shocked to find a section of the city in ruins. Nearly a whole city block had been leveled by what looked to have been a barrage of fireballs. It had obviously been the site of a major battle.

Along the way, David thought of the journey ahead, a journey to the most terrible place in the universe. He had viewed that place through the eyes of one of its former inhabitants six years ago. By opening her book in the hall of records, he had seen, as if in a vision, the horrors of the netherworld. It was an experience that had horrified him, practically brought him to tears. Now he proposed to travel there for real. It seemed like an incredibly reckless idea. Still, Heaven as he knew it might be lost if he didn't. He had to go.

Ahead, the Holy Place came into view. He was horrified to discover that it was surrounded by what must have been thousands of demonic warriors. Were they here to keep people out, or to keep the inhabitants of Heaven in? He figured that he would soon find out. He felt the weapon in his cloak and engaged its capacitor—it was ready to fire.

David was more than a little surprised when the demons moved aside to let him pass without so much as a word. He stepped into the Holy Place.

Never had David seen a crowd the likes of this. The Holy Place was a great open air plaza. The surface below him was an indeed strange material that looked like translucent gold. The plaza itself was perfectly round and eight and a half miles in diameter. At its very center was the Father in his actual physical form, surrounded by a counsel of 24 elders. On occasions, David had managed to get close enough to actually see the Father. Today would not be one of those days. There were just too many people here. He moved only about 100 yards into the great circle and sat down, facing the Father.

"Hello, my beloved son," said the Father, in what seemed to him to be an audible voice.

"Good morning, beloved Father," said David. He looked around again. "There are so many people here today. I've never seen anything like it."

"Does it truly surprise you?" asked the Father.

David smiled slightly. "No, I guess not, considering what is going on out there."

"Adversity has always brought My sons and daughters closer to Me," said the Father. "They need to be comforted, to be assured that everything is going to be all right…and it is, of that you may be sure."

"Father, why is this happening? Demons are all over, parts of the city are in ruins. Why?"

"Oh, my son, sometimes it is difficult to see through the present situation and see how trials shape the future," said the Father. "Long ago, before the age of humankind, there was a great angelic society. They were the first sentient beings in the cosmos. To a large degree, they were My hands in the evolving universe. For billions of years, the cosmos had evolved without outside intervention. The rules I had set down from the beginning, the natural laws, had governed its development, as well as that of the Earth you called home. It was not necessary for Me to intervene on a day-to-day basis. In your age, My son, people would say that the universe had been preprogrammed."

"Yes, Father, I think I see what You mean," said David. "You needed the angels to make some fine adjustments to the universe."

"Not to the universe as a whole, but to the Earth," said the Father. "I created the angels as adults, six hundred million of them. They were fully capable of survival from the instant of their creation. They already had a language with which to communicate with each other, and the innate skills to complete the tasks assigned to them. I gave them intelligence, initiative, mobility, and a vision.

"They appeared much as they do today, but they possessed far less wisdom. Wisdom comes only with experience, and experience with the passing of time. They were new creatures. However, these new creatures did not function perfectly together. They had to contend with rivalry, jealousy, and pride. None had more pride than Lucifer. I had created him as the most beautiful of all of the angels. He served Me very well until he discovered that I was preparing to create a new being called man, and that the angels would eventually be subject to him. He wanted things to remain as they were, but they couldn't. I had a plan for man, a plan that the angels couldn't fulfill. He and his followers rebelled. You see, he couldn't bear the thought of losing his position. He viewed himself as second only to Me in authority. He could not see that he was deluding himself."

"But he was not really second in power and authority, was he?" asked David. "I mean, there was Your son, Jesus."

"But he didn't know of Jesus," replied the Father. "At that time, Jesus was hidden from the minions of Heaven. The angels were my emissaries, my servants, nothing more. I loved them greatly, but they were not my children; that privilege, that honor, belonged to humanity. Many of the angels could not accept that. They had visions of an angelic order that could never exist. There was a war. Inevitably, I had to cast Lucifer and his followers out of Heaven and confine them in a place beyond the universe of man and angels."

"Outer darkness," said David.

"Yes," confirmed the Father. "Lucifer was very angry about this turn of events, as you might imagine. So great was the enmity between Lucifer and his followers, and those that remained in Heaven, that he changed his name to Satan. All of his followers changed their names. It was a symbol of their rejection of My plan, their rejection of Me. Their hatred has simmered for millennia."

"I'm sorry Father," said David. "I know that must have hurt You a lot."

"Yes it did," said the Father, "You see, I still love them, however I can not condone their actions. It was necessary to permit Satan to challenge Michael and Gabriel. Releasing Satan and his followers opened the door to potential reconciliation between the warring angelic factions, if they truly desire it. Michael and Gabriel would have you believe that none of the fault in the division between the angels lies with them, but I tell you that is not entirely true. Over the span of nine millennia, Michael and Gabriel had not attempted to establish a dialog with Lucifer and their followers. Though they have remained faithful to Me and my plan, a portion of the blame is nonetheless theirs."

David was absolutely astonished. What the Father had told him was incredible.

"I still speak to Lucifer on a regular basis," continued the Father. "Between us, the channels of communication remain open. When he last spoke to Me, he claimed to have a repentant heart. However, his actions since then say otherwise." There was a pause. "You would like Me to stop him. But I tell you that all that is happening now must transpire for My plans for man to come to fruition. The future of the entire universe, not just the future of humankind, hinges on the events that are transpiring even as we speak."

"So we are on our own," deduced David.

"Oh David, you are never on your own," said the Father, compassion in His voice. "I love you more than you know. The events of the coming days will test and strengthen your character. You will know what you are to do, because I will guide you."

David could remain silent no longer about the plan he and Nikola Tesla had devised. "You know of our plans to travel to outer darkness?"

"Of course," replied the Father, "but you aren't going. Even as we speak, your friend Nikola Tesla is preparing to leave without you."

"What!" exclaimed David. "Why would he do such a thing? He promised that I could go."

"He did not mean to deceive you, but to protect you," replied the Father. "He knows how dangerous the mission is. He never intended to put you in that sort of peril. He loves you too much."

"But You told him never to travel to outer darkness again," said David.

"I told him that for his own protection," replied the Father. "He's on his own. Yet, he goes there for the love of others, for the love of Me. Don't be afraid, David. I'm not angry with him, not in the least. But know this; your friend has to make this trip, and he has to make it alone. It is a journey in search of himself, driven by his own guilt. He accepted the salvation that brought him to Heaven only three days before his death. He has a feeling of inadequacy, of unworthiness. He feels that he must prove himself worthy of being here, when he does not."

David felt almost panicked. He couldn't let Nikola make this journey alone.

"You want to stop him," continued the Father, "but it's too late. He is in flight even as we speak. He must make this journey alone. Don't worry, David; you haven't missed out on an adventure. Before this war is over, you will have your adventure, I assure you."

David couldn't help but smile. God had seen right into the depths of his soul. "Father, You are amazing. I love You."

That comment elicited laughter from the Father. "And I love you. You are a continual source of joy to Me and to My Son. Yesterday, you stood with your mother on the field of conflict to do battle with the forces of Satan. Rarely has a human being faced such peril. You realized the danger, yet you stood your ground, ready to sacrifice much to defend a multitude of angels in need, most of whom you had never met. You didn't do it out of pride or out of a lust for glory. You did it out of love. You have learned well the lessons My Son taught you. David, remember this day, for I tell you this—there will be another day coming, a day when you will set off on an incredible journey, a journey so far away as to be almost beyond your comprehension. That day will bring to you a new definition of adventure, as well as responsibility. On that day, you will discover your life's true meaning."

David couldn't hide his excitement. "A journey to where, Father?"

Again God laughed. "You're not going to get that answer today… you're not ready for it, not yet. Just keep striving to be the best son you can be. Learn all that you can, and your eternity will become a never-ending adventure."

At last, David felt at peace. He had a confidence he hadn't had before. He would head back to Dr. Kepler's laboratory eventually, but not yet. Right now, he wanted to be with his Father. His time was coming, but it wasn't yet.

Chapter 13

The sun had not yet risen out of the early morning haze as the Spirit hurtled skyward. Its departure aroused the group still busy with the issues of war. They stepped out into the dewy grass just in time to see the craft vanish into the low clouds.

"Tesla," murmured Johann, who quickly moved to his telemetry room just off his main study. He activated the telesphere. An image of Tesla appeared in its depth. "What are you doing?"

"What needs to be done, my friend," replied Nikola, only briefly looking away from the controls of the Spirit. "You know that this journey needs to be made. I was tired of pussyfooting around about it." He glanced from the craft for a moment. "What a beautiful view this morning—billowing clouds from horizon to horizon. I'll send you a continual telemetry stream in the event that I am able to communicate with you from the other side."

"Is David with you?" asked Johann, glancing over at June who had just entered the room.

"No, he's with the Father in the Holy Place," replied Nikola. "I wasn't about to take him on this journey. This is a one-man operation. He is more useful to you there. He was expecting to go, but I had other plans. Please offer him my apologies. I know he wanted to go with me."

Johann nodded. He realized that he would be unable to convince Tesla to return. It was best to simply go along with his plan.

Spirit's landing legs were fully retracted now, giving it the neutral aerodynamics of a perfect sphere. It accelerated quickly, yet silently. The sky around Nikola went from deep azure blue, to violet, and then black, as he left the atmosphere behind, an ever narrowing arc of blue along the horizon of Heaven. He would need to leave the atmosphere if he were to make a successful dimensional jump. He glanced over at the telesphere still displaying the image of Johann. "I'll try to bring the Spirit in on the daylight side of Hell. That way, I might not be readily observed. Then I'll go into a high orbit to give the instruments a chance to scan the magnetic field strength, charged particle density, and space time density. I'll try to identify that power source. If I can, I'll send my observations back to you on the telemetry stream." Again, Nikola looked away from the telesphere. "I'm preparing to make the jump…wish me luck."

"With you, it's never luck," said Johann, concern on his face.

Nikola smiled slightly, but said nothing more. He had reached an altitude of 1,000 kilometers; it was time to make the jump. He would be running full power through the twin temporal capacitors, at more power than he had ever tested them. If something went wrong, he would briefly blaze with a brilliance twice as bright as the sun, as seen from the villages below. The hum of the drive grew in intensity as a flood of power surged into it. Then the craft simply vanished from normal space and into hyperspace, the tenuous essence that joined the 13 dimensions of the cosmos.

Brilliant ragged clouds of many colors contrasted against a background of inky blackness swept past him. Under normal conditions, the Spirit drew power directly from the wellspring of power that pervaded the entire universe, God's own Holy Spirit. But where he was going, that Spirit did not extend. At some point he would have to switch to internal power—the temporal capacitors. In essence, it was the power of God's Holy Spirit captured in a high-energy containment field. Lose control of it in the spiritual vacuum of outer darkness, the space surrounding Hell, even for an instant, and the resulting explosion would exceed the combined explosive power of every nuclear device ever detonated on Earth times three. It was not a comforting thought.

"I've gone to internal power," said Nikola looking toward the telesphere displaying the now snowy image of Johann. "It's a bumpy ride...rougher than the last time we came this way. My surroundings have faded to black. I should emerge from this wormhole in about thirty seconds, if all goes well."

The Spirit hurtled across the dimensional barrier. Nikola watched with concern as the energy levels of the twin capacitors plummeted. His calculations as to the energy requirements were little more than a guess. What would happen if he miscalculated or ran out of energy before completing the transit? He had a pretty good idea. He would be adrift in the nothingness of hyperspace until the end of eternity—another unpleasant thought.

The power levels dropped below 50 percent—no turning back now, he was committed. Still, the gages dropped: 40 percent, 30 percent, 20.... Then, there was calm. The craft was flooded from behind with amber light from Hell's red dwarf sun, Kordor. Ahead of him was the fully illuminated disk of the most terrible destination in all of creation—Hell. He had gated in right where he had planned to. This terrible world was predominantly a sphere of shades of brown, yellow, and red. No oceans of water or polar caps of glistening ice graced the ruddy orb, though much of the far side of this world was covered by an ocean of hot black oil.

He glanced at his fuel gauge. He had made it with 19 percent fuel remaining. Yep, that was about what he had figured. The onboard computer made the necessary calculations to place him in a 12,000-mile-high orbit. A large dish antenna and three other sensors emerged from the safety of their compartments just below the hull of the craft and sprung into action. The instruments were working fine; data was being gathered. Nikola turned to the telesphere—it was blank. Yep, he'd pretty much figured that too. It was time to get to work. The survey might well require the better part of two days. In about six hours he would be in position to communicate with Abaddon. Perhaps he would be able to conduct a tutorial session with

Victoria van Voth in the process. At least that was the plan. He really didn't want to drop in unannounced.

The hours passed slowly for Nikola. There really wasn't much to do. The data was being recorded automatically. He looked at the results from time to time, but nothing of particular note caught his eye. Suppose he was wrong? Suppose there was no power source here causing the increased dimensional density? Then there might be nothing that Abaddon's people could do. He might be stuck here for a long time. In good company to be sure, but stuck nonetheless.

Then again, save for his deathbed conversion, this is the place where he might well have spent his eternity. He had tried to live a decent life on Earth. He had done a lot of good in his lifetime, made his mark for the better. He'd saved George Westinghouse, a good man, from financial ruin. He'd brought light to the streets of America. Still, he'd missed the mark for so much of his life, failed to realize what was truly important. Again he gazed down on the terrible orb. He knew so many people down there, both friends and adversaries. Might he have made a difference for them?

No, he couldn't think in those terms. It was the melancholia that dominated this place, the melancholia that was the inevitable state of a mind separated from the Spirit of the living God. He'd experienced it on his last trip here, though he'd tried to put it out of his mind. He'd only been here for 13 hours that time. This time, he'd have to deal with it for a much longer period.

Then again, the last time he was here, he wasn't alone. Again, he tried to make contact with Johann and the group at his home in the forest. If he could just talk to someone for a while, he might feel better. The telesphere displayed nothing but static. Two more hours and he would try to contact Abaddon.

Within the small cave, Tim Monroe dreamed. He dreamed of his last night on Earth—prom night. He was the youngest junior in the class. He had even been on the prom committee, decorating the gym for the big night. Yes, this was to have been his big night, the night he came out of the closet.

There were rumors about his sexuality, but that was what they were, only rumors. Most of his classmates didn't take them seriously. He was a handsome youth, one of the best runners on the high school track team. His father was a Baptist minister, no, he was all right. He wasn't one of them; after all, wasn't he taking Gale Miller to the prom?

But that was the plan. His friend, Billy Nelson, was taking Sue Martin. In reality, Billy and he were the real couple, as were Gale and Sue. At the prom, they would switch partners. It was the perfect plan, or so they thought.

The four had been ejected from the prom after the third dance. But the night hadn't ended then. They'd left the prom together in Billy's car, not realizing that they were being followed by several irate homophobic classmates. What happened next was unclear. Tim remembered the pickup that had pulled up beside them at the light, the two guys in it. Words had been exchanged. There was a scream. He thought it was Gale. A shot had been fired, maybe two. Then he felt as if someone had driven a hot poker through his head. The next thing he knew, he was hurtling through a dark violet tunnel and dropped into a small dark cell in the depths of Hell. He had been forced to wear a gray ragged loincloth for his sentencing before the master of pandemonium—Satan himself. Satan had condemned him to the plunge for his sin of homosexuality.

In his mind, he experienced the sensation of standing before that terrible precipice for the first time, felt the taskmaster's whip at his back urging him on. Then came the dizzying plunge.

Tim awoke abruptly in the small cave. There were tears in his eyes. He looked over to where his small friend had been lying, almost expecting to find him dead. He'd been lying there for a day, barely breathing, but now he was gone. A surge of fear went through Tim. Then he lifted his head to find the small creature asleep, curled up in the middle of his chest. He was breathing regularly; he looked better. The small creature's eyes opened, meeting Tim's.

"Hi little one," whispered Tim. "I was worried about you. Are you feeling any better?"

Tim was surprised when the small creature smiled slightly. Yes, he was better. Then his eyes closed once more.

"I'll take good care of you," vowed Tim, "I promise. We're going to be great friends, I just know it."

Tim's comment elicited the slightest purr from the small creature and then it faded off to sleep. In that moment, Tim knew that his friend was going to make it. Tim wouldn't have to be alone here, he had a friend. A moment later, he too drifted away to sleep. The bad dreams didn't return.

Bedillia and Tom walked hand in hand across the frozen wasteland just beyond Refuge beneath an auroral display brighter and more colorful than any that Bedillia had ever seen. The aurora shifted in strange and wonderful patterns, like a multitude of curtains hung from the dark starless firmament, blowing in an ethereal wind.

There was not so much as a breath of wind, which made the 40-below zero environment slightly more tolerable, but only slightly. Their immortal bodies could feel the bone chilling cold just as well as a mortal one. The only difference was that they couldn't freeze to death.

"I now understand how vital winning this war is," said Bedillia. "We've both had a taste of eternal damnation, eternal suffering, but only a taste.

You would think that all of those years in a fiery furnace, having my flesh cooked like an overdone steak would have toughened me up. After that, taking a plunge off a cliff would have been easy, child's play, right? But it wasn't. Being released from the torments of Hell, only to return to it once more is horrible beyond belief."

"You've got to quit thinking about it," said Tom, stopping in his tracks and turning to Bedillia. "You've been going on about it for days, reliving it again and again. I can hardly imagine what you're going through, but you need to hear some of your own advice, counselor. The first thing you need to do to get the healing started is to put it behind you. Don't keep digging it up over and over again."

Bedillia smiled. "Counselors and doctors make lousy patients."

"Why not just enjoy the light show," said Tom, pointing to the dazzling display.

It was then that Bedillia noticed that Tom's eyes were affixed on just one point in the sky. A few seconds later, she discovered why. "Tom, that looks like a star. But there are no stars in outer darkness."

There was something there, not far above the western horizon, almost hidden as the curtains of the aurora shifted back and forth across it like drapes of translucent gossamer. It was not a particularly bright star, but it was there; it was no illusion.

They stood in wonder, watching it for several minutes before they realized that it was moving very slowly, rising higher in the sky. It also appeared to be growing somewhat brighter.

There were footsteps behind them. They turned to find the dark angel Lenar with a look of mild amusement on his face.

"Hardly a night for a stroll in the aurora light," he said, turning to gaze at the star that had so captivated Bedillia and Tom. "That is interesting. It must be the Spirit, Nikola Tesla's vessel."

Tom gazed back at Lenar in amazement. "Tesla...here?"

"Yes," confirmed Lenar. "Abaddon is speaking to him on the telesphere right now. He has called an important meeting, and he requests both of you to be present. Apparently, Tesla has brought information of some importance with him, along with supplies that we vitally need."

The three hurried back to Refuge, even as the lone star climbed higher into the sky. It was 40 minutes later when the hurriedly-called meeting got underway in Abaddon's audience chamber. By the time Tom and Bedillia arrived, it was standing room only. The telesphere, displaying a three-dimensional image of Tesla, had been placed in the middle of the table.

"We have much to discuss," noted Abaddon. "As all of you know, Satan and his forces have attacked Heaven. They have managed to largely isolate the angels on Heaven's different planes. The humans there are acting as pilots, ferrying them from one area to another, keeping them in touch with each other. However, at this point, Satan may well have captured a third of the angelic warriors in Heaven. If he succeeds in defeating them, the entire nature of the universe shall be forever altered."

"I really don't see how this concerns us," said the dark angel Ramiel. "We were long ago abandoned by our brethren in Heaven. When we were sentenced to this realm, not one of them spoke up on our behalf, only the human Enoch took up our defense. I will stand in defense of the humans, of that you can be sure. As for the angels of Heaven...I say this is their fight."

Several other dark angels nodded in agreement. Apparently, for them, time had not healed this deep wound.

"Have you forgotten the sacrifices that many of the angels have made on your behalf?" asked Nikola. "They have delivered supplies vital to your rebellion, at great personal risk, and have been instrumental in gathering intelligence regarding the devil's movements. You cannot allow old divisions to come between you. We all face a common enemy."

"A select few have," noted the dark angel Aziel. "To angels such as Aaron, Moriah, and Marlith, we owe a debt of gratitude. However, the vast majority remain adamant to our cause. We have been abandoned by God and the angels. Even if we were to assist them, how would it benefit us? We would still be condemned."

"You don't know that," objected Nikola. "Anyway, it's not just them… it's us, the humans of Heaven, who need your help. You are in a position to turn the tide of the battle in Heaven. You've got to put away your differences. We all have to work together."

"How can we possibly help anyone?" asked Kurt. "We're hanging on by our fingernails here."

"You are wrong," said Nikola. "You are in a position to turn the tables on the devil. There are currently some ninety million angels isolated on Earth with no way to get back to Heaven to join the fight. Satan has found a way to block the return of those angels. He found a way to increase the density of the dimensional barriers between Heaven and Earth, and Heaven and Hell. To do this requires tremendous power, and I believe that I have identified the power source. From up here, it is easy to see. It is the same power source that is generating the brilliant auroras over your heads. The auroras are literally leading me to it. It is a city on the Dark Continent, a city on the shore of the great Sea of Fire."

"The City of Sheol," said Lenar.

"Yes, that is correct," confirmed Nikola. "If it were destroyed, I am convinced that we could move the angels from Earth to Heaven in a matter of days rather than months. Think of it as opening up a second front in your war. Bottle Satan up in a long and costly war in Heaven, and you make your job easier here."

"But how do we destroy Sheol?" objected Ramiel. "If it is as important as you claim, it will be heavily guarded."

"I have aboard the Spirit the means to wipe Sheol completely off the map of Hell," said Nikola. "But I need your assistance to deliver that weapon. I can't do it alone."

"Are we ready for an operation of that magnitude?" questioned Eleazar.

"We will never be as ready as we would like," said Abaddon, "but I believe that now is the time. If Satan is allowed to consolidate his power in Heaven, our situation here will be all the worse. I believe it is time to hear of this weapon and see if we can come up with a means of delivering it."

The meeting went on for several more hours. Tesla was about to lose contact with them when the plan was finally taking shape. Within another six hours, the Spirit would be safely tucked away in the large icy cavern.

As the telesphere onboard Spirit went dark, Nikola prepared to alter course, bringing the Spirit into a tighter orbit of Hell. On the next circuit of this cruel orb, he would touch down.

Already, the twilight world of shifting auroras, fiery seas, and lava fields glowing in the dark, was giving way to the searing plains of Hell's daylight hemisphere. He gazed down at the desolate landscape. It was hard to believe that there were billions of people on that scorched planet. He would continue to take readings, but he already had all of the information he needed.

A 30-second realignment of the field generator saw the beginning of the descent. He would enter the atmosphere over the western regions of the Sea of Fire. Even at low speed, he realized that his entry into the atmosphere would be hard to miss. Fortunately, this was a sparsely populated region. Few indeed would bear witness to his arrival, and most of them would be well past caring. He would make some evasive maneuvers so as to make it difficult for Satan's forces to track him. He could ill afford to have some demon follow him to Refuge. He would keep his eyes glued to the radar.

He considered his situation again. He glanced at the fuel gauge, to confirm what he already knew. Even if Abaddon and his people succeeded at destroying the power generator and they managed to get the density of the barrier between Hell and Heaven back to normal, he might not have sufficient fuel to make the trip back. He might well be stuck here for a very long time. He put that thought out of his mind. There was work for him to do here. If the truth be known, he would probably be more useful to the cause here than he would be in Heaven.

Hell loomed ever larger as Nikola prepared to retract the instruments for atmospheric entry. He was cruising 600 miles above an active volcanic field, one of the most active regions on the planet. Anywhere else, this might be the kind of place that would spark a sense of wonder in a scientific mind. There were fountains of lava rising hundreds of feet into the air with clouds of ash and steam giving genesis to powerful electric discharges and rivers of hot molten rock flowing for miles. It was one of the great spectacles of nature, but not here.

Here, one might wonder what sort of horrors were transpiring down there? What manner of human suffering was underway in that sulfurous world of intense heat and toxic smoke? He turned away from it, concentrating on the job ahead. Forty minutes to atmospheric entry. Five minutes before that, he would throttle up the engines a final time and slow down to a fraction of orbital velocity so as to lessen the force of impact with the atmosphere. He couldn't afford to blaze like a meteor across the twilight sky in a world where there were no meteors.

He swept toward atmospheric interface. Hell's red sun had touched the horizon and was sinking into the dusty atmosphere behind him. The light in the cabin faded as the last glimmer of the star Kordor vanished into the middle of a swiftly narrowing red crescent. It would be the last time he saw this sight for a long time. He was heading into a land of eternal night and eternal cold. Five minutes to atmospheric interface—it was time.

The engines came to life not as a roar, but as a whine. Artificial gravity was pulling the spacecraft backward, putting on the brakes. Atmospheric interface occurred not at 17,000 miles per hour but at 5,000. There was some slight buffeting and a sound of wind roaring around the craft at hypersonic speeds, but no telltail trail of bright ionization.

Normally the Spirit was flown by two people. Critical events during entry into an atmosphere were fast paced and difficult for one man to keep up with, even with a computer. Yet Nikola flew it perfectly.

Fifty miles below, he crossed the shoreline of the Sea of Fire. The sea stretched out to the horizon, a hot black ocean, with currents and towering waves, topped with swirling columns of fire. Countless people floated helplessly in that vast sea, their blood evaporated in its fiery heat, their minds racked with unimaginable pain. He might well have ended up in a place like that were it not for the mercy of his Savior, Jesus. God's mercy to him still filled him with a sense of awe. He had lived 86 years without giving His creator the time of day, only to have a life-changing experience three days before he died. There, alone in his apartment, sick and in pain, he had finally turned to God.

His father had been a minister; he had grown up in a Christian home, yet somehow that faith hadn't been passed down to him. Science had been his god for so long. His father and mother had both been relieved when he showed up at their mansion in Heaven on that January morning. They had spoken to the Father on his behalf many times. Apparently, praying parents in Heaven did help, at least in his case. Still, what had he ever done to deserve salvation? That still bothered him. It was a free gift; this he knew, yet he felt that he had to do something. He had felt that way for 60 years. To a large extent, that was why he was here now.

Thirty-six miles altitude was the indication on the altimeter—time to increase power and extend the glide slope. After all, he didn't want to crash into the black sea below him, whether he deserved it or not.

No, he had to stop thinking like that. It was the absence of God's Holy Spirit that was making him feel this way. His mind wandered back to those last three years of his life, the things that had haunted him. Ghosts out of his past were what he had thought they were. Now, of course, he knew that they were not ghosts at all, but demons sent to confuse him.

Ahead, the sky was full of light, the aurora, but this time they were above him, not below. "About eighty to about two hundred kilometers altitude," he said aloud just to hear a voice. Strange, there was a time when he preferred to be alone. He would be in telesphere range of Refuge in about an hour, if all went well. Again he attempted to contact Johann, but without success.

To his right, towering ten miles above this otherworldly ocean, a powerful thunderstorm positively alive with blue bolts of lightning raged, driven by updrafts from the fiery sea below. The clouds themselves were yellow and not white like Earthly clouds. Below the base of the clouds, he could just make out what looked like a blue mist plunging to the sea. He knew only too well what it was that he was witnessing.

Like so many things in Hell, this was a distorted parody of an earthly thunderstorm. Below these billowing clouds fell a rain, not of water, but of concentrated sulfuric acid mixed with hailstones of flaming sulfur. It added yet another dimension to the torment of those adrift on the terrible sea.

His eyes turned back to his instruments. His airspeed had dropped to just under mach 2. By the time he reached 60,000 feet, he would have to be subsonic. He made another course correction, a precaution, just in case he had been observed from below.

Ahead of him the fires of the sea seemed to abruptly end. He had reached the Dark Continent at last.

Fifteen minutes found him crossing the shoreline at an altitude of just under 90,000 feet. Under the intense auroral display, he could make out landforms—mountains and valleys, mostly. The Dark Continent was rough territory, an ideal place to hide. He was anxious to get to Refuge. He would have liked nothing better than to push the engines a little harder to get there more quickly. No, he would stick to the plan.

A few minutes later, he had dropped back through the sound barrier. Now his approach would be very silent. He passed 40,000 feet, then 30,000. He became increasingly on edge. He would soon be passing into airspace traveled by demons. He frequently scanned his radar. It would easily pick up a bird if there was one—it was clear.

The sudden hiss of the telesphere made Nikola practically jump. He gazed into its depths to see a friendly face.

"Welcome to the Dark Continent," said Abaddon, smiling broadly. "My scouts on the surface tell me that they have you in sight…off to the west. Looks like you're right on course. We've set out lights to guide you in."

"Thank you," said Nikola, "I'm glad to be here."

"We are glad to have you here with us," assured Abaddon. "We have rolled out the red carpet for you. You are, after all, our first saintly guest. I look forward to meeting you in person."

The rest of the approach was uneventful. Within ten minutes, he had an escort of four dark angels flying in formation around him. They guided him into the cavern above Refuge. It was a tight but manageable fit. At last, the four spidery legs of the Spirit touched down on solid ground. Nikola put on the parka he had packed and descended the ladder. He was greeted by the applause and cheers of no less than 100 dark angels and humans. He was beginning to feel much more at ease.

"Welcome to Refuge, Dr. Tesla," said a fair-of-face human woman that Nikola recognized as Bedillia Farnsworth. She extended her hand.

Usually Nikola had problems making physical contact with others, but not this time. He shook her hand warmly. "No doctor, please, just Nikola."

He turned around to discover a stone wall behind him. Hadn't he just flown the Spirit through there?

Bedillia laughed. "It's a long story, but come, you are expected in Abaddon's audience chamber. We have much to discuss."

It was a long walk to the audience chamber, and all along the way were people eager to greet their honored guest. A human visitor from Heaven, a saint; surely, this was a first for Refuge.

Nikola knew that he was about to experience firsthand the other side of this struggle against the prince of darkness. He would now live with the reality of that struggle from day to day with those who had the most to lose if they failed. He prayed that he was up to the challenge.

Chapter 14

Nikola Tesla sat down at the end of the great marble conference table in Abaddon's audience hall. The rest of the council followed. The room was filled—standing room only as others crowded in the hall beyond to hear the words of the great scientist and engineer. There was a general feeling of hope in the air. Word was that he would be staying with them for some considerable time, that he had brought with him tools that would be critical for their survival.

Abaddon rose to his feet. "I believe I speak for us all when I give warm greetings to the great scientist, Nikola Tesla. While you are with us, you will be a member of the governing council and sit in our meetings. What we have done here would not have been possible without the assistance of you and your colleagues. Sir, you have the floor."

Nikola rose, somewhat nervously. He had never been one for speeches; now that would have to change. He had wanted to make a difference, to do something for the saints in Heaven…well…here was his chance.

"I'm glad to be with you," he began, searching for words. "Those of us on the other side of the dimensional barrier realize all that you have gone through. After all, this battle was yours before it ever became ours. I'm about to propose two missions that, if successful, will work to the benefit of all.

"First, is to utterly destroy the City of Sheol. I am convinced that it is the prime energy source for Satan and his minions operating in Heaven. With it gone, their operations will be greatly curtailed. Second, I propose to destroy the great ring on the plains. Through it, Satan traveled to Heaven. Destroy it, and he is stranded, unable to return. In doing this, your odds of defeating his remaining forces are greatly enhanced. I have brought with me the components necessary to build several high-yield explosive devices, more than capable of accomplishing these tasks. I will assemble them, but you will have to determine how best to deliver them."

The dark angel Eleazar rose to his feet. "With all due respect sir, I think that you are greatly overestimating the capabilities of our forces. We are scarcely two thousand strong. Even if only a tenth of Satan's forces remain, we face a force of twenty million. Are you expecting us to step out and expose ourselves to attack outnumbered a thousand to one—to assist your forces in Heaven who are only now facing a foe in combat that we have faced for many millennia?"

"And what do you think will happen if Satan prevails in Heaven?" posed Nikola.

"I do not know," admitted Eleazar. "I only know that you ask a great deal of us. I just wanted you to realize the situation we face, that is all."

For nearly two hours their options were weighed. In the end, a plan of attack was formulated. Yes, it was very risky; but the benefits, the necessity, outweighed the risks. Tesla would build the weapons—three of them—then the people of Refuge would deliver them.

Three days later, Nikola was completing work on the third weapon as Victoria was finishing the circuitry for the 53rd particle rifle. It had been an assembly-line process. Bill, Tom, and Kurt materialized the housing and more basic components while Victoria generated the circuitry. They all worked together in the same room, one of only three where this craft could be pursued. Even Nikola could not construct the components beyond this place. Only here did an artificial version of the power of the Spirit of God dwell. It had its limitations, but it did work.

Tesla picked up the now completed weapon, a bomb, really. It was hefty, weighing in at 60 pounds. He estimated its yield at better than 60 kilotons, nearly three times as powerful as the bomb that ended World War II. He was confident that it would work, but might it work too well? The resulting explosion would not just release energy here, but in hyperspace as well. What would the results of such an explosion be? Would it rip a hole in space time? He wasn't sure.

They would hit the City of Sheol first, within a week, after they had refined their delivery technique. When the day finally came, he would be there to observe the blast from a mountain ridge 22 miles away. If the blast was more powerful than he had counted on, if there were unexpected side effects, they might have to alter their plans regarding the next target. After observing the results of the first explosion he would make recommendations.

Tim was awakened rather suddenly. His mind wandered. For a moment he thought he was home, in his parent's home once more, but he wasn't. He was in a small cave in Hell. Opening his eyes he came face to face with the tiny creature. It had been rubbing up against his chin with its soft fur.

"Hello, you," he said quietly, petting its soft body with his hand. It responded with a soothing purr. He sat up, looking his small friend over carefully. "You look much better. I'm glad."

The creature fluttered its wings, making a short flight over to the other side of the small cave.

"You sure healed fast," said Tim, sitting cross-legged on the floor. "Who and what are you? I still don't know. I'm just glad you're here."

The creature nudged something setting on the floor. There was something in the shadows. Tim crawled over to see what it was. He reached down. He was surprised to discover that it was a silvery ring with a large yellowish stone.

"Where did this come from?" he asked, gazing at the small creature. "Is it for me?"

Tim was astonished when the creature looked straight at him and nodded vigorously. Then it extended its right front arm in Tim's direction. The creature touched it to his left several times, opening and closing his claw like fingers. For a moment Tim didn't understand. Clearly, his small friend wanted him to do something. Then he got it. He placed the ring on his finger, then he clenched his fist. He was surprised when a bright beam of light emanated from the gem. It was a beam that the best LCD flashlight couldn't beat for brightness. He opened his hand and the beam went out.

"Cool," said Tim. "Thank you."

The creature did a flip that made Tim laugh.

Tim formed a fist again and the light came on once more. He directed the beam still deeper into the cave. For the first time he got a sense of the size of this place. The tunnel continued, first narrowing then expanding into a much larger cavern. For a moment he hesitated. "Hey, are you up to going exploring?"

Again the creature nodded.

Tim had been in a mist up to this point. Perhaps his year of pain and terror had left him so. "You can understand everything I say, can't you."

The creature nodded, smiling as he did so.

"Oh my gosh," gasped Tim, leaning down in his friend's direction. "Do you have a name?"

The creature shook its head.

"Would you mind if I gave you a name?" asked Tim. "I promise it will be a good name."

The creature nodded, smiling.

"OK," said Tim. "How does Goliath sound, do you like that name? Goliath was a giant, one of the strongest men who ever lived. You're not big, but I bet you're strong."

The tiny creature cocked its head for a second then nodded.

"OK, Goliath it is," said Tim. "Let's go."

Tim crawled farther into the cavern with the help of his magical light, and Goliath followed. It was not a tight fit at all, and just 50 feet brought Tim to a tunnel that was at least 7 or 8 feet high. He continued. There was a wonderful cool dampness here that Tim enjoyed.

Suddenly they came to an abrupt halt. There was a very faint noise ahead. He continued. The tunnel opened into a sizable cavern room at least 50 feet across and 15 feet high. There were icicle-like stalagmites hanging from the ceiling, and at the center of the room was the source of the noise— a pool of liquid perhaps 20 feet wide and several feet deep at the center. Drops of liquid were occasionally falling from several of the stalactites overhead. Could it be water? Tim had almost forgotten what water tasted like. He cautiously approached the pool and stuck his hand into it. It was chilly and it didn't burn, nor did it feel slimy. He cupped his hand and took a drink. It was refreshing water.

"Oh God," he said taking one sip after another. "Oh thank You God, thank You."

Tim had grown so accustomed to his thirst that he had forgotten how wonderfully quenching it was. It was several minutes before he was satisfied. He had never realized that there was water in Hell.

He looked around and saw many tunnels that radiated away from this room, some quite large, others were very small. Some might lead to other exits. Tim had once read that even after 100 years, many parts of Carlsbad Cavern remained unexplored. It might take weeks, even months, to thoroughly explore these caverns—his own dark world. That was OK; he had all of eternity. This place was pretty cool, and he wasn't afraid. After all, he had Goliath with him.

David Bonner had been communing with the Father for two solid days. Never had he spent so much quality time with his Creator. He now understood the reason that this war had to happen. He had questioned it, even debated it, but in the end he had gained insight way beyond his years. He was acquiring a new sense of purpose, but he was also coming to realize that there were trials ahead. He was part of what was happening and what was going to happen.

The events of 9-11-2001 that brought him here, his continuing uncanny insight, his relationship with Johann Kepler, even his involvement in releasing Serena Davis from Hell six years ago—it was all starting to make sense. But now, it was time to leave.

"You know that you are safe here in My presence," said the Father. "This place shall be an island of calm in the raging storm. Those who remain here will be untouched by the events unfolding around us."

David smiled. "Yes, Father, I know."

"And you still choose to go out there?" asked the Father.

"Yes, I have to," confirmed David.

"Do you know why, David?" asked the Father.

"Because I've learned all that I need to know, for the moment, that is," replied David, rising to his feet. "I thank You, Father, for opening my eyes like never before. I've never seen things so clearly. I know I could stay here and be safe, but then I'd miss an experience to grow, to exercise my faith, and test my courage."

There was a long pause. "There was something else," said the Father. "You have one more reason that you haven't mentioned as yet."

"Yeah," said David. "There is something else. It will be more of an adventure if I go out there. I don't think I want to use the word fun to describe it, because it may not be that. I just know I have to go out there."

"Very good, My son," said the Father. "Step out there with your eyes open. You may have occasion to feel fear, but do not allow it to rule you."

"I'll do my best," said David, heading for the boundary line separating the Holy Place from the rest of the city.

The perimeter of the Holy Place was cordoned off by thousands of Satan's minions who seemed determined to corral the saints. David took a deep breath, though he never looked back. He had walked about 100 yards into the city beyond when he was finally stopped by one of Satan's own; a bat-winged demon with an indeed pale visage.

"You need to turn back," he said, pointing toward the Holy Place. "It is not safe for your kind here. It is for your own good that I tell you this."

"And I appreciate your concern," said David. "However, I am not staying in the city. I am staying with friends some distance from here. I will be staying with them until the crisis passes. I believe I will be safe there."

It was then that a second demon joined the first. David couldn't be certain, but he appeared to be a higher ranking demon. He turned to the first. "You told this young man of the dangers in the city?"

"Yes, sir," said the first, "but he insists on traveling to be with friends afar off."

The second demon looked at David carefully. "This entire plane of Heaven is a battle zone."

"But I will be traveling to the third plane," replied David.

"War on that plane has been particularly brutal," said the demon. "Indeed, we plan to evacuate humans from that region within days. Some humans there are part of the problem, rebels they are. They do not accept that a new order is coming to this place."

"I think you're counting the cause of angels to be lost, when the war has just begun," said David.

"We shall see," said the demon, who had suddenly taken an interest in the object hidden beneath David's cloak. "What is it you carry with you?"

David thought for a second what to do. Truth might be the best policy. He pulled out the pistol. "As you said, this is a war zone, so I brought a weapon to protect myself. You never can be too careful."

The demon seemed startled. "I believe it was weapons such as this that were used against our forces not far from here, by rebel forces."

David shrugged, "I cannot say one way or the other. I made this weapon myself. I assure you, it has not been fired in this war at anyone, at least, not yet."

"May I take that as a thinly veiled threat?" asked the second demon.

"Take it however you wish," retorted David. He toggled the power switch, the pistol's capacitor charged with an unmistakable pulsing hum. "I didn't come out here looking for a fight."

"That is good," replied the demon. "Our orders are clear. We are not to harm any humans here in Heaven. You are children of the Father, noncombatants. That is, unless you choose to enter this conflict of your own accord, as these rebels have. In that case, we may treat you as we would treat the angels of Michael and Gabriel…as enemies. I assure you their fate will not be pleasant."

David looked around. This discussion had drawn the attention of no less than eight demons within a radius of 20 feet. At this point, David wished that he had packed one of the particle rifles rather than this pistol. This pistol had less than half of the knock-down power of one of the rifles, and its smaller field coil required three seconds to fully charge the capacitor.

That meant three seconds between shots, compared to the rifle's one. He might get off two or three shots before the rest of these demons were on him. He also was unsure as to whether he could gate out of here so close to the Holy Place.

"We will have to confiscate that weapon," said the demon.

This encounter-turned-conflict was rapidly escalating out of control. No, David knew he had to remain cool. "That isn't negotiable."

"We could take it by force," said the demon.

"You might," said David, "but I believe that would violate your orders, to say nothing of the five or six of you I'd turn into piles of smoldering bones before you took it. How would you explain that to your master?"

The number of demons around him was growing; David knew he was pushing his luck, but he stood firm. Had he said something about looking for adventure? He might just have found it.

"Why don't you explain it to the master?" said the demon, pointing to the tall building that had once housed the angels of this sixth level of Heaven. "He has given orders to bring unto him the first member of the rebellion we find. I think that is you. You have my word that you will come to no harm."

David didn't like the sound of that at all. The Father had talked of times like this, times when his faith and courage might be tested. "How can I pass on such a kind offer?"

"Very good," said the demon. "Now you are being sensible. If you will stow your weapon, we shall be on our way."

David complied. Within a minute, he found himself carried on demon wings toward the once mighty Hall of Angels. As he drew closer, he was shocked to view the full damage this enormous structure had sustained. At many places, entire walls had been blown out. One corner had even partially collapsed.

From this vantage point, he also gained some perspective as to the damage done to the city itself. Much of it remained intact. Still, there were regions that were leveled. The greatest damage had occurred immediately around the Hall of Angels.

For the first time ever, David got the experience of entering the Hall of Angels from its rooftop entrance. In reality, there were no street entrances to this building. It had given the angels one place in Heaven in which they could truly be to themselves. It seemed to David that angels and humans mixed only when they had to. Neither had any real quarrels with the other; it was just that they preferred the company of their own kind. The mind of an angel just wasn't wired like the human mind, and as such they didn't have a lot in common. David had always viewed this as being unfortunate. On Earth, angels guarded humankind, but they didn't interact with them, except on the urging from the Father. Greater collaboration between the two races would have been of so much benefit to them both.

David alighted on the roof and was escorted by three demons down a wide, covered walkway into the interior of the building. David scanned his surroundings, taking in every detail.

This place was not at all as David had envisioned it. Its white marble corridors were wide enough, tall enough to accommodate angel's wings, but were totally blank. It surprised David to find that they were not particularly well lit. Even in its best days, this place would probably not have been particularly welcoming. Rooms that led to either side were without doors. Most contained nothing more than a network of small cubicles where the angels rested. David recalled hearing that angels rested balanced upon their knees and their wings. They didn't rest very often, nor did they require much space. The lives of angels were routine and uncomplicated, a life of service to both the Father and humankind.

They passed the large entryway to the gate room that housed a shimmering metal ring that was about 20 feet across. It was through this gate that angels came and went to the different levels of Heaven, to remote places within the same level, and to Earth. It was filled with demons, and new ones were gating in constantly. It was not encouraging.

Demons were clearing rubble from the corridor in an attempt to make travel through these passageways just a bit easier. Still, amid the commotion of repair, David could hear the sound of a great multitude crying and moaning beneath his feet. What was going on here?

At last they came to a corridor on the right that actually led to a set of ornate golden doors. There was a demon sentry standing at that double door. One of the demons escorting David walked to the sentry and spoke to him in a language that David only vaguely comprehended. The sentry opened the door and headed in as David and his demonic escorts waited.

"I suspect that Lord Satan will see you immediately," said one of the demons. "I recommend that you remember your manners in his presence. Very soon, his will be the ultimate power among the angels."

David resisted the temptation to make a flippant remark.

Curiously enough, one of the last books that David had read in the great library was a book on angelic history and etiquette. Its lessons might come in very useful today.

One side of the double door opened, and the sentry emerged. He turned to David. "Lord Satan will see you at once; you may enter."

The double doors opened again, and after taking a deep breath, David entered. He was not quite sure what to think as the double doors closed behind him and he came face to face with the Prince of Darkness himself. He sat upon Michael's throne, the very image of an angel of light. Satan was dressed in white from head to foot, his white angelic wings towering over his body. He was practically radiant.

David had seen Satan many times before, though never in person. The first time was six years ago. Using the black book of Serena Farnsworth in the Hall of Records, he had witnessed the horrors of Hell through the eyes of one who had actually experienced it. Since then he had made a virtual character study of this dark being. In many ways his face was the same. It was his surroundings that made him seem different, from his golden hair to his spotless raiment.

Satan's eyes followed David carefully as he approached. At the middle of the chamber, while he was still 30 or more feet from the throne, David stopped and bowed as angelic protocol demanded. It was an act that seemed to greatly please Satan.

"Peace be unto you, David Bonner," said Satan, rising to his feet.

"And unto you, sir," said David, walking several steps closer.

"I am delighted to finally meet you in person," said Satan, a smile on his face. "To have one of the greatest students of the great Doctor Kepler in my presence is a pleasant surprise." Satan took several more steps toward David halving the distance separating them.

"Thank you, sir," replied David, returning the smile. "I too feel honored to at last meet you in person." David took several more steps toward Satan, doing his best to suppress his apprehension—and, yes, his fear.

Satan's eyes turned to the pistol that was partially visible beneath David's cloak. "And that is the weapon that the human rebel faction is employing these days?"

"Yes," replied David, removing it from his cloak. "At least this is one of them, we have several versions. I made this one myself. As an angel is expected to fashion his own sword, I have fashioned this weapon. It is a rite of passage."

"Yes, I see," said Satan, displaying his own jewel handled sword, and pulling it partway from its sheath to show his young guest. "I too fashioned this weapon many millennia ago, in the days of my youth."

"It is magnificent," replied David, trying to appeal to Satan's weakness of pride. "I cannot say that I have ever seen its equal."

Satan nodded in approval. "I am curious, young man. If that weapon you hold is as powerful as my minions claim, why have you not been tempted to use it on me? You have the opportunity."

"But not the desire," replied David. "I am an invited guest in your home. To do so would not be, well, civilized."

Satan nodded again. "Well said, young man. May I see this wonder that you have made with your own hands?"

Oh boy, that was something David had not expected. What should he do now? He reengaged its safety, took several steps forward, and handed it to the Prince of Darkness.

Satan seemed genuinely surprised at the faith and courage of this young human. He took the weapon in hand and examined it carefully. "Marvelous craftsmanship," he said, "something quite different from that which might have been forged by angelic hands, but no less magnificent." He returned the weapon to David.

David placed his weapon to its makeshift holster. "Thank you, sir."

Satan placed a hand on David's shoulder. Though his hand was warm like any human or angelic hand, it brought a chill to his soul. "I remember well the day I faced your mentor on the plains of Heckath, in Hell six years ago. On that day, we were adversaries. Our meeting today, friendly and trusting as it has been, shows that this need not be the case. The winds of change are being felt across all of Heaven, my young friend. It need not be a foul wind. I can bring order out of chaos, uniting all of the angels under one rule."

"Yours," deduced David.

"Of course," confirmed Satan. "After many thousands of years, the rule of Michael and Gabriel has brought us no closer to unity. If anything, it has driven us farther apart. Now, with the leave of the Father, all of that will be changed. I shall take reign over the angels. There will be a new age of the angels, an age of unity."

"And where will humanity fit into this new enlightened age of the angels?" asked David.

"A fair question," replied Satan. "I admit I was wrong to oppose the will of the Father on the issue of human dominance. If he wishes man to play a part in the future of Heaven, well, so be it. There will be room for your people here *and* in Hell. Hell must exist as a place to discard those humans not worthy of standing in the presence of the Father. Surely, you must realize that."

David thought it best not to argue that point.

"But you are a student of Doctor Kepler, and a trusted one at that. You can go to him carrying a proposition from me. I will propose peace between us. Allow Michael and Gabriel to fall on their own; don't drag this war out longer than need be. I can offer something to all of you. For Doctor Kepler, it is within my power to free his wife and his mother from their torments in Hell. It would be a gesture of peace between us. No longer need his mother burn in subterranean fire, nor his wife hang suspended by her hair above the toxic boiling pits of foulness. I shall take them away from all of that…give them each a cool quiet cell where they can live out their eternities in peace.

"And as for you, I can free your own grandfather from a torment too terrible to be discussed in pleasant conversation. As you see, I have something to offer the saints. I ask not that you serve me. No, that would be too much to expect right now. All I ask is that you remain neutral, allow this war to follow its own natural course. It is not your war."

Never had David expected this conversation to follow the course it had taken. He had expected to be threatened, perhaps even worse. Instead, Satan was being civil and relatively reasonable. "You make a compelling argument, sir."

"Thank you," replied Satan. "Will you take my proposal back to your friends?"

"Yes I will, sir," confirmed David. "I can't say how they will react, but I will deliver your message."

"Excellent," replied Satan, "I will ask nothing more of you beyond this…remain as my honored guest for a few days, at least until Heaven is a bit safer. Then, I will send you on your way. You came in peace, and you may go in peace."

"How can I turn down such a generous offer?" said David.

"By the way, don't try to gate out. My predecessor made quite certain that you humans could neither gate in or out of this facility. He valued his privacy."

"Of course," replied David.

"Excellent," said Satan. "I will assign my lieutenant, Lemnok, to see to your comfort and your needs. Take this time to get to know us better. You might be surprised at what you learn. Lemnok will be your guide while you are with us. He will meet you beyond and answer what questions you might have. Please consider my home to be your home." Satan motioned to the door. "I bid you a pleasant day."

David took several steps backward, bowed a final time, and made for the door. Quite honestly, he'd had all that he could take of this guy. David departed the audience chamber.

"Are you sure that you want him here?" asked Metastopholies, stepping out of the shadows. "He is quite clever. Just because he is here rather than on Earth, makes him no less dangerous. Had you not gone to such great measures in seeing to his demise on September 11, 2001, he might well have taken millions of humans from our kingdom. Be careful, my lord, he could be a considerable adversary."

"You worry too much, my old friend," laughed Satan. "He is young and so very trusting. He will not realize what is going on until it is entirely too late."

"Take care, your pride and confidence will be your undoing," warned Metastopholies.

"My confidence is well-founded," replied Satan. "In all likelihood, his mentor and his allies will already be vanquished by the time I, well, release him from this place. They might indeed be reunited, but it will not be in Heaven. The wheels are already turning to make it so."

Metastopholies shook his head, but said nothing. He bowed and made his way back to his quarters.

Chapter 15

June opened the door of Dr. Kepler's mansion to discover eight heavily armed demons there, with more flying overhead. She cringed, but held her peace.

"Is this your home?" demanded the demon nearest her.

"No," replied June, "my home was in Zion before it became a war zone. This is the home of a friend. I am looking after it until he returns."

"And would that friend happen to be Johann Kepler?" asked the demon.

"Well, yes," replied June. "He's my son's teacher. My son and I are living here for now."

"You might be," said the demon, pushing his way in, "but for now your son is a guest of our master, until he decides otherwise."

June suddenly grew quite pale. "What do you mean?"

"I thought that would be obvious, June Bonner," replied the demon. "Your son is in the custody of Lord Satan. He is safe, so long as you and your friends cooperate."

The other seven demons entered the house and spread out, searching the rooms. From the sound of falling objects, breaking glass, and scattering papers, they were anything but subtle in their methods. All the while, June waited in shock. She had been certain that her son was with the Father. It was 20 minutes before the search concluded.

"There is evidence that things have been taken from this place, and recently," reported one of the other demons.

June looked into Kepler's study to discover the place in shambles. "You had no right to do that!" she exclaimed.

The demon wasted no time in grabbing the woman by the throat. "On the contrary, madam, I had every right to do it. The third plane of Heaven is ours. Thanks to people like you, most of the angels here have escaped us, but they are running out of places to hide. We know that you are one of the rebels. You and yours have given comfort to the enemy; you have no rights here." He threw June into the study. She flew 15 feet before crashing into Johann's overturned conference table.

June felt pain. There was blood pouring down her cheek, and she deduced that her left arm was broken. It had been years since she had felt such a sensation.

Another of the demons looked into the study to see the prone woman. "What shall we do with this one, sir?"

Their leader smiled. "Shackle her hand and foot, let her experience the burning shackles of Hell. Then secure her to that support beam over there. We shall burn the house down around her. Give her a feel for what Hell is like. She shall be an example to deter others from making the same mistake."

Another of the demons tossed a pair of wrist and ankle shackles across the floor at her. June looked at the open shackles with their barbed interiors.

She had heard of these things from her son; they were commonly used in Hell to restrain the damned. When closed about the ankles or wrists of their unfortunate wearers, they immediately welded themselves together in a searing flash of heat, severely burning then restraining them.

"There," said the demon, "lock the big pair around your ankles first, then you can do your wrists later…after the pain subsides."

June tried to clear her mind then looked angrily at her attackers. "Not likely." Instantly, a glowing field of misty stars appeared before her.

"Get her!" demanded the demonic leader.

It was too late. June had already stumbled into the mists. One of the demons lunged at her, but his claws grabbed at empty air.

"Damn it!" said their demonic leader. "These humans are entirely too slippery. When the master comes to power, we will have to have some restrictions placed on this parlor trick of theirs."

"You've become too accustomed to the humans of Hell," noted another. "They make such excellent victims, so very weak, so very helpless."

The first demon smiled slightly. "Perhaps that is the one thing I shall miss about Hell. Let's get out of here. A couple of fireballs shall make short order of this place."

The demons retreated several hundred feet from the house before their leader directed his sword at the place and let loose a fireball. It exploded on contact, engulfing the place in flames.

"Too easy," said their leader, as they departed. They would return to their staging area in the city of Paradise and make their report to the master from there. He would be pleased that the rebel base had been destroyed. It was unfortunate that the rebels had already moved on. Still, they, like the angels, were running out of places to hide.

Johann was alarmed as June materialized out of the mists and stumbled into the audience hall of the angelic general Moriah in the City of Elesia. She collapsed to the floor.

Immediately angels and humans alike rushed to her aid. It was several minutes before she was able to relate the story of the attack on Johann's forest home.

"Homes can be rebuilt," said Johann, holding June in his arms. "I am just thankful that you escaped."

"They have my son," lamented June, tears flowing from her eyes. "If they intended to burn me, what will they do to him?"

Already June's body was being restored to health. Her arm had mended, and only drying blood was left to bear witness to the deep gash that had been on her head a few minutes before.

"What now?" asked Marlith, Moriah's lieutenant. "They have David, and my commander hasn't been seen in two days."

"We proceed as planned," replied Johann. "Michael and Gabriel are depending on us. In five hours we must journey to the Mountains of Sarval at the confluence of the Marten and Salba Rivers. We have over seventeen hundred human volunteers to ferry whatever angels are at the rendezvous point to here. It won't be like the operation at the Hill of Ceranda. We should be able to evacuate a million angels in a matter of minutes, not hours. Hopefully there will be more than a million there to evacuate."

"It indeed disturbs me to see the sixth level of Heaven completely abandoned to Satan's forces," lamented Marlith.

"For the moment, we must retreat to a defensible position," said Johann. "I am not a military man, but I know that to be a sound strategy; so do Michael and Gabriel. By tomorrow we will have with us a true military man to organize the human involvement in this conflict. He will counsel directly with Michael and Gabriel to coordinate our efforts. At that point I will defer to his authority, and my group shall become his science and technology advisors, no more. Currently, he and several of his lieutenants are gathering intelligence regarding our situation, as well as pulling together a real army. Between angels and humans, we might be able to field quite a large military force.

Getting those angels out of the sixth level will be my last act as coordinator of the human forces. My people will continue to build hardware for them, mainly the Tesla particle rifles. We have about four hundred of them ready to go. We've pulled in artisans from Zion to help with the task. Once they get up to speed, we should be able to build even more."

Over 3 million angels had gathered at the confluence of the Marten and Salba rivers when the humans gated into their presence. They had been waging a fighting retreat for three solid days. Their defense had become more organized; they were fighting as a single force at this point. Still, it had happened too late. The battle for the sixth level of Heaven was lost. Satan's forces on this level alone were nearly 20 million strong by best estimates. If these angels remained here, they would surely join the estimated 30 million angels now held in captivity by Satan's minions across the seven planes.

Over the past three days, the human inhabitants of Heaven had assisted the angels in every way possible, helping Michael's and Gabriel's forces retreat to the safety of the second plane. There were better than 20 million battle-ready angels in the City of Elesia now, and with the continuing efforts of Johann Kepler and his team, several hundred angels had even made the trip back from Earth. This operation today promised to be the largest single evacuation to date.

Still, it was a dark time for the angels. There were rumors of an impending conditional surrender in the wind, but not as far as Michael was concerned. They were fighting on. They would never accept Satan as the ruler of the angels—never accept his concept of a great angelic society.

"Satan has about six million of his minion pursuing us," explained Michael. "We managed to elude them for a time, but I suspect that they will be here within two hours."

"We will have all of your people out of here well before then," assured Johann.

"A similar evacuation is planned for the fifth plane in just a matter of hours," noted Michael, "orchestrated by your new commander, General Cornelius. I have met him briefly only once, but he seems to be a competent leader."

"He is one of our best," assured Johann. "We are fortunate to have him. He has two thousand years of experience."

"And what of your Nikola Tesla; is there any word?"

Johann shook his head. "Sadly, no. We can't make communication work between here and Hell. The only person who was able to make it work has been captured by Satan."

Michael nodded. "Yes, I heard about David, I'm sorry. I know the two of you are close."

"I feel personally responsible for him," said Johann. "I will get him out of there no matter what it takes."

It took a few minutes to get the evacuation underway. The process moved along at a tremendous speed. A mere half hour saw the entire field emptied of angelic forces.

The last of the humans and angels vanished, leaving only Michael and Johann. Michael scanned the skies carefully.

"I have not seen Gabriel, have you?" asked Michael.

"No," replied Johann. "But there were so many here. He might have already gone on ahead."

"No," said Michael. "He would not have left until I too was prepared to depart the field of battle. He was leading a group of about fifty of our fellows, searching for stragglers. Now I am very concerned for him."

"Perhaps he was cut off," suggested Johann. "He might turn up later."

They waited for more than 20 minutes. Then a dark cloud appeared on the horizon. It grew by the minute.

"Satan's forces," said Michael. "They were closer than we had thought. We must leave."

Johann scanned the sky a last time before opening the portal. They vanished into the mists. There would be no further mass evacuations from this level of Heaven. The City of Zion and all of its surroundings were now firmly in the hands of Satan.

David Bonner sat on the edge of the roof of the Great Hall of Angels in the City of Zion with his escort, the demon lieutenant Lemnok. It had been an interesting experience, having a calm and civil discussion with a demon. Lemnok had told him quite a bit about the philosophy of demonkind, even bits and pieces of Satan's plans. Assuming that it was not misinformation, it might be quite valuable.

"Would you answer me one question?" asked Lemnok.

"Sure, ask," replied David.

"Why would you want to support the angels of Michael in their struggle against us?"

David didn't need to think too long on that one. "Well, for one thing, they are our neighbors, and they have been good neighbors. Second, they have safeguarded humanity from, well, you guys on Earth. No offense meant."

"I asked a question, you have answered it honestly," said Lemnok. "Why should I take offense?"

"Good point," said David

"Still, you are not totally correct," continued the demon. "Suppose I were to tell you that demons persecute humans not because they are human but because we are at war with the angels. It is nothing personal regarding you and your people."

"I would say that I have never heard that point of view," replied David. "I thought it had to do with Satan's jealousy toward man because he thought that God loved man more than the angels."

"There might be some truth in that," admitted Lemnok. "However, the real conflict is between the angels, not between us and the Father or humanity. It really has very little to do with humankind. You and your people are meddling in a war that has very little to do with you."

"Am I to just forget what your people do to mine in Hell?" objected David.

"In Hell we follow the commands of the Father," said Lemnok. "It is He who commands that we torment humanity. We are just following orders. It is not a good idea to disobey the Father."

David had real issues with that statement. He knew the Father. The Father was not a torturer. Still, he would not pursue the issue.

"But you must be tired," said Lemnok, "A quiet place has been prepared for you, a place where you may rest."

David followed Lemnok back into the great hall. They proceeded down the corridor to a room just beyond Satan's chambers. Unlike most of the rooms along this hallway, this one had a large golden door. Lemnok opened the door to reveal a small white room illuminated by what appeared to be a small skylight. The room was broken up by several small partitions.

"I regret that the accommodations are so Spartan," said Lemnok. "This room was used as a resting place for Michael's chief lieutenants. Since angels rest upon their wings, there are no beds. It is an inadequacy that I will endeavor to correct soon. But it does offer a door that will provide you some measure of privacy."

David looked around and smiled slightly. "Thank you, Lemnok; it will be more than adequate."

"Then I will take my leave of you," said Lemnok. "There are matters requiring my attention. Please feel free to call upon me if you have any specific needs."

"Thank you," replied David.

Lemnok bowed slightly and departed the room, closing the door behind him. David breathed a sigh of relief. He walked around the room, scanning behind the partitions to confirm what he already knew; there were no windows. He then walked quietly to the door. It was difficult to determine its exact composition. It looked like gold, but it might be composed of angelic metal, a substance with several times the tensile strength of steel. It had a golden handle. He gently pushed upon it, applying ever more force. His suspicions were confirmed; it was locked from the outside. Apparently, they weren't taking any chances on his snooping around. Despite their assurances, he was a prisoner.

David considered his options. He concluded that it might be best if he gated out. Could it be done? Satan claimed that it couldn't, but that was certainly no guarantee. He would try to gate a short distance. His bedroom two miles away was a good choice. Try as he might, the gate wouldn't form. Apparently there was a barrier or field that was preventing it. He leaned up against the wall and considered his options.

He considered the particle weapon. What would it do to a door of angelic metal? He wasn't quite sure. It would probably blow a hole straight through it, one inch in diameter, maybe two. No, that was no good. By the time he blasted his way through, there would be 100 demons waiting for him on the other side.

His mind focused on the problems of gating. What prevented the gate from forming? Was it a barrier or some sort of damping field? There was a difference. If it was a damping field, any gate either made by human or angel would not function within these walls. There was one way to find out, though he had never tried it. Again he attempted to open a gate. A misty field of stars appeared before him. He stepped in and emerged 12 feet away, on the other side of the room.

"Yes," said David. Now he knew what he was dealing with. It was not a damping field, but a barrier that probably surrounded the whole building. Again he tried to gate out. This time he was just outside the wall of the building. Again no luck; the barrier must be right at the outer wall itself. He could gate anywhere within the building, but not beyond it.

He had a scheme to get out, but it carried with it considerable risk. In reality, it was downright crazy. He sat down on the floor and began to concentrate. In midair before him, a particle rifle began to appear. Slowly it assembled itself, from barrel to stock. The process went slower than usual. It was the better part of 40 minutes before the task was complete, and it left David feeling rather drained.

"Yes, much better," he said, giving the weapon a quick once over. This would be far superior to the particle pistol, if it worked. He had some concerns. How would he test it?

There was a commotion out in the hallway. David put his ear to the door. He heard a myriad of footfalls. Then he heard the double doors of Satan's chambers across the hall opening. What was going on? An idea occurred to him. It was crazy, but he had a good feeling about it. He took a deep breath as a misty field of stars appeared before him. He stepped in.

He emerged into the semi-darkness behind the deep blue curtains at the back of Satan's audience chamber. He had made it. He had about 3 feet between the curtain and the wall behind it. He cautiously peered through a tiny gap between the curtains to see a group of about a dozen demons in the chamber, gathered in a circle. Satan was among them, though this time he had taken on his characteristic dark visage. In the middle of their circle knelt an angel whose white robes were spattered with blood. His wings were torn to shreds.

Wait, David knew this angel—it was Gabriel. He felt sick to his stomach.

"Well, well," said Satan. "Who do we have here? Why, I do believe that it is the archangel Gabriel. My, my, you have been careless this day."

"Please spare the melodrama," said Gabriel, pain in his voice.

"You're losing this war," announced Satan, "you know that. Now I have you, and that meddling youth, David Bonner. I shall be transporting both of you to Hell, there to find your own terrible eternities. For you and your angels, it shall be a fiery cavern in the depths of Hell. You have been a pain in my side entirely too long, and now you shall pay the penalty. As for that boy, he helped Serena escape from me, and now he will take her place in the great Sea of Fire."

"You don't have the right," insisted Gabriel. "He is a child of God."

"And a combatant in this war," interrupted Satan. "I have every right. He is mine."

Satan turned as he heard the sudden low hum from behind the curtains. Out stepped David, his particle rifle in hand. "So I'm yours, am I? I think that is a matter of opinion."

The other demons immediately went for their swords, as David trained his weapon on the master of darkness himself.

"I wouldn't do that if I were you," said David, his voice calm. "This weapon is quite capable of turning your master into a footnote in history, and you know it. One pull of this trigger and your war is lost."

"And after you do, my minions will be upon you in seconds," retorted Satan. "You won't get out of here."

"That might be true," admitted David, "but you won't be around to see it, and I suspect that several of them won't be either. The way I look at it, it will be more than worth it to remove you from this universe. One life in exchange for the eternity of billions…I'm cool with that."

Gabriel looked to David. "Shoot," he gasped. "This is your one chance. Without him, his followers will be lost, his war will be lost."

"A strong argument," replied David, drawing closer. He turned to Satan. "What do you think? Shall my friend and I depart, allow you to live to fight another day, or should I blow you to subatomic particles right here and now?"

Satan's rage was in his eyes, but it remained contained there. "And how will you get out? You can't…you are trapped here."

"Actually, I'm not," replied David. He turned to Lemnok. "Remove that angel's shackles. I'm taking him with me."

"You can't gate out," said Satan. "I told you."

"Actually, I can," said David, looking at Satan's minions. "Now, here's the deal. Gabriel and I are walking out of here. Anyone tries to stop us, and your boss gets it."

There was a long silence. It was Satan who finally broke it. "Release the angel…do as he says."

The wave of Lemnok's hand was all it took to make the shackles around Gabriel's wrists and ankles release.

David glanced but a fraction of a second at Gabriel. "Can you walk?"

"Yes," said Gabriel, "but I can't fly."

"You only need to walk." David brought his weapon to within inches of Satan's back. "Sir, we are going to the roof; your people here aren't coming with us. They set foot out of this room within the next five minutes or sound an alarm, and you will live on only in history books. Do I make myself clear?"

"Abundantly," said Satan, barely in control.

By now Gabriel had risen to his feet.

"Ready to go?" asked David.

"Yes," replied Gabriel.

David motioned for Satan to walk to the door, while David walked behind. Gabriel walked at David's side. The others stood in stunned amazement.

"You will instruct the sentry to clear the hallway," said David, who once more looked to Gabriel. "You will need to watch our backs." David drew the particle pistol from his belt and switched on the power. Then he handed it to Gabriel. "Do you know how to use this?"

"Yes," confirmed Gabriel.

"I hope you don't have to," continued David. "But if someone draws a sword, don't hesitate. If that happens, I'm afraid that things are going to fall apart very quickly. Then I'll have to take out this guy first. At this range, that is going to be messy...very messy. Then we'll blast our way out of here, taking out anyone who gets in our way."

Gabriel looked at David incredulously, but said nothing.

"You understand what that means, I assume," said David to Satan.

Satan nodded.

"You have my word that if you cooperate, if no one gets in our way, I will not harm you. You will be free to continue this war of yours." David paused. "You almost had me convinced earlier, convinced that you might be able to change. I was wrong."

Satan didn't reply. He opened the doors to see the sentry beyond. "You are to clear the corridor at once," he commanded. "Instruct all you see that there is to be no violence. These beings are leaving."

The sentry looked into the audience hall briefly, then bowed to his master. "It shall be as you command, my lord."

They waited at the door for at least two minutes. David eyed the other dignitaries in the room suspiciously, almost expecting them to make a stupid move; they didn't.

"It's time," said David, placing the point of the weapon at Satan's back. "Let's move."

As David suspected, the corridor was empty. He figured that it was over 100 yards to the ramp leading to the roof. It was the longest 100 yards he could imagine. They began the journey. From side rooms and passages, demons watched their progress. It would only take one to start a bloodbath, a firefight that would surely have only one outcome.

"Do you really have a plan?" asked Gabriel, holding the pistol in two hands.

"Of course," replied David.

The entire walk to the ramp couldn't have taken more than two minutes, though it seemed much longer. Another minute and they were on the roof, 50 yards from the edge. The place seemed deserted. They made their way toward the edge.

Yes, David had a plan—but it kept changing. Perhaps they should take Satan with them as a hostage. That would surely have put a crimp in his plans for the conquest of Heaven. If Gabriel had been in better condition, if there were three of them and not two, he might have considered it. As it was, escape was their prime goal. Another minute and they were at the edge of the roof. There was no safety railing, no warning sign, nothing to keep a careless traveler from going over the edge. David peered down to confirm that there was nothing between them and the street. It was time.

"You have nowhere to go but down, boy," said Satan. "The drop reminds me of one of the cliffs from which the homosexuals of Hell are forced to cast themselves. Are you prepared to take the leap?"

"Yes," confirmed David. "Let's just call it a leap of faith."

"We have company," noted Gabriel, as several dozen demons stepped onto the roof and began walking in their direction.

"OK then," said David. "Can you run?"

Gabriel looked at David in surprise. "Run where?"

David pointed to the edge of the roof.

"Human humor has always eluded me," said Gabriel.

"I ask again, can you run?"

"Yes," replied Gabriel.

"OK, we have about ten yards to get up some speed. Take my hand and don't let go. We take the plunge feet first. On the count of three, run as fast as you can. One, two, three!"

David and Gabriel darted toward the precipice as Satan watched in disbelief. Then they were airborne. Barely two seconds later, a cloud of stars appeared in their path. The human and angel vanished into the vapors. By the time Satan reached the roof's edge, there was no trace of them. His minions burst into the air in pursuit, yet he knew that they might already be a world away.

David and Gabriel plummeted through the cool mists for several seconds. Then they saw the blue glistening waves before them. They hit the water hard, descending into the depths a good 12 or 15 feet before coming back up to the surface.

David still held onto Gabriel's hand as they broke the surface amid the sounds of flapping gulls and pounding surf. A hundred yards away, the waves broke on a sandbar, and beyond that was a sandy beach.

Gabriel looked around in amazement. "Where are we?"

"The Crystal Sea of the forth level of Heaven," replied David. "It's a great place to surf. We hit harder than I thought we would. I'll do better next time."

"Next time!" exclaimed Gabriel.

"Never mind, just more of that human humor. We need to get to shore. After all, we might well still be in enemy territory. I hope angels can swim."

Apparently they could, especially when the tide was with them. Nevertheless, David had to assist his angelic companion, whose wings were more of a hindrance than a help when it came to swimming. Five minutes saw them staggering onto the white sand beaches, under the amazed eyes of a group of tanned surfers.

"You OK, brother?" asked one of them.

"Apparently this place is not as yet in the hands of Satan's forces," said Gabriel, gazing at the seven concerned onlookers.

"Maybe demons can't swim," suggested David, turning to face the crowd. "We're OK folks, just cliff jumping."

"Cliff jumping…what do you mean dude?" asked one of the bronze-skinned surfers.

"Gotta go," said David, creating another gate. He led Gabriel through and into the mists. A matter of seconds found them before the smoldering remains of Kepler's forest home. The smile quickly evaporated from David's face. "What happened?"

"It would appear that Satan's minions got here before we did," said Gabriel. David walked toward the ruins that were still very hot.

"Old slewfoot is gonna pay," said David, anger in his voice.

"We cannot remain here," cautioned Gabriel. "I doubt that Satan's forces are far away. We must get to the City of Elesia as quickly as possible."

David nodded as he opened another corridor in space and time.

They emerged dripping wet in the audience chamber of the angel Moriah. They, in very fact, interrupted a meeting of the war council. Their appearance was a relief as much as a surprise.

Johann rose immediately from the table and rushed over to David, hugging the shivering youth. "Praise God, you're safe," he said, nearly in tears. "Your mother was told that you had been captured by Satan."

"I was," replied David. "I just turned out to be a bit slipperier than he had anticipated. I even managed to put a healthy scare into him. I believe that few people can make that claim."

"I am very certain that I owe my continued well-being to the incredible bravery of this young man," said Gabriel. "He rescued me from Satan's own audience chamber, and there threatened the Prince of Darkness with his very own existence."

By now, everyone at the conference table had risen to their feet. What they were being told sounded almost unbelievable.

As David recounted the story of his capture, and the subsequent rescue of an archangel, the group was abuzz with amazement. This was the greatest story of heroism of the war—perhaps any war. Holding the devil himself hostage was, well, incredible.

Still, David's action was not without its criticism and that criticism came from a most unlikely source. "You had the opportunity to assassinate Satan," argued Gabriel. "At any point between the audience chamber and the roof it could have been done. Why didn't you do it?"

David didn't seem in the least offended by the comment. He pointed the particle rifle at a nearby wall, charged its capacitor, and pulled the trigger—nothing happened.

"The weapon got wet, now it won't fire?" deduced Gabriel.

"No," replied David, "it never would have fired, not in the audience chamber, not on the roof. I was in too much of a hurry when I assembled it. I was pretty sure that I'd botched the field coil. When I heard it change that first time in the audience chamber, I knew I had. I didn't have time to correct the mistake, how could I? So I went with what I had, and prayed for the best."

"So, it was a bluff?" asked the angel Marlith.

"Afraid so," replied David.

"You would have made a formidable poker player, or a fine field officer," noted General Washington, one of the members of the human delegation. "I salute you, sir."

"Thank you, sir," replied David, who was now beaming with pride. To have the father of his country offer him such a compliment would be something he would treasure for all of his eternity. Indeed, David had not recognized Washington among the group until now. He appeared so much younger than his picture on the dollar bill.

"But to jump off of a nearly three hundred foot tall building," said Johann, "not knowing for certain if you would be able to gate out during the fall was a terrible risk."

"It was an exceptional situation," said David. "It was the only option that I could see at the time. Anyway, it worked…we're here."

"You need to go see your mother right away," said Johann. "She has been worried sick about you."

"Yes, sir," said David, turning to leave.

He didn't have to go far. Having heard of his miraculous return, his mother met him right beyond the door. She cried tears of joy as they headed down the hallway together.

It was nearly a minute before Gabriel continued. "Satan claims to have captured over fifty million of our people during the past several days. He plans to offer them a choice. If they swear their allegiance to him, he will spare them. They will assume the simple duties of the lowliest of the angels. Some will even assist in tormenting human souls in Hell. Those who refuse will be condemned to some vast furnace he has contrived, a furnace that will reduce us to little more than a flaming heap of glowing bones. He plans to send the first group there in a matter of days, once his entire army is here."

The war council looked at each other. Was this just one of Satan's boasts, or could he make good on this terrible threat?

"Satan claims he will eventually have a force of 160 million," continued Gabriel. "How many have we gathered here in Elesia?"

"From all of the planes, twenty-seven million," replied Michael. "We know that there are other angels scattered here and there about the planes. There could easily be fifty or sixty million. But they are not an effective fighting force as it is. We will continue to make efforts to contact them. Still, I fear that Satan's forces will capture most of them before we can rescue them. They are just too scattered and disorganized. If we could only return those trapped on Earth more rapidly, our numbers here would swell to 100 or 130 million. Then, we might be able to face him on the field of battle."

"I have had some success in recruiting saints with military experience for this conflict," said General Washington. "I believe you can count on about a hundred thousand within the next few days. Equipped with those special rifles, they might make a formidable force, despite their numbers."

The commander in chief of the human military, General Cornelius Decius Galeo, stood to his feet; the council chambers grew silent. "Never in all of my twenty centuries have I heard of a weapon of the sort described by the honorable Doctor Kepler. Its effectiveness and the bravery of those wielding it allowed three hundred thousand angels to be evacuated from Ceranda. You have literally rewritten the book of warfare. If we had a sufficient number of them, human foot soldiers could become the pivotal factor in this war, even if the angelic forces were outnumbered. Can you produce a large number of these weapons, Doctor Kepler?"

Johann shook his head. "My people have produced about two thousand of those rifles to date. To equip an army of the size of the one General Washington speaks of would take a month, at least."

"We don't have a month," objected Gabriel. "Eventually, Satan will completely control all of the planes of Heaven, save this one. By then our captured brethren will no doubt find themselves within a terrible furnace in Hell. And I assure you, the time will come when he breaches the wall that protects us. Perhaps he will force humans to gate his people across. Perhaps he will discover another way, but I doubt that we have a month."

"Then it's up to my friend Nikola Tesla," said Johann. "I have faith that his mission to Hell was not in vain. He will find a way to open the gates to Earth, make clear the path of the angels trapped there."

"He had best do it soon," said Marlith. "I fear that soon there may not be a Heaven to send them to…at least not as we know it."

Chapter 16

For five hours David sat on a stool working on the telesphere. He was tired, but he just couldn't give up on this project, too much was riding on it. The small cluttered suite of rooms that had become Johann's new laboratory in Elesia was a mess. They had pulled out of his old lab quickly, and from the looks of things, none too soon. Several others were doing their best to set up the other equipment. Some of the instruments had required months to calibrate, and so wouldn't be working again anytime soon.

June was asleep on a comfortable couch nearby. She insisted on being near her son. David didn't mind in the least.

"Done," whispered David, placing the new circuitry module into the base of the telesphere. The idea to do this had come to him during his visit with the Father. In very fact, it was God's guidance that made this thing possible. Now it was time to test the new signal discriminator.

The telesphere began to glow. Abruptly, a sphere of snow appeared before him. There was something in the snow, but he couldn't quite make it out. Was it a face?

"Come on," whispered David, adjusting the new discriminator, in an attempt to pull the distant signal out of the static. It was a person, he could see that now, it was becoming clearer.

"David, is that you?" It was a faint voice, just perceptible above the static.

"It's me," said David, making further adjustments. "Is that you Nikola?"

"Yes," came the reply, stronger this time. "It's good to hear your voice. I am sorry about the other day. Understand that I had to do it."

"It's OK," said David. "I guess I'm needed here. OK, here goes." Suddenly the strength of the signal increased ten fold. It was still a bit snowy, but better than David had anticipated. He could see Nikola clearly. He was in the lab along with two other men. "I'm sending you a schematic diagram that will help you make the necessary upgrades on the telesphere over there. Then we should have a much better signal."

"Got them," said Nikola. "You need to know, we found the power source; it is in the City of Sheol. We plan to hit it with an explosive device in about four or five days, once we work out a few problems in the delivery method."

"The sooner the better," said David. "Things here are not so good. We need to get the angels on Earth back here."

"I'll keep you informed of our progress," said Nikola. The signal was starting to degrade. "I'll contact you in twenty-four hours. In the meantime, I'll upgrade the telesphere. Tesla out."

"Way to go, son," said June, placing her hand on David's shoulder. "The Father has given you a priceless gift. We're going to get through this, so long as we have people like you. Now, why don't you get some sleep? You're going to have to be at your best in the days to come."

David nodded and rose to his feet. He would let the others know about the new telesphere modifications then get some sleep. Right now he felt really great; he was making a difference.

Two days later, dark angel Lenar was climbing high into the starless sky. Rarely had Lenar felt so very uncomfortable. He carried the dummy bomb in the harness attached to his chest, below a sky filled with shifting green aurora. The bomb wasn't that heavy, but the combination of high altitude, cold, and the exertion needed to reach an altitude of five miles were taking their toll.

"If God intended angels to fly this high, He would have given us bigger wings," he grumbled. He knew why he was up here—no demons. Who in their right mind would fly at this altitude? It had to be negative 60 or 70 degrees.

Below, he saw the faint glow of the crystals that had been set out to mark the target. It was time. He had done this four times already today, five times yesterday, and each time he had dropped the bomb a bit closer to the target. When was Tesla going to be satisfied? He slowed his speed and prepared to make the drop. He made a steep 180-degree turn to the right, then he took the bomb in his hand and dropped it. He accelerated and descended, heading for the high mountains to the east.

Five miles below, Nikola and Abaddon watched the sky. They couldn't make out Lenar amid the shifting lights. This was a good thing. If they couldn't, then neither would demons guarding the city.

"The bomb has been dropped," said Tesla, looking at the small gray box in his hand. "It will be a couple of minutes before we know."

Abaddon turned to the great human scientist. "How many times does Lenar need to do this? He has this thing mastered."

"I want to see how he does this time," said Nikola, barely looking up from the readings on the box.

"You said that last time," objected Abaddon.

Nikola remained focused on the readout before him. "If he gets it this time…we do it for real tomorrow."

The bomb made a whistling noise as it fell through the thickening atmosphere. Nikola couldn't help but smile as it struck the ground, a mere 150 yards from the target. They were ready.

An hour later, Nikola was on the telesphere in the Spirit communicating with David and Johann. Since he'd made the modifications David had recommended, the image produced by the unit had returned close to its normal clarity, even with the increased inter-dimensional density.

"I'm still a bit concerned with the yield of the bomb," admitted David. "I mean, sixty kilotons, do you really think you need that much yield? I'd think five or ten would be more than enough to destroy Sheol. Keep in mind, this isn't a typical nuclear explosion. Its effects will likely extend into higher dimensions."

"They had fears like this regarding the trinity test—the first nuclear detonation on Earth," said Nikola. "Those fears were unfounded. As I see it, we're only going to get one shot at this. If we don't do the job the first time, I doubt we will get a second chance."

"It's your call, my friend." said Johann, "Do what you think best."

"But sixty kilotons," repeated David. "Look, could you send me your telemetry data from the flight? Maybe it will tell me more about the risks."

"Transmitting," said Nikola, turning to the Spirit's computer terminal.

"When will you make the drop?" asked Johann.

"Tomorrow at 1430 your time," replied Nikola. He paused. That is, 1430 hours, your time at the mansion. I am sorry for your loss."

"That place was near and dear to my heart," replied Johann, "a gift from God. But, it was a thing, and it will be replaced when this war is over. My concerns are with you. Take care my friend."

"I shall," replied Nikola. "By the way, be certain to close your gate and the one in Elesia in the event that there is a powerful electromagnetic pulse from the detonation. I doubt that there will be, but we'd best err on the side of safety. You should be able to move the angels from Earth back to Heaven by 1440."

As the sphere went blank, Nikola turned off most of the Spirit's electronics. He descended the stairway, where he was met by Abaddon and Lenar.

"We are all set for tomorrow," he announced. He turned to Lenar. "One or two more drops, and you can retire from bomber duty."

Lenar smiled. "I don't mind in the least. I was just tired of dropping those duds, as you call them."

"I assure you, the next two will be quite real," said Nikola. "Just make sure that you fly fast enough to get out of the blast range. Believe me, this will be an explosion like none you have ever seen before. Don't look straight into it."

Lenar considered telling this eminent scientist that his last comment made no sense, bright light would not damage his eyes, but he decided against it. Right now, he was just eager to drop the bomb.

Abaddon had seemed deep in thought until now. "My friends, before we drop that thing, there is something else I wish to see to. In the lower caverns, millions of my children rest in hibernation for lack of food. I propose to release all but half a million of them into diverse regions of Hell, give them an opportunity to renew their strength, live off the land. We've been waiting for the right time; I believe that time is now."

Lenar smiled broadly. "Yes, I like that idea."

"Live off the land?" asked Nikola.

"Yes," replied Abaddon. "My children are most remarkable. They have the ability to read the aura of any living creature. They can recognize a soul that is relatively pure, and one that feeds upon evil. Their instincts are indeed simple. They will release and defend those whose hearts are truly repentant, even as they feed upon those who are evil—unrepentant humans and demons alike. They hunt in packs to this end. They are numerous enough now to raise true chaos in Hell. In the process, they would grow stronger, be fruitful, and multiply. I shall send them forth in groups of a hundred thousand through the portal, to places of relatively benign climate. I had already decided the where and how; it is just a matter of when. That *when* is now."

"It should create an interesting diversion," said Lenar.

Within an hour, all had been set in motion, and the children of Abaddon set forth from their resting places, flying through the tunnels of Refuge and into the now active ring. They emerged into a multitude of places where the hunting would be favorable. The exodus continued for the better part of four hours. Hell would now have a new army of tormentors, and an army of deliverers.

With the communications concluded, the sphere went clear in the laboratory in Elesia. David turned to Johann, but said nothing. He wondered if he were the only one concerned with the size of the blast proposed by Tesla. Apparently he was.

He needed to keep producing particle rifles for the war effort, but right now he was too troubled. He removed what looked like a small sliver of glass from the telesphere, replacing it with another. Then he proceeded to another room that contained his computer. It really didn't look much like a computer. It lacked a mouse, keyboard, and even a monitor. It was a small light gray box with nothing more than an on switch. He pressed it and placed the small shard in a small port in the front. The computer responded to the weak electrical impulses produced by his own mind. In reality, it was an extension of his mind, solving in seconds problems that might have otherwise taken him days.

An image of the pictures and numerical data produced by the Spirit's scientific instruments appeared in midair as a three-dimensional display before him. For the next three hours he stared at it. Tesla's conclusions were correct; the demonic City of Sheol was the source of the field that was preventing the angels from moving from Earth to Heaven.

Sheol wasn't a city, really, it was a launching point where demons left their physical bodies and traveled to Earth as spiritual entities only. Their physical bodies were left there in Sheol. It was composed of a repeating series of glowing crystalline pillars and crossbeams built upon what appeared to be a huge marble slab over three miles on a side. Exactly how this place worked had remained a mystery to everyone here. Now that was a question he should have asked Lemnok while he had the chance. He wondered if Lemnok even knew. He dove still deeper into the data; there wasn't much time.

Nikola Tesla and Abaddon emerged from the misty field of stars to set foot on a 4,000-feet-high mountaintop, 22 miles north of the City of Sheol. It was distinctly chilly here, only a few degrees above freezing. Yet compared to the barren frigid wasteland around Refuge, it seemed almost warm. Sheol looked so much like a human city from here, a dazzling network of lights laid out in true geometric precision.

Here, the aurora seemed to descend to the surface in a narrowing and brightening cone of light. Never had he seen such a sight. Where was a camera when you needed it?

Three miles to the east, the great Sea of Fire extended to the horizon, a glowing ocean of horror and pain. This mountain formed part of a range that paralleled the coast for hundreds of miles. It prevented the warm winds from the sea from penetrating far into the interior of the Dark Continent.

"At any given time there might be millions or even tens of millions of demons in that city," noted Abaddon. "Yet their spirits are far from this

THE WAR IN HEAVEN

place, creating chaos on your own world. With the war underway in Heaven, I cannot say for certain how many demons remain in the city."

Nikola scanned the city carefully with his binoculars. "It's too far away to tell how many demons are there. It is, however, the perfect place from which to observe the detonation of a sixty kiloton bomb." He glanced at his wrist watch with the red LED display. "Kurt and Lenar should be gating in right about now."

"They are closer to the blast than we will be," noted Abaddon.

"Yes," confirmed Nikola, "fourteen miles. But they will not be in a direct line of sight of the blast, far from it. There are two high mountain ranges between them and ground zero. I didn't want Lenar to have to fly very far to his extraction point. Don't worry, they'll be just fine. In a little less than two hours, Sheol will cease to exist."

Lenar and Kurt gated unto a high mesa a few hundred feet down from the western summit of the westernmost of two ridges that separated the great Sea of Fire from the interior of the Dark Continent. A near freezing breeze swept down from the ridge as they carefully scanned their surroundings. It took several minutes to confirm that they were indeed alone.

"I don't like this wind," noted Kurt. "It will move the fallout from the detonation in our direction."

"We will be out of here long before that happens," assured Lenar.

Kurt helped Lenar prepare for his flight, as he had for all of the test flights. They got the weapon secured to the harness and calibrated the small digital altimeter and compass that Lenar would wear on his wrist. As expected, the compass pointed directly toward Sheol. Last, they tested the small radio communications device that Nikola had fabricated.

"It's not too powerful as two-way radios go," said Kurt, pulling his own unit from his belt. "In that you will have a straight line of sight, you should be able to stay in contact with both Nikola and me...but the mountains will prevent me from contacting Nikola and visa versa. You may need to relay messages."

"We've gone over all of this before," noted Lenar, wearily. "I'll take off to the west, gain altitude, then swing east. I'll release the bomb on Nikola's signal. You'll hear my release announcement. Just be ready to depart on my return."

"We've gone over this before," replied Kurt.

Lenar smiled, though slightly. "I think we're ready."

"May the Father guide and protect you," said Kurt.

"And you," replied Lenar. "Remember, if any demons show up, just get out of here, I'll get back myself."

Kurt nodded and stepped back as Lenar bolted skyward, heading out across the rolling hills to the west. It would take well over an hour for him to reach the proper altitude. Now it would be a waiting game. There were a bunch of things that could go wrong in the meantime. They would pray for the best.

The displayed figures before David had long ago become a blur. He now sat asleep before his computer. In his sleep he dreamed. He dreamed of lightning and thunder; against the backdrop of a black starless sky, a mighty whirlwind swept up everything in its path. The whirlwind was consuming the entire world like some insatiable dragon. The portion of the world that was being devoured was being swept away into some netherworld realm, scattered to the ethereal winds. Yet, it didn't end there. Even as the world was being destroyed, the ethereal realm was being poisoned by the shattered world's very essence. He was watching it all from a hill that stood above the whirlwind. From the hill, he could see all of these things and the dire consequences of this terrible event. It was horrifying.

Then the very Earth shook beneath him, as if in a terrible earthquake. It knocked David to his knees. The whirlwind that was consuming the world around him expanded, threatening to draw the hill on which he stood into the maelstrom as well. The roaring wind was nearly deafening. Then fire erupted from the whirlpool of chaos before him. He fell on his face, terrified.

"Oh Lord, save me!" cried David, covering his head and closing his eyes.

Then there was total silence. It was half a minute before David looked up to see only a bright glowing star in the darkness.

"There was an earthquake, but I was not in it," said a quiet voice. "Then came the mighty wind, but I was not there either. Nor was I in the raging fire that followed it."

David rose slowly to his knees, looking into the brilliant light. He knew that voice, knew it well. It quieted his fears. "Father, what have I just seen? I don't understand."

"Yes, you do," said the Father.

David thought back to the incredible tragedy he had just witnessed. He tried to clear his mind, see deeper into its symbolism. The world he saw being ripped asunder was not just any world; it lay at the very heart of outer darkness; it was Hell. And this was no normal whirlwind of air shaped by the clashing of contrasting air masses. It was something far more primal—a rip in space time itself, a wormhole.

David had dealt with wormholes before, many times, everyone in Heaven did. The saints used them routinely to cover vast distances in seconds. Jesus had used one on Earth when He entered the locked room where His disciples hid in fear from the authorities after His resurrection. But this one was different. Those wormholes were a bending of the fabric of space and hyperspace. This one was not so subtle. It was an actual rip, punched in the fabric of space, like a black hole.

Everything was falling into place. In that moment, he understood a great mystery—the real secret of Sheol. In a hyperspherical universe, it was the south magnetic pole.

"Of course," he whispered. "Why didn't I see it earlier?"

"Because it wasn't time," replied the Father.

"Sheol—it was built at the confluence of the magnetic lines of force. It is the south magnetic pole of the universe. I don't know how else to describe it, but I understand. I know why Satan built Sheol where he did. From there a spirit could ride the field lines effortlessly to anywhere in the universe he desired. It's how demons ride to Earth and back again, expending practically no energy."

"Yes, continue," urged the Father.

"But he's not sending demons to Earth this time. He's sending gravitons, gravitons that are making the barriers between dimensions more difficult to cross, preventing angels from returning to Heaven from Earth."

"But there is a danger in this," said the Father.

"Yes," replied David, who had now forgotten his fear. "The injection of gravitons is further weakening the fabric of space time at the point where space time is already very tenuous." Then the reality hit him. "And we're going to detonate a sixty kiloton bomb right there. Space time will breach! That is what I saw in the vision! I can't allow it to happen."

Instantly, David was awake. He looked around…the lab was empty.

"Time?" he asked the computer.

"1411 hours," said a synthetic female voice.

"Oh no," gasped David.

There was no time to contact Johann, no time to explain what he had just witnessed to anyone. He rushed to the telesphere at the far end of the room and opened a channel to Refuge. He prayed that he got an answer. It took only a few seconds to make contact. Within the sphere of light, he saw Bedillia.

"Hi David," she said smiling. Then she saw his grave expression. "What's wrong?"

"We've got to call off the bombing of Sheol," said David, his tone frantic. "If that bomb goes off, it will rip a hole in space time that will wreak who knows how much havoc. It could destroy all of Hell, or even worse; it will scatter a huge cloud of highly ionized plasma, right in the direction of Earth."

Clearly Bedillia didn't understand all that David was talking about, but she did get the picture—it was really bad. "How long do we have?"

"Less than half an hour," replied David.

"Did you discuss this with Dr. Kepler?" asked Bedillia. "Does he agree with you on this?"

"There isn't time," replied David. "Look, you've just got to trust me on this. I had a vision. I know how crazy that sounds, but you've got to help me."

Bedillia paused for just a few seconds. "No, it doesn't sound crazy, David, I believe you. Look, I'll try to reach Nikola, stop him if I can. I'm heading to the ring room right now. I only hope there's time."

The sphere went clear. David looked back to the computer, which now displayed the time—1413.

David ran off to locate Johann and the others. He knew pretty much what they would say. He might find himself in a good bit of trouble. Right now, that didn't matter. He just hoped that he hadn't acted too late.

Chapter 17

On the way to the ring room, Bedillia had more than a few misgivings about what she was doing. Suppose David was wrong? He was little more than a kid, certainly not a senior member of Kepler's science team. They had discussed the importance of this mission. If something wasn't done, and done soon, Heaven might well fall to the forces of Satan. Then she encountered Julie. Someone else had to know what had happened. She filled Julie in on her encounter with David and what she had been told as they rushed toward a secure storage room, which housed spheres that were used to power return trips to the ring room.

The dark angelic sentry at the door to the room that held this most precious commodity in Refuge also insisted on being told why a sphere was being requisitioned without prior approval. All the while, the clock kept ticking. Bedillia was almost tempted to go through the gate without a sphere, hoping that she gated to the exact location to which Abaddon and Nikola had gated several hours before. Eventually, the sentry yielded to this highest ranking human, and Bedillia and Julie were on their way to the ring room.

"Won't you need a heavy coat?" asked Julie.

"No time," replied Bedillia. "It isn't that cold where I'm going. My only concerns are getting there in time, and hoping that I gate in at the right point. Since I wasn't going on this mission, I wasn't paying that close of attention to the coordinates. I think I remember them, but I'm not sure."

"But if you're wrong, you might freeze or be captured," objected Julie.

"I'll just have to take that chance," replied Bedillia. "I'll give you the coordinates before I leave. Anyway, if worse comes to worse, I have my ticket back." Bedillia held up the small sphere. "I'll make sure not to lose it this time."

In a couple minutes, Bedillia stood before the ring. She took a deep breath. "Lord, let my memory be sharp on this one." Then she stepped through the ring, into the misty stars, and vanished.

A few seconds later, she was on a windy mountain ridge. She could see the city of Sheol far to the south. There was a strange sound in the air, almost like static electricity. To the east, she saw the dreaded Sea of Fire glowing brightly in the night. Far off on the eastern horizon, she saw the blue lightning of a distant brimstone and sulfuric acid storm. Her mind wandered back to stories of her daughter, adrift on that awful sea.

She looked around the ridge. Abaddon and Nikola were nowhere to be seen. No, she had to be close. She scanned the ridge again. It was a full minute before she picked out two figures, a good 300 yards farther up the ridge. Yes, she was fairly certain it was them. Should she yell out to them? Suppose she was wrong? She started to run in their direction.

The aurora that arched up from the city and scattered out into the sky overhead added illumination to the scene, still, depth was hard to determine, and the ridge was very rocky indeed. After several minutes, she had scarcely covered a third of the distance. Still, she couldn't be sure it was them. She looked to the sky; there were no demon sentries, not this far out from the city. She would have to take the chance.

Bedillia cupped her hands around her mouth and cried out in her loudest voice. There was no response. Maybe it was just an oddly shaped rock formation that she was seeing, and not Abaddon and Nikola. She called out again; still nothing. She quickened her pace.

"I'm at altitude," announced Lenar, into the two-way radio. His wings beat erratically. He seemed to be in difficulty. "This climb has been the hardest of all. I don't understand why. I'm right at the edge of this thin glowing mist. It is cold, and there is a strangeness here, like electricity all around me. That couldn't make this thing blow up, could it?"

"Absolutely not," replied Nikola. His voice was full of static. It had gotten worse and worse as Lenar had approached the rising mists. "You've got eight minutes to release."

"Eight minutes," confirmed Lenar. "I hope I can make it."

From the ground, Abaddon watched the proceedings. He again examined the silly looking goggles with dark tinted glass. He shook his head. Tesla seemed to be having fun with this whole operation; he was sure of it. He was eager to use the largest, most powerful toy he had ever had. But Abaddon just wanted to get it over with and get everyone back to Refuge safely. Right now, he was concerned about Lenar.

Abaddon turned to the side; he was certain he had heard something. It sounded like a voice. He looked down the ridge to pick out something moving amid the rocks. He turned to Nikola. "Hand me the binoculars, if you please."

Totally absorbed, Nikola didn't so much as look away from the readings on his gray box as he gave the binoculars to Abaddon.

Abaddon turned the binoculars on the moving form. "It looks like a person," he said, focusing on the mysterious figure. "It's a woman. I think it is Bedillia."

"Bedillia?" asked Nikola. "What would she be doing out here?"

"I will find out," said Abaddon moving several steps away, and preparing to take flight.

"Get back right away," warned Nikola. "I don't want you in flight when the bomb goes off."

"Why not?" asked Abaddon, "Lenar will be."

With those words he took to the air, heading in Bedillia's direction. Nikola glanced away from his readings for just a few seconds before focusing upon them once more.

Bedillia held her breath as one of the two figures took flight and headed her way. She was relieved to see that the flying being's wings were like those of a bird and not a bat.

"Bedillia, what are you doing here?" asked Abaddon, landing but a dozen feet in front of her. "We are only minutes from exploding this bomb of Tesla's."

"That's the thing," said Bedillia, who by now was both breathless and shivering. "We have to call it off. David said something was wrong. There is no time to explain; we have to stop this."

"OK," said Abaddon, "we call it off." He took Bedillia in his arms and bolted skyward. He prayed that it was not too late.

It took only 30 seconds to make the flight back to Nikola. He looked at Abaddon incredulously when he heard the news.

"David has opposed this mission since yesterday," he objected. "I don't see why, nor do I agree with his conclusion. This is going to work, trust me."

There was a moment of hesitation. "As the leader of Refuge, it is my duty to weigh the merits of all points of view. We might decide to do this mission later, but for right now we are calling Lenar back...calling this thing off. That is my decision."

Nikola appeared disappointed but did not press the issue. He pressed the transmit button. "Lenar, we need you to abort the drop, I repeat, abort the drop. Return to the extraction point and gate out."

He released the button. All he heard was static. He repeated the order still nothing.

"What's wrong?" asked Abaddon.

"It must be the ionization in that plume about the city," replied Nikola. "The signal isn't getting through."

"So what's he going to do?" asked Bedillia, scanning the sky, trying to make out the form of a dark angel.

"We'd anticipated this," continued Nikola. "In the event that Lenar lost contact, he was to drop the device on schedule. Don't even think about it, Abaddon, you'd never reach him in time. I'm sorry. But I assure you, nothing is going to happen except the destruction of that city. I'll keep trying to reach him, but I don't think it will do any good."

High above the city, near the brightest region of the glowing plasma, Lenar prepared to make the drop. He was in considerable pain. His skin burned as the electricity coursed through his body. Again he tried to contact Tesla, but with no success.

He was losing altitude. He was 300 feet below the agreed upon drop altitude, but he didn't have the strength to climb. Indeed, he couldn't even maintain this altitude. He banked hard to the left, pirouetting 180 degrees, before returning to level flight. He put the radio away and took the bomb in hand. This was it.

It was so difficult to see. He lined up the shot and released the bomb. It plunged swiftly into the lights of the city, vanishing from sight. He increased his angle of descent to gain speed and flapped his wings with all of his might, what was left of it.

"The bomb is away," announced Nikola, staring at the display on the gray box. "There is nothing we can do now. But I assure you, nothing out of the ordinary is going to happen. This is going to work. Within minutes of the detonation, angels will be able to move freely between Earth and Heaven." He turned to Bedillia. "I'm afraid I don't have an extra set of glasses for you. You'll need to look away when it detonates."

Tense minutes passed. The bomb would detonate a mere 500 feet above the city to maximize the effect of the blast. The group took cover behind a nearby set of boulders. It was almost time.

Bedillia felt a sense of terrible dread. She couldn't explain why, but she believed David totally.

"Ten seconds," announced Nikola, putting his dark glasses on.

Abaddon held Bedillia close in an attempt to keep her warm as the last seconds went by. Then there was a flash, the likes of which had never been seen in Hell. For a moment, this realm of eternal night became as bright as day. There was no sound, at least not immediately, just light and intense heat.

Nikola stood there, most of his body protected from the heat by the boulders. Never in his life had he seen such a sight. A billowing mushroom-shaped cloud whose stem was as bright as the sun, rose into the sky. Along the ground, an ever expanding luminous fog spread out in all directions, blasting then melting everything in its way amid unimaginable heat.

As the cloud expanded, its luminosity slowly diminished. Nikola removed his goggles to see the work of his own hand in all its splendor. The glowing mists that had emanated from the city were gone, as was the city for that matter, hidden from end to end in a hot cloud of radioactive dust.

Abaddon scanned the destruction in amazement. "It is a fitting end for a place intended to promote the fall of humankind to damnation. I never thought I would see a day such as this."

Then the sounds of the apocalyptic demolition reached the trio as a deep ground shaking rumble. By this time, the mushroom cloud had risen a full four miles into the air. Nikola scanned the destruction with his binoculars. Here and there he saw fires burning beneath the fading clouds of destruction rolling along the ground. Secondary explosions of an unknown nature erupted here and there within the city. Then he went for his radio. He tried several times to contact Lenar, but the airwaves were crammed with static.

Fear gripped Bedillia's heart as Nikola called out to him on the radio again and again. She had heard that Lenar was having trouble just before the bomb drop. Suppose he hadn't made it?

A somber atmosphere had fallen over the group. They didn't want to contemplate the possibility that something had happened to Lenar, something very bad. However, it was looking grimmer by the second. Nikola turned up the volume of the radio.

"Lenar calling Tesla," said a breathless voice through the relentless static of the radio. "You never told me that blast wave would be that hot. I don't think my wings will ever be the same."

The whole group moved closer to the radio. It seemed like a miracle.

"It's good to hear your voice," said Nikola who barely hid his emotions. "Sorry about the heat. Where are you?"

"Above the valley between the first and second ridge," came the reply. "I've been trying to call you, but I couldn't get through. My strength came back quickly after I got away from those glowing mists, or whatever you want to call them. I don't think I've ever flown as fast as I have these past two minutes. I should be at the extraction point in about ten minutes or so. I will probably lose contact with you once I cross the mountains."

"Right," replied Nikola. "We're going to stay here for a short while to see if there are any strange aftereffects from the blast. We'll meet you back at Refuge in about half an hour."

"See you then," replied Lenar. His voice was fading as he drew close to the limit of the range of the radio. "By the way; congratulations on your accomplishment." There was another message after that, but it was hidden by the static.

The three remained for 20 minutes as the fires faded and the cloud dispersed. It was the rising radiation level that finally compelled Nikola to abandon their position.

"An unusual amount of radiation," noted Nikola, "a bit more than I would have expected…and of a different type too. We might want to monitor this over the next few days."

"I guess David was wrong after all," said Bedillia, as the team gathered up their equipment. "I was so sure he was right. Maybe I was foolish coming here."

"No, you were being prudent," said Abaddon. "I think we were just lucky today."

The three travelers vanished into the starry mists, leaving a smoldering radioactive city in their wake. But amid the radioactive wasteland something was happening. In the midst of growing electrical discharges around ground zero, a strange breeze was blowing straight into the center of the blast from all directions.

It was 1452 hours when a continuous stream of angels from Earth began to pour through the gate at Elesia. Still others entered the second level of Heaven through the hastily prepared gate that Johann and his collaborators had brought from his house before it had been destroyed. Tesla's plan had succeeded.

An hour later, Nikola Tesla contacted the war council by telesphere from Abaddon's audience chamber in Refuge. The bomb had been successful; Sheol had been destroyed. He was the hero of the day.

When David Bonner was called before the 20-member war council several hours later, he realized that he had much to answer for. He had nearly jeopardized the angelic position in Elesia, based on what might well have been nothing but a dream.

"You didn't even consult us," objected Michael.

"There wasn't time," replied David, who seemed totally unrepentant for his actions, "and I'm afraid this isn't over yet. You had better get as many angels through from Earth as you can…while you can."

"And why is that?" asked another angel.

"Because the gate is going to shut down again," replied David. "Still, you might have enough time to get the angels across. After that, the bomb that was dropped on Sheol is going to change everything."

"Because?" asked Michael.

"Because that was not a normal nuclear bomb that was detonated," replied David. "The explosive radius of that bomb had hyperdimensional characteristics. It exceeded the mean cohesive strength of the space time continuum in the region of Sheol."

"Please," interrupted Washington. "Would you tell us what you think is going to happen in a language we might all understand?"

"OK," said David. "The bomb destroyed Sheol, but now you have a different problem, one that is potentially far more serious. In a normal explosion, like those you are familiar with general, the blast extends out, up, and across from the point of the explosion in three dimensions, but not this one. This blast extends across all of the extra dimensions of the known universe, all thirteen of them. That makes this explosion vastly more destructive. The worst place in the universe to use it was Sheol."

"But why?" objected Gabriel.

"I was wondering the same thing," admitted Johann. "We've known that Sheol was special, that it was the departure point for demonic spirits on their way to Earth, but we never understood why. I suppose you are going to tell us."

"I am," confirmed David. "Sheol was built at a natural weak point in space time, the magnetic south pole of the universe. In that way, demonic spirits could easily make the trip from Hell to any place within the universe by simply riding the lines of force. It is one of only two places in the universe from which it is possible."

"I assume that the other would be the north pole of the universe," replied Washington.

"Yes," confirmed David. "Think of space time as a thick pane of glass holding water in a huge aquarium. What we have just done in setting off that bomb is to go off and strike that pane at its thinnest point with a sledge hammer. It sent a radiating set of cracks all around the point of impact, and at the point of impact is a hole, not a big hole, not yet, but it is growing. Ever more water is rushing out of the aquarium. What is worse is that the environment beyond the aquarium reacts violently with water. That is why the glass was there, to keep them apart."

The blank look David got from the council, told him that he still hadn't got his point across. They still didn't understand the gravity of the situation.

"Hell itself is going to be consumed at an increasing rate," said David, "pulled into hyperspace ever more rapidly. As it falls into the hyperspace, it will be converted into a stream of high-energy particles. Satan had been blocking the route of the angels between Earth and Heaven by injecting a stream of gravitons into hyperspace, a beam directed at Earth. The high energy particles entering this hole will follow that same route. They will eventually irradiate the Earth to such a degree as to strip off its atmosphere and sterilize all life on its surface. That is what we are looking at. That is what I was trying to prevent."

"It is just a theory," said Johann. "How could we know such a thing had happened?"

"The hole would be easily visible," replied David. "It would emit large quantities of X-rays. That's how you'd know."

"If this thing has happened, how could we close this hole?" asked Cornelius.

"I don't know," admitted David. "The hole is at the south magnetic pole of the universe. Perhaps we could increase the flux, the power of the magnetic field at the north pole? That might drive the particles, the charged plasma, back through the hole. It might even seal it. I don't know. Thing is, I couldn't even begin to guess how to do it."

"But where is the north pole of the universe?" asked Johann.

There was a long pause. It seemed a crazy notion—the north pole of the universe.

It was Cornelius who broke the silence. "I think I know. The opposite of the depths of Hell would be the summit of Heaven. It is Zion, in the holiest place. Psalms 48:2 says, 'beautiful for situation, the joy of the whole earth, is mount Zion, on the sides of the north, the city of the great King.' The side of the north? Why would it be the side of the north? Unless it is at the north pole of the universe."

"Yes, of course, that makes sense," said David. "I always wondered why it said the side of the north, rather than any other cardinal direction."

"But there is no evidence that there is a problem," objected Gabriel.

"Believe me, there will be soon," said David.

Nikola couldn't sleep. He had paced the tunnels of Refuge for hours. This should have been the most glorious day of his life, but it wasn't. He knew what David was going through in Heaven. David was so certain of his figures. Yes, he was just a child in comparison to his years; however, during the past several years he had come to take what this youth said seriously. His mind was made up. He headed for Abaddon's audience chamber. He was not surprised to find the dark angel there at the end of the table, alone, deep in thought.

"I would have thought that you would have been in bed by now," he said, without even looking up.

"I've been thinking about what David said," admitted Nikola. "Suppose he is right."

"Then I would say that we are all in considerable trouble," said Abaddon.

"I'd like to go back there," said Nikola.

Abaddon looked up in surprise. "When?"

"Right now," replied Nikola.

"But you said that it would be highly radioactive," objected Abaddon.

"Not to us," replied Nikola. "Our bodies regenerate so rapidly that I don't think residual radiation is much of a threat."

"Very well," said Abaddon, rising to his feet. "Grab your gear. We shall depart in one hour."

Cordon was sitting at the round granite meeting table of Governor Molock's audience chamber with his aide and long-time friend Lieutenant Rolf when a messenger brought the news of the destruction of the City of Sheol. He looked up from his paperwork astonished. "How?" he asked.

"Some terrible weapon that brought destruction to the entire city in one great flash of light," replied the messenger. "Afterward, a great billowing cloud towered over the city."

Cordon had heard enough to surmise what had happened. He had seen such a thing when he had journeyed to Earth many years ago. Then, he had been assigned as a tempter and general malefactor. It was a task that he took no great pleasure in. It had been a waste of his talents. But that sight had intrigued him—the detonation of a nuclear bomb in the Mohave Desert.

"Lord Beelzebub is no more," continued the messenger. "He and his lieutenants vanished in the blast. My lord, you are now the ranking minion in Hell. I await your orders."

For a moment Cordon was stunned. Never had he imagined such a situation as this unfolding. This morning, millions of small flying creatures had appeared all over Hell, and now this, the destruction of Sheol. They were linked, of that much he was certain. Still, he had to organize his priorities. He had to support the master. He could not allow Heaven to be reinforced by angels from Earth. He wasn't sure how he could prevent it, or even if he could prevent it. He would first need to consult with experts. "What of the minions Cerenak and Wormwood?"

"They were in Sheol when it was destroyed," replied the messenger. "They are gone with Lord Beelzebub."

This just kept getting worse. "Very well, I will go to Sheol with Lieutenant Rolf to assess the damage myself. Thank you. See that this message is sent through the portal and delivered to the master. He needs to know."

The messenger bowed, then quickly departed, leaving Cordon and Rolf to their thoughts. A moment of silence passed between them. Rolf spoke first.

"I don't know whether to congratulate you or offer my condolences."

"I need to know how many troops are available for a mission right here in Hell," replied Cordon.

"Not as many as you might like," replied Rolf. "Our forces are spread thin keeping the humans in their places of torment. If they were to become aware of our current weakness they might rebel. These small creatures of which we have heard might very well have been released so as to incite just such a rebellion."

"I agree," replied Cordon. "From what you know of our situation, how many minions could we spare to attack the rebel base?"

"Two…perhaps three million," replied Rolf. "But that assumes that we know the location of their base of operations."

"We do," replied Cordon. "We have had a stroke of luck. When these legions of flying beasts emerged from their tunnels they left a trail behind them. Two skillful seers witnessed the emergence of legions of these beasts from two separate locations and reached the place from which they appeared while their trail was still warm. They gave me coordinates from whence they came. I have only now completed the final calculations. They are on the Dark Continent, my friend. I have pinpointed their location to within five hundred square miles."

Rolf scowled, "That's a lot of territory, Cordon; I mean, Lord Cordon."

Cordon shook his head. "Just Cordon, my friend, I haven't changed. I'm not as pompous or arrogant as the master. And it isn't that much territory when you know what you are looking for. Their base has to be underground, and it has to be somewhere there is heat below the surface. A community as large as I think this one is leaves traces. Furthermore, I'm betting that there is a cave access to the surface. We will send a thousand of our best trackers out to search the area. We will find them, Rolf, and when we do, we will hit them and hit them hard. I will send dark angel and human alike to their eternal fates."

Chapter 18

Nikola and Abaddon stepped through the ring and once more were transported to that dark ridge from which they had viewed the destruction of Sheol. It would be too risky to venture closer. Surely there would be scores of demons combing the wreckage of the city for survivors. Nikola set up a sophisticated telescope to scan the ruins of the city from here.

Here and there, fires still burned. Through the telescope, Nikola could see the demons moving about like ants swarming over the ruins of a destroyed ant hill. The ground was like a mass of melted glass. Only the very edges of the city retained any semblance of what had once existed in this place.

Nikola focused on ground zero. If anything out of the ordinary was going on, it would be there. He saw several fires in that area, but nothing else immediately caught his eye. It was a gathering of demons around a particular spot that drew his attention. Something was there, but Nikola could not make it out from this distance. There were short bolts of what appeared to be lightning emanating from a very small but bright region. It might be a remnant of the otherworldly circuitry that most surely ran the length and breadth of this facility, a dying ember in a dying city. He gave it no further consideration.

There was still radiation emanating from the city, but not much more than he had expected. His fears had not been realized. If there was something here, some inscrutable fracture in space time, it wasn't obvious. He felt a sense of relief. He would check back in a few days, but he didn't expect to find anything.

Twenty minutes later, he and Abaddon departed. He would sleep easily tonight, and tomorrow begin to plan the destruction of the great ring. David was a bright lad, there was no doubt about it, but he was prone to be a bit melodramatic. This was one of those times.

It wasn't ten minutes later that a second pair of visitors gated in from Satan's audience chamber and unto a windswept ridge, some nine miles south of what was once the City of Sheol. Cordon and Rolf scanned the desolation that was once the empire's greatest accomplishment.

"A terrible tragedy," said Rolf, shaking his head.

"I doubt that the likes of it shall ever be built again," noted Cordon, scanning the desolation with his telescope-like sphere.

"I'm confused," noted Rolf. "You spoke of Cerenak and Wormwood as being the experts on this place."

"Yes, they were the chief architects," confirmed Cordon. "That was over six thousand years ago. It seems like an eternity. But why does this confuse you?"

"If my memory serves me correctly, you were the third architect of this place," said Rolf. "You speak as if you knew nothing of its construction."

"That is not exactly true," said Cordon. "Still, it was Cerenak who was the creative genius, and to a lesser degree, Wormwood and myself. It took years to figure out how to build it, and centuries to perfect it. There were secrets about its construction known only to Cerenak. Now he has taken them with him into oblivion."

"This I never knew," said Rolf, stepping forward to gaze upon the destruction below. "You could not build a second one?"

There was a pause. "I suppose I could," replied Cordon, "given sufficient time. I might even manage to build a better one."

"But?" asked Rolf.

"I lack the desire to build it," admitted Cordon. "I have no interest in tempting humanity, luring additional humans here. There are already too many. I would like to discover a method by which I might ship some of them out."

That comment elicited a chuckle from Rolf. "I think I can understand that. It would make our lives easier."

Cordon nodded. "Cerenak and I were the designers of the ring that teleported us here. Did you know that?"

"No, I didn't," noted Rolf.

"Satan ordered that only one be built, one for him. There were to be no others."

"I feel uneasy using it without the master's permission," said Rolf.

"I don't," replied Cordon. "After all, I designed it. At this point, I'm not sure I much care what Satan thinks."

That comment caught Rolf by surprise. Disobeying the master's commands was not a very good career move. He considered what had happened to Rathspith, though he wasn't quite sure what that was at this point.

Cordon once more called for the portal, and a moment later they appeared at the very edge of the city to view an indeed eerie sight. What remained of the crystalline pillars and crossbeams of this region had the appearance of blocks of ice that had thawed in the midst of a great windstorm, only to freeze once more, forming icicles that stretched horizontally away from ground zero rather than downward.

Rolf starred in wide-eyed surprise at this place. It was as if its moment of destruction had been frozen in time.

"I sense something strange ahead," said Cordon. "Come…let us travel to the center of the city."

They walked across the still very warm glassy surface of the city. Rolf cringed when not far away he saw the skeletal form of a demon, frozen in the depths of the melted glass. At some places the twisting sheets of glass that once formed the great pillars of the city still glowed with a dull red heat.

It was a difficult walk with many obstacles. Ahead, the ground rose, then fell into a crater-shaped depression 200 yards wide. Before them, half way down the inner slopes, stood a group of demons looking at a strange apparition about 3 feet above the very center of the crater. It glowed and flickered as bolts of electricity arced around it. About 20 feet to its left and about 10 feet higher was a second phenomenon like the first, only much smaller.

Cordon and Rolf stepped into the midst of the group. They all bowed before the now ranking demon of Hell.

"My lord, the greater light you see before you was here when we first arrived," said one of the demons. "The second one appeared only a few minutes ago."

Even as they watched, a third appeared about 100 yards farther away. Its appearance authored a wave of concern from all of those around.

"Do you feel the wind," asked Cordon, looking to Rolf.

"Yes," confirmed Rolf. "It blows toward that thing, whatever it is."

"It blows toward it, no matter where we stand," said the demon who had first addressed them.

Cordon turned to the other demons. "You are all to leave the city at once. There is great danger here. Tell all you see to back away. Now, go."

The demons obeyed, taking flight. Within a minute, Cordon and Rolf were alone.

"It is worse than I thought," said Cordon. "The great barrier that separates our reality from the ether beyond is crumbling. It will continue at an ever increasing rate until it consumes our very world."

Rolf had an indeed puzzled look. Cordon was not at all certain that his friend understood what he had just said.

"What can we do?" asked Rolf.

"I don't know yet," admitted Cordon, "but finding the rebel's hiding place has suddenly become our top priority. We must know exactly what it is they did, if we are to have any hope at all of stopping this." He hesitated. "If it can be stopped."

A moment later, they took to the air, even as a fourth rent in the fabric of space appeared. The destruction of Hell had begun.

It had been over 36 hours since the dropping of the bomb when the first signs of trouble appeared. It was during a routine telesphere communication with the City of Elesia from Abaddon's audience chamber. The report that nearly 30 million angels had arrived from Earth was interrupted by an increasing amount of static in the image.

Nikola did all that he could, but the signal continued to deteriorate until it was lost in a mist of snow. All efforts to restore communications failed.

"There is nothing wrong with the unit," said Nikola, after he had worked on it for an hour. "The interference must be coming from somewhere else."

By now a crowd of about a dozen humans and angels had gathered in Abaddon's audience chamber. Speculation as to the nature of the problem abounded.

"David said that something like this might happen," said Bedillia, looking over Abaddon's shoulder.

"Perhaps it is time to return to the mountaintop to see what new things have transpired in Sheol," suggested Abaddon.

Nikola nodded. He was feeling ill to his stomach. Suppose he had been wrong after all?

Half an hour later, Nikola and Abaddon once more stepped into the ring. It had been difficult to get a lock on the mountaintop, and what was usually a calm walk through the mists was anything but. The normally blue mists were a shade of yellow and swirled wildly around them. They were practically thrown onto the ridge.

A strong wind blew from their back and into the most nightmarish maelstrom either one of them had ever witnessed. It was a swirling vortex, easily a half mile across, directly above the city. It was surrounded by lightning bolts that reached out for at least a mile. They watched in disbelief as it gobbled up a sulfur storm drawn in from the sea. Blue fire and brimstone hurtled into the swirling clouds.

"Oh my God," gasped Nikola, "what have I done?"

"I suggest that you find out," insisted Abaddon.

Nikola quickly set up his instruments to categorize this beast that he had created. The initial results confirmed his fears.

"High levels of hard X-rays," said Nikola, "just as David had predicted. The blast has created a tear in space time."

"Fine," said Abaddon, who seemed increasingly agitated. "How do we fix it?"

The long pause that followed was not encouraging. "I don't know," admitted Nikola. "We need to get back to Refuge with the information I've collected. Maybe we can figure something out from there."

They quickly gathered up the scientific gear to make their retreat. When they tried to gate out, nothing happened.

"The space time around here is too badly distorted to make the trip back out," said Nikola. "We'll need to get farther away."

"How much farther?" asked Abaddon.

"Perhaps another twenty miles," replied Nikola.

"I'll carry you," said Abaddon. "Only take what you absolutely need."

Two minutes later, Abaddon was in flight, carrying Nikola to safety. It took a journey of eighty miles and two hours into the frozen interior of the Dark Continent before they were able to successfully gate back to Refuge. There they met with Tom, Bill, and Vikki, and informed them of their dire predicament. They had some of the best minds in Hell all together in one place to work on the problem. Yet they realized that their time was indeed limited. They were not hopeful.

In Heaven, all attempts to reestablish communications with Refuge met with failure. Even David's expertise with the telesphere was insufficient to overcome the mysterious new interference. To David, the meaning of the relentless static was clear—the rip in space time was spreading.

For days he wracked his brain for a solution to the problem, but he was at a loss. There was only one solution; he would need to return to the Holy Place and consult with the Father. But how? It was surrounded by the minions of Satan. He couldn't gate in, and he couldn't walk in.

It was within the modest makeshift living quarters granted them by the angels that David spoke to his mother of his intentions to find his way back into the Holy Place in Zion once more, blasting his way through if needs be. He couldn't deceive her and sneak off secretly; she had to know. He was surprised when she didn't object to his plan.

"You can't possibly make it alone," she said. "I'm going with you. We make a pretty good team, if you haven't noticed. Anyway, I know that God will guide and protect us, I feel it. When do you plan to leave?"

"Tomorrow morning," replied David. "But you mustn't go. I couldn't bear anything happening to you. You've already had one close call."

"Listen to me David Bonner," said June, in a mother's stern tone. "You're not going to go alone and have all of the fun, I'm going with you."

David looked at his mother in total shock. It wasn't a laughing matter, but he was laughing nonetheless. "I'll pack a particle rifle and pistol for the trip; hide them under my cloak. You need to do the same. Maybe we can just walk in, but I'm not taking any chances. If we have to fight our way in, so be it."

David was up late that evening making final plans and praying like he never had before. Yet his mother went out for several hours without explanation. She returned after midnight, offering no explanation. They would gate to a meadow some miles to the north of the city at first light, then gate to the cover of their condominium in Zion from there.

David didn't sleep well at all. Maybe he was beginning to move beyond the need for it. More likely, however, he was just too wound up. Taking his mother was not a good idea, but he was unlikely to make it without her. He knew that he would draw courage and strength from her.

June awoke her son just before daybreak. "Time to go, son," she said. Already, she was dressed for the trip. "I'll be waiting for you outside."

It took only three minutes for David to prepare himself for the journey ahead. Despite his prayers and his faith, he was uncertain as to what this day might hold. He stepped out into the hallway and was surprised to find Don and Karen, two of Dr. Bohr's students, standing beside his mother, dressed in white robes, weapons ready.

"Four pilgrims have a better chance of success than two," said June.

David was amazed and grateful to have such good friends accompanying him on this quest that he had feared he might have to make alone. A minute later, they gated out to the meadow.

Here, David was in for another surprise. Standing before him was someone he hadn't seen in a very long time. It was Jennifer Davis, Serena's mother-in-law, who stood amid the tall grass. She too was armed with one of the rifles. In the six years since his adventure of rescuing Serena, they had lost touch. Yet his mother had formed a bond with this special woman, and they had become close friends.

"Hi everyone," Jennifer said, a broad smile on her face. "June, thank you so much for inviting me. For a very long time I have wanted to make a somewhat stronger statement to those who caused my daughter-in-law so much pain. Today might be that day."

"No revenge," said June. "This is not what this trip is about."

"Of course not," said Jennifer, "I'm just going to make a statement, if need be."

David didn't quite know what to think about that one, so he said nothing. He was glad to have her along. At least, he thought so.

After a round of introductions, last moment thoughts, and more than a few prayers, they were ready to go. They walked together into a cloud of stars, appearing in the condo in Zion just a few seconds later. Nothing much had changed here since their last visit. Apparently, the demons had left it alone.

Hiding their weapons beneath their long cloaks, they ventured into the empty streets and advanced toward the Holy Place.

"Look, we don't want a fight," said David. "If we can get into the Holy Place without firing a shot, let's do it."

"You don't have to tell me that," said Karen. "I have faith, but I'd really rather not test it at odds of hundreds to one."

"Amen to that," said Don, looking about nervously. "I've lost enough limbs in battle for one eternity."

No one opposed their progress as they worked their way through the sometimes rubble cluttered streets. They were 200 yards from the Holy place when seven demons descended from the sky, landing in the street before them.

"Just keep moving," urged David. "I don't think they will try to prevent us from entering the Holy Place. They didn't last time. They seem more concerned with keeping humans confined there once they arrive."

They drew closer to the demons as four more joined their ranks. The tension increased. What were they going to do? No one was sure. The fact that several of them had drawn their swords was not encouraging.

"Stop, humans!" roared the one who stood closest to them. "It is forbidden for your kind to be within the city."

"We are going into God's presence," said June. "Surely you will not prevent us from doing that."

"None may pass," said the demon. "The five of you are in serious trouble. You are violating the orders of Satan."

"What do you want us to do?" asked June.

The demon smiled, but slightly. "You will come with us to our command post where you will be questioned and searched. If we are satisfied that you are not members of the rebel faction assisting the angels, we will allow you to enter the Holy Place. If, however, we have reason to suspect that you are, you will be confined until this war is over."

Don was trembling. It became all too clear where this was leading. Still, he was not about to surrender to these minions of Satan.

"You have no right to do this to us," objected David.

Another demon came forward, eyeing this young man carefully. "We have every right, David Bonner." He turned to the others. "This one is a rebel. I've seen him before."

"Seize them," said the first demon.

Their cover was blown. It was Jennifer who drew and powered her weapon first. "The time for talk is over," she cried. She opened fire on the demon leader. Her aim was dead-on accurate. He was blasted into a million pieces that scattered across the street. "That was for Serena," she yelled, turning her weapon on a second target.

Don's weapon found the second target first. Then David joined the fight. Their demon adversaries never stood a chance. Within 15 seconds, all of them had been cut down and butchered right there in the street.

"To the Holy Place!" cried David, leading the charge forward.

The group ran toward the safety of the Holy Place. Still, 200 yards had never seemed so far. Already they could see dozens of demons moving to block their path. They had a firefight on their hands.

From the Holy Place itself, thousands, then tens of thousands of worshipers stopped and took note of the battle transpiring so close. Never had the battle between the angels and demons raged so near. But wait, this was not a battle between angels and demons, but between demons and fellow saints. It was a realization that filled them with horror. Many fell to their knees in prayer.

The five human warriors were about 120 yards from their goal when they realized the pure futility of their efforts. Hundreds of demons now blocked their path. Some were on foot, others flew, but all were deadly obstacles.

"They are going to launch fireballs!" warned David.

The group took cover behind a set of marble columns, the only cover between them and the Holy Place. They opened fire on the encroaching demons, cutting down a score of them. The demons responded with an equal number of fireballs.

The fireballs exploded all around them, engulfing the area in flames. None were spared the terrible burning fire of the most dreaded of demonic weapons. All suffered horrendous burns. Yet just a few seconds later, they returned a round of equally devastating particle beam fire. It was a fight to the death in a place where death was not easy to come by.

The demons prepared to launch another volley of fireballs, yet only a few of them made it to their targets. The demonic forces were overwhelmed by a sea of humanity streaming from the Holy Place. Armed only with God-given courage and determination, the demons were trampled under foot by the swelling multitude.

The demonic forces were caught totally by surprise. They took to the air or retreated into the streets of Zion. Within a minute, the swelling mass of saints had reached their fallen brethren. More than a few had felt the thrust of a sword wielded by an angry demon along the way, yet they had not hesitated. Now borne on the loving arms of their fellow saints, David and his friends were carried into the safety of the Holy Place.

By this time the demons had regrouped and were quickly overtaking the saints who were withdrawing into the Holy Place.

"Make them pay for their arrogance!" screamed one of the demons. "Ready your fireballs…burn them all!"

The demons, thousands of them, collectively drew their swords and prepared to discharge fireballs. These humans would be made to pay for their insolence.

Abruptly, 12 men robed in white materialized between the retreating crowd and the demon hoards, forming a thin defense line. Each wore a crown and held a golden scepter.

The man near the middle who had long dark hair and dark eyes stepped forward. "Be gone from this place," he commanded in a mighty voice. "You are forbidden to touch the children of God."

One of the demonic multitudes flew forward, landing on the cobblestones a dozen feet before the robed human. "Who are you to make demands of us, human?"

The man never flinched. There was not a trace of fear on his countenance. "Who I am is not important. It is He whom I serve who commands you. But, if you must know, my name is Peter; I'm a fisherman."

The demon smiled, then laughed. "I have brought fear and pain to men more formidable than you. I have made them beg for mercy."

"Withdraw your forces," said Peter. "I will not give you another warning."

"No, you won't," snarled the demon. "Your head won't be attached to your neck."

He drew back his sword as Peter extended his scepter forward. The sword came down, yet it struck an invisible barrier before reaching Peter. In rage the demon stepped back and summoned forth a fireball. It was propelled toward Peter; again the weapon was deflected by the same barrier, returning it from whence it came.

The demon was engulfed in fire. He screamed a high pitched tone as he was rapidly reduced to a pile of smoldering ashes.

The other demons launched their fireballs, yet they were deflected long before they reached the crowd. The demons retreated in panic as the last of the humans crossed the threshold into the Holy Place. For the first time in days, the Holy Place was not completely surrounded by the minions of Satan.

David and his friends were laid upon the golden floor of the Holy Place. Although they were regenerating rather quickly, they were still in great pain. The crowd backed away as Peter and his 11 compatriots drew close to David and the others. Peter knelt down at David's side and placed his hand upon his still red forehead.

"You have done very well indeed," said Peter. "Your example caused the people of God to respond, to put away their fears and confront the forces of Satan face to face. What they have done once, they will be able to do again more easily. But for now, sleep; when you awaken your pain will be gone."

David gazed into Peter's eyes as the world went dark around him. He couldn't stay awake. Then a quiet calm darkness engulfed him—a darkness without fear or pain. Then, nothing.

Chapter 19

It had been 89 hours since the dropping of the bomb when a new problem started. Fully 72 million angels had made the trip from Earth when arriving angels began to complain of a turbulent and even painful trip. Within a few minutes the pathway had closed again. Another of David's predictions had come true. But by now David was nowhere to be found. Word was that he had made the trip to the Holy Place in Zion, in the company of several others, but no one was really sure.

Still, they had accomplished miracles. They had also managed to rescue an additional 4 million angels from the other planes of Heaven. Many came through the assistance of an unknown saint, who departed even before his deed could be recognized. They now had some 117 million battle-ready angels, and their numbers were growing by the day. This represented fewer than a third of the angels of Heaven, but it was, nonetheless, a formidable fighting force. It would be several more weeks before they would be ready to go on the offensive, and even then they would be outnumbered, but for the first time there was a glimmer of hope.

Satan sat alone in his new audience chamber. He'd had his old throne and scepter transported from Hell to here. It made him more comfortable, made this place seem somewhat more familiar.

Angelic resistance to his armies had virtually evaporated on six of the seven levels of Heaven. There was still some random resistance here and there, but it was fading. It was the second level of Heaven that posed the greatest threat. It had been little more than a mouse hole, into which the angels had been able to find refuge; now, Satan feared that it had become more akin to a fortress. It had been the second setback of the campaign.

Satan had never taken setbacks well. Word of the destruction of Sheol and the loss of some of his highest ranking minions had been the first. True, if he succeeded in conquering all of Heaven, Sheol would have been relegated to little more than a chapter in his success story. It would no longer have served a purpose. The ability to travel from Hell to Earth in spirit form would be little more than a parlor trick, a thing of the past. Why travel to Earth as a spirit when he and his minions could have used the ring at the Hall of Angels to travel there in their physical form? Indeed, he might have found it necessary to tear down the city anyway, to further isolate the angels who would eventually be relegated to Hell as its eternal prisoners.

Yes, Sheol was the source of power for the seven crystals that enhanced the strength of his armies, but he had barely touched these reserves. The fully charged crystals were, at this point, little more than an insurance policy that he probably wouldn't need.

But still, the timing of its destruction was bad. The barrier generated by Sheol had served to keep the last two pockets of angelic resistance isolated until he was ready to deal with them. Now, he was certain that those two pockets had combined to form what might be one large and effective angelic army, the last angelic army, bringing him back to the second setback. Satan knew that, eventually, they would strike. After all, it was their move.

And where would they attack? It had been a topic of debate in his war council. Zion itself seemed the most likely target. Satan had repositioned his forces in such a way as to make mobilizing them easier; still, he was troubled. For the first time in the campaign, his victory seemed to be in question.

The altercation here in the Hall of Angels with young upstart David Bonner had been the last foul weed in the garden. David had moved himself way up on Satan's hit list. He had done something few had ever managed to do—humiliate him in front of his followers. He would have to deal with David very soon.

Satan's thoughts were interrupted as the first member of his war council entered his chambers. Their daily meeting was about to commence. He would have to seem positive before them. The Prince of Darkness could not be viewed as faltering or indecisive. His doubts would have to remain hidden.

In deep space between the orbit of Uranus and Neptune, the New Horizons spacecraft was accepting new commands from Earth, 2 billion miles away. It turned its battery of high tech instruments toward the new Comet Florence. It was pure serendipity. The only spacecraft in this region of space was going to pass a mere 19 million miles from the comet, close enough to gather much valuable data. It would be observing the comet for several weeks, determining its size, temperature, composition, and most importantly, its exact position. In conjunction with telescopes on Earth and from orbit, they would determine the comet's location and orbit exactly, and hopefully confirm that it was *not* on a collision course with Earth.

Right now, the comet was 36 million miles away, closing rapidly. The powerful LORRI imaging camera detected the tiny ball of ice on the very first try, snapping its picture against the background of stars using a variety of filters and exposures.

Despite the huge increase in the number of charged particles flying through the solar system these past four days, the images were crisp and clean. Scientists at the Jet Propulsion Laboratory were elated by the beautiful images of the comet. It was the first time they had observed a comet at such short range while it was still so far from the sun.

Yet, observing of the comet from Earth was not nearly so easy. The skies above the Discovery Channel Telescope in northern Arizona were ablaze with curtains of shifting red and green light. This was the third day of record auroral activity, as charged particles streamed into the Earth's atmosphere above the magnetic pole. The mystery: where were the charged particles coming from? The sun was quiet, in the midst of a Maunder Minimum. The source of the aurora was not a solar flare. But if not a flare, then what?

Power blackouts were already rampant in northern countries including Canada, Russia, and Norway—outages related to high energy charged particles entering the atmosphere. Even far southern countries such as New Zealand and Argentina were beginning to feel the effects.

High above the Earth, the mysterious particles were manifesting themselves in yet another way—one satellite after another experienced catastrophic failure and went silent. These were the satellites in the most vulnerable positions beyond Earth's protective magnetic field, and the danger was growing as the intensity of the radiation grew.

Radiation at the International Space Station was approaching dangerous levels. Soon, this off-world outpost would have to be abandoned. For the first time in 20 years there would be no human presence in space.

In addition, commercial spacecraft flights had been suspended. Even jet aircraft operations above 40,000 feet were off limits.

"This one isn't going to work for us either," complained Sam Florence as he scanned the image from the control room of the Discovery Channel telescope. "I never thought aurora would spoil an observing run for me."

Ken, the observatory assistant, looked at the image and shook his head. "The comet is getting low in the sky, Sam. You aren't going to have too many more chances tonight to get an image, and tomorrow there's a front moving in."

Sam started the seventh exposure of the comet. "Then we just have to pray for a small break in the aurora."

Ken smiled. "Yep, I reckon it worked before, didn't it?"

"Yeah," said Sam, smiling, "it did. New Horizons is taking its second set of images of the comet right now. It would be very good to get an image of it taken from Earth at the same time."

"Word has it that this particle radiation that has our skies full of aurora is highly localized," said Ken. "The New Horizons spacecraft is experiencing it too, but not nearly as badly as we are here on Earth. Even the Mars orbiting satellites are recording a somewhat lower level of radiation, although, we lost Mars Odyssey to the radiation yesterday. It's just creepy. Take that and this potentially doomsday comet together and it almost seems like the end of days."

Sam just nodded. The same thought had crossed his mind several times during the past several days, though he hadn't voiced it. It wasn't the sort of thing that one spoke of too loudly around the professors at the university.

Five minutes later they got their first good image of the comet that night. Amazingly enough, it was followed by one more good image six minutes later before the comet dropped too low in the western horizon.

Other observatories around the world were following the comet as well. Word of the new comet had circulated widely through the professional and amateur astronomical community. It was touted as potentially the comet of the century. Nominally, it would pass well within 2 million miles of the Earth, though the exact distance was still hotly debated. There was even a possibility of impact, though the 1 in 60,000 odds didn't seem to alarm the general public.

The comet had been spotted while it was still so far out that there was plenty of lead time before its arrival. There was even talk of a robotic mission to study it close up, perhaps even land on it.

Still, others saw it in a different light. To be visible from such a distance, it had to be a very large object, probably larger than the comet that brought the reign of the dinosaurs to an abrupt end 65 million years ago. Might this object be capable of turning humankind into a footnote in the cosmic history of Earth? It seemed a preposterous idea, yet the governments of Earth were taking the threat very seriously. Within the next two weeks, they would have an orbit for the comet that was refined by a factor of 100. They hoped that the observations that were being made now would prove that the Earth was not in the gun sight of Comet Florence.

Slowly, David Bonner was coming around. His eyes opened to see his mother kneeling over him. Her clothes were tattered and singed, but she seemed little the worse for wear.

"Hey," she said, stroking his cheek with her hand. "We made it, we're in."

David looked up to see that the others were here safe and sound. That was a relief.

"Welcome back, my son," said the Father.

"It is really good to be back," said David.

"Was your adventure all that you had hoped it would be?" asked the Father.

David nodded. "Father, I've had enough adventure for a long time. You know, I thought I wanted something exciting to happen, to live a life full of intrigue, full of danger. I can't believe I could have been so foolish, so childish."

"You are being far too harsh on yourself," replied the Father. "Understand this: your eternity can be an adventure, or simply a long journey…it is totally up to you. You live at the very center of creation, everyone does. Do your best to take every advantage of the opportunities it affords you. I know that the past days have been difficult for you, but you have learned so much, and you will learn still more."

"Yeah, that's what I'm afraid of."

David's comment elicited a hearty laugh from the Father. "David, you survived these past few days because you place your faith in Me. You handled yourself well in the presence of the deceiver. You displayed courage and wisdom. You became My instrument in delivering Gabriel from the hands of Satan. Furthermore, you must not hold yourself accountable for what has transpired in Hell. I assure you that what is happening there is what must happen, that My plan might be fulfilled."

"So, what am I to do now?" asked David.

"Nothing, for now," said the Father. "What you must do now is relax, regain your strength. Spend some time with Me. I'll try to make it interesting."

This time it was David and his mother who laughed.

God continued. "When the time is right, I'll tell you exactly what is to be done. Your mother was right when she said that the two of you made a good team. The time will come when I send you out together."

The dark angel practically stumbled into Abaddon's audience chamber, interrupting the ongoing meeting between Abaddon, Bedillia, and his four top human scientists.

"Sir, the sentries report that the skies overhead are practically filled with demons, perhaps several legions of them."

"Might they simply be passing through?" asked Abaddon.

"No," replied the dark angel. "They are circling, and their numbers increase by the minute."

"Then, this is it," announced Abaddon. "Raise the alarm. Get all angels and humans alike ready for battle. Summon the war council. It looks like we'll have to fight."

The angel bowed slightly and quickly departed. The silence that followed was indeed ominous.

Abaddon turned to the members of his science team. "How many of those rifles have you produced?"

"There are currently about thirteen hundred," said Bill, "tested and ready to go. The majority of our people know how to handle them."

"And how many power cells do you have for them?" asked Abaddon.

"There is the problem," said Bill. "Even with the extra cells that Nikola brought us, we have fewer than three thousand."

"Twenty or thirty rounds per rifle," deduced Nikola. "That's not much."

"We also have nearly a million of my children in the lower caverns," said Abaddon. "Within the close confines of the caverns, they would be formidable adversaries."

"I think we can beat them," announced Tom.

Bedillia looked toward Tom and smiled. At last, her positivity had rubbed off on him. "They will regret the day that they came here looking for us," she said.

"My war council will be here within a few minutes," announced Abaddon. "I wish for the science committee to remain. I need to know all of my options. Keep in mind, they might not know we're here. We hide if we can, and we fight only if we have no other choice."

The group nodded. They knew that they could give the demons a fight they would not soon forget. They would fight as long as they were in one piece. The consequences of defeat were too horrible to contemplate. Still, they had limited resources. They might drag this thing out for days or even weeks; nonetheless, things weren't looking bright. They really weren't ready for this fight, not yet.

In the dark, minus-40-degree air beyond Refuge, Cordon and Rolf had set up headquarters in the midst of a narrow canyon. A series of fireballs had been used to bring the walls to near red heat to lessen the bite of the frigid weather. Overhead, darkness ruled the night. The auroras that often dominated this land were strangely absent.

"The one large cave is several hundred yards in that direction," said one of the scouts, pointing up the canyon. "Though some effort has been made to mask the tracks, we found evidence that humans or dark angels have been there recently. However, there is currently no one living within. They might already have fled."

"Take us there," said Cordon.

Cordon and Rolf were escorted up the narrow canyon and into the mouth of a truly enormous cavern. They made their way through the tunnel cautiously, using the crystal light from their rings.

"A lava tube," said Cordon. "In some ancient epoch of time, molten rock flowed through this dark tunnel."

"It seems warmer in here," noted Rolf.

"Totally normal," assured Cordon.

It was several minutes before the huge tunnel came to an abrupt end.

"There does not appear to be any side passages," noted the scout. "We've searched thoroughly."

"Not thoroughly enough," said Cordon, moving his hand along the walls, slowly and carefully. "They're here, I know it. See the way this lava tube turns? It's not natural. By the looks of it, the tube should fork here."

"But it doesn't," replied Rolf.

Cordon looked toward his lieutenant, a slight smile on his face. "Doesn't it?"

Fifteen minutes of silence passed before Cordon stopped. By now, Rolf stood at his side. Rolf too had his hands on the wall.

Cordon looked to his lieutenant. "Do you sense it, Rolf, the vibration, the sense of power in this wall?"

Rolf's eyes opened wide. "Yes, I think I do."

"This wall is an illusion," announced Cordon. "It is a very good illusion, but it is phantasmal."

A rock bounced off of the wall not far away, a rock thrown by the scout. "With all due respect, my lord, it seems solid to me."

"Ah, that is because you believe it to be." Cordon stood motionless for a few seconds. He seemed deep in thought. Then he stretched forth his hand. It passed right into the wall and back out again. "It is a simple matter of faith, my friends."

Rolf reached out to the wall. It still seemed solid. "I don't understand," he admitted.

"You will," assured Cordon.

"Are we then to prepare the troops, march them into this cavern?" asked Rolf.

"No," replied Cordon. "The plan has been changed. As I told you, we need these people as much as they need us."

Three hours later, Cordon's entire army was assembled; a demonic force nearly 2 million strong. Within the cavern, before the phantasmal wall, several thousand of those demons were assembled. They looked on with disbelief as Cordon dropped his sword to the ground and picked up a large white flag.

"What are we doing?" asked Rolf, as they stood before the wall.

"We are going in under a flag of truce," replied Cordon.

"Do you really believe that they will honor it?" asked Rolf, who, under his commander's orders, had also dropped his sword.

"I'm not sure," said Cordon. "If you don't return within three hours, they are under orders to begin the assault. They have my battle plans. I do hope it doesn't come to that. Are you ready?"

Rolf took a deep breath as he took his commander's hand and walked into the wall into which he had vanished just an instant earlier. For a moment, they seemed to be walking through a mist. They emerged into an illuminated cavern. They were facing over 100 dark angel and human warriors—their weapons trained on them.

"We ask you not to shoot," said Cordon, holding his white flag before him. "We are unarmed. We come under a flag of truce."

A dark angel stepped forward, eyeing the two carefully. "Let me guess. You are, no doubt, going to ask for our surrender, guaranteeing us merciful terms if we turn over the humans to you."

"On the contrary," said Cordon, "I am not asking for your surrender or the humans in your care. You can keep them for all I care. I am asking for your help. I wish to speak to your leader, Abaddon."

"You have found him," said the dark angel. "I am Abaddon."

Cordon bowed slightly, as in an angelic greeting. "I am Cordon, and this is my lieutenant, Rolf."

"So, you are Cordon," replied Abaddon. "I know of you. Why would I wish to speak to you? My words would be with your superiors."

"Sadly I have no superiors," replied Cordon. "You have seen to that. I am the ranking minion of Hell."

"So what business would you have with me?" asked Abaddon.

"The thing that your people created," replied Cordon. "It is something that now threatens us both…a hole in the thing that the humans call space time. I am prepared to help you close that hole."

"How would you know of such things?" asked Abaddon.

"Because I am one of the original designers of Sheol," said Cordon. "The only one still remaining. We don't have much time. If you will accept my help, it is offered. I might have an idea as to how to close that hole. If you agree, I will send Rolf back through that wall of yours and my forces will withdraw. On the other hand, you could destroy us and have some temporary satisfaction before my forces level this place. What shall it be? Revenge? Or do we get to work on saving our world?"

"And if we could close that hole, what would happen afterward?" asked Abaddon.

"A treaty," replied Cordon, "a treaty that would stand so long as I ruled Satan's domain. Personally, I do not believe that he is coming back. Trust me when I tell you, I would be more than reasonable. You might be pleasantly surprised."

Lenar stepped up to Abaddon's side. "I seriously doubt that he can be trusted."

Abaddon looked into Cordon's eyes. "Send your minion through the wall and call your forces off. So long as you stand by your agreement, I will stand by mine. Come with me."

"I am hesitant to leave you here alone," said Rolf. "I fear for your safety."

"Don't," replied Cordon. "I feel that I am in good hands." He looked toward Abaddon.

Rolf nodded, and after taking a deep breath, walked back through the wall.

Cordon walked at Abaddon's side, flanked by both human and dark angelic warriors. They proceeded to the audience chamber.

Cordon's presence was met with disdain, confusion, and fear as they made their way through the maze of tunnels. They had almost reached the audience chamber when Cordon encountered his one-time prisoner, Julie, standing along the corridor. He paused.

"Julie, child, I am glad to see you again."

Cordon moved on. His presence had sent a shiver through her very soul.

They entered the audience chamber where several members of the war council and the science committee, including Nikola, sat. They rose at the sight of a demon in their midst. After a brief introduction, Cordon had the floor.

"Destroying Sheol in the manner you did was reckless," began Cordon, "but we don't have time to discuss that now. I believe I can assist you in developing a device that will close the fissure in space time you created. A series of graviton pulses set off from the other side of the fissure might close it. I have no way of getting there or powering the devices, but I suspect you do. As I see it, we need each other."

For 20 minutes the debate raged as to whether one of his kind was capable of telling the truth, but they eventually permitted him to join the group. They prayed that it was not a mistake.

Tim's life in the cave was becoming more routine. Occasionally his small friend, Goliath, brought him a present. Lately, the gifts had taken the form of small luminous crystals, from places unknown, that brought ever more light to his dark world. It took only a few to illuminate his favorite cavern room—the one with the pool. Yes, he could get use to this. Being a cave dweller was infinitely preferable to the alternative. In fact, he never so much as stuck his nose out of the cavern entrance. The hot dry world above could be the realm of the demons, but this cool damp world below was his.

He spent hours exploring the many side passages. Most went only 100 feet or so to dead ends, or led to tunnels too narrow to crawl into. Others went much farther and deeper, to other cavern rooms with their own branching tunnels. Always, Goliath was there when he explored. He would have felt ill at ease without him.

Then came the day when Goliath brought a friend home with him—another of his own kind. It took just a passing glance for Tim to realize that this one was a female. Like Goliath, she accepted this human as a friend. Tim decided to name her Cindy, for no particular reason. Like Goliath, she took up residence in the cavern. Tim couldn't have been happier. They stayed close to Tim when they were in the cavern, often sleeping directly on or around him. Their presence was reassuring, and he talked to them for hours, mostly about himself and how much he appreciated them. They seemed so attentive. It helped him to know that he wasn't alone.

Tim wondered if eventually there would even be more of them, tiny ones. He supposed that he would just have to wait and see.

Chapter 20

For the better part of three days the scientific and engineering debate as to what could be done with a hole in Hell's space time raged. At first, the group shunned Cordon and his ideas. He was, after all, a demon, a dark minion of Satan. Yet, they quickly discovered the wealth of knowledge he possessed on the subject. In addition, he was very much unlike any demon they had ever dealt with before. He was highly focused, yet soft spoken and not prone to anger.

They also discovered that he was true to his word. His army had withdrawn totally. Abaddon's scouts reported that they were nowhere to be found within a 100-mile radius of Refuge. He was here alone and unarmed, and he offered constructive ideas, as well as new often unheard of technologies. The others were beginning to accept him.

Slowly a plan was emerging, developed mainly by Cordon and Nikola—a means of closing the hole in space time. They realized why they needed to work together. Neither side alone had the means of deploying this technology. It was a sort of anti-graviton bomb, powered by the same technology that powered the Spirit and the device they had used on Sheol. Still, the delivery of the device was fraught with danger. They had neither the time to test the device or run extensive simulations on it. It would have to operate properly the first time. Nearly one percent of Hell's atmosphere had vanished into the maelstrom already, and now even the Sea of Fire was being pulled into the void.

In the audience chamber, a multidimensional model of the terrible rent in space time was displayed above the conference table using equipment borrowed from the Spirit.

Tesla pointed toward the great whirlpool. "This rift in space is like nothing you've ever seen before. It is not a black hole or wormhole; there are no tremendous gravitational tidal forces associated with it. It will not reach out and grab you. However, the atmospheric pressure here is forcing the atmosphere into the vacuum on the far side producing gale force winds in its vicinity. There, powerful radiation is ionizing it and whatever else is pulled in. Those charged particles are directed by magnetic fields toward Earth. There it emerges from hyperspace to create havoc. If it is not stopped, it will eventually sterilize our world."

"This crisis started with a bomb, and it is a bomb of sorts that shall end it," continued Tesla. "Cordon and I will need to fly the Spirit into hyperspace, but not through the rift...attempting to enter the rift would be nothing short of suicide. We will enter from approximately a hundred miles up. There, we shall approach the rift from the far side. We will release three devices. They will utilize a drive system not unlike that of the Spirit to hover just beyond the rift. Once they are placed, we will back off to a safe distance and detonate them. Each will produce a tremendous anti-graviton pulse that will fuse the space time continuum and seal the hole. Ironically, the power to produce this pulse will be obtained by scrapping the explosive element from the remaining two bombs I brought with me."

Victoria van Voth looked to Cordon. "Have you ever tried something like this?"

"No," replied Cordon. "But the technology will work. It has been tested for other applications, just not this one."

Abaddon looked at Cordon suspiciously. "What purpose would such a device serve for a demon?"

"I prefer the term fallen angel, if you don't mind," replied Cordon. "We used this technology on a smaller scale to make Sheol work, to slip the spirit of one of our kind into the magnetic stream of the ether and, from there, journey to Earth."

"I believe it will work," said Nikola. "I have sufficient fuel on board the Spirit to get us there and back. I'll need Cordon with me because he knows this anti-graviton technology better than I do. I'd never even considered such a technology until just a few days ago."

"The rift is growing," said Cordon. "If we wait much longer, I do not believe this plan will be effective. It will take two days to build the devices."

"And at least that long to modify the Spirit to do this job," noted Nikola. "We need to begin now if we are going to pull this off."

It took over an hour, but eventually the rest of the committee concurred with Cordon and Nikola's plan. Now all eyes were on Abaddon; his would be the final word.

"Do what you need to do," said Abaddon. "The matters of which you speak are beyond my experience. I shall defer to the decisions of the experts. I hope you are right."

The work started. Cordon briefed Victoria as to the nature of the circuits that she would have to create. It was not an easy task. The technology of the angels and fallen angels was very different from anything she had ever seen. Yet, she produced work that met or exceeded Cordon's expectations.

Through it all, Julie acted as Cordon's lab assistant. In the past two days, not a dozen words beyond what related to the business at hand had passed between them. It was a difficult assignment. Never had she thought to see him again; now they worked together. He brought back memories of those nightmarish years on the altar. Yet, he had also been the one who took her from them, and indirectly brought her here. He made it a point to be kind to her and made no reference to those terrible days, but it was festering within her soul. She had to confront him.

It was during a break from their labors that she found him alone in the lab. She had brought a cup of water to him, as he had once done for her.

"I didn't know if you drank water or not," she said.

Cordon smiled, accepting the cup. "Not often; it is Hell, after all. I do, however, like to drink water from time to time. Thank you, Julie."

Julie was leaning against the wall, drinking her own cup of water, trying to find the strength to confront him. Yet, now she didn't know what to say.

Cordon made eye contact with his former prisoner. "It must be difficult for you Julie. I can understand that."

"I'm sorry?" she replied.

"It's OK," continued Cordon. "You have nothing to fear from me. Nor am I in any way angry that you escaped from your cell that day. It is just as well that you did. We were nearly out of time. Soon I would have had to return you to the cycles of torture that all humans must endure in Hell."

"And you were comfortable with that?" asked Julie.

"I was numb to it," replied Cordon. "I was neither comfortable nor happy with it. Sometimes I found some sense of irony in granting people what they asked for before they realized they had asked it. There are no pleasant destinies in Hell, Julie, understand that."

"After I gave you the name, the name of the angel that saved Tom, what were you going to do to me?"

Cordon turned away. "Julie, you really don't want to know that, do you?"

"Yes, I do," replied Julie. "I'm trying to understand who you are...why you are helping us now."

"Why I'm helping you now," replied Cordon, "is because we must work together if we are to survive. A crisis makes strange allies." There was a pause.

"Let me tell you something Julie, something that I wouldn't tell just anyone. I have no love for Satan. In fact, I despise him. I would prefer that he never returns. In very fact, I do not believe that he will. This war in Heaven will be his downfall, but he is too mad, too egotistical to see it. The old order in Hell will soon pass away, and there is nothing that I can do about it. Indeed, I will be glad to see it go. However, I do not wish to be a victim of its passing. I can see in which direction the wind is blowing. I will not fight against it; I will soar with it. If that means allying myself with Abaddon, so be it. At the end of the day, I will still be standing, as will my people."

Julie looked at Cordon in amazement. She wasn't sure if she could believe him or not.

"You might find that this new order you seek has more problems than you or even Abaddon can now see," continued Cordon. "I do not know if there is a solution to our problems, or if the lot of you are up to the challenge of solving it. I can only tell you this…if we can negotiate an equitable peace, I will not be one of the problems." Again there was a pause. "Regarding your initial question, I had intended to melt a section of the permafrost in a particularly swampy portion of the Dark Continent using several fireballs. Then, after shackling you hand and foot and weighing you down with heavy ballast, I would throw you in. Where I intended to drop you, you would probably have sunk a dozen feet before the muddy ice froze around you. There you would have remained for all times, suffocating in the quiet frigid darkness. It would have been your eternal hiding place."

A long silence passed between them as Julie digested Cordon's words. "I know…there are no pleasant destinations in Hell," Julie said.

Cordon hesitated. "I was under orders. I did what I was told to do. This has been the nature of my existence."

Julie shook her head sadly. "In the history of Earth, so many people have done such terrible things, caused so much pain and sorrow, only to say later that they did it because they were following orders. Why should it be any different here?"

Cordon placed his hand gently on Julie's shoulder. Strangely, she didn't pull away. "I truly hope that I have the opportunity to get to know you better in the new world we might forge. I hope that down the road, you might find it in your heart to forgive me, even to call me a friend."

Julie nodded, a slight smile came to her face. "I hope so too, Cordon... really."

It was three days later when construction of the last of the anti-graviton devices was completed. The craft's equipment bays in the belly of the Spirit that normally held scientific instruments had been specially modified to hold launching racks that would send the projectiles on their way.

"I thank God for the ability to turn blueprints directly into a completed product through directed thought," said Nikola, walking around the craft. "Without it, modifying the Spirit's science instrument bays would have been a daunting task requiring months."

"Your human technicians did a superb job of installing them as well," noted Cordon. "To have made such a modification to your craft in such a short time is nothing short of miraculous. When we lift off, you may be assured that you will have total cooperation from my people."

"I heard we had a visitor earlier," noted Nikola, examining the starboard seam where the rack folded into the fuselage as several technicians continued to make fine adjustments on the port rack. "It seems strange that demons should be flying in and out of Refuge."

"Perhaps it will become a common sight," suggested Cordon.

"Perhaps," replied Nikola. "We should be ready for liftoff in three hours. If you have any last minute preparations, you had best see to them."

"I am always ready," assured Cordon.

Three hours later, Nikola was carefully maneuvering the Spirit through the large tunnels that led to the surface. Reaching the narrow canyon just beyond the mouth of the cave, the Spirit made a vertical sprint toward space.

From the main deck, Cordon watched the Dark Continent drop swiftly away as they headed toward a curtain of aurora straight overhead. This was his first experience seeing Hell from this vantage point.

"We'll make the jump as soon as we clear the atmosphere," said Nikola, glancing back at his lone passenger.

They were surrounded by the auroral curtains when Nikola instituted the jump. The disk of Hell vanished below them, to be replaced by the shifting clouds of faintly glowing plasma usually associated with hyperspace. All the while his eyes were on the power levels. He was just barely crossing the barrier into hyperspace. It shouldn't have taken much fuel. Yet, at the completion of the jump, he was looking at power levels below 10 percent. This wasn't good.

"There it is," said Cordon, pointing to a beam of brilliant blue light that seemed to erupt out of nowhere and continue into infinity.

Around the beam were swirling clouds filled with powerful bolts of lightning. The lightning shifted unpredictably, seeming to wrap around the beam. It was an awesome yet frightening sight.

"Bring us in slowly," said Cordon. "Mind the lightning. It is no doubt several times stronger than any lightning bolts you have experienced on Earth or Heaven."

Nikola swung the Spirit toward the beam. There was no way to judge distance out here. Radar didn't work in hyperspace, and it was easy for the human senses to be fooled.

As he got closer, he was able to determine the dimensions of the phantasmal beam more precisely. The bright shaft of shifting luminous plasma at its heart was about 100 yards wide, but the coursing blue lightning and swirling clouds extended out from the beam for a half mile in all directions. It grew larger and more menacing as he drew closer.

It was 15 minutes before Cordon advised him to hold position. Right now, he was just beyond the reach of the lightning bolts. Cordon was standing at his side, eying the phenomenon over carefully.

"Follow the beam toward its source," said Cordon. "We will need to hold position when we close to within about two of your miles of the rift. Then we'll release the first anti-graviton device. Be careful...the rift doesn't have a strong gravitational field, but it is unpredictable and shifting. We wouldn't want to be swept into that beam of plasma."

"Yes," replied Nikola, "that might ruin our day."

Cordon looked at Nikola and smiled slightly. "Or our eternity, as in the end of it."

The Spirit was jostling and quivering in the gravitational eddies as they came to a stop and a port on the bottom of the craft opened to reveal the first of the three devices.

"OK," said Nikola, "I show a green board for the first device. Everything is functioning normally."

"Release it," said Cordon. "It should travel about fifty yards and then go to station keeping."

The 5-feet-long bomb was propelled out of the port and toward the rift. It stopped as programmed, 50 yards ahead of them.

"It has enough fuel to stay there about thirty-five minutes," noted Cordon. "We need to position the other two devices and get to a safe distance before then."

"I know," replied Nikola, who was becoming weary of Cordon's continual instructions.

He maneuvered the Spirit around the beam to the second release point. All the while, the gravitational turbulence fought with him. Several times he feared that it might pull them into the midst of the realm of lightning surrounding the swiftly flowing plasma, but he managed to keep on course. The second device turned out to be an easier placement than the first. He was well ahead of schedule. He moved in to place the third. That was when the trouble started.

"I'm getting an error light on the drive system of the third bomb," said Nikola, pointing to a display that seemed to float in midair.

Cordon looked at the display carefully. "Could it be a false reading?"

"It could be, but I doubt it."

"Go ahead and try to deploy it," said Cordon. "If it doesn't pull free of the rack, we will know."

Nikola nodded. He opened the bay, activated the electronics, and engaged the drive. The device didn't move. "We have a problem—no drive. Can we seal the rift with two bombs if we readjust their positions?"

"No," said Cordon, "it requires three to shape the pulse properly. Does the anti-graviton emitter seem functional?"

"Yes," confirmed Nikola. "Perhaps we could pull back a few miles, release the clamps on the bomb, and shoot it off toward the rift from there. Once it was in position, we could manually detonate the other two with it."

"In the midst of those gravitational eddies?" asked Cordon. "It is hard to say where the device would end up. The three devices have to be precisely placed if this is to work. I could go out there and examine it, see if it is something simple that could be repaired in a few minutes."

Nikola looked at Cordon incredulously. "It's a vacuum out there, you would suffocate. Even if you didn't, how could you maneuver?"

"With my wings," replied Cordon. "You humans don't know everything about the nature of angelic flight."

"Then there is the radiation," continued Nikola, "you'd receive a lethal dose in minutes. Yes, I know that it wouldn't kill you, but it would take days for your body to recover."

"If you have an alternate plan, I'd be more than happy to hear it," said Cordon.

Cordon's statement was answered with silence.

"I noticed that you have an airlock," continued Cordon.

"It has never been used as such," explained Nikola. "It is used mainly to prevent passengers from tripping into the stairwell, but it is airtight."

"Good enough," said Cordon, grabbing the tool pouch. "If I can't repair it in ten minutes, then I suppose we will have to come up with an alternate plan."

Nikola reached into a compartment to his left and pulled out a small breathing device. "Here, if you insist on going out there, take this. This won't help much. You'll still be exposed to the vacuum and the radiation, but at least it will provide you with breathable air. It is lightweight and will function for about twenty minutes, converting your exhaled carbon dioxide back into oxygen."

"I don't have time," insisted Cordon. "Keep it. You might need it later. Open the airlock, please."

Nikola nodded. "Be careful out there."

Cordon nodded, but said nothing.

The floor panel slid open and Cordon carefully descended into the belly of the ship. It was close quarters with his large wings, but he managed. The panel slid shut above him. A few seconds later, the air in the small compartment bled away.

It was a most uncomfortable experience for Cordon. In fact, it was downright painful. Perhaps he had been just a bit too confident. The belly of the craft opened and the stairway extended. The port housing the device in question was only a few feet away from the open hatchway. Cordon pushed off, grabbing the edge of the port. In the weightless environment, working with the device was a frustrating experience. It required five minutes just to remove the housing. Inside, no obvious problems caught his eye. They had checked all three of these devices before liftoff. What could possibly have gone wrong? He had hoped to find a loose plug or tripped relay. No such luck. Whatever was wrong was more fundamental. He replaced the access port.

He felt physically ill as he jumped back to the main hatchway. He climbed in and pounded on the inner hatch. The outer hatch closed behind him and a second later, air rushed in, filling his oxygen-starved lungs. The inner hatch slid open and he stepped onto the main deck, only to collapse.

Nikola looked down from the flight deck with concern, yet he was battling with increasing gravitational turbulence and could not come to Cordon's aid.

"No luck," said Cordon in a breathless voice. "I hope you have a plan."

"I do," replied Nikola, "but you're not going to like it. There should be no inherent problem with setting off the device while it is still in its cradle on board the Spirit. I could move the Spirit into position and arm the device. I would keep it in position, at station keeping until then. If you can fly through hyperspace, you might be able to reach a safe distance before I detonate the warheads."

"You call that a plan?" asked Cordon, rising to his knees.

Nikola shook his head. "We have only twenty-two minutes before we must detonate the devices, what else can we do?"

"Can you program the Spirit to hold its position without human assistance?" asked Cordon.

"Yes," replied Nikola, "I would use the same program I used in the three bombs."

"Then do it," said Cordon. "Get the Spirit into position for the detonation. The longer we wait, the less time I have to get you to safety."

"You want me to go out there?" asked Nikola, a sudden look of fear on his face.

"Yes," replied Cordon.

"But where would we go?" objected Nikola. "We would be stuck in hyperspace with no way to get out."

"There is a way out," said Cordon. "I left orders to engage the great ring, to set it to link to itself."

"Say what?" asked Nikola.

"I'll explain it another time," promised Cordon. "Let's just say that it is a way to link into hyperspace without creating a rift, and having Hell's atmosphere bleed away. Just get us into position, set the automatic detonator, and I'll do the rest."

Nikola nodded. He really didn't have much choice. It took about three minutes to maneuver into position and set the autopilot. He looked around for a moment. It had taken years to build this vessel. It was almost a part of him. Abandoning it, blowing it up, was almost more than he could bear.

"Are you ready?" asked Cordon.

"Yes," said Nikola. "Detonation of the three devices will occur in eighteen minutes." He again tried to offer Cordon a life support mask. Again he refused it.

"How many of those things do you have?" asked Cordon.

"Just these two," he replied.

"You are likely to need both of them," said Cordon.

"So, you are going to go out there and search for a hole in the hyperspace medium that is what…thirty or forty feet across? You don't have any points of reference. You don't know how far, or even which way to go."

"Do not proceed to tell me what I can and cannot do," replied Cordon, just a trace of anger in his voice. "I have studied the sciences for a hundred times longer than you have existed. I can sense distortions in space time or hyperspace that you could not even begin to detect with your most sensitive instruments. I know how far and in what direction. If you will finish your good-byes to this vessel and depressurize it, we will be on our way."

Nikola put on his heavy coat and one of the masks while he stuffed the power supply and filter of the second one in a small pack he would take with him. It would be easier to change out the components than switch masks. If only he had more of these things. If only he had thought ahead.

He was very afraid as he entered the command to open the inner airlock and depressurize the main cabin. The computer offered him the option of aborting the command. No, he would have to see this through. He confirmed the order and activated the mask.

There was a loud hiss as the depressurization began. His ears felt as if they were about to explode as the air pressure in the cabin plummeted toward zero. This air mask of his was intended as an emergency rescue device only. The road ahead promised to be very unpleasant indeed. It would be worse when the filters of this device saturated and its power supplies died. Then he would start to suffocate. At least that is the way it would feel. Yet it wouldn't kill him. Death was a once in an eternity experience.

The sound of the hissing dropped away. In fact, all sound ceased. He opened the outer airlock.

Cordon took him by the hand and led him to the place where his world ended and eternity began. They walked down the steps and took the plunge. The second that they were beyond the Spirit's gravity generator the sense of falling ceased. Cordon held him in his arms and began to fly.

Nikola looked back, amazed to discover just how fast they were traveling. He could feel what seemed to him to be an electric radiance coming from the beam, combined with a sense of intense cold. Cordon made a turn to the left and what to Nikola seemed downward. Again, they were flying in a straight line. Nikola glanced at his watch. There were 13 minutes to go.

Eleven minutes later Nikola again looked back. He couldn't make out the Spirit at all from this distance. The beam radiating out from the rift was little more than a thread of light against the backdrop of the eerie gossamer clouds of hyperspace. Soon he would know if this had all been worth it.

Then there was a great flash, filling the twilight world of hyperspace with light. For a moment, the bright star-like light kept him from seeing anything else; for that moment, the hard cold softened a bit. When the light faded, the thread of plasma was no more. It seemed to have worked. Instead, there was a roiling hot sphere of gas expanding in all directions, expanding fast. Nikola looked away, then at his watch. The instrument that was sparing him the discomfort of suffocation was nearly expended. It had just two minutes of operating life remaining. The filter would probably saturate first, allowing carbon dioxide to build up. He vowed to milk every ounce of oxygen out of it he could before switching to the second filter and power source.

The minutes ticked by. This breathing apparatus was working better than he had projected. He'd coaxed 28 minutes of life out of it. In the end, it was the power supply that gave up the ghost first. The flow of air slowed then stopped. As calmly as he could, he unscrewed the power module and replacing it with the second unit. Then he replaced the filter as well. Good air was flowing again.

He looked back to see the huge red ball of fire released from the explosion. It had dissipated as it had expanded, but not as much as he had hoped. It looked like a huge red sun, and its heat and size were growing. He might not have to worry about suffocating after all. He might end up flame broiled before then.

With the passage of ten more minutes, the translucent ball of fire had come to dominate this region of hyperspace. It was not unlike a great hot soap bubble growing thinner and cooler as it expanded. Yet its proximity had long since driven away the cold, turning this corner of hyperspace into an inferno. It would overtake them in minutes. The heat within it would surely be far worse, to say nothing of what it might do as it passed them.

Abruptly, Cordon changed course, climbing and banking to the right. Nikola looked ahead to see a yellow star. No, not a star, it was daylight! It was the open gate. Cordon's wings flapped ever harder.

Surely Cordon must have realized that he could have made better time if he released this human. That was Nikola's fear. This was, after all, a demon. Yet, he held on to this human all the more tightly. There was a shuttering, then a sense of being in an out of control spiral. Nikola's ears pained him terribly as the darkness was replaced by light. Cordon emerged from the blackness of the ring into the open air of the plains. The barren ground swung wildly in front of him before stabilizing. Then there was a sudden jolt as Cordon landed.

Nikola stumbled forward, removing his mask. He turned to find himself surrounded by demons of all description, and they didn't appear particularly friendly. He started to fall, yet Cordon got hold of him, stabilized him.

"Just have a little faith in me," said Cordon, smiling, even as he gasped for breath. "I told you I'd get you to safety."

"Yes, you did," said Nikola, reaching for Cordon's arm. "Please forgive me for doubting you, my friend."

A second later, an enormous cloud of fire erupted from the great ring, accompanied by a loud roar, startling everyone. Then the ring went silent.

A demon approached Cordon, bowing slightly. "My lord, it is good to see that you are well. We were growing concerned." He looked toward this human. "What would you have us do with him?"

"First of all, give him a few minutes to gather his strength. He has been through a lot," said Cordon.

"There isn't time," said Nikola, struggling to stand on his own once more. "I need to know if it worked, if the rift is sealed."

Cordon nodded. "As do I, my friend. Let us travel straight away to the ruins of Sheol, and see the results of our labors."

Suddenly, a dark circular portal appeared before them. Nikola was startled. "A gate? You can create your own gates?"

"Yes," confirmed Cordon. "It is a technology that I myself developed thousands of years ago. I thought that it would revolutionize travel here. But Satan commanded that only one device of its kind should be built, and that it was to remain in his hands exclusively. The instrument itself sets in his audience chamber. Over the years, I have improved it, but there is still but one. Now in his absence, I and Rolf have the power to call upon it as our needs require. I assure you, it is quite safe."

The two stepped into the dark portal, vanishing from the plains, en route to a place half a world away.

Chapter 21

David had been in the Holy Place for days with his mother and their friends. They had traveled about, spoken to others, spreading the news of the crisis that could well bring life on their home planet to an end. As incredible as their story was, no one doubted it. This was a place of truth, and these were the words of brothers and sisters in Christ. Those people, in turn, told others, and so the word spread through the multitude, which numbered over 100 million.

David spoke to the Father as well. The Father confirmed David's worst fears, but spoke of a time and a season to act. This was not that time. However, He did not discourage the mission of David and the others to spread the word. David had faith in the Father, but he also possessed an impatient spirit, so this ragtag messenger continued to spread the word.

He was often stopped by others who wanted to know more of the events in Hell, of how he even knew anything of the goings on there. He spoke of the events of six years ago—of Serena and Chris, of a love that spanned the distance between the most distant places in the universe, and how seemingly impossible prayers had been answered. He spoke of a struggle in the dark domain that went on even to this day. He spoke of his memories of loved ones there, of an aunt, a grandfather, a cousin, forever lost. He had asked the Father for those memories, to remember with crystal clarity all those he had known in life on Earth, and they had been granted to him. Yes, it hurt, it hurt a lot, but in the truth, the entire truth, he had become a whole individual with his eyes wide open.

Now there were others who came to ask the Father for the restoration of those memories. To all who asked, a solemn warning was given. Never again would their world be the same. They would be both a sadder and wiser individual. Many withdrew their request, but others sought the knowledge despite the consequences. For the first time there were tears in Heaven. It was the end of a sort of childhood that for many had lasted for centuries. They were ready to move on. They were sons and daughters of God still, yet childhood was over.

Ahead, a woman approached David. David prepared to greet her.

"Peace be unto you, David Bonner," she said.

David prepared to return the greeting. Then he realized who she was. "Peace be unto you Mary Magdalene. Oh, wow."

"Oh wow?" she asked, smiling slightly.

"Yes, I mean, I'm honored to meet you, ma'am. What I mean to say is that I feel privileged to be addressing someone who actually walked with the Lord while He was on Earth."

"I'm just another of the Father's children," replied Mary. "But I'm here for a reason. The words you and your fellows have spoken have reached all who are in attendance. The time has come to act…to spare the world of our birth."

"How?" asked David.

"You already know," replied Mary. "All of us here stand ready to help you."

"We need to send an enormous magnetic pulse out to seal the rip in hyperspace," replied David.

"Your friend Nikola Tesla has already sealed the rip, but the job is not complete," said Mary. "If it is left as it is, the repair will not hold. I do not understand it all, but my understanding is that we need to smooth it out. The Father told me that much. He said that you would understand."

"I do," confirmed David.

"The power of the Father's Holy Spirit will be called upon by all of the saints here," continued Mary. "It is you who will direct it, for the Father has already placed the knowledge of what is to be done within your heart. It is for this reason that you came here. Stand ready, for the moment shall be upon you soon."

Nikola and Cordon stepped forth into the City of Sheol. It was a realm of yawning chasms and ridges radiating out from a vast central crater miles across. It took several minutes for them to navigate the chaotic terrain, to a point from which they could clearly view the entire scene. What they saw was perplexing. There was no longer a great vortex here, but it was not a peaceful place either. Black oil from the Sea of Fire had breached the walls of the crater forming a circular bay of fiery fury. Here and there, narrow shafts of constantly shifting blue electricity coursed from dozens of points of light hanging in the sky above the bay like so many tiny stars. From the middle of the bay, the black sea churned and smoked.

Cordon shook his head. "Not enough. It was a noble effort, my friend, but it was not enough. We patched the rift, but I fear the patch will not hold very long."

Nikola looked around, trying to come up with a plan. They had almost succeeded. They had bought themselves some time at least. "You are the expert on this phenomenon. How long do you think our patch will hold?"

"I can't be sure," admitted Cordon. "Perhaps a few weeks, maybe months, I just don't know."

There was nothing more to be said. For the moment at least, Nikola was out of ideas.

They started to depart when it happened. It was like a wave in space that seemed to radiate from the very heart of the distortion. It practically knocked Nikola and Cordon off of their feet and caused the ground to shake violently. It all passed in a matter of seconds. Then there was silence.

Nikola rose to his feet to discover that the threads of blue electricity and the points of light were gone.

"What happened?" asked Cordon, gazing about in disbelief.

"I was hoping that you could tell me," replied Nikola.

"I can't feel it," said Cordon. "The rift is totally gone. Everything has returned to normal."

For a few minutes, they stood there bringing up one possible explanation after another but nothing seemed to fit. In the end, Cordon called for the portal and they were off again—this time to Refuge.

They emerged just inside of the phantasmal wall before a dozen human and angelic guardians. Over the next few hours, they would recount their story again and again to a grateful people. Their mission had been a success—or had it? Perhaps they would never fully understand what had happened.

Cordon stepped from Abaddon's audience chamber into a crowded hallway to be greeted by the cheers and applause of hundreds of humans and dark angels. Cordon was overwhelmed. Never in his long life had he ever imagined being greeted so warmly by so many humans. While shaking hands and listening to the outpouring of grateful hearts, he pondered the future.

From the midst of the crowd, Julie stepped forward to thank the fallen angel. "I guess you'll be leaving us now?"

"For now," said Cordon. "However, I hope to return from time to time. It is my sincerest wish that the future might offer peace and cooperation between our peoples. I hope to see you again, Julie. You are a most interesting human...I enjoy your company."

Julie hesitated, then kissed Cordon on the cheek. Cordon seemed surprised. A growing smile graced his countenance.

"Until we meet again, my friend," she said, stepping back into the crowd.

"Until we meet again," echoed Cordon.

As Cordon prepared to depart, arrangements for another meeting on neutral territory were made. A delegation from both sides would meet. It was an almost inconceivable concept—a peace treaty between the people of Refuge and the demons of Hell. Only time would tell if this fantasy could be turned into reality, but the groundwork had been laid.

Cordon and Rolf stood before the great portal in Hell. The low sun glistened off of its surface.

"The great gate no longer functions," explained a demon warrior. "We have tried to send needed reinforcements to the master but have been unsuccessful. I fear that recent events have damaged it, perhaps irreparably."

"A pity," said Cordon, looking at the gate, then back at the demon. "You've done your best. You are needed at the fire pits of Kroll. Word is that there is a human uprising underway. These are a particularly dangerous lot. Take your minions and see that the humans are returned to their torment. I have some experience with this technology; I shall see what can be done here."

The demon bowed before his master and departed, along with his 53 compatriots. Cordon waited until they were well out of sight. Then he proceeded to the ring.

"Is this gate truly a thing of the past?" asked Rolf. "Will it function no more?"

Cordon placed his hand upon the ancient stone on the left side of the ring. "I suspect that it is but a temporary problem, a static buildup in its depths. It should function normally in a few days."

"Then we should act quickly," suggested Rolf.

Cordon only nodded as he removed the small explosive device borrowed from his friends at Refuge. He touched a hidden pressure plate, causing a panel to slide to one side. Within, he beheld a series of crystals and crystal strands. He reached in, placing the small explosive device inside. Then the panel closed once more, even as Rolf did the same on the right.

The task done, Cordon and Rolf retreated several hundreds of yards away. For a moment, Cordon gazed upon the magnificent ring.

"In a way, it is regrettable that we must destroy it," said Cordon. "It is part of our history. But I can ill afford Satan retreating back here. He took his most loyal followers with him. Those left behind might well be convinced to follow a new course…the one I establish for them. Nonetheless, there might be consequences associated with what we do here today. Are you still sure that you wish to be part of this?"

Rolf smiled. "I'll take my chances."

Cordon removed the detonator from his cloak. He armed the bombs then pressed the plunger.

A barely perceptible detonation emanated from the ring. For a moment, a reddish glow engulfed the entire device. Then it was hidden in smoke and dust. When the dust cleared, the ring looked much as it had before, but it was now only an ornament in the desert, a monument; it would never function again.

Cordon and Rolf walked away. They had just burned Satan's bridge behind him. He and his minions would never walk this parched land again, nor would they draw support from it. Now Cordon was in control. Was he now the master of Hell? He doubted it. The old Hell was gone, as surely as its tyrannical ruler. Now, with only limited resources, Cordon would have to forge some sort of coalition government. He could not rule Hell alone. He would need Abaddon's help. He was not optimistic about the future. There was still much distrust between the demons and dark angels, but surely pursuing this route was the lesser of two evils.

With the restoration of telesphere communication between Refuge and Heaven, and the opening of the gate between Heaven and Earth once more, the stage was set for an angelic counterattack. During the following week, 15 million more angels made the trip between Earth and Heaven, and the number of armed human fighters soared to nearly 100,000. They could not allow Satan to consolidate his position. They had to attack as soon as possible, and that attack would come at Zion. They would throw everything they had into a single battle.

Intelligence indicated that there might be countless millions of angels imprisoned in the Hall of Angels at the heart of the city. Releasing them would be the first step in a long-term strategy of the liberation of Heaven. Nonetheless, it promised to be a long campaign, perhaps taking years.

Word arriving from Refuge indicated that Satan's bridge had been burned behind him. He could not retreat to Hell. Therefore, he would no doubt fight to the death, employing whatever means necessary to secure victory. And they couldn't forget that he still held a four to three numerical advantage, and had probably fortified his position. Their work was cut out for them.

The atmosphere at the final meeting of the war council in Elesia was cautiously optimistic. Come tomorrow, they would mobilize one of the largest angelic armies ever assembled. At 137 million strong, its numbers almost defied comprehension. They would be facing a force of 170 million battle-hardened demons.

The plan was simple, at least on paper. They would make use of their one advantage—superior mobility. They would begin their attack on the demon-held city of Sarel, on the fourth level of Heaven. Six million angels would be committed to this fight; yet, it was only a rouse, an attempt to draw Satan's forces away from Zion as angelic forces gated unseen into the cover of the dense forests just four miles north of the great city. Six hours later, those forces, virtually all of Michael's and Gabriel's angels, would attack as the original 6 million were withdrawn to reinforce their numbers. Their primary mission would be to release captive angels from Satan's compound at the heart of the city. They only hoped that the devil would fall for it.

As morning dawned, 6 million battle-ready angels led by 10,000 human volunteers gated out of the fields north of Elesia bound for Sarel, even as a far larger force prepared to gate into the dense forests north of Zion. It would take many hours to transfer so huge a force. They could only hope that no wandering demons discovered them.

The demonic messenger practically tripped over his own wings as he burst into a meeting of Satan's advisory council. His clumsy and totally inappropriate entrance drew the attention of all.

"My lord, millions of angels are attacking the city of Sarel. They came out of the west, supported by their human allies. Lieutenant Kazat, the city commander, reports that the garrison is in danger of being overrun. He is holding out for now…barely, but his forces are being pushed back. He requests reinforcements."

Satan was uncharacteristically calm as he replied. "We all expected this. It was the where and when that was in question. How many legions do we have guarding that city?"

"One," said the messenger, "but they are greatly outnumbered."

Satan turned to General Krell. "General, I need you to dispatch two legions to Sarel. I assume that you have that many troops ready to be deployed."

"And more," confirmed the general. "You want only two, my lord?"

"Yes," confirmed Satan. "I suspect that shall be sufficient. Once they are dispatched, I want you to put everyone else on high alert. Activate all of our reserves and bring them here. As for this city—I want to execute our perimeter plan at once."

"The perimeter plan…here in this city, not Sarel?" confirmed the general.

"Yes, that is correct," confirmed Satan. "I need you to do this thing now."

The general rose from his seat. "It shall be as you command." He departed, leaving Satan and his other four advisors at the table.

"I don't understand, my lord," said Governor Molock. "If the attack is in Sarel, why are we fortifying our position here?"

"Because the attack on Sarel is but a distraction from the angels' true mission," said Satan. "I know Michael; his real objective is Zion. I assure you he will attack here within hours. He can do nothing less. In his mind, his first priority is to liberate the holy city. I have been preparing for this."

Metastopholies raised his eyebrows in dull surprise, but said nothing. Usually he could discern the outcome of a set of events, but not today. The currents of time were too swift and turbulent this day. He would have to hope that it cleared in the near future. Until then, he would offer no advice to the master.

Gabriel gazed upon the City of Zion from the edge of the forest; all was quiet. Could he be so fortunate? Might Satan have diverted the majority of his forces to the City of Sarel? He would soon know.

At the appointed moment millions of angels took flight, a mighty wind arose from the combined breeze of their beating wings. They set course for the city. At first, it looked like they might not be challenged. Then they saw the black hordes arise from the former Hall of Angels. Apparently, they had not caught Satan completely by surprise.

From the edge of the forest, guarding the left flank, General Washington gazed up at the magnificent sight of so many angels in flight. His troops were ready to move once the first ranks of angels reached the outer walls of the city. He turned to his troops. For the first time in his career, there were women in the ranks. Nearly 40 percent of his 30,000 troops were of the fairer gender. Many of the warriors pulled down the visors on their helmets and shielded their eyes against the dust raised by the winds sweeping in from the meadows as the angels passed overhead.

Washington looked to his right to see his commander, Cornelius, step from the shadows of the forest a mile away with his 40,000 troops. They would be on the move in another two minutes. Still, there was something missing; Washington missed his horse. He was certain that Cornelius felt the same way. Rare was the day that he had not led his troops into battle from horseback, as had Cornelius. He gazed down at the sword in his scabbard. He smiled, but slightly. He imagined that there were few humans in the ranks who still carried a sword. Yes, he had a particle rifle and a pistol, but he couldn't imagine going into battle without his sword. In reality, he had never imagined leading troops into battle again. Today, he would face the most vile foe of his career, humankind's worst enemy.

He watched the first wave of angels cross the wall; it was time. He motioned for his troops to advance. The forest was suddenly alight with mists and stars as the troops advanced through the ether toward the city.

Five thousand steps would be covered in about five. Washington pulled the visor down on his helmet and stepped into his own portal. The next stop was the Via de Gloria, one of the most important avenues in the city.

Washington and over 1,000 of his troops materialized in the middle of the golden street. They quickly scanned their surroundings; the street was deserted. In the skies behind them, a vast multitude of angels were swiftly advancing, while in the skies ahead, an equally formidable formation of demons was closing on them. The demons would be within range of their particle weapons within a minute. Washington and the others were preparing to find places of cover which offered a clear view of the encroaching demon forces, when the sound of multiple loud detonations erupted from a neighboring street, somewhere to the west.

Washington turned to see motion within a neighboring building. Then there was a brilliant flash, as a fireball roared from a second floor window and into the street. His troops were thrown in all directions by the blast. The realization of their situation hit him immediately. "Take cover!" he yelled. "It's a trap!"

From all quarters the demons emerged, thousands of them. The street was ablaze in explosive fire. Washington's forces were caught by surprise. They returned fire, yet they were largely firing blind.

In seconds, Washington found himself face to face with a huge demon, his sword drawn. Washington's reaction was automatic; he went for his own sword. Titanium alloy met angelic metal with a resounding clash and showering sparks. The demon seemed surprised to find himself crossing blades with a human. They maneuvered for position. The demon went for the kill with a quick thrust to the heart only to have his blade deflected by Washington's swift sword.

It became obvious that this human would not be a quick kill. Yet the battle between them lasted for another few seconds before Washington's demonic adversary was blasted into a cloud of vapors by a particle beam at point blank range. Were it not for Washington's helmet and heat resistant uniform, he would surely have been seriously injured.

Washington stumbled toward a shop at the edge of the street. He prayed that he would encounter no more unpleasant surprises along the way. A particle beam emerging from a window of the shop told him that he was making for friendly territory. Within, he found three soldiers who had dug in for the firefight.

Another round of fireballs rendered portions of the street itself into a semi-liquid state. The screams of his own men and the blazing inferno radiating from beyond the temporary safety of the shop told him that this skirmish was lost.

"There is a back door that leads into an alleyway," said a fourth soldier, entering the room from the rear. "It looks clear." The soldier spotted Washington, saw his rank insignia. "Sir, we've gotta withdraw."

"You're sure it's clear?" asked Washington.

"Far as I can see, sir."

"Then we'd best retreat," said Washington. "Never have I taken such a licking in a battle so quickly. They knew we were coming. Perhaps some of the other companies have faired better." He went for his radio. It was full of frantic reports and crosstalk. It sounded like everyone was in a fix. He ordered a retreat to anyone who could hear him. He didn't want his troops to gate back to the woods and leave the angels on their own. That would be a last resort. They were to fall back to the Manasseh Gate. They would try to make a stand there.

Seventeen blocks away, Cornelius heard Washington's order to fall back. His troops were taking a pounding too, but they had managed to dig in and hold amid the ruins of a deserted marketplace. He wasn't prepared to sound the retreat—not just yet. He knew that they were tying down demonic forces that would otherwise be free to attack the angels who were even now passing overhead. Some of those angels were breaking off, joining the fight in the streets, reinforcing his position. No, he would have to hold out.

The second wave of Michael's angels had crossed the walls of Zion when no less than four legions of demons swept in behind them, emerging from their hiding places within the buildings. An aerial battle of enormous proportions ensued as the swords of millions of angels and demons clashed.

Farther to the west, a great barrage of fireballs erupted into the air scattering and burning the third wave of angels as they crossed the wall. An orderly advance was turning into a fierce and chaotic battle that ranged from the ground to an altitude of several thousand feet.

A steady stream of angels continued to enter the battle from the north and northeast as the demons reinforced their ranks from the south and west. Neither side was willing to budge an inch, so the battle continued to escalate.

At the Holy Place, millions of demons streamed in, surrounding the saints. The saints could not be allowed to enter the war on the side of the angels. The saints would be secure, so long as they didn't step beyond the bounds of this greatest of all temples. This fact was made abundantly clear to them; step beyond the bounds of the Holy Place, and face dire consequences.

There were those within the Holy Place, those enlisted by David and the others, who were more than ready for a fight. Armed with their newly made particle rifles, they were ready to face the most deadly enemy of humankind. Not the least of these was Thecla, a follower of the Apostle Paul. An inspiring orator, she was more than willing to step boldly from the Holy Place and stand toe to toe with their foes.

"I will face them with a weapon in my hand or armed only with the power of the Holy Spirit," she cried. "No demon from Hell will be able to stand before us. After all, if God is for us, who can be against us?"

She had more than 1,000 followers, mostly women, willing to follow her into harm's way, assured that they would be safe. Yet Peter and the elders urged Thecla and her followers to quiet the angry spirit within them; their time was not yet. Still, unrest among God's people was mounting. They could hear the battle raging and see the flashes of weapons fire in the north. Passions stood near the boiling point.

God's word to His people was the same—they could enter the war if they wished, but for the moment, He would not interfere. Up until now, many of the saints felt that statement had implied that participation in the war placed them both out of God's protection and His will. But now they weren't so sure. One thing was certain—they would not accept Satan as the ultimate leader of the angels. If push came to shove, they would fight him.

It was the wee hours of the morning when Elizabeth awoke to hear someone calling her name. She found her modest forest home filled with glowing fragrant mists. There was someone standing there, a slightly glowing figure near the door. Perhaps she should have been afraid, but she wasn't. She boldly rose from her bed and walked directly toward the figure.

She was halfway across the room when she was finally able to discern his features—it was Jesus. A smile appeared on her face, one to match His. "Lord, it does my heart good to see You."

"Peace unto you, Elizabeth," said Jesus. "I have come to ask you why you have been hiding from our Father."

Elizabeth was confused. "But Lord, I haven't been hiding from the Father, I've been right here."

"Don't you see, the others need you?" continued Jesus. "In Zion, at the Holy Place, the saints need a leader. You are that leader. You hold the key to victory in your hand, yet you have stayed away."

"But Satan and his demons control the city," objected Elizabeth.

"Does he?" asked Jesus.

Elizabeth was silent. She truly didn't know what to say.

"Go to Zion, daughter of God, you will know what to do."

Jesus faded away with the mists. Elizabeth awoke from her sleep. She looked around; it was dark and quiet. Only the light of the fireflies illuminated the forests beyond her open window. It had been a dream. What was she to do? She didn't have to ask that question, she knew. She lit the oil lamp and went to fetch her best white robes. She was going to the City of Zion.

Chapter 22

At the edge of the forest, Michael and his lieutenants evaluated their situation and their options. They were now five hours into the battle for Zion. They had fully anticipated battling on the rooftop of the Hall of Angels at this point. That hadn't happened. The battle was raging in the streets of Zion and in the air above, scarcely a quarter mile within the walls, and that battle had virtually leveled the northern regions of the city. Indeed, much of it was in flames, and the fires were spreading. Michael had hoped to take the city virtually intact. It wasn't working out that way.

Overhead, ever more angels were gating in to join the battle, but that influx was nearly at an end. They were sending in reserves at this point, and that resource was nearly tapped. Still they weren't making headway. In fact, during the last two hours they had been pushed back.

Angels who had fallen into enemy territory were quickly stripped of their wings and shackled hand and foot, to be picked up later and imprisoned. Since the beginning of the war, over 150 million angels had gone missing. Where they were was anyone's guess. Certainly they couldn't all be held prisoner in the Hall of Angels.

"We've held eleven million of our best warriors in reserve, according to your command," said one of Michael's lieutenants.

"We want to open up a new front right here," said Michael, pointing to the far western fringe of the city on the map. "If Satan is slow to respond, we might drive deep into the city, perhaps all of the way to the Hall of Angels."

Colonel Borst, commanding the last 5,000 human reserve troops, looked at the plan and scowled. "I suppose you'll be asking me to throw my troops into the city in advance of your forces?"

"I doubt that our plan will succeed without ground support," said Michael.

"May I remind you that General Washington suffered a nearly fifty percent loss supporting your forces," countered the colonel. "Who can say what Satan's minions did with them. I can't condone turning my men and women into fireball fodder."

"Your superiors agreed to this plan," countered Michael.

"I'm aware of that," replied the colonel, "I just wish to enter my protest for the record. My people will be ready when called upon." The colonel walked away from the table.

"The humans and their weapons have not been as effective or reliable as they have been in previous engagements," noted one of Michael's lieutenants.

"Don't be so critical of them," replied Michael. "The colonel happens to be right. They are taking heavy casualties, often gating into regions of fierce resistance unaware. This whole operation is going badly. I believe Satan has been studying our tactics and has adapted. Even if we do turn the tide, I fear Zion will be reduced to little more than a pile of rubble before this operation is complete. Unless things begin to improve, and quickly, we may be forced to withdraw."

"It is the uncanny resilience of Satan's troops that has disturbed me," noted Gabriel. "They were not created by the Father to be warriors, yet they seem to have more stamina, more strength, than our most seasoned veterans."

"I am at a loss to explain it," replied Michael, but I am not willing to withdraw, not yet. Let us see how this new attack goes before we make such decisions."

Gabriel nodded. Yet he was beginning to lose hope that this battle could be won.

Thirty minutes later, the new offensive began—the results were little better. The battle lines ground to a halt less than a mile into the city, and the casualties, especially on the human side, were appalling. Best estimates indicated that the angelic forces had lost over 5 million of their own, and nearly a third of their human allies. They could ill afford to continue the fight, yet they could not afford to withdraw either. Their hopes of ever regaining control of Heaven were fading before their eyes.

None of the combatants had noticed the woman who had just materialized at the Manasseh Gate. It was here that Elizabeth had always materialized when she came to Zion. This war would not cause her to change her habits.

Passing through the gate, Elizabeth looked on in horror at the damage that had been done to the most beautiful city in the universe. It first brought tears to her eyes, but her grief was slowly being transformed into anger.

She made her way around the rubble as the battle raged on over her head. It was about ten minutes before she came upon a wounded angel, his right wing sliced nearly in half by the sword of a demon. She rushed to lend assistance, and helped him from the street to the shelter of a still standing awning in front of a bombed-out business.

Then she heard movement behind her. Turning, she found a demon approaching her, his sword drawn.

"You are aiding the enemy," he said. "That makes you an enemy. I will shackle both of you and take you back to the master."

"Run," bid the angel, doing his best to stand up.

"I will not," replied Elizabeth, growing anger in her voice. She walked toward the demon as the angel looked on. "Leave my presence at once," she demanded.

"What gives you the authority to make such a demand of me?" asked the demon.

"I am a child of God, sanctified by the blood of his Son, Jesus," she replied.

"I am not impressed," retorted the demon, pointing his sword at the apparently unarmed woman.

"You should be," replied Elizabeth. "This is my last warning."

The demon only laughed. "Or you'll do what, wench?"

"Or I'll reduce thee to a pile of ashes here and now. I assure thee, that it is a most painful experience…I've done it to others of your kind. Be thankful that I am giving you a choice. Now, go."

Again the demon laughed. He was becoming weary of this woman. "I believe it is time to teach you some manners before I send you on to Satan."

That was it. Instinctively, she stretched out her hand toward the demon. Instantly, he was engulfed in a sphere of pure fire. So great was the heat that Elizabeth was compelled to pull back a good 20 feet. A minute later, her threat had been made good.

The angel looked on incredulously. "How did you do that?"

"The power of the Holy Spirit," she replied.

"But you used neither sword nor rifle," objected the angel.

"I have not the time to explain," said Elizabeth, helping the angel find cover. "Remain here. Fly to safety once you have healed. I fear I must be on my way to the Holy Place."

Elizabeth did not wait for the angel to respond. She moved on. Though this time she made an effort to stay under cover as much as she could. What had just happened had been a leap of faith. She hadn't been certain what would happen, only that God would protect her, as He had with Daniel in the lion's den.

Along her route the sounds of fighting overhead, of explosions and weapons fire, filled the air. Elizabeth had reached the Via de Gloria when she was confronted with yet another horror. Here, men and women in military attire, hundreds of them, were shackled hand and foot in groups, thrown into the center of the street like garbage set out for collection.

They were bound in such a way that they could hardly move. The logic was clear. If they were bound together, if they couldn't move, they couldn't gate out. She approached the first group—three men and two women— their heavy ankle and wrist shackles intertwined in such a way as to render them a helpless pile of flesh.

"Help us, please," pleaded a man on the top of the pile. His arms were shackled behind his back, intertwined with those about the ankles of another, while his ankle shackles were looped around the wrist shackles of still another. It forced him into a most unnatural bent back position.

Elizabeth examined the shackles. They had no release point, not so much as a seam. She could think of only one thing to do. She touched the shackles with her hand. "In the name of Jesus, be released," she said.

Immediately the shackle cracked in half, as did every shackle that held the soldiers within the pile. They rolled apart, and then helped each other to their feet.

"Remove thee from here," warned Elizabeth. "You've suffered enough."

The soldiers didn't have to be told twice. They quickly gated away.

She proceeded to another pile of humanity and repeated the act that freed the first. She offered them the same warning.

Again and again the miracle was repeated as she continued her journey to the Holy Place. She praised God for His mercy and His Son for the act that had brought humanity salvation. Amazingly, the demons overhead were too preoccupied to give the acts of this lone woman any heed, at least for the moment.

Not long after she moved on, demons dispatched to gather up the captured humans were surprised to find that their helpless captives on the Via de Gloria had vanished without a trace. The search was on for the person or persons responsible for the theft of prisoners who were rightfully the property of the master.

Elizabeth was not far from the Holy Place when the demons overhead took note of the lone human wandering through the city. When she was scarcely 100 yards from the Holy Place, three of them descended to intercept her.

"You are trespassing in territory that is rightfully ours," announced the first demon who had landed about a dozen feet in front of her.

"This is not thy territory," replied Elizabeth, not the slightest sign of fear on her countenance. "This is the kingdom of the Father and of His children. You gave up your rights to it long ago."

Anger flared in the demon's eyes. He was not accustomed to humans speaking to him in such a manner. He took a step toward this bold woman. "It belongs to us now, wench."

"So you say," was the reply.

"You would doubt it?" asked the demon to the first one's left.

"It isn't a matter of doubt, but of record," retorted Elizabeth.

"She is the bold one," said the third demon, amusement in his voice.

"Perhaps she needs to be taught a lesson in humility," said the second.

The demons continued their verbal assault on this slight woman as she stood in silence. It had become a game to them, one to pass the time of day.

As the confrontation continued, it had drawn the attention of David Bonner and several of Thecla's female followers at the threshold of the Holy Place. The incident stoked the fires of their anger.

"These demons are such pigs," said one of the women. "They choose to confront those smaller and weaker than themselves."

"Don't underestimate them," warned David. "They can be formidable opponents."

The confrontation beyond the Holy Place was quickly escalating as more and more demons surrounded the young woman. Elizabeth had felt it best to pursue a policy of silence up to this point, yet the odds were turning against her. Then the demons' conversation took a new and more threatening direction.

"Someone has stolen prisoners of war from the master," said one of the demons. "I believe that someone is you."

Elizabeth considered her options, sought guidance, and then answered the demons' accusations. "You have trespassed into Heaven, brought down this city with your foul warfare; now you complain of stolen prisoners, prisoners you have no right to in the first place. I tell you this: depart this place while you still can, seek God's pardon for this transgression. For I tell you now—if you do not, your existence shall come to an end this very day. The saints shall judge you, and you shall be found wanting."

The demon stepped forward and forcefully struck Elizabeth, knocking her to the ground. For a moment she was stunned.

"Answer the question wench," demanded the demon. "Did you aid the enemies of Satan?"

"Of course," said Elizabeth, "I could do nothing less."

At the threshold of the Holy Place, Thecla, June, and Jennifer had joined the mounting crowd. Thecla watched as the demon struck Elizabeth. For her, it was the last straw. She had been known to take incredible leaps of faith during her life on Earth. Now she was prepared to take the greatest one of all.

"Enough!" she roared. "It ends here. We have cowered from those demons long enough! I am going out there, even if no one else follows."

"I'll go with you," cried more than a dozen of her followers with one voice.

David was surprised to hear the voice of his mother and Jennifer among them. He turned to Don and the others.

"We're with you if you go out there," said Don.

The others nodded in agreement. Thecla was right—the time was now.

"I have a few spare weapons," said David. "It would only take a moment to teach you how to use one."

"Thank you for your offer," said Thecla, "but I don't need your weapon."

David looked at her incredulously. "You can't go out there unarmed."

"I can do nothing less," said Thecla. "I will place my life in the hands of the Father as I always have. He has never abandoned me in the past…He will not abandon me now."

There was no further discussion, not even a plan. Thecla and over 30 of her followers, mostly women, stepped from the safety of the Holy Place and into harm's way.

"It's going to be one of those days," said Don, charging his rifle.

"Tell me about it," replied David, doing the same.

A growing hum arose from around them as several dozen men and women equipped with newly made particle rifles charged their weapons. This was it; they were really going to do it. They moved out to join Thecla and her followers. They marched to not only aid Elizabeth, but to declare all-out war on the demon hoards.

To the credit of the children of God, it was the demons who fired first. Over a dozen fireballs roared in their direction from above. Amazingly, all but two were detonated by particle rifle fire, well short of their mark.

Elizabeth looked up at the tightening ring of demons about her. She saw the encroaching saints. It was time. She reached out toward the closest demon. A blinding beam of light emanated from her palm. The demon was sent flying. He was reduced to dust long before he reached the ground. She followed the first shot with two more before being hit by a fireball at close range.

Seventy yards away Thecla witnessed what Elizabeth had done. Now it was her turn. "Lord, grant me the power I need to rid Heaven of this plague in the name of Jesus."

She stretched forth her hand toward a nearby demon. A ball of expanding yellow flame erupted from her hand engulfing her adversary. He writhed in agony as he was reduced to little more than ashes within the span of half a minute.

Meanwhile, David and the others fired round after round using their particle rifles. David was amazed by the faith of Thecla and several of her other followers who now also displayed the unique gift. Converting the energy resident within God's Holy Spirit directly into a weapon of such power without any sort of instrumentality went beyond his comprehension. Perhaps that was the reason he couldn't do it—he just didn't have the faith to make it work. For now he would use this rifle; later, when there was more time for reflection, he would seek this new gift.

The gap in the ring of demons encircling the Holy Place was widening as ever more saints found the faith to set forth from the sphere of protection to do battle with the enemy. Some had even managed to form an effective shield of protection to protect themselves from incoming fireballs.

Though severely burned, Elizabeth rose to her feet in the midst of the demons. She swung about swiftly, engulfing all the demons around her in the flames of vengeance. The demons who had assaulted her were burned to dust as Thecla and her followers arrived to surround and protect Elizabeth.

Even more saints emerged from the protection that the Holy Place offered, to face the ultimate battle. Most were armed with nothing more than faith, reinforced by the deeds of a growing number of others. That faith yielded a weapon of immense power. The demons were falling back in confusion. Their worst fears had been realized—a second front in the battle for Zion had opened up. Their real troubles were just beginning.

In Satan's audience chamber, the news of the events transpiring around the Holy Place reached him even as he had begun to glory over his perceived victory over the angels and humans in the northern regions of Zion. Now he weighed his options. If these two forces met, his task might be greatly complicated. He could not allow that to happen.

He needed to mobilize all of his forces from all of the plains of Heaven and bring them here to Zion to join the battle. This was the critical moment.

The humans at the Holy Place would probably not want to risk expanding their battle front too swiftly. They were, after all, little more than a disorganized rebel faction. They had offered only token resistance up to this point. They might not have the stomach for a prolonged battle. He might have many hours to focus his full effort on the collapsing angelic front. Once they withdrew, he could concentrate on this new human threat.

Under the full weight of his army, they would fold quickly enough. No, this day wasn't lost—far from it.

At the southern edge of the forest, the leaders of the coalition forces of angels and humans were also weighing their options. This battle had gone very badly. Their hopes had been so high. There seemed little to be gained in continuing the struggle. They had lost still more angelic and human warriors.

Yet, a series of indeed strange reports had been filtered to them—reports of a woman who had rescued an angel, slain a demon with the wave of her hand, and rescued no less than 100 human captives who were helplessly awaiting their transportation to Satan's new domain. Who was she? Word was that she had been on her way to the Holy Place. Might she have made it?

"I don't want to imagine what might have happened to us had she not found us," reported one of the human recipients of the mysterious lady's grace. "The shackles fell from us with just the touch of her hand, and we managed to escape and make it back here."

"I would like to know if she made it," said Cornelius. "I could take a hundred human volunteers deep into the city, just short of the Holy Place. We could fight our way in from there, question those who have sought refuge there. Then we would report what we found by radio, assuming that is not too far." He turned to Johann Kepler.

"No, that is not too far," confirmed Johann. "While you're there, you might try to locate David and the others. I am deeply concerned about them."

Cornelius nodded. "I shall do as you ask."

The council gave their approval to the plan, and within a matter of 20 minutes, Cornelius had found the volunteers to make this mission work. They all realized that they might well be walking into a hornets' nest of demons, but they would have to take that chance. A few minutes later, they walked into the starry mists, bound for the very heart of Zion.

They were not quite prepared for what they found on the other end of the gate. They walked into a bustling crowd of humans. For a moment, they thought they had walked right into the Holy Place itself, but no, they had emerged right on course. The men and women were marching out in all directions, singing songs of praise to God. The soldiers could do little more than go with the crowd.

Before them they could see flashes of light and hear peals of thunder. What was happening here?

It took a few minutes to piece the events of the past couple of hours together. It was incredible. Cornelius radioed his findings back to the war council. In light of what had happened, they dared not withdraw. They had to fight on, hold out. Time was on their side if they could weather this storm.

A new plan was hastily drawn up. They would send angelic warriors directly into the heart of the city to join the swelling human throng. They could be ferried there by human pilots, gated there through the mists.

At the same time, they would double their efforts to the north of the city. Somehow, they would hold. The very knowledge that help was on the way would strengthen their resolve.

The demons were waging a fighting retreat against the swelling human force. More and more they were compelled to pull demonic reinforcements from the northern front in an effort to shore up their defenses in the heart of the city.

Within his throne room, Satan's air of calm was swiftly evaporating. The old prince of darkness was back. He paced back and forth like a lion in a cage as his court stood before him, awaiting his commands.

"I will not be defeated now!" he raved. "I will be master of Heaven." For a moment he stopped, then he turned to his advisors. "Yes, I know what we shall do. General Krell, pull thirty legions from the northern front. Those that remain will hold Michael's forces at bay until the mission of these legions is complete. Order the thirty legions to completely surround the humans. God cannot claim that they are anything but combatants. They are fair targets. Once the legions are in position, they will fire the most massive fireball barrage that the universe has ever known. The humans shall be reduced to burnt meat. Then they will fire a second volley to finish the job. Only then shall they once more focus their attention on the angels at our northern wall."

Krell looked his master with a look of astonishment. "My lord, two fireball assaults of that magnitude would drain our already low resources. Since the destruction of Sheol, the crystals are no longer being renewed. Our warriors have been engaged in battle for many hours, they have drawn the power in these crystals down to a quarter of their capacity. Such a use of force would nearly exhaust them. If the attack failed, we would be most vulnerable."

Satan flew into a rage. "Are you questioning my orders? I hope not. For if you are, there are others who would gladly accept your position as master of the armies."

Krell dared not question the master again. "It shall be as you command."

"Then go do it!" demanded Satan.

Krell bowed and walked from the room as the others watched in silence. Yes, the old Satan was back.

"Governor Molock," said Satan. "You will assist in a little project that I have been preparing. Proceed to the gate room and oversee its progress. You will be my eyes and ears. You will see that it is completed in a timely manner."

Molock had no idea what project the master was referring to. Yet, he was not about to question it. "I live but to serve," he said, bowing before his master and making his way to the gate room, leaving Satan and Metastopholies alone in the chamber.

"We have spoken of this before," said Metastopholies.

"Of what?" said Satan, who had made his way back to his throne.

"Your anger," replied Metastopholies. "When you are in this state, you make poor decisions. Krell was right. If your fireball attack fails, matters will be worse."

"It will not fail," replied Satan. "Why must you be so negative?"

"To counter your rash overconfidence," replied Metastopholies. "Someone has to. The others fear to do so; therefore, the task falls to me."

"Be careful where you tread, old friend," warned Satan, simmering anger in his eyes. "Do not test our friendship."

Metastopholies showed not a trace of emotion as he stared into the master's eyes. "Then know this, my lord, heed my words well; today your leadership will be tested. I see a place of darkness, cold and foreboding. It is a place of total isolation, where chains will bind you for a thousand years. It has been awaiting you since eternity began. Beyond it is something even worse, a realm of unquenchable fire. There may yet be a way out for you, but will you find it? The decisions you make here and now will have a profound impact on your destiny. Are you a prisoner of that destiny, my lord?"

With those words, Metastopholies left his master's presence. He did not ask his permission, nor did he bow, as was customary. He simply walked out the door without so much as a glance back. No one else would have gotten away with such an act of insolence.

Satan sat down, pounded his fist on his throne, and was silent. What was happening? Why was his victory unraveling? No, he would triumph. Though all would question his leadership, he would triumph. It would take but an hour to institute his plan, see it to completion; then, everyone would see and understand his genius. It was his destiny to rule.

Chapter 23

Satan stood at the edge of the roof of the Hall of Angels gazing upon the city below. In the distance, he could see the human contingent advancing away from the Holy Place. They had covered nearly half of the distance from their circle of safety to his stronghold here.

To the north, he could see that his forces had pushed the angels completely out of the city. He was amazed that they had not withdrawn totally. Here, he also saw his encroaching forces, 30 million strong. The sky was darkened as they passed overhead and began the task of encircling the human rabble. What he was about to witness was a first. Never had he ordered such a barrage to be launched against an opponent.

Would they expect what was about to happen? He doubted it. He looked on in anticipation. It would take his forces about 20 minutes to get into position. They would form a shroud of death about their human adversaries. After which, they would choke them out.

What would he do with so many prisoners? He had been unable to reestablish communications with Hell. If he had his way, he would send them all there, throw them into the Sea of Fire, though he suspected that the Father would forbid it. Fine. Perhaps when this was through, even if the humans lacked any real respect for him, they would have a new fear for him.

David was struggling to keep up with Thecla and her entourage, which now included his mother, Elizabeth, and Jennifer. Behind them, a great multitude followed. Amidst the city streets of Zion, many of which were cluttered with debris, the going was slower. The crowd was fanning out in all directions, though their numbers were thinning as they moved ever farther from the safety of the Holy Place. They sang and glorified God as they went, confident of their victory.

More and more were discovering the powerful God-given gift that allowed them to become the judge, jury, and executioners of Satan's minions. However, their numbers were still small, perhaps a few percent of the whole.

So far, they had met with only token resistance and David knew it. The devil was capable of much more.

What was going on around him? Was this march an act of pure spontaneity, the response of a crowd following a bold leader, or was there more behind it than that? David really wasn't sure. They had no plan beyond spreading out into the city, reoccupying the land that had been taken from them.

A small number of angels had now, with the help of human navigators, gated into the midst of the human contingent, giving their human allies support from the air. It had been many days since the marching humans had seen angels in the skies over their heads. It gave them a sense of renewed hope.

Yet, what David had feared seemed to be coming to pass. A great black cloud appeared on the horizon before them. It grew larger by the minute and moved around them, encompassing them in a wall of darkness. David had never seen so many demons in one place.

Within a matter of minutes the dark cloud had completely encircled them, casting an ominous shadow over the assembled multitudes. David wanted to open fire, but they were well out of the effective range of his weapon.

By now he had caught up to Thecla and the others. He urged them to slow down; to allow others to catch up, to consolidate their position, but Thecla would hear nothing of it.

The wall of demons around them darkened even more. Then they were abruptly bathed in a bright orange glow coming from everywhere.

"Fireballs!" yelled David. "The demons have launched millions of them!"

Thecla and the others came to a halt. Elizabeth stretched out her hands, her eyes closed tightly.

David looked around—there was no place to take cover in this bombed-out region of Zion. He had, maybe, 45 seconds before they hit. He racked his brain for ideas. His mind tried to calculate the amount of heat such a barrage would generate. Surely the land around him would reach a temperature of 1,000 degrees, at least…perhaps more. Then it came to him—a strange and powerful thought that seemed to have emerged from someplace else. As he pondered it, it was voiced by another and then another around him.

"Gate out!" came the cry. "Gate out and wait in the mists beneath the wings of God!"

It was a proclamation that was echoing through the ranks. Already, scores of people around him were vanishing into the starry mists. David hesitated, then followed suit. He walked only a few steps into the mists and came to an abrupt halt. He seemed to be standing on a cloud. All around him were the cool blue vapors. He had only intended to gate a distance of 20 feet. Only once before had he attempted to gate such a short distance. He looked back; only mists met his eyes, no doorway back to the City of Zion. Looking around, he saw other people in the mists, some nearby, others almost obscured in the haze.

"What are we doing," asked a man who appeared about 30 or so feet to David's left. He spoke in a thick British accent. "I feel like we've just taken refuge from the blitz in a fallout shelter."

"I think we have," replied David. "Those were fireballs coming toward us. We should be safe here."

"I've never stopped halfway to my destination," continued the man. "I can't even tell you why I did it. It was like the Holy Spirit was urging me to do it."

"Same here," said David.

David was actually somewhat surprised when he felt the temperature of the mists rise noticeably for about 10 or 15 seconds, then fall. It wasn't hard to figure out what caused that.

"That must have been it," said the man.

"Yeah, I think so," said David.

"Little the worse for wear," noted the man. There was a momentary pause. "I know you. You're one of those scientists who built those ray guns. You know all about this stuff. How long can we stay here in the mists, neither here nor there?"

Now there was a question. How long could someone stand in the middle of a hyperspace tunnel—between two realities? "I really don't know…I guess, we'll find out," replied David. "Just hold tight, I don't think we'll be floating out here for very long."

The man nodded. They gazed out into the infinite, a place with absolutely no points of reference.

Then a man robed in white appeared in the mists. He hadn't walked toward David and into view; he had simply materialized about 15 feet in front of him. Like all persons in Heaven, David knew him. But it went beyond that, he had met him before. It was James, the brother of Jesus.

"Listen to me," he began. "Don't be afraid; you are completely safe here. You are in the hands of our loving Father. The time has nearly come to deal a crushing blow to the enemy of all humankind. The city beyond the mists is glowing red hot with the fire that was rained down at the command of Satan in an attempt to destroy God's people. They are preparing to strike us again. Do not venture forth. Remain where you are, under God's wings. Try to be comfortable; you are going to be here for some time. When the time at last comes to vanquish the enemy, God will give you the power to do so; doubt not. Their time of judgment has come."

The image of James faded. David could see where this was all leading to and he liked it.

"Did you hear and see that?" asked the man to David's left.

"Sure did," said David.

"It was James, the brother of Jesus," said the man. "He appeared right here in front of me."

"To me too," echoed another voice from the mists.

"I think he appeared to all of us," said David.

"With the Father's help, we'll give them a shellacking for sure," replied the man. "Praises be to the name of Jesus."

"Amen to that," said David.

In the very midst of the glowing blue mists David heard songs arising— the songs of praise of the saints. Now David saw the plan, and he rejoiced in it. This crowd had no plan beyond that of their commander—the Creator of the universe. David was both proud and thankful to be part of it.

Again, he felt a moment of heat. The temperature of the air around briefly increased, only to fall once more. After two fireball barrages, the ground beyond the safety of this place must surely have been glowing hot. He prayed that all of the saints had found their way to safety. Most assuredly, any that had not taken shelter were surely enduring an ordeal the equal of any they might have experienced in Hell.

From the roof of the Hall of Angels, Satan watched with glee as the second barrage of fireballs hit their mark. The land around the Holy Place glowed with an intense heat beyond description. So great was the heat that the demons who had launched the attack from a mile away were burned by its radiance and had been forced to pull back. Satan could feel the heat from here.

This plan had succeeded well beyond Satan's expectation. After the glare of the first barrage had faded, that region of the city had been reduced to glowing red rubble. Only a few isolated pockets of humans, protected by some form of shield, had apparently survived the attack. Now after the second attack, even those had vanished from the landscape. It had taken virtually all of his reserves, but he had persevered.

The now exhausted demons who had launched the assault had landed, too weak to fly. Satan would grant them a couple hours of rest. All of the crystals, save one, were totally drained, but it had been worth it.

Metastopholies walked to his side to survey the destruction of the once great city. Around the dead zone, fires were spreading out of control. Satan had reduced this city to desolation.

Satan looked to his closest advisor. "Look, come see, is it not as I told you?" he said triumphantly, stretching out his hands to the city. "I have neutralized the threat posed by the humans. If anyone remains, I shall take them prisoner. Before the Father bids me to release them, I will give them reason to fear me. Admit it old friend, I was right."

"I have already said all that I am going to say," said Metastopholies. "Ages ago I warned you not to oppose the will of the Father. Yet you would not be swayed from your path. I followed you in those days. I followed you because I felt your cause was right. Humans were not and would never be worthy to be our masters. But you have defiled your own cause. What gave us the right to torture the humans that over the years joined us in our fate, our separation from God? I looked on in disgust through it all as we defiled ourselves as surely as we defiled the humans, yet I said nothing.

"After all of the cries of pain we caused, the screams of terror we evoked, are we one step closer to our ideals, our goals? No. In doing so, we have become as detestable as those humans…no, even more so. This invasion was your last opportunity to recapture those ideals. You could have negotiated a peace from a position of strength; you had your opportunities, yet you squandered them. I am through with you."

Satan stood in stunned amazement as Metastopholies turned and walked away. No one under his command had ever spoken to him as Metastopholies had this day and not suffered for it. "Wait, I have not granted you permission to leave my presence!"

"That doesn't matter," replied Metastopholies, "I am departing nonetheless."

Satan drew his sword. "Stop! I command it!"

"And what will you do?" asked Metastopholies. "Will you run me through with that sword? Do you propose to do battle with me?"

Metastopholies leaped into the air, heading westward, away from the battleground. Satan, in his anger, was tempted to follow him, but sheathed his sword instead.

"Go then," he said. "Go into oblivion for all I care. Your services are no longer needed."

Satan once more turned his attention to the ruined city before him. Within two hours, when the heat finally dissipated, General Krell would lead his forces into the now baked dead zone around the Holy Place. How would he ever deal with so many prisoners? Well, he would deal with that problem when the time came.

He thought back to a time when he and his minions stood before God in the Holy Place. Heaven was so different then, the City of Zion especially. There were no elders around the throne, only the Father, and he led the worship to Him. Those days were so much simpler. Sometimes he still longed for those times—the era before man. Those were the days of his glory. He had loved the Father so much, led the praise to Him so well. Why hadn't the Father exalted him, placed him in a position above the other angels? He should rightly have been at the Father's right hand. Even if he won this war, things would not be as they were.

No, he couldn't think like this. The latter days would not be as the former; however, they would be no less glorious. If he played it right, today might well be the last great battle of this war. There might be more battles, but this would be the formidable one, the one that shaped the destiny of men and angels.

For hours, David and the others had remained in the cool hyperspace tunnel. From time to time they had experienced visitations from other elders including John, Matthew, Paul, and Thomas. All gave them encouragement, rousing their spirits for the battle to come. But now the time had come to depart. There was a battle to be won.

"Arise," proclaimed Enoch, he who had never known death. "Now is the time to go forth and claim the victory which has even now been placed before you."

David paused—perhaps he wouldn't use his weapon. No, it had served him well enough up to this point. He hoped that his viewpoint would not be seen as a lack of faith. He powered it up.

In unison, the saints moved forward. They all materialized within a few seconds of each other. They had emerged into a sea of demons searching for humans that they figured would be little more than moving lumps of still charred flesh.

There had been some humans, though few, who had not escaped the fireballs, humans who had either not comprehended the message or didn't perceive the danger despite the warning. The demons had been busy immobilizing them before they fully regenerated when the others who had found sanctuary materialized in their midst.

There was hardly a second of hesitation before the saints attacked. A mixture of bright white particle beam fire and the bright yellow radiance of the God-given weapon of the saints filled the air.

The demons were confused and completely surprised. They were still weak from the exertion of generating two fireballs in rapid succession to offer up any meaningful resistance. Within the course of 15 minutes, tens of millions of demons had perished, reduced to little more than soot and smoke.

With renewed determination and a more focused mission in mind, the saints were on the move once more. Only this time they were far more deadly—an unstoppable force bent on Satan's defeat.

Tens of thousands of the saints gated away, materializing near the northern edge of Zion where they offered assistance to the angelic army, which had finally managed to stem the advance of Satan's forces. Within an hour, the demonic forces were in full retreat, amid losses running in the tens of millions.

From the roof of the Hall of Angels, Satan watched his armies fall back on all fronts. The war was over and he knew it. He could not retreat back to Hell, and a retreat to another plane of Heaven would only delay the inevitable. Reports coming in from all over painted the same story—he had been defeated. If the most pessimistic estimates were to be taken literally, he had lost somewhere between 30 and 50 percent of his forces within a matter of hours. With defeat inevitable, some of his forces scattered into the countryside, while others formed an ever shrinking circle around the Hall of Angels.

Satan sat alone in his throne room where he had been for the past hour. With word that General Krell had fallen in battle, came the realization that he was virtually alone. All of the other members of his war council, save Governor Molock, were gone. He couldn't go out like this. What would the universe be like without him?

"My lord," announced a voice from the doorway.

Satan looked up to see Governor Molock. He looked at him with a blank stare and said nothing.

"My lord," repeated Molock. "Michael and his forces are almost upon us...we must flee."

"Yes, governor," replied Satan, his voice strained and distant. "I had assumed as much."

"My lord, you told me to inform you when all was in readiness," announced Molock.

"Yes, of course," said Satan, rising slowly to his feet. He retrieved a sizable box from aside his throne. "Let us be on our way, then."

Satan and Molock made their way down the hallway to the gate room. Molock seemed stressed, in a hurry, yet Satan continued at a somber pace. Along the way, they finalized the last details of their plan. Neither of them had thought it would come to this. They walked into the gate room where several hundred demons awaited them. Some held boxes not unlike their master's.

"My lord, we might be able to hold the gate open for twelve minutes, no more," said one of the demonic technicians. "That doesn't give us very much time to get our people through. What are your orders?"

Satan turned to his minions. "Our plans have changed. These are my new orders. We are going to Earth, my brethren. I want you all to take on a human form before you enter the gate. I cannot be sure that you will be able to do so afterward. Nor can I guarantee you how many of your powers you will retain. For the first time in millennia, we will walk on the surface of Earth in physical form, and not merely as spirits. That form must be human if we are to blend in among their people. We will travel in twenty-six teams, each sent to a different region of the globe. We shall bring about a dark age the likes of which humankind has never known. They shall know in their hearts that Satan and his minions walk among them."

The group stood at attention about the master, focused on his every word, even as the sounds of battle beyond the walls of the Hall of Angels grew ever louder. They had already been fully briefed by Governor Molock. They really didn't need this pep talk.

"I shall lead the first group," continued Satan. "Our destination is the City of New York on the continent of North America. It is the financial center of the Earth, it shall yield unto us great wealth that we shall utilize to further our plans. Governor Molock will lead the second team to Europe to breed unrest among its people. The rest of you have your assignments. Establish yourselves as quickly as you can, utilize all resources at your disposal. I expect us to be fully networked within a year. Remember, nearly ten million of our brethren still roam the Earth in spirit form. Make contact with them; make full use of their services. With our superior knowledge and wisdom, we should easily be able to dominate this pathetic world."

A particularly large detonation shook the room. Their time was indeed short.

Satan scanned his minions one final time. "We will try to get as many of our people through as possible. The time has come. Open the gate."

The area within the great ring took on the form of a dark foggy tunnel. They were ready. Satan took on human form—that of a middle-aged man in a dark cloak and business suit—and entered the tunnel followed by a steady stream of his minions who also took on the form of human men and women.

As the minutes passed the exodus became ever more hurried and chaotic. Few relished the thought of living on Earth in human form, but it beat the alternative by a large margin. The demon technicians did everything they could to keep the gate open for as long as they could. It was nearly 14 minutes later when they themselves joined the exodus fleeing through the gate. Thirty seconds later, the corridor to Earth was severed, leaving several thousand of Satan's minions adrift for eternity between worlds.

The remaining demons did the only thing they could, they turned to fight their last battle. Seven minutes later, that battle had spread to the gate room itself. Five minutes after that, it was over.

It was several hours later when the archangel Michael stepped into the gate room. The beaten demonic warriors had already been removed to a place of confinement, and the captured angels and humans within the great compound were being released.

"Our captured brethren were being held in unimaginable conditions," reported one of Michael's lieutenants, shaking his head sadly. "They were shackled together and thrown into the lower levels like garbage. They were piled to the ceilings in the resting rooms and the corridors. I cannot even begin to estimate how many there are or how long it will take us to get to all of them."

"Make it a high priority," said Michael, who had turned his attention to another of his lieutenants.

"They used the ring to escape," said the second. "There is no way to tell how many of them went through before their power faded."

"Where did they go?" asked Michael.

"Earth," replied the lieutenant.

"Then we will hunt them down there," announced Michael. "I will alert our brethren on Earth about their presence. Still, it may take a very long time for us to find them and bring them back to justice. The Father has ordered that all of Satan's minions who have not already perished face judgment. There will be trials convened within the judgment hall starting in a few days. I suspect that those judged guilty will not be cast from the Father's presence as it was in the first war, but will face total annihilation. At least I pray that this shall be so."

That thought brought a smile to the lieutenant's face. "At long last, the Father is going to destroy our enemies. It is long overdue."

Gabriel shook his head. "No, my friend, you do not understand, it will not be the Father who passes judgment upon them, but His children."

The smile vanished from the lieutenant's face. "His children? You mean the humans?"

"Exactly," confirmed Michael. "The Father shall convene the trial, He shall carry out the sentences Himself, but He shall not act as the judge. That honor shall fall to the humans. And it shall not only be the demons who are judged, but us as well."

"The humans will judge us?" asked the lieutenant. "They are but children. I have always thought of them as such."

"They are children no longer," replied Michael, they are the sons and daughters of God. We are to treat them as we do His firstborn." There was a moment of silence between them. "It was they who saved this day. Were it not for them, Heaven might well be in Satan's hands by now. The saints are just. I feel confident that we shall find favor in their eyes. But the Heaven we knew is changing, my friend. No longer will we be the guardians and tutors of humanity, these sons and daughters of God. We will be their trusted servants. It is our destiny, and I suspect that it is not such a terrible fate. It is, after all, what we were created for."

Four days later, the council chamber of the angels in the great City of Elesia was packed with both angelic and human leaders alike. It was a sort of conference call with their counterparts in Refuge, at the far pole of the universe.

"We will be meeting with Cordon and his people in five days," said Abaddon. "It still seems strange to me to be negotiating with one of Satan's minions. I cannot say what will come from it. Cordon and his lieutenant, Rolf, seem very different from any demons we have had dealings with; still, I have my doubts. We are to meet with them on the Plains of Sardon. Supposedly they are setting up a meeting place for us."

"Do you really trust them?" asked Gabriel.

"To a certain extent," replied Abaddon. "I don't think that they are going to ambush us or take us prisoner at the meeting, if that's what you mean. I trust Cordon to be civil, diplomatic, and even honorable. Still, our positions are worlds apart. I suspect that we will both be doing a lot of compromising before the process is complete."

Nikola Tesla stepped up to the telesphere. "Is there any way that you could get me back there with you? Hell is an interesting place to visit, but, well, you know."

"Yes, I can imagine," said Johann. "Right now, the Father has decreed that all travel between Heaven and Hell is to be totally suspended. Even on Earth, the spirits of the dead are remaining in the tomb. They will not rise until the rapture or the Day of Judgment. I do not know when that will be.

The Father will not tell any of us. David and I are preparing to build the Spirit Two. Perhaps, at some time, God will allow us to fly to Hell and bring you back. Still it may take some time to construct it. After all, I don't have Heaven's greatest inventor here to help me."

Nikola looked at David from the telesphere. "Oh, I think you do."

"And what of your war in Heaven?" asked Abaddon, "What is the latest news?"

"We are in control of all of the planes of Heaven," announced Michael, stepping up to the telesphere. "There remain a few stragglers of Satan's ill-fated campaign hiding within some of the more remote regions, but we will root them out in time. The war is over. The trials of the demons are scheduled to begin in only a few days, while those of the angels are likely to begin some time in the next year or so. We have been assured that we have nothing at all to fear. David and Johann have both been invited to act as jurors in some of the early trials. Eventually, all of the saints will have the opportunity to participate in the process."

"I sure wish that we could be judging old slewfoot along with them," noted David. "He is the one we really should be putting on trial."

"I shall not argue that point," replied Abaddon. "Has there been any decision about the demons still here in Hell or my people here in Refuge? Will they be judged during this coming trial?"

"There is no word on that as yet," replied Johann, "though I will bring the issue up when I serve. I will fight for your right to be heard...to be acquitted. You have a lot of friends in this hall, Abaddon. Be assured that we will all do whatever we can on your behalf."

"And what of us?" asked Tom, who stood at Abaddon's side, along with Bedillia. "Is there any word as to what is to become of us?"

"Your case isn't going to be heard by our tribunal," said Johann. "That will be an issue addressed at the great White Throne Judgment. That is still over a thousand years away. I'm afraid that, for the moment, your case is in limbo. I'm sorry. I wish I could offer you more hopeful news."

"Maybe, it is just as well," replied Bedillia. "Perhaps it will take a thousand years of penitence in Hell to prove our worth. A thousand years to make up for sixty or seventy wasted years on Earth. Maybe even that won't be enough, but I for one, intend to try."

There seemed to be a general agreement among the other humans standing in the crowded audience chamber in Refuge. They had a thousand years. It was nothing compared to eternity. Perhaps they could do something useful with it. After all, if all were to be judged guilty at the White Throne Judgment, why have a judgment in the first place? They would live with that hope in mind.

"It is my understanding that Satan did extensive damage to the holy city of Zion during your war," said Abaddon. "It sounds like you are going to be rebuilding for some time to come."

The smiles that followed his comment were, at first, puzzling.

"The city has already been restored," replied Johann. "With a wave of the Father's mighty hand, all was restored to what was. Even my mansion and laboratory were restored to their former nature. Praise be unto the Father."

That comment elicited a round of amens from both sides of the telesphere.

"Already things are returning to normal," noted David. "No, it is even better than normal. You never know what you have until it is taken away. The children of God have gained a new maturity through it all. We are ready to put away childish things and get on with developing our own character. We are ready to stop playing around and start being more like Christ. We have a destiny to fulfill. It's time to get to it."

As their conference came to an end, it was obvious that, at least for the immediate future, their only contact with each other would be through the telesphere. Both David and Nikola had ideas for the design of a matter transporter—a device not dissimilar in concept from the telesphere. Such a device would allow them to transport small items back and forth between Kepler's lab and Refuge. Refuge currently depended heavily on power spheres that could only be manufactured in Heaven. Establishing a new way to send them to Refuge was a high priority. Between their responsibilities at the tribunal and the lab, David and Johann had their work cut out for them.

Chapter 24

A mentally tired Abaddon, Bedillia, Nikola, and Lenar stepped from the large tan-colored tent on the windswept Plains of Sardon after 11 straight hours with their counterparts in the demonic camp. The large red sun, the star called Kordor, sat upon the hazy horizon a third hidden by the featureless plains. When they had begun the meeting, the entire sphere had been above the horizon.

"This is one of the very few places in Hell that still experiences day and night," noted Cordon stepping from the tent behind them. "Perhaps, together, we can change all of that, get Hell spinning more rapidly, allow this whole world to know day and night."

"Perhaps," said Abaddon, smiling slightly.

"I don't wish you to become discouraged by the seeming lack of progress we had today," said Cordon. "We will come to an accord, I am certain of it."

"At least we are talking," said Bedillia. "That is more than we were doing a month ago."

"Exactly," said Cordon. "We can resume the talks two days hence. Kordor will have then set completely. You will be surprised how much cooler it will be."

No more was said between the two parties. The four moved toward their gate out point.

"Not a promising start," noted Bedillia. "I for one am quite disappointed. I thought that now with Cordon in command things would have gone better."

"I really didn't know what to expect," admitted Abaddon, "therefore I was not disappointed by the results."

"We did get a nonaggression agreement with him," said Lenar, who wanted to accentuate the positive aspects of the meeting, such as they were.

"But we made no progress on the issue of repentant humans released by my children from their torments," argued Abaddon, who seemed less optimistic than Lenar. "We are to sit idly by while his minions round them up and send them back to their torments. These people need to be with us. Then he expects me to call off my children, to instruct them to feed only on the unrepentant humans of Hell. He expects us to give him so much, while he offers nothing in return but a promise not to attack."

Nikola remained silent. Cordon had saved his life—no two ways about it. Yet, he too seemed disappointed with the day's results, or lack thereof. To him one thing was certain, Hell had become a far more unstable place. It was ripe for revolt. Cordon couldn't control so many humans with his limited resources. Why was he being so stubborn? They had come to an agreement on exploring ways to moderate the environment of their world. That, at least, was a positive outcome. Still, he was troubled. He couldn't see a pathway to a more just and yet workable realm. It was a long road that lay ahead, and like it or not, he would be stuck here for a long time.

At the tent, Cordon and Rolf watched as the four Refuge delegates gated out. Cordon glanced back at the other two demonic delegates. He practically had to threaten them to keep them from being openly hostile to their guests, so great was their dislike of humans. He knew that he wasn't going to change their attitudes.

"That could have gone better," noted Rolf.

"Yes, that could have gone better," echoed Cordon. "Our people will never accept the humans as equals, even if their very existence depends upon it."

"And it does," interjected Rolf.

"Probably," said Cordon, turning toward the setting orb in the west. "The master was able to bend our people to his will through a combination of fear and appealing to their desire for vengeance. I doubt that I can do that. If I give these humans much more than I already have, I may very well have a revolt on my hands."

"And if you don't?" asked Rolf.

Cordon shook his head. "If I don't, I'll have a revolt on my hands, one of a human nature."

"So, what is to be done?" asked Rolf.

"I was hoping that you could tell me," said Cordon.

"You are the master of Hell," said Rolf, a very slight smile on his face.

"Yes, that is the problem," noted Cordon.

Tim Monroe was overjoyed when he discovered that Cindy had given birth to three young ones. They looked like miniature versions of their parents. Goliath marched proudly back and forth around his new brood.

Tim was hesitant to approach at first, but quickly discovered that Goliath and Cindy didn't mind in the least. Tim was their friend; they trusted him. Goliath went out frequently during the next few days, bringing back small pieces of stringy red flesh with him. Tim wasn't so sure that he wanted to know its source.

Goliath's and Cindy's children ate voraciously, and grew at a startling rate. Within three days, they were over half the size of their parents. Unlike human babies, they were not helpless, at least not for long. Within a few hours of their birth, they were moving about quite well on their own. They learned quickly, and they took a liking to Tim right away. He played with them for hours on end. They added a new dimension to his life here.

More marvelous still was the arrival of more of the tiny creatures. His world was becoming ever more populated, and he didn't mind a bit. Every one of his guests seemed happy to share the cavern with their human host. They all liked to be talked to, and when he was in a talking mood, they all gathered around to listen. Tim had a name for each and every one of them.

Within two weeks of the birth of Cindy's children, the population of his little community passed 50, and the number was increasing daily, as more continued to join him or were born right there in the caves.

Tim knew only too well what these creatures were capable of, yet he was not afraid. Tim, the protector of one, had become Tim the protected by many. Tim was getting ideas. What could an army of these wonderful creatures do? One day he might well find out. Until then, he would bask in their friendship and love, giving back what was given to him. Perhaps with the right leadership, they might reshape the face of Hell. He would endeavor to be that leader. Until then, he would bide his time.

"Now keep it simple," said Clarence Booth, the U.S. ambassador's administrative liaison, as Sam Florence prepared to enter the chambers of the UN Security Council. "These aren't scientists, you know; they are career diplomats. But don't talk down to them either. They are highly educated people. As the discoverer of Comet Florence, it was deemed appropriate that you give this presentation rather than someone from the NSF."

"I appreciate the opportunity, Mr. Booth," said Sam, looking through his note cards one last time. "I've given talks to rooms full of very picky planetary scientists. I'm sure this crowd will be no rougher on me."

"But remember, don't talk to them like they were scientists," repeated Booth.

"And don't talk down to them," said Sam, anticipating Booth's next sentence.

"Right," confirmed Booth. "Now, we've got the projector set up for you, and your PowerPoint slides are all ready to go. They'll be calling for you in just another minute or so. Just relax, OK?"

"Sure, no worries," said Florence, taking a deep breath. He knew that what he had to discuss tonight was going to be, to say the least, alarming. It wouldn't hit the Internet and the news networks until tomorrow. Tonight would be like dropping a bomb in the room. He wondered how the general public would take it. He'd find that out tomorrow. There would be no hiding it.

There had been reports about the comet for nearly a month. A large bright comet that preliminary estimates said would pass within 2 million miles of the Earth was big news. It would be the comet of the millennium—filling the sky and blazing as bright as the full moon. Thing was, Sam knew differently.

"You're on," said Booth, ushering Sam into the meeting room.

After a brief introduction by the U.S. ambassador, Sam walked to behind the podium with butterflies in his stomach. He would break it to them as gently as he could. Still, it was a daunting task. He spoke about discovering the comet at the edge of the solar system, almost to the orbit of Neptune. He spoke of the Discovery Channel Telescope and the instruments that had been used in producing the initial images of the comet. Never in history had a comet been discovered while it was still so far from the sun. It gave them plenty of time to prepare for the comet's coming, time they desperately needed. He told them about the orbital calculations and how images from the New Horizons Spacecraft made those calculations all the more precise.

Then came the bombshell.

"This is a large comet, estimated to have a diameter of approximately twenty-five miles. Based upon more than five hundred observations over three months, we have determined that this comet poses a serious impact hazard to Earth…the most serious to date." Sam paused, yet no one immediately jumped on his statement.

The French ambassador finally commented. "Sir, with all due respect, define *serious* for me. Are we talking one or two percent?"

Sam prepared for the onslaught. "No, Mr. Ambassador, we are talking between ten and fifteen percent. This is a serious threat."

"Is this in anyway related to the mysterious radiation we were hearing about just last month?" asked the Nigerian ambassador. "There were auroras seen even in the equatorial regions of Nigeria. Thankfully it ended before it did serious harm."

"No," said Sam. "That was a totally different phenomenon. It was just coincidence that these two events have occurred in the same year."

"How long?" asked the Chinese ambassador. "I mean, how long do we have before this comet gets here?"

"Less than fifty-three months," was the reply.

"We hear often that it was a comet that wiped from the Earth the dinosaurs," noted the Argentinean ambassador. "Is this one bigger or smaller?"

"I'm afraid that it is much bigger," replied Sam. "Add to that its almost certainly higher velocity and you have an impact that could potentially be four to six times as devastating as the one that ended the age of the dinosaurs. It could well wipe out ninety percent of all the species on Earth."

"Except for the cockroaches," said the Canadian ambassador, almost under his breath.

"It might end life for them too," said Sam.

"So where does that leave us?" asked the Canadian ambassador. "Can we blow it up before it reaches us…maybe with nuclear weapons?"

"No," replied Sam. "It's just too big. Blowing it up would create a swarm of smaller objects. Some might miss us, but others will hit. It's like comparing a shot from a forty-five to that of a twelve-gauge shotgun. Either one has the capacity to kill."

"OK," said the Canadian ambassador, "then what do we do?"

"We deflect it," said Sam. "The comet is going to spin around Jupiter. The Europa Orbiter will be there by then. We make sure to get plenty of images of the comet as it passes. That will give us its exact course." Sam advanced the PowerPoint presentation to show the U.S. government's plan to deflect the comet.

"We will need help from all of your governments…from all of the governments of the world. If we start now, we should have enough time. We propose a four stage attack. Within eighteen to twenty months, NASA feels confident that they could have the Ares Five heavy launch vehicle ready for flight. Thirty-one and thirty-four months from now, four of them would be used to deliver a set of high yield nuclear devices to two points in space, one just this side of Jupiter, and the other about half way to Jupiter.

"From there, we would launch the devices toward the comet, detonating them about two to four miles out. The tremendous heat would vaporize that side of the comet, acting like a huge rocket engine, pushing it off course. We would have several opportunities to deflect and measure the amount of deflection of the comet at both points. We might succeed the first time, but we would have a second, third, and forth chance if the first one failed."

"But suppose we discover that the comet is going to miss the Earth?" asked the French ambassador. "We would spend hundreds of billions of Euros for nothing."

"I won't deny that," replied Sam, "but consider the possible consequences of doing nothing."

"I agree that we need to act," said the Russian ambassador, "and I assure you that you will have my government's support. However, have you considered the possibility that the blast might, despite all of your precautions, fragment the comet, sending not one but hundreds of smaller pieces in our direction?"

"Yes we have," said Sam. "That is why we will need additional spacecrafts positioned along the comet's path, closer to Earth. These crafts would deflect or destroy any smaller fragments still on a collision course with Earth. We are confident that we can avoid this tragedy if we all work together. With God's help, we can beat this thing…we can save our planet."

That comment brought a few raised eyebrows from the delegates, and even an amen from two. Having God on your side was a good thing. There would be a lot of prayers said before it was all said and done. None debated that.

By the end of the meeting, the delegates were in agreement. They would recommend that their governments participate in this project—they could do little else.

The following day, the news hit the streets. There was deep concern, but something short of outright panic. After all, there was at worst only a 15 percent chance of impact. The United States government spoke with confidence about their plan to deflect the comet. They had the time and the technology. They had the money and the resources. On this thing, the governments of the world were united. They were confident of success. The world would not end in October 2018.

Epilogue

It was after 11 o'clock as Serena Davis walked down the half mile long gravel lane, flashlight in hand. It had been the last night of their revival meeting in this eastern Nebraska farming community. She and her husband had been staying with the pastor of the church on his farm these past three days. It had been a wonderful and restful experience, a break from spending another night in their small motor home.

Serena and her husband had traveled more than 100,000 miles during the past six years, spreading the Gospel, telling their story of their adventures in Heaven and Hell. They had even written a book about their exploits.

Over the years, her story in particular had drawn a lot of criticism. After all, who could really escape from Hell? Her story of meeting the devil, and the dark angel Abaddon, of swimming for months in an oily sea of fire, was almost beyond belief. Even many Bible-believing Christians criticized her testimony. They claimed that it was no more than a dream or a wild story fabricated to bring her money and fame. It hurt that brothers and sisters in Christ felt that way about her, but it didn't stop her mission. She was determined to warn the world about what had happened to her—of what could happen to them. She was determined to tell the world that Hell was real and terrible beyond imagining. If people criticized her for that, then so be it.

They would be moving on to South Dakota tomorrow. They would be leaving early in the morning. She needed to get some sleep. She hadn't noticed the man standing by the big oak tree along the road.

"Hello, Serena," said a voice from behind her.

She turned with a start to see the man leaning against the tree. He wore an old straw hat and overalls. He looked like the stereotypical farmer.

"Hello," she said uncertainly.

"I'm sorry," said the man. "I hadn't meant to startle you. I thought that you had seen me."

"No, I didn't," she replied. "I guess I was too deep in thought."

There was something about that voice. It was so very familiar, yet she was having trouble placing it. He stepped out of the shadow of the tree and into the light of the nearly full moon. His face was smooth, without blemish. His eyes practically sparkled in the moonlight. The face too was familiar, very familiar, yet it seemed out of place on this man. What was missing? Then she knew what was missing—great white feathered wings.

"Oh sweet Lord…it's you, Aaron!"

"Yes," confirmed Aaron. "It is wonderful to see you again Serena, back here on Earth where you belong."

Serena ran and gave him a big hug. "I never saw you take human form," she said. "It looks good on you."

Aaron laughed. "Why thank you, Serena. It seems to me that the years have been kind to you as well."

"But what brings you back to me after all of these years?" asked Serena.

"I am just doing my job," replied Aaron. "It is a job that I do with great joy." Aaron handed Serena a stack of four letters. She quickly accepted them. "Two are addressed to you, and two to your husband."

Serena first held them up to the moonlight, then directed her flashlight upon them. All were addressed in the usual format, yet the return addresses were, to say the least, unusual. Her heart skipped a beat when she looked at the first one: Abaddon, care of Refuge.

"Refuge?" she asked.

"Yes," replied Aaron. "It is the great subterranean fortress of the dark angels and free humans on the Dark Continent of Hell."

The second one was addressed to her husband. It was from his good friend, Professor Kepler.

"Oh, Chris will love getting this one," said Serena, who moved onto the next envelope also addressed to Chris. Tears came to her eyes when she read this one. "It's from his mother in Heaven…oh, how he will treasure this."

Yet the greatest thrill was yet to come. She brought the last letter to the top of the pile. Her eyes opened wide with amazement as she read the return address: Bedillia Farnsworth, Refuge. Tears of joy ran down Serena's cheeks.

"My mother has been freed from that awful furnace?" said Serena in a trembling voice.

"Yes," confirmed Aaron. "Abaddon released her nearly six years ago, shortly after you left. She has been at his side, his closest human companion ever since. I do believe that he once promised you that he would do it. I assure you, she is well and quite safe. There is much that I must tell you, and we have little time."

"Can't you come back with me to the house?" asked Serena. "I'm sure that Chris would be thrilled to see you again."

"Perhaps some other time," said Aaron. "Right now there are things that you must know. I bring you a warning about things that have happened and about things to come."

"About the comet?" asked Serena.

"In part," confirmed Aaron, "but there is much more. Even as we speak, Satan is here on Earth in physical form."

That comment sent a chill up Serena's spine. "I think you had best tell me the whole story."

For more than 20 minutes, Aaron related to Serena the events of the past months. It was an incredible story that led Serena to the only conclusion—the last days are nearly upon the world. Time to get the word of salvation out was growing short.

The glare of a second flashlight from the porch of the house told Serena that Chris had grown concerned and had set out to look for her. She flashed her light in his direction. He was heading her way.

"Oh, won't you stay just a few more minutes?" asked Serena.

"It just isn't possible," said Aaron. "Please give your husband my regards and my apologies that I could not tarry. I assure you, I'll see the two of you again soon." Aaron gave Serena a kiss on the cheek and stepped back. A few seconds later, he vanished into a cloud of mist and stars.

Serena looked down at the letters in her hand—they were real; she hadn't imagined them. Less than a minute later, Chris was at her side.

"I was getting worried," he explained. He looked around. "I thought I saw you talking with someone out here."

"You did," confirmed Serena. "It was Aaron."

"Aaron? You mean the angel?"

Serena smiled broadly. "Yes, dear, the very same. He said I should give these to you." Serena handed Chris the two letters addressed to him.

"From my mother?" gasped Chris, tears welling up in his eyes.

"Yes," confirmed Serena. "It would seem that she has had quite an adventure. I'm sure she describes it in her letter." She showed her husband the letters she received as well. "Let's go back to the house where we can read them in the light."

Chris shook his head. "How are we ever going to explain this to Pastor Wilson, to other people? Many of them already think we're crazy...or worse."

"Who said that they have to know anything about these letters?" replied Serena, a broad smile on her face. "After all, they're addressed to us, not to them. They're very personal and precious letters. Why don't we keep them our little secret?"

Chris shook his head in wonder. "Our *big* secret is more like it."

"All the better," said Serena. "Let's have this quiet moment with the words of our loved ones. I'll tell you what Aaron told me afterward. No one else needs to know what happened here tonight. It's enough that we know. There is a storm coming, Chris, that much I can tell you. It will be a battle of terrible proportions, a battle not only against flesh and blood, but against principalities and powers as well. Let's have this moment of peace before we step out to face it."

Hand in hand, they walked back to the house, knowing of the dark times that would soon fall down around them. But tonight they would share in the joy and encouragement sent to them by loved ones long gone from this world. Serena was reminded of the words of Paul to the Ephesians as recorded in chapter 6 verse 12:

> For we wrestle not against flesh and blood, but against principalities, against powers, against the rulers of the darkness of this world, against spiritual wickedness in high places.

Although Satan would bring to the world the greatest darkness it had ever known, yet they would endure, come what may. Greater is He who is in them than he who is in the world. They would face the coming days without fear.

Another Book by Kenneth Zeigler

AB NEGATIVE

Welcome to America 2052. The Corporate Collective, a mighty alliance of mega-corporations, dominates every aspect of life in the United States. Its elite military force struggles to suppress the growing discontent spreading across a nation in the midst of the darkest economic depression in its history.

In this America of broken dreams, Kendra Olson faces a grim decision. Soon her parents and younger brother will be compelled to leave the homeless shelter, their only source of food and warmth, to face a cold and slow death on the streets of New York City.

Her only hope of escape rests in the hands of her oldest brother, Lieutenant Kenneth Olson, a member of the Army's Special Forces, and a small group of unlikely rescuers. Yet, there is more at stake than just her life. One of the Collective's most terrible secrets awaits Lieutenant Olson upon a surgical couch at the very gates of the Collective's own private hell.

AB Negative carries you on a roller coaster ride through a world of the not too distant future. Welcome aboard!

Paperback: 266 pages

Publisher: Windsor House Publishing Group

ISBN: 1881636429

Available through Amazon.com

About the Author

Kenneth Zeigler teaches advanced chemistry to gifted high school students in the Phoenix area. He holds a master's degree in chemistry, and his graduate work was in quantum chemistry. He is married and has two grown step-children. A former consultant for NASA, he continues to do research in planetary science.

Additional copies of this book and other book titles from Destiny Image are available at your local bookstore.

Call toll-free: 1-800-722-6774.

Send a request for a catalog to:

Destiny Image® Publishers, Inc.
P.O. Box 310
Shippensburg, PA 17257-0310

*"Speaking to the Purposes of God for This
Generation and for the Generations to Come."*

For a complete list of our titles,

visit us at www.destinyimage.com.